The Chickens of Atlantis
and Other Foul and Filthy Fiends

The
Chickens of Atlantis and Other Foul and Filthy Fiends

Being the memoirs and musings of a
time-travelling Victorian monkey butler.

Adorned with annotations and illustrations by

Robert Rankin FVSS*
★ Fellow of the Victorian Steampunk Society

GOLLANCZ

LONDON

Copyright © Robert Rankin 2013
All rights reserved

The right of Robert Rankin to be identified as the author of this
work has been asserted by him in accordance with the
Copyright, Designs and Patents Act 1988.

First published in Great Britain in 2013 by Gollancz
An imprint of the Orion Publishing Group
Orion House, 5 Upper St Martin's Lane,
London WC2H 9EA
An Hachette UK Company

A CIP catalogue record for this book
is available from the British Library

ISBN (Cased) 978 0 575 08645 6
ISBN (Export Trade Paperback) 978 0 575 08646 3

1 3 5 7 9 10 8 6 4 2

Typeset at The Spartan Press Ltd,
Lymington, Hants

Printed and bound by CPI Group (UK) Ltd,
Croydon, CR0 4YY

The Orion Publishing Group's policy is to use papers
that are natural, renewable and recyclable products and made
from wood grown in sustainable forests. The logging and
manufacturing processes are expected to conform to the
environmental regulations of the country of origin.

www.thegoldensprout.com
www.orionbooks.co.uk
www.gollancz.co.uk

FOR MY BEAUTIFUL GRANDDAUGHTER

LAYLA

HERE IS A BOOK ABOUT A MONKEY

I HOPE IT WILL ONE DAY MAKE YOU SMILE

AND FOR

PETER HARROW FVSS (ETC!)

WHO KNOWS WHY, OR SHOULD.

Acknowledgements

A degree of blame must be
placed like milk upon the
doorsteps of the following:

Steve Campbell, Tim Mavrick, Richard Scott, Richard Fair-
gray, Stu Dall, Nick Reekie, Jonathan Crawford, Lee 'Prist'
Hughes, Ali Salmon, Gavin Lloyd Wilson, Ian Crighton, Kit
Cox, Robert Otley, James Southard, Rachel Ball Rat, Steve
Lowdell, Xymon Owain, Richard Warne, Spike Livingstone,
Jenny Owen, Trevor Pyne, Nigel Haveron, Jon Sykes, the
lovely Rachel Hayward and the real Mr Cameron Bell.

The late, great James Stuart Campbell.

'All ideas are true somewhere.'

Leonard Susskind

'It is only by attempting the impossible
that we achieve the absurd.'

Norman Hartnell

'Absurdity is the only reality.'

Frank Zappa

'The past is the new future.'

Darwin (The Educated Ape)

1

1

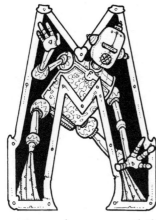y name is Darwin and I am a monkey butler.

I have travelled through space, I have travelled through time, and I have had many adventures.

My earliest memories are not pleasant to recall, full of stench and of ghastliness, of many bells chiming, of coarse cries and clamour and I all alone and in fear.

I awoke to sensibility in a cage on a Tilbury dock. The year was eighteen ninety; the month, I believe, was May. I have no knowledge of my parents, my tribe or even the country in which I was born. Upon my passport and papers of travel I am now identified as 'a citizen of London', and I take pride in this, for within that great and ancient city I have enjoyed more happiness than sorrow, made more friends than enemies and acquainted myself with artists and musicians, knights and noblemen and members of the Royal Household.

I recall too clearly the kicking at my cage and a great face, all red and wildly whiskered, calling upon me to dance. The breath of this face was tainted with liquor, and the eyes of this face were fierce.

At that time I spoke not a word of the Queen's English and as such was limited in my means of communication. My response to the assault upon my tender senses lacked then the sophistication I now enjoy and I make no pretence to the contrary. And so it was there, upon that clamorous, foul-smelling dock, that I committed my first social gaffe. For I produced dung and hurled it!

This act, construed no doubt as one of defiance, was met with a brutal rejoinder: a shaking of my cage, which increased in vigour until it reached an intolerable degree and I passed from consciousness once again.

Cold water awakened me to a room with air made dense by tobacco smoke. A roguish type in a colourful suit wrought a brisk tattoo upon the bars of my little prison with the business end of a swagger-stick and called out to an audience before him. I was announced as, 'Lot thirty-two. A monkey of cheerful disposition. Eager to learn and as fine a fellow as might grace an organ-grinder's in-stri-ha-ment and lure many pennies into an old tin cup.'

Hungry then was I and bitter at the shaking I had received. And so, I confess, I did not exhibit that cheerful disposition attributed to me by the chap in the colourful suit. I made loud my protests in my ancestral tongue and had I been capable of producing further faeces I would gladly have done so. And gladly hurled them, too.

I was sold for the princely sum of twelve shillings to a gentleman named George Wombwell, the proprietor of a travelling menagerie, and it was he who named me Darwin.

Mr Wombwell was a kindly man, whom I feel harboured a genuine love for the animals in his charge. At the time when I accompanied him on his meanderings along the highways and by-roads of southern England, he owned a pair of charming elephants, a lion of evil intent, numerous trained kiwi birds and performing chickens, a 'pig of knowledge' and a mermaid.

The mermaid was a fascinating creature. It appeared for all the world to be part-monkey and part-fish, although the monkey portion never spoke to me. Around and around that creature swam in a vast spherical bowl and many were the heads that shook in wonder. It was many, many years before I saw its like again, and then in somewhat outré circumstances.

Although initially belligerent and uneager to cooperate, I found myself gently won over to Mr Wombwell's wishes. I learned that to please him garnered rewards which, like as not, came in the shape of bananas. To displease him, however, occasioned a falling from grace characterised by an absence of these yellow delicacies.

I learned quickly and became most obliging.

I could write much regarding my travels with Mr Wombwell, for indeed my days with that singular gentlemen were rarely ever dull. We moved from town to village and likeabouts, mostly bringing happiness to those who patronised our performances. I became adept at juggling, tomfoolery, pratfalls and 'tricks above ground'. I well remember the happy cries of children and the merry jingle of Mr Wombwell's brass cash register. I learned tricks enough to please him and gained an understanding of the English tongue, although at that time I was unable to vocalise and express myself through words. There was the occasional unpleasantness.

I will not belabour my reader with tales of the travelling life. Mr Wombwell has published his autobiography, and although his recollections differ somewhat from my own regarding the extent of his successes, the gist is very much the same as any account I could give.

Now, a man must adapt to what he cannot control, and so too must a monkey. I have lived upon other worlds and encountered beings who, although sharing a common sun with men of Earth, inhabit such strange forms and hold to such quaint manners as to baffle my small senses. These beings do not cogitate like men, but they do exhibit certain attitudes which display, to my thinking, what might be described as an all-but-universal constant.

That of tribalism.

My first experience of this was with Mr Wombwell's Travelling Menagerie. Showmen and circus folk consider themselves a race apart. The 'hicks' or 'rubes' or 'billy-docks' or 'nadgers' who attend their performances and fill their coffers are 'not as they'. Showmen and circus folk are of a tribe that keeps itself apart. They look after their own and hold most others in the lowest form of contempt. Such, sadly, I have found to be the case throughout all levels of society, on this world and elsewhere.

History records that in the year eighteen eighty-five, King Phnarrg of Mars declared war upon the British Empire. He sent a mighty fleet of space-going warships to attack and destroy the subjects of Queen Victoria. Few there are, however, who understand that this was a religious crusade. The Martian tribe considered itself composed of God's chosen people and Mankind to be an impure race of idolaters, fit only for extermination.

Tribalism is the tragedy of the sentient being, and I, who have visited the past and the future, can see no end to it.

I gathered what learning I could from Mr Wombwell and also from others in his employ, for although I was at that time unable to utter words of English, I was perfectly able to converse with others of my 'tribe': to wit, the animal kingdom.

A rooster named Junior talked long into the nights with me. He was a prodigious conversationalist and a cock of a religious bent. Junior held to the belief that Mankind had descended from chickens, that the first fowl had been placed upon the Earth by Lop Lop, God of the Birds, and the Great Mother Hen who dwelt on her cosmic nest. I later came to understand that a gentleman whose name I shared held to not dissimilar beliefs – his, however, involved ape-like antecedents.

I will not at this juncture inform the reader as to which of these theories is correct. Although the title of this tome might have released the pussy of metaphor from the sack of obfuscation, thereby saving it from a drowning in the village pond of Penge.

In the year of eighteen ninety-four, I resigned from Mr Wombwell's employ. I am of a mercurial disposition and have what my good friend Sigmund Freud would term 'a limited span of attention'. I had by this year gained sufficient understanding to realise that the itinerant life held little charm for myself. I had become an ape of ambition and now held to the conviction that I should seek my fortune in the great, good-hearted City of London.

My opportunity to take my leave came one night after a performance at the Egyptian Hall in Piccadilly. An inebriate cage-boy had inadequately secured the fastenings upon my quarters and I stole quietly away into the night.

The closing years of the nineteenth century were, regrettably, characterised by debauchery and decadence. Whether this is the case in every century, I know not. My experiences in several, however, lead me to believe that this is the rule rather than the exception.

During these years, well-to-do ne'er-do-wells behaved with shameless abandon – ingesting morphine by means of gold-plated syringes, guzzling Vin Coca Mariani, a wine laced with cocaine, and concluding their extravagant dinings with a desert of strawberries soaked in ether.

As for myself, I have always preferred Treacle Sponge Bastard for afters.

The literature of this period reflected its social mores and I well recall a popular erotic novel of the day called *Fifty Shades of Earl Grey.**

I was free, but all alone once more. From lofty rooftops I viewed others of my tribe, sporting slave-wear of the waist-coat and fez variety and chained to the barrel organ. *Not for me*, thought I. *I am cut from richer cloth.* Perhaps I felt I was more of a man than a monkey.

Reality impinged upon such ill-founded graces when I was taken by Lambeth's Monkey-Catcher-in-Residence and found myself once more put up for auction. On this occasion, perhaps on account of the rather smart velvet suit Mr Wombwell had clothed me in and my knowledge that flinging dung brought few rewards, the hammer came down at the sum of one guinea and I became a member of a most exalted household.

That of Lord Brentford, whose stately abode, Syon House, occupied lands between London's most beautiful borough (Brentford) and the fields of Isleworth.

I was greatly taken with his lordship, a gentleman in every sense of the word. He delegated one of his minions to school me in the noble arts of monkey butlerdom, and these I took to willingly and without complaint. The duties were not arduous, the tasks simple but specific. My accommodation was almost luxurious and bananas were in plentiful supply.

* *This may strike the reader as a rather tired and worn-out gag, but do remember that Darwin encountered this book in 1897. (R. R.)*

Looking back now, I know that Lord Brentford cared deeply for me. He *was* and *is* a good man and my times in his employment lacked not for adventure and excitement.

He, too, named me Darwin, which seemed a rare co-incidence. Only later did I come across the velvet suit that I had worn during my years with Mr Wombwell, laundered and folded in a drawer of my dresser. By that time, my knowledge had increased and I read the label on the collar, which said 'Darwin, property of George Wombwell's Travelling Menagerie'. Lord Brentford might well have chosen to return me to my 'owner', but he did not. Because he cared for me.

I am grateful that he did and glad to have known that noble lord, for it is because of him that I became what I am today.

The world's first and only talking ape.

The Ape of Space.

The Ape of Time.

The ape who would, through a twist of fate, become the father of all apes and the father, too, of all Mankind.

And many many tribes.

2

have chosen to set down my musings and memoirs in 'the first monkey'.

This is, I do not hesitate to add, in direct opposition to the wishes of my publishers, who advised strongly against such a course of action, stating that my prose was dense and idiosyncratic and suggesting that I – and here I employ the parlance of the nineteen sixties – 'dumb it down in the cause of increased sales'.

My response to this did not involve the employment of dung, for I am now above such acts of grossness. Rather I explained to them, with patience and good grace, that I valued quality above the worship of Mammon, adding that as the world's only speaking ape ever to publish his memoirs, I felt that the reading public might be persuaded to meet me halfway and look up any difficult words in the *Oxford English Dictionary*.

You may consider my decision rash, or indeed vain, and suggest that one of England's great writers should have been engaged to better tell my tale. Perhaps even Robert Rankin himself might have been presumed upon to take up this endeavour.

And indeed I have, in the spirit of altruism, made the

concession of allowing Mr Rankin to lend the considerable weight of his literary celebrity to this venture by adding illustrated letters and annotations to the text at appropriate intervals.

I will confess that after my initial meeting with my publishers, I repaired to my suite at The Dorchester, where I regathered my wits in the company of Château Doveston champagne and vowed, using another term I encountered during my sojourn in the swinging sixties, to 'stick it to the man'.

I briefly touched upon the matters above because it is now my wish to touch upon other matters connected therewith. To wit, how I arrived at that estate of Man characterised by speech and literacy.

It all came about in this fashion.

I had become Lord Brentford's 'man' in that I was now his monkey butler, engaged as a gentleman's gentle-monkey to aid his lordship with his daily endeavours, to ensure that the niceties which should be accorded to a person of noble birth were occasioned with correctness.

A monkey butler's duties are those of the valet. To attend to his master's dressing room and maintain order and tidiness therein, replenishing the jars of pomade, moustache wax and gentlemen's special creams when necessary. To assist his lordship in dressing or otherwise. To accompany him upon outings and be aware at all times of the correct social etiquette. To be on hand, when so required, for anything as may be required.

Naturally, the duties of a human butler go beyond this and extend to the hiring and firing of staff, the admittance of and making of polite conversation with guests, the ordering of supplies and the keeping of household accounts. And, of course, the occasional thrashing of wayward bootboys.

My size and communicative abilities precluded me from several of these duties. Much to my regret, as I would dearly have loved to thrash those wayward bootboys.

It was during the summer of eighteen ninety-five that I accompanied Lord Brentford on what was intended to be the first circumnavigation of the globe by airship.

The *Empress of Mars* was a magnificent vessel, a gigantic pleasure craft almost a third of a mile in length. The very cream of London society was booked on board for this historic flight and history was to be made. The *Empress* would rise from the Royal London Spaceport, which spread beneath the Crystal Palace at Sydenham, and I would be amongst the history-makers.

I confess that I was wary, but the prospect of such a journey held great charm for me as Lord Brentford explained that the airship would pass over Africa.

'Where you were born, young Darwin.'

Sadly, his lordship did not return in triumph from the maiden flight of the *Empress of Mars*. That beautiful silver ship of the skies went down in a terrible storm and plunged into a distant ocean. Lord Brentford was lost and I returned to London in the company of Mr George Fox, later dubbed a knight for his services to Queen and country.

It was at this time that I first attained great wealth.

Lord Brentford, it transpired, was not a man who looked favourably upon his family; in fact, he held them in utter contempt. He had taken the sensible precaution of updating his will before taking passage aboard the *Empress of Mars* and had removed the names of his 'nearest and dearest' and sub-stituted my own.

I had suddenly become an ape of wealth. The lands, the investments, the great house of Syon – all indeed were mine.

I was deeply touched by this act of Man's humanity to

Monkey and vowed that I would raise a monument to Lord Brentford. Possibly a bronze statue of himself to adorn the vacant plinth in Trafalgar Square.

Just as soon as I had attended to one or two more pressing matters, to wit, the laying down of banana plantations in the grounds and the construction of a Bananary to adorn the rear of Syon House. And in order to achieve these admirable ends, it was essential that I gain the ability to speak the Queen's English, to read and also to write.

I had overheard conversations regarding a mysterious gentleman known only as Herr Döktor, who held to certain radical theories, most notable amongst them his conviction that the evolutionary progress of the simian species could be advanced through human tuition, and that apes might eventually catch up with Humankind. Herr Döktor's goal was to bring spiritual enlightenment to Man's hairy cousins, that their souls might be saved through knowledge and worship of the Almighty.

Sir George Fox, with whom I had formed a bond of friendship, had a beautiful wife named Ada. I had achieved some success at communicating with her through the medium of mime, and when I made my wishes known, she arranged for Herr Döktor to attend me at the great house and put me through an intense course of instruction.

Dear reader, I could write at great length of the travails endured upon both sides during the months of my training. And I confess that in times of great frustration I did resort to the flinging of dung. But Herr Döktor endured and so did I, and six months later I shook the hand of this remarkable visionary, thanked him and said farewell in all-but-perfect 'Man'.

And here I must express a certain measure of regret, for I did not use my new-learned talents as wisely as I might. I craved excitement and I craved to be as men are. I shaved my facial whiskers and the hairs from my hands; dressed as a sporting toff, my tail tucked out of sight; represented myself as an English country gentleman; and took myself off to the gaming tables of Monte Carlo.

Within several short hours I had lost all that Lord Brentford had left me. I stood once more at poverty's door, a sadder yet wiser monkey.

I learned that evening a bitter lesson. But my life has been a series of lessons learned and it has also been an adventurous and often carefree one, filled with the joys of genuine friendship and love. Thus I no longer offer excuses for my early foolishness.

Happily I had retained my papers of employment, drawn up for me by Lord Brentford himself and bearing his heraldic seal. With these I presented myself at the offices of Blackfrond's, London's premier employment agency.

Blackfrond's specialised in placing registered non-human workers into suitable employ. Here, upon any given day, the sapient pig, the equine wonder, even the spider of destiny might be found in the plushly furnished confines of Blackfrond's Waiting Hutch, patiently preparing for placement.

I was fully aware that as the world's first speaking ape, a simian prodigy if ever there was one, I could reasonably expect to turn a pretty penny by exhibiting myself before a paying public. But my travels with Mr Wombwell had convinced me that discomfort outweighed monetary benefit in that line of work. I had grown to love the finer things of life. I determined to take once more to what I now considered my vocation and return to being a monkey butler.

It was a wise decision.

I took employment with a venerable ancient by the name of Colonel Katterfelto.

My adventures with this worthy fellow have been chronicled within Mr Robert Rankin's admirable book *The Mechanical Messiah and Other Marvels of the Modern Age*, and I can do no better than to recommend the reader purchase and peruse this finely crafted tome.

After a life of heroic service to his fellow man, Colonel Katterfelto died in my arms. He was one of the finest and most noble individuals it has ever been my honour to call friend. Indeed, he called me his little brother, and tears fill my eyes at his memory.

After that I fell in with Cameron Bell.

Mr Cameron Bell is a most singular individual, even in an age that appears overpopulated with singular individuals. He is, by calling, a consulting detective and owns to a number of literary friends and acquaintances, two in particular being worthy of note here – Messrs Charles Dickens and Sir Arthur Conan Doyle. Mr Dickens based the looks of Mr Pickwick upon those of Cameron Bell, and Sir Arthur Conan Doyle modelled the deductive reasoning of his most notable creation, Sherlock Holmes of Baker Street, upon that of Mr Bell.

A most singular individual indeed.

Mr Bell's observational skills, his capabilities as a consulting detective, his discretion and his boundless enthusiasm for his vocation have made him the greatest detective of the Victorian age and something of a darling with the well-to-do.

He has solved cases for most of the royal houses of Europe, and in eighteen ninety-nine, with my invaluable assistance (as he and I had formed a partnership under the name of Banana and Bell), he saved Her Majesty Queen Victoria from assassination.

Mr Bell was awarded the Royal Victorian Order for his services to the sovereign and became a Knight of the Grand Cross.

I received neither medal nor commendation. But, like the Fuller's 1900 Millennial Double Chocolate Stout, I harbour no acerbity.

The case that led to Mr Bell saving the life of Victoria, Empress of both India and Mars, involved two dreadful harpies: Lavinia Dharkstorrm, a witchy woman, and Princess Pamela, twin sister of Queen Victoria and, as it turned out, the female Antichrist.

It was a hair-raising adventure and I have many hairs that might be raised. Especially whilst in the company of Mr Bell, who is known to me as the World's Most Dangerous Detective due to his immoderate use of dynamite.

I would mention here, because it is of importance, that Mr Bell and I had been taken into the confidence of the pre-eminent chemist Ernest Rutherford, the gentleman who created the world's first Large Hadron Collider, which was cunningly disguised as part of London's Underground Railway System – the Circle Line.

This piece of advanced technology powered yet another.

Mr Ernest Rutherford's time-ship.

Through a series of what the mean-spirited amongst us might describe as unlikely events, I became the pilot of Mr Rutherford's time-eliminating conveyance and returned from the future to save my past self. In doing so, my future self was shot dead by Lord Brentford, who had not in fact died when the *Empress of Mars* went down, but had survived and taken shelter on a cannibal island. It is all rather difficult to explain, and rather than waste the reader's time doing it here I would recommend perusing a copy of *The Educated Ape and Other Wonders of the Worlds* by Mr Robert Rankin, where all is set out in the most meticulous detail.

I write these words in the elegant city of Brighton, in the year two thousand and twelve. I know that I must return to the year eighteen ninety-eight to save my younger self, and I know that in doing so I will be shot, in error, by Lord Brentford.

This is my fate. So it must be.

But between the time when I set off in Mr Rutherford's time-ship in the company of Mr Cameron Bell and the time of my inevitable extinction, there have been many years of travel and many adventures, and it is these that I intend to write of here.

Mr Bell assured me that once he had cleared up the single case that he had so far failed to solve, we would travel back in time to watch Beethoven conduct the Ninth Symphony and thereafter begin our adventures.

Things did not go quite as he had planned.

But they did get very exciting.

And it all began when we sailed the time-ship back to eighteen ninety.

1890

3

ain was falling and it was falling hard.

Had it not been for the quality of my sou'wester, Ulster coat and India rubber galoshes, I would have felt the chill of this midnight hour more cruelly than I did.

As I am possessed of considerable skills when it comes to piloting a space vessel, I was able to steer the time-ship (a back-engineered and greatly modified Martian war craft) gently down to a secluded area of Hyde Park. One frequented, when the weather was fair, by slosh-pots and Muff Mary Ellens, but deserted upon a night such as this.

'I shall remain here whilst you conduct your business,' I told Mr Bell as we sat in the time-ship's cabin, peering out at the night. 'I am reading a book about tea that I'd quite like to finish.'

Mr Bell shook his hairless head at this. 'I contend,' said he, 'that we should not become separated during our journeyings through time.'

'Surely there will be times when we must part,' said I, for I had learned to take privacy whilst engaging in latrinal excursions.

'And we will have none of *that*.' Mr Bell made the firmest of faces. 'An adventure through the ages seasoned by toilet talk and innuendo would be one too rich for my palate.'

'Look,' said I, removing the ignition key from the time-ship's dashboard and hanging it on its chain about my neck. 'We have agreed that you will solve your one unsolved case and then we will go back to see Beethoven conduct the Ninth. We even swore a great oath to this effect – your idea, as I recall – and shook hands on it and everything.'

'I wanted things to be absolutely clear,' said Mr Bell, 'so there would be no later disagreements or unpleasantnesses.'

'Then go off about your business and I will await your return. Or better still, let us both remain here until the weather clears up.'

'It rains all night,' said Mr Bell. 'And what must be done, must be done now and by both of us together. The quicker it is done, the quicker you can experience the Ninth, played as it truly should be played and conducted by the great man himself.'

And so we left the *Marie Lloyd* (for such was the name of our time-ship) and trudged off into the rain. Mr Bell hailed a cab at Hyde Park Corner and directed its driver to take us to the British Museum.

The cabbie, who rode aloft in the rain sporting an Ulster coat not dissimilar to my own but for its lack of quality, called down to us through the little roof hatch that he might enliven our journey with tales of those who had brought him honour by deigning to ride in his cab.

'I 'ad that Winston Churchill in the back o' me 'ansom the other night,' he told us. 'Now there's a rum young gentleman if ever there was one. Very fixed in 'is opinions, is our Mr Churchill. I touched upon the matter of public Ladies' Excuse-mes, or *conveniences* as may be, and 'ow to my reckonin' they would be a blessing to the dear ones, who aren't as good at 'oldin' it in as would be a chap, and—'

Mr Bell drew shut the little hatch. Toilet talk, as he had said, was not at all to his liking.

As we had some distance to travel, I made polite conversation by asking my friend just what he knew of the villain he sought and just what the unsolved crime might be. Mr Bell had recently been all but defeated by a woman, and women appeared to be rising in prominence during this period of history – as evidenced by the spread of public Ladies' Excuse-mes and suchlike. Was this villain a lady? I asked Mr Bell.

The great detective shook his head and his hat showered me with raindrops. 'A man,' said he. 'Most definitely. There is always talk,' he continued, 'of a criminal mastermind, some secret orchestrator of the capital's crimes. The Moriarty, who my good friend Arthur set against his Mr Holmes. This is the work of such a fellow and a very strange business indeed.'

I yawned, rather too loudly, perhaps, but I was still a growing ape and it was after my bedtime.

'An evil overlord,' Mr Bell continued some more, 'one capable of manipulating even the most powerful in the realm through blackmail and tergiversation. I have spied evidence of his sinister handiwork in everything from headlines in the broadsheets to acts passed in Parliament. Rumours abound as to his identity.'

'Or indeed as to his very existence,' I suggested in a tone of casual flippancy. Mr Bell raised an eyebrow to this and then went on to say more.

'He is known as the Pearly Emperor,' he said. 'For as the cockneys have their Pearly Kings and Queens and Her Majesty is Empress of India and Mars, this would-be usurper of thrones has chosen such a title for himself. He is said to have risen from a humble background in the East End, and seeks to rule this world and all the others that roll about our sun.'

'A man of great ambition,' I said, snuggling down in my Ulster coat and searching out my mittens. 'A worthy adversary for your good self. You being the uncrowned King of Detectives, as it were.'

Mr Bell peered at me through his gold-framed pince-nez. 'Are you,' he asked of me, and here he employed suitable cockney patois in the form of rhyming slang, 'having a *gi-raffe* at my expense?'

'Heaven forfend,' said I, a-putting on my mittens. 'Here I am, rattling along in this uncomfortable conveyance, in bitter cold at an ungodly hour and all but freezing off those parts that will escape mention lest I be accused of toilet talk, bound for the British Museum. There to foil the evil intention of the Pearly Emperor, a monomaniac intent on world domination and—'

But here I paused as I could, even in the limited light available, observe the reddening of my friend's cheeks and the infuriated expression he now wore. I felt it would probably be best to keep my own counsel.

I did, however, make the observation that to my limited knowledge there had never been a single crime of any significance committed at the British Museum that had not gone unsolved.

My good friend's face had now become purple, and when next he spoke it was as one possessed. 'A crime *did* occur,' he cried into my little ear. 'A crime covered up by the authorities – no doubt in the pay of this *monster made flesh*.' (I mouthed the words *monster made flesh*.) 'This vile creature's minions have committed numerous crimes on his behalf. I could name dozens of them. I have been involved in solving dozens of their felonious cases. But the criminals never turn King's evidence, they never betray their master. He is never there when the crimes are committed. But tonight, tonight he will be there. I know it. My studies of case histories have led me to this conclusion. I know that I am right.'

'Quite so,' I said. 'I am sorry if I misled you into believing that I harboured any doubts.'

'He will be there tonight, and I will have him. Tonight, a seemingly impossible crime will be committed at the British Museum. I will be there to see how it is done. Then I will capture the criminal mastermind – or destroy him, if need be.'

'Ah,' I said. 'Destroy?'

'If need be,' said my companion.

'You brought your ray gun with you, then?'

'Of course.' Mr Bell patted a pocket.

'And dare I ask if—'

'Ask away.'

The hansom made an alarming lurch and I said, 'Dynamite.'

'I *have* taken the sensible precaution of bringing along a few sticks in case they are required.'

I groaned dismally, but silently.

'Do not worry,' said Mr Bell. 'I am well prepared.'

'But,' I said, for I felt that I must, 'it *is* the British Museum. It is filled with wonderful, beautiful things. Please do not blow up the British Museum, please, Mr Bell, oh please.'

Mr Bell smiled as to offer me comfort. 'It is a sturdy building,' he said. 'Have no fear for its collapse.'

'But the wonderful, beautiful things—'

'Let us hope it will not prove necessary.'

'But it *always* proves necessary to your reasoning.'

I noticed a certain twinkle come into the eyes of Mr Bell,

for most surely this fellow's love for explosions was equal to his love for justice. I sighed deeply and inwardly and prayed to my chosen deity that the British Museum would still remain standing after our departure from it.

And also that the rain might stop.

The driver raised the little hatch and called down, 'British Museum, guv'nor.'

The British Museum truly was a beautiful building and it was my dearest hope that it would remain so.

Built in that neoclassical style so popular during the reign of Queen Victoria, designed by Sir Robert Smirke and containing no fewer than eight million artefacts at the time of my visit, it was a thing of great splendour.

In those days it also housed what would come to be known as the British Library, a collection of some twenty thousand, two hundred and forty volumes bequeathed by Sir Thomas Grenville. Exactly how a single individual had managed to acquire so vast a collection of books within a single lifetime was *at that time* quite a mystery to me.

Later, all would become very clear.

The sky above was not at all clear. Thunder rattled chimney-pots and lightning flung brightness and stark shadows about in a manner that was most alarming. The rain poured down and down and down and I grew quite afraid.

Mr Bell, being the kindly man that he was, brought what comfort he could to me with light but caring pats upon the shoulder. Then, when the hansom had departed and we were left in an otherwise deserted street before the big locked gates, he drew a stick of dynamite from his pocket.

'Surely not *yet*?' I cried upon sighting it.

'But we must open the gates,' said he, 'to gain entry. My portly form will not permit me to shin over them.'

'My slight and nimble one will, however, permit me to do so,' said I. 'I assume that keys might be found within that little brick house there marked Gatekeeper's Lodge?' For the lightning periodically illuminated such a building.

Mr Bell nodded, and as I swarmed up the rain-drenched iron gates, I swear I heard his distinctive chuckle moment- arily made audible amongst the thrashings of the storm.

I returned at length in the company of keys.

'The gatekeeper slept?' asked Mr Bell.

'The sleep of the inebriate,' I said.

'Or possibly the *drugged*.' Mr Bell availed himself of the keys.

'Please hurry now,' I said. 'I am growing most chilly.'

Within minutes, we had entered both gates and building. The museum, a pleasant enough place by daylight, looked far from pleasing now, lit only by periodic flashes of light- ning. The statues and ancient artefacts became fearful in this untender and uncertain illumination and I trembled from more than just cold.

Mr Bell perused his pocket watch, a gift from a grateful Jovian plutocrat for sorting out a delicate business that involved an actress, a bishop and a kiwi bird called Cuddles. 'It nears the hour of one,' he whispered to me, though his whispered words echoed terribly within the great atrium. 'We must set ourselves to hiding in the Egyptian Gallery. Follow me.'

I did as I was bid and followed Mr Bell through deserted galleries and up a broad flight of marble steps. I tugged at my friend's trouser leg and asked him what, precisely, was the nature of the crime that was about to be committed.

'Ah,' said he, with a certain lightness of whisper. 'The sarcophagus of the God-Pharaoh Akhenaten will be stolen tonight from its unlocked cabinet.'

'Having acquired a set of keys to this museum myself with very little bother,' I said, 'I cannot imagine unlocking a cabinet would present much of a problem to a determined thief.'

'No key unlocked that cabinet,' said Mr Bell.

I shrugged.

'And anyway,' he went on, 'it was not merely the sarcophagus that was stolen – which alone weighs several tons and was removed without leaving a single trace of *how* it was removed. It was something more than *that*.'

'Something more than *that*?' I whispered. Thoughtfully.

'Something more indeed,' said Mr Bell. 'All at once and all in a single night. Gone without trace and never seen again.'

I raised my eyes and said, 'What?'

'The entirety of the British Library,' said Mr Cameron Bell. 'All twenty thousand, two hundred and forty volumes.'

'All in a single night?' said I. 'Now surely *you* are having a gi-raffe.'

4

We were making a cautious passage through the Etruscan Gallery when first we heard the chanting. I looked up at Mr Bell, and in the uncertain light I saw him put his finger to his lips. Together we crept forward until, upon reaching the far doorway, we espied them.

Nubians!

I knew them to be such because I had most recently read an article in *The Times* newspaper penned by Mr Hugo Rune concerning the construction of ancient monuments. I will not tire the reader here with Mr Rune's theories on the subject as they may be found written up in considerable detail elsewhere.* The article in *The Times* had been profusely illustrated. A Nubian slave was pictured beneath a paragraph that claimed the Great Pyramid was merely the capping stone of a far larger obelisk that had sunk into the desert sands due to inadequate foundations.

'Nubians,' I whispered to Mr Cameron Bell.

'Nubians indeed,' this fellow whispered back to me. 'And take a peep to see what they are doing.'

* *In several of my wonderfully written novels, now available for the Kindle. (R. R.)*

I took such a peep and noted well that they had formed a human chain, which stretched through the doorway and off into the distance towards the Egyptian Gallery. The human links in this chain were passing from hands to hands what must surely be the contents of the British Library.

'There are dozens of Nubians,' I further whispered.

'Hundreds,' said Cameron Bell. 'And all in the employ of the Pearly Emperor.'

I must confess that the sight of so many Nubian slaves, so very far from the Nile Delta and stripped to the waist upon such a chilly night, caused me not only considerable concern, but did tend to lend credibility to Mr Bell's suspicions. Which should, of course, have caused me to give credit where credit was due, had it not been for the obvious thought that they were so many and we so few in number.

This obvious thought was in turn followed by another. That the explosively inclined Mr Bell might well choose to even up the odds through the employment of dynamite.

'What do you suppose they are chanting?' I whispered, perhaps in the hope of distracting him from any such thinking.

'*Aom eeom Aten*,' said my friend. And, surprising me with his arcane knowledge, he added, 'In the ancient Egyptian sacred tongue, the chant means "living spirit of the Aten" and is spoken in praise of the God-Pharaoh Akhenaten.'

'He of the mysteriously stolen sarcophagus,' I remarked.

'Precisely.'

'And how do you know of such stuff?'

'I did my research,' said Cameron Bell. 'Here amongst the tomes of the British Library.'

I was about to ask further questions, but Mr Bell once more put his finger to his lips and then beckoned with it that I should follow him.

We crept forward to gain a better view of the nefarious goings-on and caught sight of a mysterious yellow glow emanating from the Egyptian Gallery, many yards and many book-passing Nubians in the distance.

'Do you have that new-fangled portable telephone,' I asked, 'which Mr Tesla gave you as a reward for sorting out that delicate affair concerning the actress, the bishop and the collie dog called Daisy? You might well now employ it and call for police reinforcements.'

Mr Bell offered me a certain glance, which I observed but briefly in the flashings of the lightning. 'I fear not,' said he, 'for it has yet to be invented.'

And I mused upon this.

Mr Bell delved into his pocket.

And brought forth, to my great relief, his ray gun.

'Ah,' whispered I. 'Then blast away, do, Mr Bell. I shall wait here for your victorious return.'

'You will accompany me,' said the great detective. 'But in truth I wish no harm to come to you, so climb up onto my shoulders for now, but be prepared to take cover.'

I took off my sou'wester and mittens and tucked them away into my Ulster coat, then clambered onto the shoulders of Cameron Bell. 'What *precisely* is your plan?' I whispered at his ear.

'Each floor's galleries are joined together to form a quad-rangle,' Mr Bell replied. 'We will retrace our steps, then skirt all the way around the building and enter the Egyptian Gallery from its most distant door rather than its nearest. Do you understand what I mean?'

I shook my head. 'Of course I do,' I said.

And so we did skirtings about, through further deserted and lightning-lit galleries, eventually to come upon the most distant door of the Egyptian Gallery.

Through which we furtively peeped.

Mr Bell drew back of a sudden. 'Well now, indeed,' whispered he.

'What did you see?' I asked him.

'What I had hoped *not* to see, but suspected that I might.'

'Which is?'

'Akhenaten himself,' said Cameron Bell.

And indeed, as the two of us now peeped forwards, there was certainly no doubt in my mind that my friend spoke the truth. My knowledge of ancient Egypt is not profound, but even *I* know that Akhenaten was the *strange* pharaoh. The one with the weird long face and un-Egyptian features. The one that never seemed to fit. The one who messed about with the ancient Egyptian religion. The being that now stood in the Egyptian Gallery, bathed in a curious yellow light and directing the Nubians to load the contents of the British Library into his *own* sarcophagus, could, in my opinion, be none other than Akhenaten the odd God-Pharaoh himself.

I now became once more afraid. 'Surely,' I whispered, 'his body lies in that sarcophagus. This must be the ghost of Akhenaten.'

Mr Bell nodded without conviction.

'This is not work for a detective,' I further whispered. 'This is work for a priest and exorcist.'

Mr Bell said, 'We shall see,' and cocked his ray gun.

Then he said, 'Hold on tightly, Darwin,' and marched through the open doorway.

Akhenaten was a being of considerable height, towering well over six feet tall and surely nearing seven. He wore the robes that a pharaoh should wear and that curious hat with the cobra motif and the big, long, dangly ear flaps. His body was gaunt yet his belly was large, his arms gangled long and his fingers weighed heavy with rings.

At first he did not notice Mr Bell, but merely kept right on directing his Nubians to load more books and still more books into the apparently bottomless sarcophagus.

Mr Bell made loud coughing sounds, then uttered the words, 'Good evening.'

Akhenaten swung about and the coldest pair of eyes I have ever seen turned down their glare upon Mr Cameron Bell.

'Gawd strike me down,' said Mr Bell, affecting the manner of the cockney. 'I fort you was Bill, me assistant. Can I be as 'elpin' of you?'

Akhenaten's eyes grew wide and his mouth fell hugely open.

'I will 'ave to ask you, sir, to return them books to the library,' said Mr Bell. 'You can only take three out at a time and not wivout a ticket.'

Akhenaten's mouth gaped wider still. And then he threw back his queerly shaped head and began to loudly guffaw. The Nubians had ceased their hands-to-handsings and their loadings-in and now stood like statues, blankly staring on.

Akhenaten's guffaws suddenly ceased. He wiped away a tear from his eye and spoke to my companion.

'Well, well, well,' he said to him. 'My old master, Mr Cameron Bell.'

And, 'Well, well, well,' the other replied. 'My old boot-boy, Mr Arthur Knapton.'

I looked from one to the other of them.

'And this must be the famous Darwin,' said Mr Arthur Knapton. 'The talking anthropoid. Say 'ello, little fella.'

'I am most confused,' said I.

To which Arthur Knapton, if such was this fellow, guffawed and guffawed again.

'I recall well that most annoying laugh,' said Mr Bell to myself. 'Arthur was my bootboy when I was at Oxford, a lad of low breeding but high ambition.'

'I 'eard that,' said Arthur in the tones of a genuine cockney. 'You always thought so well of yerself and thought so little of me.'

'You were a petty thief,' said Mr Bell. 'The last I heard of you was that you had been shipped off to Australia for stealing a bunch of bananas.'

'Ah,' said I, 'bananas.'

''Tis true enough,' said Mr Arthur Knapton, now folding his arms and idly tapping a toe. 'But as yer peepers will attest, I 'ave now arisen to somewhat greater 'eights.'

Cameron Bell now levelled his ray gun at Mr Arthur Knapton.

'A short-lived career, I'm afraid,' said he, 'for you are now under arrest.'

I must confess that the further guffaws that now issued from the mouth of Arthur Knapton, I, too, found annoying.

'Under arrest?' he croaked, between his outbursts of hilarity. 'Look at yerself, little man, why doncha? *You* dare t' threaten *me*?'

Mr Bell nodded. 'Do you have an overcoat with you?' he asked. 'Otherwise you might get a trifle wet in that fancy-dress costume when I escort you in handcuffs to Bow Street.'

And once more those guffaws rang loudly in our ears.

'Best gag him, too,' I suggested.

'Oh, please stop it.' Arthur Knapton raised his gangly arms and waggled his over-long, beringed fingers. 'I ain't bein' taken nowheres. And this ain't no fancy dress.'

Cameron Bell shook his head.

Arthur Knapton continued, 'I 'as come a long way since last we met,' he said. 'A long way an' a good many "whens".

An' I ain't Arthur Knapton no more. I'm Akhenaten, lord high muckamuck of ancient Egypt, I am. An' I'll 'ave you talk civil when in me presence, or I'll 'ave yer 'ead chopped off.'

'I don't think he's coming quietly,' I said to Mr Bell.

'*Begone!*' the cockney pharaoh shouted, and then strange things occurred.

The yellow glow grew to a blinding light and Mr Bell was flung backwards from his feet. I dodged nimbly away at this point to avoid being squashed by the most substantial detective.

There then came a mighty crackling as of static electricity, which caused every hair I possessed to stand up aloft from my person.

I heard a great clamour as of chiming bells, a scurrying of sandalled feet upon marble floor and then what sounded to me like water escaping from some mighty bath down a plughole.

And then, in what appeared to be the very blinking of an eye, Mr Bell and I found ourselves the only occupants of the Egyptian Gallery. The book-shifting Nubians had gone and so, too, had Arthur Knapton, Akhenaten as he claimed, along with his mighty sarcophagus.

Mr Bell arose from the floor and said, 'Well now, yes indeed.'

'He vanished away,' I said in reply. 'He and his band of Nubians. And, I rather suspect, all of the British Library with them.'

'He certainly did,' said Mr Bell. 'And I should have seen it coming.'

I cast a questioning glance at Cameron Bell. 'You *knew* that something such as that was likely to occur?' I said.

'I suspected something of the sort, yes.'

'Then he has defeated you once more.'

'Not yet,' said Mr Bell. 'The game has only just begun.'

'*Begun?*' I made a further questioning glance. 'He vanished away to who knows where. He clearly has magical powers. We have probably seen the last of him. A shame for you, but it cannot be helped.'

'It *can* be helped,' said Cameron Bell.

To which I shook my head. 'You had your try and you failed,' I said. 'It was a brave effort, but now it is my turn and I choose that we depart for eighteen twenty-four to watch Beethoven conducting the Ninth.'

Mr Cameron Bell now shook his head.

'You are shaking your head,' I told him.

'I am indeed,' this man agreed, 'because you and I both swore an oath that we would travel to wherever and whenever *you* wished once I had apprehended the criminal mastermind. But not *before* then. We shook upon this but an hour ago. I am sure that you remember.'

'I do,' I said and I hung my head. 'And I recall your distinctive chuckle.'

Cameron Bell chuckled now. 'I shall have Mr Arthur Knapton,' he said. 'No matter where or when.'

'*When?*' I said, in a somewhat leaden tone.

'When indeed!' said Cameron Bell. 'Because, as must surely now have dawned upon you, we are dealing with no ordinary criminal mastermind with delusions of world domination, but rather one in command of most singular skills. One who can travel through time.'

5

felt that Cameron Bell had deceived me and my teeth fairly ached to sink into some tender part of his anatomy. And most surely they would have done so had it not been for the clamorous sounds of alarm bells ringing that now grew loud to our ears.

'The game is afoot,' said Cameron Bell, 'and we had best be away.'

We returned to the time-ship in silence. Which is to say that no words passed between us as we sat side by side in another hansom cab and were driven along through the rain.

Once more aboard the *Marie Lloyd*, Mr Bell had the temerity to tell me that I should cheer up because a great adventure lay ahead.

I bared my teeth to signify contradiction. 'Not *my* big adventure,' was what I had to say.

'We will travel, I think, to ancient Egypt itself.' And with no more words spoken than that, Mr Cameron Bell took himself off to his cabin to select suitable apparel from his ample wardrobe.

I sat in the pilot's chair and I confess I sulked. It was quite clear to me now that I had been tricked from the very start.

Mr Bell, whose powers of observation and deduction were at that time unequalled by those of any other man on the planet, had clearly deduced *before* we launched into our journey that it was probable his adversary, the Pearly Emperor, was a fellow traveller through time. And that it was also probable that he might not be able to apprehend him at the British Museum and so would have to pursue him *through* time. And to draw me into this unfinished business of his, he had enticed me to share an oath which, on the face of it, had looked to be advantageous to myself.

In short, he had played a very mean trick upon me, and when he returned to the main cabin his duplicity became clearer still.

'These are for you,' said Mr Cameron Bell.

I turned about in the pilot's chair to peruse what 'these' these might be.

'A white linen three-piece suit with fitted tail-snood and matching pith helmet,' said Mr Bell. 'I ordered it from your personal tailor. It has your own personally chosen lining, too.' Mr Bell flashed this lining at me. It was the one I had designed myself, blue silk with banana motifs.

It was a very beautiful suit, but I viewed it with a very jaundiced eye. 'You *knew*!' I said to Mr Bell. 'You *knew* that he was a traveller of time.'

'*Suspected*,' said the smiling Cameron Bell. 'It appeared to be the only logical conclusion, but in eighteen ninety no other time machine was available in which I could pursue him. I had to *bide my time*, so to speak.'

'You are a very deceitful man,' I said most bitterly. 'You should have been honest with me from the start.'

'And then you would have readily agreed to pursue this criminal rather than simply swan about through history attending concerts or wandering the galleries of the Great Exhibition?'

'Ah,' I mused, 'the Great Exhibition of eighteen fifty-one. I remember reading that they displayed a prodigious selection of cultivated bananas there.'

'Precisely,' said Mr Bell. 'And I do wish to enjoy these pleasures with you. But you must understand, I am driven by my vocation. I am a detective. This is what defines me as a human being. I must bring Mr Arthur Knapton, the Pearly Emperor, to justice before I can consider doing anything else. I am sorry that I was not altogether honest with you. Would you care to try on the suit? White linen favours your complexion and it does have your personal lining.'

'Well . . .' I said, with some hesitancy.

'And for desert travel one would also need one of *these*.' And Mr Bell produced from the inner pocket of the suit he intended for me a bright and shiny object.

He placed it in my hands and I gave it my attention.

'It is a little hip flask,' I said.

'Turn it over,' said he.

I turned it over and read what was engraved upon it: ' "For my very best friend and partner Darwin, from one not so noble as he. Cameron Bell, 1900." '

A tear sprang up into my eye and I gave my *best* friend a cuddle.

'Then we work together and bring this rogue to justice?' asked Mr Bell.

'We do,' I said. 'But I have not quite forgiven you as yet.'

'I understand,' said the detective. 'Even so, let us plot a course for Egypt and adjust the time counter to the day of Akhenaten's ascension to his throne, and we will be off.'

'Why *that* particular day?' I enquired.

'Because that will be *before* our paths crossed at the British

Museum, and so at that time he would not even have guessed that I would be on to him in the future.'

'I can see that I will find time travel *very* confusing,' I said.

'Not just *you*,' said Cameron Bell. 'Let us set the controls and get the ship in motion and then I suggest we take some supper. I brought along a rather special bottle of Château Doveston champagne. Best crack it now, as ever, don't you think?'

I grinned towards Mr Cameron Bell. 'I do so like champagne,' I said to him.

How long, I am occasionally asked, does it take to travel from one time period to another? Do you travel at several years a minute? Do you accelerate or decelerate, or does no time whatsoever pass within the confines of the time-ship as you travel?

All of these are questions which might well demand answers, but I have no answers to give. On gazing occasionally through the portholes during our periods of travel, it always looked to me as though we were simply travelling through space. Planets appeared to pass us by and distant galaxies wheeled. Once in some while or another, a queer thing was to be seen. Once I swear that I saw an angel pass by, but Mr Bell and I *had* been drinking Vin Coca Mariani at the time, whilst celebrating the fact that it was Mr Bell who had been responsible for bringing down the walls of Jericho.

That, however, is quite another story. If I recall correctly, it only took about five minutes for us to travel back to eighteen ninety, but journeying more than two thousand years into the past was probably going to take a little longer.

★

We enjoyed a most delectable supper and refreshed ourselves with champagne. And then we took to our bunks with jovial goodnight-to-yous.

Which, looking back, was not perhaps the wisest of things to do, because several hours later we were both awakened by the crash.

The *Marie Lloyd*, unpiloted, had reached her destination and we plunged down without due let or hindrance into the Sahara Desert at a rate of knots that was to say reckless, if it were to say anything at all.

I said, 'Eeeek!' and, 'Help!' and, 'What is going on?'

And then we struck the sand a thunderous blow.

Many things that had been distributed along the length of the time-ship now found themselves plunging helter-skelter towards the rear, for when travelling backwards through time the *Marie Lloyd* naturally flew in reverse. Myself and Mr Bell, issuing from our cabins, found ourselves accompanying the multifarious objects in their pell-mell rearward dash. Happily, neither of us was badly injured, and as I was wearing my nightshirt, I avoided besmirchment of my new linen suit.

Mr Bell, however, was not quite so lucky. He found himself intimately involved with the HP Sauce dispenser, the contents of which had smothered him head to foot.

I tried so very hard not to laugh.

But sadly I utterly failed in this endeavour.

When order was restored and Mr Bell had showered and changed his clothes, we ventured from the time-ship with a certain trepidation, fearing greatly that we might already have damaged it beyond any reasonable hope of repair.

I sported my new suit and pith helmet and cut a rather dashing figure. Mr Bell looked somewhat hot in his tweeds. He had a large pair of binoculars strung about his neck, a mighty knapsack on his back and was carrying a fine stout walking cane.

The *Marie Lloyd* was well dug in to the desert floor. But the soft sand had clearly cushioned the impact and our limited inspection appeared to reveal that no great damage had been done.

Mr Bell produced a compass from his pocket, a lovely gold affair – a gift, he assured me, from a grateful Venusian ecclesiastic for sorting out a delicate business concerning an arch-druid, a pantomime dame and a whistling racoon named Frisky.

'That way to the east,' said Mr Bell, pointing off towards nothingness.

I looked up at my friend the detective and asked him if he was sure.

'Never more certain,' said he.

'Only it looks to me to be a very large desert and the sun is shining brightly from a very cloudless sky.'

'You have your hip flask?'

'Yes, and some fruit for my breakfast.'

'Excellent. Then we set forth to seek the city of Akheta-ten. It is known that Akhenaten built this city in honour of the God Aten, Aten being an aspect of himself.'

'That comes as little surprise,' I said. 'But given matters so far, I must insist upon hearing your plan before we set forth.'

'My plan,' said Cameron Bell.

'Your plan. So that as your partner I might offer my considered opinion as to its validity. You do actually *have* a plan, I suppose? You were not simply thinking to strike out into a desert beneath a blazing sun, en route to an appointment with who knows what, without any plan at all?'

We returned to the *Marie Lloyd*.

★

An hour later, we re-emerged from the *Marie Lloyd* and I climbed up to the time-ship's pointy nose to have a good look around through my friend's binoculars. Then I climbed down and returned them to him.

'There is a very large city in *that* direction,' I said, pointing towards the west. 'It looks to be a little less than a mile away, so it won't take us long to reach it.'

We marched in a spirited fashion. We even sang a music hall number or two, and Mr Bell told me a joke about a lady who grew parsnips in her window box. I laughed politely but did not understand it. Presently we climbed to the crest of a sand dune and gazed towards the mighty city beyond.

It rose from the sand like some fairy-tale creation, towers and cupolas shimmering in the heat. It held to such a rare beauty that I was touched to behold it. Mr Bell dusted sand from the lenses and peered at it through his binoculars.

Then he suddenly said, 'Oh my, oh my,' lowered his binoculars, then raised them once again.

'They are building a pyramid,' he said. 'A gigantic pyramid.'

'They did a lot of that kind of thing at this time,' I replied. 'Mr Hugo Rune believes that pyramids are just the tops of ob—'

'I think you had better see for yourself,' said Mr Bell, and he handed his binoculars to me.

I adjusted them to fit my face and raised them to my eyes. Then I fiddled somewhat with the focusing.

Then I beheld the sight of a half-completed pyramid. And something more that caused me to gasp and lower the binoculars.

'You see them?' asked Cameron Bell.

'I see them,' I replied. 'Thousands and thousands of them, hauling great blocks of granite up ramps to build the pyramid.'

Mr Bell nodded. '*And?*' said he.

I raised the binoculars and stared once more through their lenses. '*And*,' I said, when I had done, 'they are not men who haul those blocks, but thousands and thousands of chickens.'

6

'h my dear dead mother,' said Cameron Bell.

And I, too, expressed considerable surprise.

We both took turns with the binoculars to assure ourselves that we had not fallen prey to some desert mirage. But there they were, large as life – thousands and thousands of chickens.

'I must express my extreme disappointment,' said I.

And Cameron Bell asked me just why this was.

'Because it has been my conviction,' I explained, 'that the race of Man descended from Ape, as popularised by the theory of my namesake, Mr Darwin. The Ape being God's noblest creature, as you yourself would attest, having spent so much time in my company.'

Mr Bell rolled his eyes somewhat at this. Perhaps he had some sand in them.

'It certainly puts a new perspective upon history,' he said.

'Not one that *I* will readily embrace,' I replied. 'There will be some rational explanation, I am sure. Perhaps they are a special breed of worker chicken bred by an ape of the scientific persuasion.'

'As likely an explanation as any, I suppose.'

Mr Bell shrugged and I, having nothing better to do, joined him in shrugging.

'Will this affect *our* plan?' I asked, when I had tired of shrugging.

'In no way.' Mr Bell arose and dusted sand from himself.

'That there may be no misunderstandings,' I said, doing likewise, 'please outline to me *precisely* what your intentions are.'

'Certainly.' My friend drew from an inner pocket a hip flask that greatly dwarfed my own and acquainted himself with its contents. 'Today is the day of Akhenaten's coronation. The city will swell with visitors, many many visitors, from all parts of this ancient realm. We will be able to move unnoticed amongst them—'

I made a coughing-mumbling sound, which signified a degree of uncertainty. Mr Bell continued undeterred.

'And we shall take ourselves to a hostelry and learn what there is to be learned. Our aim is ultimately the capture and return to London of the elusive Mr Knapton. This we *will* achieve, but by what means depends upon the intelligence gained within the city. I can offer little more in the way of specifics than this.'

'Perhaps we should return once more to the *Marie Lloyd* and iron out the details,' I said. 'I recall that I made several suggestions earlier which do not now appear to be included in your scheme.'

'Darwin,' said Mr Bell, 'do you wish to see Beethoven conduct the Ninth, or do you not?'

'Let us hasten to the city,' I said. 'I am confident that the details will iron themselves out soon enough.'

★

It was fearsomely hot. We trudged over sand dunes and eventually found ourselves upon a paved road. Here we fell in with other travellers, some on horseback, some upon camels, some simply plodding on foot. All were bound, as we were, to the great city of Akhetaten, and none paid us any attention.

Mr Bell had suggested that it would be better if I did not display my vocal skills whilst in unfamiliar company, but that I might instead employ my considerable talents as an actor by posing as his servant. He was quite profuse in his praises for my acting skills and likened me to a simian Henry Irving.

I had acquiesced to this on the condition that I remained in my white linen suit and pith helmet and was not required to don the hated fez and waistcoat.

Onward we marched to Akhetaten.

I confess to no little sense of awe. For here was I, actually in the past, amongst people of history, walking towards a city of a biblical persuasion. I had become the first Ape of Time and this was my first adventure.

Those we marched amongst were certainly striking to behold. So much so, in fact, that I feel the need to versify.

There were tall Zoroastrians all the way from Persia.
Gaunt Ethiopians in colourful attire.
Princes of Atlantis and of Narnia and India,
Who travelled to the music of the flute and lute and lyre.

There were worshippers of Hanuman, of Hathor and of
  Horus,
Freya and Fortuna, Marduk and Mummu.
Dagon and Demeter, Ganesha and Fanjita,
Achilles and Adonis and Agamemnon, too.

I will, in the fullness of time, add other verses to this text to bring the reader further joy, but those two for now are sufficient. Mr Bell identified to me Babylonians, Mesopotamians, denizens of Phoenicia, Nineveh, ancient Greece and Rome. It seemed as if all of the antique world had been invited to attend the coronation of Akhenaten. And given Mr Arthur Knapton's intentions for world domination, this was not altogether surprising.

A thousand thoughts must have whirled their way through my mind as we moved on towards the great city. Many many questions sprang forward, but few answers moved to greet them.

We passed rather too closely to one of the half-built pyramids and viewed the chickens that worked upon it. They were fearsome chickens.

Each one of them was the height of a man and possessed of considerable strength, for they hauled those granite blocks with ease. I looked up at Mr Bell and caught sight of a most quizzical expression upon the great detective's face. It was evident to me that Cameron Bell was baffled by those chickens.

We entered the city through a gateway that yawned between two monstrous statues of Akhenaten, seated and stately and striking to behold. I have seen several of the capital cities of Earth during my travels and also once Rimmer, the capital city of Venus. But I had never before seen such a city as this.

Its architecture was daunting to the eye, its scale beyond an ape's ability to encompass. It was not as if the mighty buildings rose up from the ground, but rather that they appeared to soar down from the sky. They conformed to a curious geometry that played havoc with perspective and brought troubles to the mind. This was indeed a biblical city. And new thoughts crowded my head. I thought of those mighty men of old, the patriarchs and prophets, of Moses, Aaron, Isaiah, Ezekiel, Abraham and the rest. Did their feet, in these ancient times, walk upon the pavements of this city? Were such Old Testament heroes here at this very moment?

Mr Bell was searching for a public house. Whilst I gazed up in awe at obelisks inlaid with tiger's-eye, chalcedony, chrysoprase and jasper, he sought out a bar. I knew Mr Bell to be a man of integrity and ingenuity, but also a man who was keen to haunt taverns.

'Aha,' said he of a sudden, and drew me from the throng that was now pressing hard about my small self. 'Here will serve us fine, I do believe.'

He pointed up to a row of hieroglyphics above an open doorway.

And once more proved the extent of his arcane knowledge by interpreting them.

'Fangio's Bar,' said Mr Cameron Bell.

'*Fangio's Bar!?!*' I would have said, but I was sworn to silence.

'Let us enter and see what we can see.' Mr Bell dusted down his tweeds, removed his pith helmet and, in the company of myself, entered Fangio's Bar.

It came as a surprise to me on this occasion, but would fail to do so upon others, that a bar looks just like a bar no matter which where or when you happen to be. And this one was ever so typical.

It was long and low and loathsome, dimly lit and evil-smelling. A bar-counter ran the length of the far wall and a cockroach was sauntering along its length. The floor was cobbled with sandstone and clothed with rotten rugs. The walls were dressed with sporting prints and I viewed what looked to be a number of Spanish souvenirs behind the bar-counter amongst the optics, along with several picture post-cards and a scale model of Noah's Ark.

It was not a big bar and my eyesight is acute.

Patrons of this sorry establishment lounged upon rough wooden stools, taking their Egyptian porter from earthen-ware tankards and mumbling in those Neanderthal tones common to bar patrons the whole world over, throughout the length and breadth of time.

Having taken it in, I turned to take my leave.

Mr Bell, however, would have none of that.

'We shall stay,' said he, a-pushing me forward. 'We will taste ale and *I* will chat with the locals.'

I mentioned in passing that this bar was evil-smelling. Much of this foetor clearly emanated from the patrons, who were surely not of princely stock. The beer had a mal-odorous quality that was all its own and I felt disinclined to sample it.

Mr Bell approached the bar, one hand upon my shoulder. A barman, of filthy aspect, viewed our arrival with a jaundiced expression, a jaded eye and a nose with a boil on the end.

'Two measures of your finest ale,' said Mr Cameron Bell.

The barman just stared on and made no movement.

'*Two . . . measures . . . of . . . your . . . finest . . . ale*,' said Mr Bell once more, this time more slowly and more loudly, for as any Englishman knows, Johnny Foreigner *can* under-stand the Queen's English if he chooses to, and if you say what you have to say *very* loudly and *very* slowly he will eventually acknowledge this fact and you will get what you require.

Fellow time traveller Hugo Rune suggested that to enforce a point in circumstances such as these, the employment of a stout stick had an educational effect. Mr Bell did carry such a stick!

'I said . . .' said he, '*TWO . . . MEASURES . . . OF*—'

'There's no need to shout,' said the barman. 'I heard you the first time.'

'Oh,' said Mr Bell.

'And I would have answered you the first time, too, had I not become overwhelmed by wonder.'

Mr Bell was now speechless. For after all, here was a barman, in the historical city of Akhetaten, who spoke Her Majesty's tongue.

'Wonder?' said Mr Cameron Bell in a very small voice indeed.

'Wonder as to what a gentleman such as yourself is doing on a hot day as is this, wearing a three-piece suit of Boleskine tweed more suited to a spot of grouse-shooting on a Highland moor, and in the company of an ape got up in more appropriate apparel. An ape, I might add, as carries himself in such a manner as to affect a certain snootiness. And—'

'A Scotsman,' said Mr Cameron Bell, extending his hand for a shake. The barman took this hand for a shake and gave it a thorough shaking. I had learned through keeping company with Mr Bell that *certain* handshakes had *certain* significances, and I felt that this particular handshake was one of those.

'Have you travelled far?' asked the barman.

And whispered words were now exchanged.

'Well now,' said Mr Bell, a-settling himself onto a tall and rugged stool set against the bar-counter. 'A Scotsman serving ale in the city of Akhetaten. How could I possibly have guessed?'

The Scotsman offered an enigmatic smile. 'You don't think the tam-o'-shanter, the clan cloth and the kilt give it away, then?' he asked.

And Mr Bell laughed somewhat.

'I do not think that you are altogether surprised at all,' said the barman. 'I would have you down as a seasoned traveller, would I not, sir?'

'You would,' said Cameron Bell.

'And one who has acquainted himself with many bars in many places.'

'That, too,' agreed the detective.

'And in each of these bars, all over the world, there is one thing notable?'

'More than just one thing,' said Mr Bell. 'But perhaps the most notable is that no matter in what far-flung reach of civilisation one finds oneself, if there is a bar to be found, there will like as not be found also a Scotsman standing be-hind the counter.'

The barman nodded. 'They predict that in a future time it will be an Australian,' said he.

'Pray that it be not so,' said Mr Bell. 'But it is a pleasure to meet with a fellow son of the isles I call my home.'

'A joy indeed,' said the barman. 'It will be a pleasure to shoot the breeze and chew the fat, talk the toot and drink the drink with your good self, a fellow lover of equality, liberty and egalitarianism.'

Mr Bell nodded.

'So what shall it be then, sir?' asked the Scottish lover of freedom, equality, liberty and egalitarianism.

'Two measures of your finest ale,' said Mr Cameron Bell.

'You are a thirsty gentleman indeed.'

'One, of course, is for my servant.' Mr Bell smiled upon me.

'No,' said the barman, smiling not. 'We don't serve *his* kind in here!'

7

'ou are surely jesting,' said Mr Cameron Bell.

'Indeed I am,' agreed the barman, displaying a toothless grin.

Mr Bell shrugged, the barman continued.

'I am of a whimsical disposition,' he explained, 'and levity lightens the burden of work.'

'I see,' said Mr Bell.

'Oh no you do not, sir.' The barman pointed at me. 'This little chap here,' he said, 'had me thinking. And I thought to myself, would it not be humorous to suppose that he was an ape of singular talent, who might one day choose to pen his memoirs?'

Mr Bell raised an eyebrow. I raised both of mine.

'And that set me to thinking,' the barman went on, 'as to how amusing it might be for him to end a chapter upon my words that "we don't serve *his* kind in here!"'

'Truly mirthful,' said Mr Bell. 'Although a most unlikely proposition.'

'And therein lies the mirth, sir,' said the barman. 'As unlikely a proposition as you in your tweeds *there* coming across me in my kilt *here*. Would you not agree?'

'I think the matter would be best not dwelt upon,' said Mr Bell. 'Especially by one with a mouth so dry as mine. Might I have the two ales that I asked for?'

'You may.' The Scottish barman drew ales from a copper can and introduced himself to my companion as Sandy MacTurnip.

'My name is Cameron Bell,' said Mr Bell, 'and this is Darwin, my simian servant. Nod to the gentleman, Darwin.'

I nodded with little enthusiasm, but with sufficient vigour as to have my pith helmet fall from my head. Which occasioned much mirth from the fun-loving barman, who told Mr Bell that he had once owned an ape but had beaten it to death for biting him. And then he turned his toothless smile once more towards myself.

I had no smiles to offer in return.

Presently our ales were served, mine in a sherry glass which MacTurnip explained had previously been held in reserve for titled ladies. Should any ever choose to enter his establishment. Mr Bell and I quaffed ale and I found it less noxious than others I have sampled.

MacTurnip served customers, few as they were, and then fell into conversation with Mr Cameron Bell.

The detective asked him, in as subtle a manner as he could manage, what the barman knew of Akhenaten.

'Now you are asking,' said the Scotsman, and his voice sank to a whisper. 'A queer enough fellow by any reckoning. A God, they say, and with the miracles that he causes to occur, who amongst us is to doubt it?'

'Miracles?' said Mr Bell, in the blandest tone he could muster.

'They say he came down from the Heavens,' MacTurnip whispered, 'in a flying sarcophagus inlaid with agate, opal, amethyst and bloodstone. And also with blue labradorite, which shines like crystal sky.'

'And have you yourself witnessed such an extravagant descent?' asked Mr Bell.

'Not as such, but we live in a time of wonders, and who is to say what is truly real or not?'

'What became of this city's previous ruler?' asked Mr Bell.

The barman gave his nose a tap with a grimy finger's end. 'There's much conspiratorial talk,' said he. 'Many say the chickens were behind it.'

'Ah, yes.' Mr Bell finished his ale and indicated that his mug should be refilled. 'I was going to ask you about the chickens. Where exactly did *they* come from?'

'Where did the chickens come from?' The barman pulled further ale. '*You* are asking me *that*?'

'I am,' said Mr Cameron Bell.

'Then I shall tell you,' said the barman, 'where *exactly* the chickens come from. They come out of an egg.'

'You are a born comedian,' said Mr Bell, lifting his pince-nez to mime the mopping of laughter tears from his eyes. 'You are surely wasted as a barman.'

'Are you having a gi–raffe?' asked the Scotsman, which possibly dated that expression.

'Are not *you*?' asked Mr Bell.

'I certainly am *not*. A foreigner you may be to these parts, sir, but know that here there are certain things that are not to be questioned. The chickens built this city. They are still at work on those pyramids, but should have them up in a couple of weeks.'

'But where *did* they come from?' asked Mr Bell.

'Out of the egg, as I told you. The cosmic egg that rests in the holiest of most holy places within the holy temple of the holy Aten. Where too rests the flying holy sarcophagus of the holy God-Pharaoh Akhenaten.

'Interesting,' said Mr Bell, a-nodding his head.

'I should keep such interest to yourself,' said the barman. 'You and your ape would not be let within fifty cubits of the holy temple. Strictly for the high muckamucks of the sacred faith, that is.'

'Are *you* not one of the faithful?' enquired my companion.

'I favour no particular credo,' said the barman, presenting Mr Bell with his mug of ale. 'Rather I adhere to a syncretic world-view – that there is a little bit of truth to everything. The rationalist within me holds to the opinion that he who claims to know everything labours under delusion, and that he who wishes to know everything would possibly be better employed drinking ale and finding himself a girlfriend. You will notice there, Mr Bell, how I tempered wisdom with wit – to pleasing effect, I believe.'

Mr Bell looked towards myself and we both rolled our eyes.

'The coronation itself,' said Mr Bell. 'That will take place within the holy of holies, I suppose.'

The barman MacTurnip shook his head. 'No,' said he. 'In a public place, but you are too late to get tickets.'

Cameron Bell now shook his head. 'Tickets?' said he. 'To the enthronement of a pharaoh? Tickets?'

'I might know where I could get you one.' The barman's finger once more tapped his nose. 'Seeing as how you have clearly travelled far across land and sea to be present upon this historic occasion.'

'I would be very glad for that,' said Mr Bell. 'But herein lies a difficulty – I hold no local currency and would expect such a ticket to come at considerable cost.'

The barman looked Mr Bell up and down. 'You are

adorned with numerous curious items,' said he, his gaze lingering upon Mr Bell's binoculars. 'Although clearly each is of little value by itself, together they might *all* add up to the price of a ticket so rare and so dearly wished for.'

Mr Bell made throat-clearing sounds. 'Once more you are displaying your finely honed and deeply refined sense of humour,' said he. 'The items that I carry upon my person are of great financial value, as a gentleman of discernment such as yourself must be well aware. I might, perhaps, deign to part with these magic eyeglasses in exchange for the ticket.' And here Mr Bell stroked at his binoculars.

'Magic, you say?' said the barman, and his hands took to rubbing together. 'And how does this magic manifest itself?'

'You look through this end,' Mr Bell indicated the same, 'and the thing you look at becomes magnified in size.'

'I see,' said the barman, in the manner of one intrigued. 'And this is the product of magic?'

Mr Bell nodded solemnly.

'So not the product of an alignment of convex lenses, as in a standard pair of binoculars?'

'Ah,' said Cameron Bell.

'Ah indeed, sir. You will be telling me next that your pocket watch functions by means of captured imps under your command animating its mechanism.'

'I had considered telling you something of the kind,' said Mr Bell, 'if you proved to be unimpressed by the binoculars.'

'As I told you, sir, we live in an age of wonders. Now do you wish to bargain for this ticket or do you not?'

'I do,' said Mr Bell. 'But before I do, tell me this. Is this ticket a *numbered* ticket? An *authentic* numbered ticket and one for a seat in a favourable position?'

'All of those things,' said the barman, and with a flourish

produced the ticket in question. It was of papyrus, but colour-fully printed with numerous hieroglyphics.

Mr Bell studied this ticket.

And then he looked up at the barman.

'I believe this ticket to be genuine,' he said, 'and the ceremony is to be held in the Annularium. I do not believe I am acquainted with this particular word.'

'It means Oval,' said the barman. 'The ceremony is to be held in the cricket ground.'

8

'he cricket ground,' said Cameron Bell, and he said these words most thoughtfully. 'The coronation of Pharaoh Akhenaten is to be held in the cricket ground.'

'Well, it *is* the national game,' said the barman. 'The Egyptians *did* invent cricket.'

'The Egyptians did *not* invent cricket,' said Cameron Bell.

'No,' said the barman. 'Of course they did not. I was only joking. The chickens invented cricket.'

I had taken to standing upon a bar-stool next to Mr Bell. I now took to rattling my sherry glass upon the bar-top to signify that it required refilling. The barman ignored this.

'Of course, it was originally called "chicket",' he said. 'But you know the way Egyptians lisp.'

Mr Cameron Bell sighed deeply.

'The chickens invented cricket,' he said, in that thoughtful tone of his.

'The chickens invented everything,' said the barman. 'Cricket, pyramids, binoculars, the Great Games with the fox races and so on.'

'I fear to ask,' said Mr Bell, 'but *fox* races?'

'You may recall how the Scots invented greyhound racing,' said the Scottish barman, 'in the time of the old heroes. A hare is set loose, and the hounds pursue it. The fox, as you know, is the chickens' natural enemy. The fox races are held in the arena. A fake chicken is set in motion through mechanical means and the foxes chase after it. The chickens eat the winner. And all the rest, too. Actually.'

'Chickens, it would appear, have an even more perverse sense of humour than yourself,' observed Mr Bell. 'So let us talk business: you may have my binoculars *and* my pocket watch in exchange for your ticket.'

'Most amusing.' MacTurnip shook his head, raising a small cloud of dust that drifted slowly down to the bar-top. I covered my glass with my hand. Mr Bell just sighed once more.

'What would you say was your most valuable possession?' asked the barman.

'My integrity,' said Mr Cameron Bell. 'But that is not for sale.'

'Well said,' said the barman. 'So let us remain with physical possessions.'

Mr Bell now shrugged.

'How about your monkey?' said the barman.

'Darwin?' Mr Bell now shook his head.

'Come, come,' said the barman. 'A monkey *is*, after all, only a monkey.'

'Darwin is much more than *that*.'

I smiled up at Mr Bell. He was my friend and his words gained my appreciation.

'That is my price,' said the barman.

'Then I must refuse you.'

The barman cocked his head upon one side. 'I think not,' said he.

'It is not a matter open to debate,' said Mr Bell.

'I do so agree.' The barman now delved beneath his bar-counter and brought into the uncertain light something that looked for all the world to be a brass blunderbuss.

'Invented by chickens?' asked Mr Bell.

The barman nodded. 'Hand over that monkey,' he said.

The emergence of the blunderbuss had quite a sobering effect on the bar's other patrons. It was to be suspected that they had viewed this weapon of terror on occasions past and possibly borne witness to its effects when triggered. What-ever the case, as one they rose, finished their drinks, bade their farewells and departed.

'And you have cost me trade, too,' said the barman, 'so I will avail myself of your binoculars and pocket watch also. In fact, clear out your pockets – I think I will take all that you have.'

I was not at all happy about this grim turn of events and I felt my heart beat faster. I confess that I trembled somewhat, too, and I looked towards my friend to offer comfort.

Mr Bell just stared unblinkingly at the barman.

'Hurry now,' said this villain. 'Turn out your pockets, I say.'

'Gladly, then,' said Mr Bell, suddenly finding his voice. 'But might I have the ticket?'

'Over my dead body,' said the barman.

Mr Bell made the saddest of faces.

And reached into the inner pocket of his tweed jacket.

It was a very favourable seat, high in the grandstand and shaded from the sun. I sat upon Mr Bell's lap and licked at the ice cream he had purchased for me with currency drawn from the barman's cash box.

'He certainly deserved what he got,' I said to Mr Bell. 'I am glad you did not forget to bring your ray gun.'

'A most unsavoury individual,' said my companion, 'and a most disagreeable circumstance. But a lesson learned, I suppose. These are *not* our times and the folk who live in these times do not necessarily share the same moral codes as we.'

I made my most thoughtful face. 'It does occur to me,' I ventured, 'that shooting him dead might not have been the most appropriate course of action.'

'I acted out of self-defence,' said Mr Cameron Bell.

'That is not what I mean. I was thinking more of the future.'

'As was I.'

'Not of *our* future, but rather that of the barman's descendants. Surely by killing him you will have changed the future?'

'Ah,' said Mr Bell, 'perhaps. But surely to no great account. This world has never lacked for Scotsmen.'

'I am sure you are right,' said I. 'No doubt there will be millions of his clan around by the end of the nineteenth century.'

'Millions,' said Mr Bell, chewing away at his ice-cream cone. 'Millions and millions of MacTurnips. I'm sure.'

Then he accidentally bit his tongue.

There was a fair old hubbub in that grandstand. A lot of excitement in the air. A lot of ice creams being eaten and big pointy-fingered hand-shaped gloves with 'I ♥ AKHENA-TEN' (although displayed in hieroglyphics) being waved about. A party spirit, you might say. A convivial atmosphere.

Mr Bell finished his ice cream and dabbed at his chin

with his handkerchief. 'I am not at peace with any of this,' he said.

'I do not care much for those chickens,' I replied. And there were indeed many chickens to be seen in the grandstand. 'I never cared much for the ordinary sort. I find *these* most upsetting.'

'They are certainly an enigma,' said the great detective. 'And, to my mind, anomalous. This case grows ever in complexity. There is more to every aspect than I should wish.'

'Let us go and see Beethoven conducting the Ninth,' said I. 'We could come back here ten minutes ago, afterwards. So to speak.'

'One thing at a time,' said Mr Bell. 'You'll see the Ninth soon enough.'

But sadly there was no truth in these words.

A chap in red silk robes and a broad-brimmed hat now strode out onto the neatly mown grass of the cricket pitch. He came from the pyramid end and took up a position of square leg. And then he bawled at us through an ivory mouth-trumpet.

'Peoples of the world,' he called, in good plain English. 'Peoples of the world, welcome one and welcome all to this glorious occasion.'

I whispered into the ear of Mr Bell. 'Am I to understand,' I whispered, 'that English is the universal tongue of this period?'

Mr Bell made grumbling sounds. 'Invented by chickens?' he muttered.

The chap in the hat continued. 'We want you all to have a really good time today,' was what he said. 'So let us get into the spirit of the thing by beginning with a wave.'

Folk in the grandstand waved to the chap. The chap

waved back at them. 'That is not precisely what I meant,' he called out through his mouth-trumpet. 'People in the far end of the stand there—' and he pointed '—raise your hands, then the people seated to the right of them do so, then those to the right of *them*. Let's have a go. When I say . . . wait for it . . . *go*!'

And the people at the far end of the stand raised their hands, then those next to them and so on. And when our turn came we raised ours, too, and it was rather fun.

'It is called an Egyptian Wave,' shouted the man standing on the nicely mown grass.

We did the Egyptian Wave a number of times. But it eventually became subject to the law of diminishing returns and the chap suggested that we should all introduce ourselves to our neighbours and then went on to entertain us with several popular songs of the day. Which were jolly enough in their way, but somewhat similar in content as each consisted of nothing more than praise for Akhenaten. By the time he led us all in a chorus of 'For He's a Jolly Good Pharaoh', I for one felt that perhaps Mr Bell and I should quit the grandstand for a while and seek out the cricket club bar.

Mr Bell clearly felt likewise, for he was shaking and shaking his head. 'Wrong wrong wrong,' said he, through tightly gritted teeth. 'This will all have to be stopped.'

'But surely it *is*,' I said. 'For none of this nonsense will be found in the pages of history.'

'Good point,' said Mr Bell. 'This twisted version of events *is* unknown in our time.'

'Probably because *you* will put it to rights,' I said, which pleased Mr Bell, for he was a man who responded favourably to compliments.

There now came to our ears sounds of a fanfare and a great cheer arose from the grandstand crowd.

Colourful folk were marching out onto the cricket pitch – ladies most immodestly dressed, wearing very little at all, in fact, plus jugglers and clowns and elephants, too. This had more the appearance of a circus parade than a coronation. But as there were monkeys also, my enthusiasm for it went undiminished.

The monkeys called out and I called back. Called back in the monkey tongue.

And now came chickens, which I did not care for, each dressed in robes and supporting the flag of some nation or other. Then there came a mighty palanquin draped with many colourful silks and supported upon the shoulders of many Nubian slaves.

Mr Bell raised his binoculars once more to study the figure who lounged atop that palanquin, upon many a comfortable cushion amidst concubines wearing no clothes at all, munching eel pie and mash with liquor.

There was no doubt at all as to who this figure was. And why would there be, for this was to be his coronation. This was Akhenaten, God-Pharaoh of Akhetaten, known to my companion and I alone as Arthur Knapton, erstwhile cockney bootboy, Pearly Emperor and a man of considerable ambition.

Mr Bell cried out, 'Oh no!' and pointed with some wildness. I followed the direction of these wild pointings and my eye fell upon their cause.

The God-Pharaoh's palanquin was flanked by bodyguards, as one might reasonably expect. It was the nature of these bodyguards, however, that gave Mr Bell, and indeed myself, considerable cause for concern.

For these bodyguards were not Nubian slaves and nor were they those horrible overgrown chickens.

The bodyguards were something more and something they should not be.

'Your dear dead mother,' I said to Mr Bell. 'Those body-guards are *Martians*!'

9

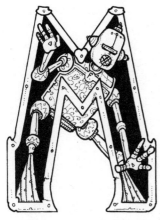r Bell reached for his ray gun.

I cried, 'No, don't!' in his ear.

For although my companion prided himself upon his marksmanship, I felt it imprudent to take pot-shots at a pharaoh whilst in the midst of a grandstand full of his followers.

'You are right,' said Mr Bell, and he patted my head and told me not to worry.

But worry I did about those horrid Martians.

There are several things known to Mankind which I believe are referred to as 'Eternal Verities', such as the fact that a swan can break a man's arm with its wing, that there is no such thing as a seagull, and that you should never annoy a wasp. Or indeed that if you come face to face with a tiger in the jungle, you should turn slowly around, bend over and put your head between your legs. This will scare away the tiger.

All right, gentle reader, you might have your doubts about the last one, but in the world I grew up in, it was considered an 'Eternal Verity'. Something you just *knew* to be *true*.

Something like the fact that *Martians cannot live upon Earth because Earthly bacteria are fatal to them.*

Everybody knows *that*!

'We are leaving,' said Mr Cameron Bell. 'Come, Darwin, follow me. We shall away from here and formulate a plan for Akhenaten's destruction.'

'But we have such a good seat,' I complained. 'And though I do not care for the looks of those Martians, I would really rather stay and watch the show.'

'Everything is wrong,' said Mr Bell. '*Everything*. We must return to the time-ship and reset the controls. Perhaps we have fallen into some alternative past by mistake. I will need to think long and hard about these matters.'

'Mr Freud says that music is a good therapy,' I said, and then I ceased to speak.

Because suddenly it became rather clear to me that the crowd in our immediate vicinity were no longer viewing the goings-on upon the cricket pitch. Rather they had become intensely interested in the conversation that Mr Bell and I were having.

A conversation which to their ears must have been of considerable interest, it apparently being that between a would-be assassin and a talking ape.

I had on several previous occasions seen a crowd *turn ugly*. I recall well the lynch mob in Wormcast, Arizona, which marched upon myself and my then-employer Colonel Katterfelto in the company of flaming torches. It had all been a misunderstanding, really. I had entered the general store and enquired regarding the availability of bananas. There ensued something of a furore amongst these uneducated townsfolk, who drew the conclusion that Colonel Katterfelto was a black magician and I a witch's familiar.

That situation was not quite so far removed from the one in which I presently found myself.

'Settle down, *please*,' cried Mr Cameron Bell in a most

authoritative tone. 'I am the Great Mage Bellinski and this talking ape is the creation of High Magick.'

I was not altogether certain that Mr Bell had chosen an entirely appropriate bogus explanation. But he went on.

'This beast is a present for my dear friend Akhenaten. Should anyone harm either him or myself, the great God-Pharaoh will have them boiled alive. Do I make myself understood?'

The ugly crowd showed no immediate signs of beauteous transformation.

'Sing them a song,' said Mr Bell.

'I should do *what*?' I replied.

'Sing them a song. It will ease the situation.'

I shrugged my shoulders. Because for the most part I *did* trust my companion's judgement.

'I would like to sing you a song,' I called out to the crowd that now glowered upon us. 'It is a popular music hall ditty and goes by the name of—'

Articulating phrases such as 'Kill the heretic!', the crowd closed in about myself and the erstwhile Mage Bellinski.

Now, being the agile and nimble fellow that I am, I hastily swarmed up one of the decorated columns supporting the grandstand roof and from a place of safety on high made forceful representations as to my opinion of the crowd.

The crowd responded by hurling things up at me – shoes, coins, heavy and dangerous objects. These failed singly to strike my person and instead descended to alight upon members of the crowd, evoking cries of pain and distress.

Mr Bell had his ray gun out and I had no objection whatsoever to him using it.

'Stand back from me!' he shouted, daring the crowd to approach him further. But he was hopelessly outnumbered and the crowd closed in upon him.

As Mr Bell went down beneath a welter of blows, my only resource was to drop my trousers, produce and fling down dung.

But sadly this did not ease the situation.

Had it not been for the intervention of the chicken militia hens, I fear that those bad folk would have killed poor Mr Bell. I gazed down from on high to see the beastly birds, easily six feet in height, wading forcefully through the crowd, flinging folk to the left and to the right with their muscular wings. It caused me to think of the power of swans' wings, but only for a moment. Mr Bell was hauled to his feet and hauled from the grandstand. I fled up and over the roof and made good my escape.

The chickens were not kind to Mr Bell. I swung from one high vantage point to another, keeping him ever in sight. At length, he was dragged into what I took to be the police station and his protestations of innocence, mingled with the sounds of blows, were swallowed up to silence.

I sat upon a rooftop and fretted.

I could not bear the thought of further harm coming to my dearest friend, but there appeared to be a terrible inevitability that further harm would indeed come. And probably terminate in that good man's execution.

I would have to rescue Mr Bell.

The street before the police station, itself a monumental edifice of pink and purple marble, was deserted. All of Akhetaten, it appeared, had gone to the cricket ground. I descended with caution to the street and crept about the building, seeking the door with the catflap.

I will make no bones about it being a tradition, or an old

charter, or something, that every police station has a police station cat. It does. You know it's true. It does, it has done, it always will do. And so I sought out the catflap.

It was a most substantial flap and so I had no difficulty entering the building. I slipped along a corridor and soon found myself to the rear of the main entrance hall.

It was a large and cavernous room, high of ceiling, its walls frescoed in the Egyptian style. Pictorial representations of torture and death found great favour here and did not raise my spirits one little bit. I did, however, spy Mr Bell, held between chickens and facing a great administrative desk.

Behind this desk, decked out in a dark blue tunic and trousers, with his bottom parts towards my direction, sat a fellow of considerable girth who spoke in a basso profundo and appeared to be in the very grumpiest of moods.

'Name?' this fellow roared at Mr Bell.

'I have told you my name,' said the great detective. 'I am King Cameron of Albion and you would do well to release me at once, amidst a flood of profuse apology.'

'I said, *name*!' roared the fellow once more.

'And I have told you my name,' said Mr Bell.

'I see.' The fellow leaned back upon his stool, his big bottom cheeks straining at his dark blue trouserings. 'So I will find your name in the *Register of Visiting Royalty*, where each official representative from a foreign realm is to be found? Yes?'

'I use a number of different names when travelling,' said Mr Bell bravely. 'Call out a few and I will tell you which is one of my own.'

'Sir,' said he of the prodigious bottom cheeks, 'I would dearly have loved to be watching the coronation, but my duty dictates that I must sit here for the balance of the day.

I frankly care not whether you are Solomon or the Queen of Sheba. You caused a public nuisance, and for this the sentence is death. Do you have anything to say in your defence before I pass this sentence?'

'Much,' said Mr Bell.

'I thought so,' said the other. 'But I am not inclined to listen. Officers, remove this condemned man to a cell. We'll have him executed first thing tomorrow.'

'I protest,' said Mr Bell.

'And *I* would be surprised if you did not.'

'Be it upon your own head, then,' said Mr Bell. 'Let history remember you as the man who drew down the vengeance of Albion upon Akhetaten and brought about its destruction.'

'You will recall that we have failed to establish your credentials,' said the chap with his rearward end to me, 'and as such the validity of your threats remain a matter for debate. I will take my chances with the pages of history. Off to the cells with this criminal.'

And with that he waved away Mr Bell, whose further protestations were stilled by further blows.

I crept past the big-bottomed man and, keeping to the shadows, followed Mr Bell as he was thrust down stone steps to that horrid subterranean realm of cells and torture chambers.

I passed by many doors. Some were clearly those of cells, but I passed one door marked PRIVATE RECORDS KEEP OUT. Crudely scrawled in English, these words were, and I viewed them with some puzzlement.

At little length, Mr Bell was flung into a cell and the door closed and bolted upon him. I hid as best I could as the chicken militia hens swaggered back along the corridor and took their leave.

I watched the horrid things depart and trembled not a little.

And then I set to the task of releasing my bestest friend.

10

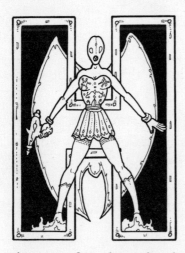

ow nice it was to see a smile on the face of Mr Bell.

When eventually I peeped in through the little grille in his cell door and blew a raspberry at him.

I say 'eventually' because I had waited for what I considered to be a respectable length of time before seeking to effect his rescue. I felt that my friend might do well to endure a solitary period during which he might engage in valuable contemplation. To dwell upon the error of his ways and, hopefully, given the mortal danger that embraced him, to abandon this wretched venture and accompany me instead to Beethoven's concert.

I counted up to one thousand, but went no further as I could abide the smell of this dismal place no longer.

'Mr Bell,' I called as I grinned in and waggled my fingers. 'I have come to rescue you.'

Mr Bell smiled back at me. Although he did it with difficulty as his face displayed many a graze and a bruise.

'You are as ever a hero, Darwin,' he said.[*]

I put up a struggle with the bolt and finally opened the door.

Mr Bell tousled my head and thanked me for saving his life.

'Let us return to the *Marie Lloyd* and be off upon our way,' I said. 'There is nothing more we can do here. When they find your cell empty they will hunt you down. It is obviously far too dangerous for us to remain here.'

'I do so agree,' said Mr Bell.

And I was glad for that.

'However, there are certain things that must be done first.'

'Lunch would be nice,' I said, for my stomach grumbled. 'But in a part of this city far distant from here.'

'It is *here* that these things must be done,' said Cameron Bell.

As we made our way back along the grim passage, Mr Bell stopped of a sudden.

'Our investigations begin *here*,' said he.

We stood before the door that had the words PRIVATE RECORDS KEEP OUT scrawled upon it in English.

I looked up at Mr Bell, who tapped his snubby nose. 'I caught a glimpse of this as I was being bullied down the corridor,' said he. 'The crude lettering of my old bootboy Arthur Knapton was instantly recognisable to me.'

---

[*] *There is no way of telling whether Cameron Bell actually said this, and by now the reader will have noticed numerous inconsistencies in the text. True, the book is penned by a monkey and this must be taken into account. Also there is always the problem of self-aggrandisement, which is so often to be found in autobiographies. My own I, Robert, soon to be published by Far-Fetched Books, suffers from none of this. (R. R.)*

And Mr Bell examined the door. 'Locked with a key, this one,' he observed.*

I turned to take my leave.

'Not quite yet, Darwin.'

And I turned back to find Mr Bell tinkering in his trouser pockets. Presently he drew out his little roll of house-breaking instruments and set to an act of lock-picking.

I glanced fearfully up and down the passageway. I had no wish at all to remain here and cared not at all for whatever PRIVATE RECORDS this locked room contained.

The locked room soon became an unlocked room. Mr Bell pressed open the door and entered it. I followed hard upon his heels and closed the door behind us.

We stood in darkness a moment or two, then the room came to a sudden illumination and we cried out in some surprise at all that lay before us.

Mr Bell was examining a switching arrangement upon the wall. His finger rested upon it. 'Electrical lighting,' said he.

'But look.' And I pointed. 'See all of this.'

My companion now viewed the contents of the room that spread all around and about us. We stood within a vault of considerable size, in what appeared to be—

'A library,' said Mr Cameron Bell. 'And if I am not entirely mistaken—' and he plucked a book from one of the nearest shelves and examined it with interest '—the British Library. All twenty thousand, two hundred and forty volumes, I suspect.'

The shelves diminished into hazy perspective.

They appeared to me to go on and on for ever and ever.

* *It is generally believed that keys did not exist in ancient Egypt (nor indeed dark blue policemen's trousers). But given all that has gone before, who would argue about such small details? (R. R.)*

'Surely there are many more books than *that* in here,' I said.

Mr Bell nodded at this. 'I would hazard a guess that this vault contains some of the great lost libraries of history. The Alexandrian Library, the Library of Ephesus. Perhaps even—'

Mr Bell replaced the book, hitched up his trousers and strode forward. I followed on, a-shaking my head as Mr Bell 'oohed' and 'ahed' and pointed here and there.

Eventually he stopped and said, 'He has acquired them all.'

I shrugged and said I did not understand.

'He has acquired the books from *all* the lost libraries, including those that were presumed to be purely mythical – those of Mu and Lemuria and Atlantis.'

'How can that be?' I enquired.

Mr Bell did thoughtful head-noddings. 'I have a theory,' he said, 'and I will tell you all about it. But not here.'

'That is much to my liking,' I said. 'Let us depart at once.'

'Not quite so fast.' Mr Bell shook his head. 'I am set upon a course. That course is to bring Mr Arthur Knapton, the Pearly Emperor, to justice. The easiest way to achieve this is to catch him unawares, some*where* and some-*when*.'

'I am in agreement with *that*,' I said. 'But the *when* is not *now*, I am thinking.'

'Myself also. *Here* and *now* are dangerous places to be. I must reason out, by the study of this collection, when certain items were stolen and from where. Then we can travel to this given time and location and catch the villain red-handed.'

'But surely you already tried that at the British Museum.'

Mr Bell made a grunting sound.

'In fact, though,' I said, 'why don't we go back there again

– to the night when he stole the British Library? This time in the company of many armed constables?'

'Cannot be done,' said Mr Bell.

'Of course it can,' I said. 'I have but to reset the controls.'

'No no *no*.' And Mr Bell shook his head. 'We dare not return to any specific time that we previously visited in the time-ship, for if we do so, then all sorts of chaos might occur.'

'Well, we would not want *that*,' I said.

Mr Bell raised an eyebrow. 'If we do that, there *will* be chaos,' he said. 'There will be two time-ships there. Two sets of us. There is no telling what could happen.'

I gave my chin a good stroking. 'All right,' I said. 'You have a search about, do your detective work. But I would ask of you one favour.'

'Which is?'

'Find us some*where* and some-*when* that are relatively safe,' I said. 'Not Pompeii an hour before the volcano goes off. Or indeed Atlantis ten minutes before it sinks into the sea. Some-*where* and some-*when* where we will not be in mortal danger.'

'Agreed,' said Mr Bell, and set off on his way.

I was left to my own devices, nervous lest we be discovered, somewhat hungry and indeed rather cross. I was not enjoying myself at all and it all felt terribly unfair.

Here I was, the very first monkey to travel through time, and *here I was*. Right *here*! In an underground vault full of musty old tomes. It was no fun at all.

There was nothing whatsoever that I liked about this particular time. I did *not* like those gigantic chickens and I did *not* like those Martians and I hadn't liked that nasty Mr MacTurnip one little bit, either. But at least Mr Bell had shot *him* dead with his ray gun.

And . . . And here I peered down at myself. My lovely white linen suit was thoroughly spoiled. It was begrimed with dust from all the shinning over rooftops I had done and stained with something horrid.

I took a sniff.

'Oh dear,' said I. 'And I never washed my hands.'

I sighed a long and dismal sigh, then called to Mr Bell to hurry up. Then I mooched about the shelves and peeped at all those books. There were so many of them. All those words and all that knowledge, all those works of wonder.

From first I learned to read I have been taken with books. The earliest that I read, the one from which I was taught by Herr Döktor, was the Bible.

I greatly enjoyed the Old Testament, although there is hardly a mention of a monkey to be found. Many animals gain starring roles but not the noble ape. In fact, I was only able to find two references to my kind in the Old Testament: in 1 Kings, chapter ten, verse twenty-two, and 2 Chronicles, chapter nine, verse twenty-one. And in both instances, apes are listed as nothing more than cargo. And not only that, but the verses are all but identical. Clearly a bit of cribbery went on amongst those who penned the Old Testament. Examine these verses for yourselves if you doubt my words.

And whilst we are on the subject of the Old Testament, some of the allusions made to animals are quite absurd. Take, if you will, the fourth chapter of the Song of Solomon:

1. Turn away thine eyes from me, for
   they have overcome me; thy hair is
   like a *flock of goats* that appear
   from Gilead.
2. Thy teeth are as a *flock of sheep*
   which go up from the washing, whereof
   every one beareth twins and there is
   not one barren among them.

3. As *a piece of pomegranate* are
    thy temples within thy locks.

The italics are my own, but you no doubt gain the picture. Barking mad! I ask you, indeed – *As a piece of pomegranate are thy temples?*

In the fifth verse, the author goes on to add:

5. Thy breasts are like *two*
    young roes that are twins.

And we will leave it there!

'Aha!' I heard the cry of Mr Bell, stirring me from my biblical reverie. 'I have it, I do, I have it!'

He was clearly in high spirits and he approached me at the trot, carrying a bundle of papers beneath his arm.

'I have a place and a date,' said Mr Bell, 'and I think you will be pleased by both.'

I expressed relief at his conclusion.

'We shall take our leave of this time and place,' said Mr Cameron Bell. 'Come, Darwin, let us return to the *Marie Lloyd*.'

Mr Bell put out his hand and I most gladly took it. We left the room of many books and with great care and courage stole away from the police station and the city of Akhetaten.

After hot and breathless desert trudgings, we returned at last in safety to the *Marie Lloyd*, where we hastened to our bathrooms. And I was glad for that.

We ensconced ourselves once more within our time-eliminating conveyance and I enquired of Mr Bell just where and when we would be travelling to.

'Home,' said Mr Cameron Bell. 'Home to London, it is.'

And I was very happy to be going home.

To the safety of London, the heart of the British Empire.

'Shall I set the controls for the year nineteen hundred?' I asked.

Mr Bell now shook his head. 'A little way on from there,' he said to me.

I must have made a worried face at this, but my friend and companion assured me that all would be well. He knew London intimately, he told me, and I would have nothing to fear in the heart of the great Metropolis with him by my side.

'London is London and always will be,' said Mr Cameron Bell.

'So what year are we travelling to?'

'Nineteen forty,' said Mr Cameron Bell.

11

e agreed that we should land the *Marie Lloyd* at the Royal London Spaceport in Sydenham, which spread beneath the hill and the Crystal Palace.

I set the controls for the date, month and year that Mr Bell instructed me to and we were off.

'And so,' I said to my friend, 'explain to me, if you will, just why we are going to this particular time and place.'

'To catch our thief,' the great detective said.

'Yes,' I agreed. 'I am aware that this is your goal. Now please offer me some *specifics*.'

'Specifically, then,' said Mr Bell as he uncorked champagne, 'I discovered these papers –' and he indicated those that were spread about upon the navigation desk '– which suggest that Arthur Knapton will have dealings here with a secret organisation in London during the year nineteen forty. There are dated memoranda. From numerous meetings.'

'Meetings about *what*?' I enquired, for this seemed a reasonable question.

' "The employment of top-secret technology",' said Mr

Bell, reading from a memorandum. 'Mr Knapton is going to be engaged in discussions with the Ministry of Serendipity.'

'I believe this Ministry is unknown to me,' I said as I helped myself to a banana from the bowl and accepted a glass of champagne.

'But not to myself,' said Mr Bell. 'It is said that the Ministry of Serendipity has been the "power behind the throne of England" for several hundred years.'

'I like not the smell of that,' I said.

'The Ministry upholds the interests of the British Empire as a whole. Rulers come and rulers go, but the Ministry remains.'

'That all sounds somewhat sinister,' I said. 'Almost criminal, in fact.'

'Not a bit of it,' said Mr Bell. 'We . . . I mean *they*, do what is for the best.'

' "*We* . . . I mean *they*"? You mean *you* are an agent of this Ministry?'

Mr Bell nodded and toasted me with champagne. 'I could possibly get you an honorary membership,' he said.

'Ah,' I said. 'So then I might have a say in the running of the country?'

'No, not as such. But you could use the Ministry's bar and you get a discount on hansom cab fares.'

'Do you think they will still have hansom cabs in nineteen forty?' I had emptied my glass of champagne now and held it out for refilling.

Mr Bell took to this refilling. 'All vehicles will be electrically powered by nineteen forty,' he assured me. 'It will be thrilling to see the future, will it not, Darwin? To see the great strides forward Mankind will have made. I will wager you that the British Empire will rule not only the planets in our solar system, but many others also.'

I dearly wish I had taken Mr Bell up on this wager.

'I predict that it will be idyllic,' my companion prophesied. 'All men equal. Peace and harmony. The races of Ape and Man living in perfect unity.'

Oh, how I wish I had taken him up on *that*.

'So let us be clear,' I said to Mr Bell. 'You know, from the documents you found in the vault, the dates and times of Arthur Knapton's meetings with members of the Ministry of Serendipity in nineteen forty?'

'I do,' said Mr Bell. 'And with one member in particular.'

'Go on.' I took my refilled champagne glass and set about its emptying.

'An old friend of both yours and mine – Mr Winston Churchill.'

I snorted champagne from my nose. 'Mr Churchill?' I said.

'By the evidence of these papers, Mr Churchill has attained to the rank of Prime Minister in the era towards which we are heading.'

'Ah,' said I. 'Mr Churchill and I are indeed acquainted. A rather headstrong fellow, Mr Churchill. Always up for a fight, as it were.'

'But a man, you will agree, who holds the Empire close to his heart.'

'On *that* I *will* agree.' And I toasted Mr Bell and the ship crashed down without warning and he and I fell on the floor.

'We are going to have to work on our landings,' said my friend, when he had once more found his feet. 'We cannot go on crashing the *Marie Lloyd*.'

'Well, it is not *my* fault,' I said to him. 'There is no way of judging how fast this ship travels through time.'

Mr Bell helped me to the pilot's seat and I examined the dials and year-counters.

'We have reached the Royal London Spaceport,' I said. 'It is seven o'clock in the evening on the twenty-seventh of July in the year nineteen forty, and according to the barometer we can expect rain later, so we had best take our umbrellas.'

Now came the question of what would be the appropriate apparel to don for the year nineteen forty. All Mr Bell had to offer on this subject was that we ought to wear 'something smart'.

So we repaired to our respective wardrobes and presently emerged in something smart.

Mr Bell wore a full dress suit, with evening cape and top hat.

I wore the rather spiffing Germanic military dress uniform that Queen Victoria's cousin Baron Claus von Zeppelin had given to me. Mr Bell had successfully solved a case for this great man. One that involved, if I recall correctly, a music hall dancer, a biscuit tin and a wiener dog named Fritzy. I remain somewhat hazy regarding the significance of the biscuit tin. But it was a *really* spiffing uniform, bedecked with a great deal of braid, smart golden epaulettes and German eagle motifs.

With the jodhpurs and jackboots I looked very smart indeed!

'Dashing,' said Mr Cameron Bell as he looked me up and down.

'You yourself look smart enough,' I said. 'Are we going somewhere special, then, tonight?'

'I thought we would visit the Electric Alhambra,' said Mr Bell. 'That will bring back a few memories, eh?'

'Not altogether good ones,' I said. 'Colonel Katterfelto and I performed there, as you know. He had a knack for dodging the fruit and veg that was thrown by the crowd. I, however, did not. And also that was where the colonel died.'

'I will treat you to a box seat tonight,' said Mr Bell, 'after supper at my club.'

And on that merry note we left the *Marie Lloyd* . . .

. . . To step out onto the cobbled stone of the Royal London Spaceport . . .

'Where has the London Spaceport gone?' I asked Mr Bell. Because the *Marie Lloyd* was parked upon grass that spread away to the distance.

Mr Bell made sad sounds in his throat and pointed up towards Sydenham Hill.

'Where has the Crystal Palace gone?' he asked.

We had certainly landed in the right location – there were landmarks which attested to this. But the spaceport, its runways and buildings were gone, and so too the Crystal Palace.

'I bet it burned down once again,' I said to Mr Bell. 'But on the bright side, at least this time it wasn't your fault.'

Mr Bell angled his topper and said, 'Let us search for some transport.'

We marched away and found the road and with it a building that both of us recognised. A hotel in which I had lodged and Mr Bell had visited. A hotel known as the Adequate.

But it was known as the Adequate no more, for it had been renamed the British Bulldog. A swinging sign imaginatively depicted the coloured representation of a bulldog wearing a Union Jack waistcoat and some kind of iron helmet, and smoking a cigar.

'If we have now found ourselves in a time where bulldogs rule the world,' I said to Mr Bell, 'I would like to take my leave at once.'

Mr Bell put his finger to his lips and said, 'Now, listen to that.'

Somewhere from far in the distance, a curious metallic wailing sound reached our ears, followed by a number of dull but definite thumps.

All at once, a gentleman appeared from the doorway of the British Bulldog. He wore upon his head a helmet not dissimilar to the one the dog on the sign was wearing, but his had the letters 'ARP' painted upon it.

'Gawd strike me down!' he exclaimed as he viewed myself and Mr Bell. 'Surely it's Count Dracula and Kaiser Bill 'iself.'

Mr Bell grinned painfully. 'What is that woeful wailing sound?' he asked.

'The air-raid siren?' asked the chap. 'Are you kidding of me?'

'Air raid?' said Mr Bell slowly, and I swear I saw the colour drain from his face.

'Are you with the circus?' now asked the chap.

Mr Bell nodded. His thoughts were clearly elsewhere.

'Well, you'd best get inside, mate. You know you can be shot for a looter if you're out after the siren.'

Mr Bell perused the chap, his gaze moving from the fellow's shoes to his trouser-cuffs, to his waistcoat and shirt-collar. Mr Bell drew a sudden breath. 'We are at war,' he said.

'And the geezer in the topper wins a big cigar,' said the chap in the helmet. 'Now inside with you both and let's 'ave no more nonsense.'

Mr Bell looked down at me and shook his head in sadness. 'This is very bad indeed,' he said.

The interior of what once had been the Adequate had not changed very much, a tad shabbier, perhaps, and duller to the eye, and the carpet was now threadbare. The lighting, however, was electric.

The hotel reception area now served as a saloon bar, littered with ill-matched tables and chairs. These were adorned by working types, who upon viewing us displayed expressions of dire perplexity.

Someone said, 'Are you 'avin' a gi-raffe?' But this offered no comfort. A poster pinned to a nearby pillar displayed the words WALLS HAVE EARS, which I found most perplexing.

'They're with the circus,' said the chap with the painted helmet.

Mr Bell doffed his topper and said, 'Greetings, one and all.'

The working men returned to their conversations as the chap in the helmet led us to the bar.

'This is Doris,' he said, indicating a vast woman who swelled behind the bar-counter, her costume a floral symphony, her face a crimson sunset. 'She will serve your needs. I 'ave a call that must be made.' And with that said, the chap in the helmet bowed and took his leave.

Doris smiled upon Cameron Bell, then turned her gaze towards me. 'And who is this cheeky little rascal?' she asked.

I opened my mouth to reply.

'His name is Darwin,' said Mr Bell, thrusting a rough hand over my face to stifle my conversation. 'Naturally he cannot answer for himself –' Mr Bell gave me a meaningful glance '– but he is a highly trained circus ape. House-trained also and not at all fierce.'

I bit the hand of Cameron Bell, but not hard enough to draw blood.

'A cheeky rascal indeed,' said Mr Bell. And his eyes turned towards the row of handpumps.

'Only bottled, I'm afraid,' said Doris. 'And only pale ale, I regret.'

'I'll take one of those, then,' said Mr Bell, 'and a bowl of water for Darwin.'

I showed Mr Bell my teeth and a second pale ale was swiftly added to the order.

'One and six,' said Doris, serving same.

Mr Bell dug into his trouser pocket and produced a half-crown coin that bore the head of Queen Victoria on its shiny face.

Doris received it, examined it and bit it, smiled and said fair enough and took herself off to the till.

I climbed onto the counter-top and poured my pale ale into a waiting glass. This received applause from the working men. I raised my glass and mimed a toast and they clapped once again. Doris brought change to Mr Bell and he examined this.

'It's real enough,' said Doris.

'King George the Sixth,' said Mr Bell.

Doris said, 'God save the King.'

And all around folk raised their glasses and also said, 'God save the King.'

I raised my glass, too, but did not speak.

I became gloomy in this future time.

Queen Victoria would now be long dead and a king sat on the throne of England. Winston Churchill was the Prime Minister and the Empire was under attack by raids from the air. Not Martians again, I hoped.

Mr Bell noted my disposition and patted me on the back. 'All will be well,' he said to me. 'Do not worry yourself.'

And at that very moment, the soldiers entered the British Bulldog.

They were rather fierce-looking soldiers and they entered in the company of the chap in the painted helmet.

'That's them,' said this chap to the soldiers, and he pointed his finger at me and Mr Bell.

'German spies, the both of them,' said the man with the painted helmet.

12

oldiers are very like monkeys.

In that they are noble, brave and loyal.

But prone, at times, to great excitability.

Monkeys have, of course, at times been likened unto soldiers, as in the famous case of the Hartlepool Monkey. The story goes that during the Napoleonic Wars, a ship sank in a storm off the coast of Hartlepool. The sole survivor of this tragedy was an ape, which happened to be dressed in a French uniform and which floated ashore upon flotsam from the wreck.

The simple townsfolk of Hartlepool, never having seen a Frenchman in the flesh, assumed the monkey to be one and hanged the poor beast.

I can personally vouch for the untruth of this particular story as *I* was the ape in question and I escaped the hangman's noose through the timely intervention of my good friend Cameron Bell.

It is a very interesting story, as it happens, being one of the many time-travelling adventures Mr Bell and I shared. But I shall not recount it here in detail, especially as I have rather given away the ending.

But soldiers, as I have said, can be very like monkeys, and those who now pointed their fixed bayonets towards us did indeed make sounds that would have been more at home within a jungle. And as to the demand from the 'superior officer' that Mr Bell and I both raise our hands in the air *and* show our papers simultaneously, there were definitely simian qualities to that chap, I am thinking.

We were bundled from the British Bulldog and out into the night. The night, it felt to me, was full of menace. Smells came to my nostrils, of burning wood and spent gunpowder, and of blood and other things beside.

I looked up in no small fear to Mr Bell who was now being thoroughly searched by two of the soldiers.

'Oh ho,' cried one, 'and what do we have here?'

He had lifted Mr Bell's trouser-cuffs to reveal that the detective had concealed a stick of dynamite in each sock.

'And what of *this*?' cried the soldier's comrade-in-arms, drawing Mr Bell's ray gun from his inner jacket pocket. 'Some piece of Nazi super-technology, I'm thinking.'

The soldier waggled the ray gun about. I ducked for cover and Mr Bell counselled for caution.

It was as much of a surprise to me as to the soldiers exactly how much concealed weaponry Mr Bell had about his person, and the grins upon the faces of the soldiers at each disclosure were negatively mirrored by the growing look of gloom that spread about the face of Mr Bell.

By the time we had been pushed into the rear of a motorised vehicle, Mr Bell was shivering in his vest and underpants and I had been reduced to my boots and spurs. Most undignified! I was quite prepared to signal my disapproval through the medium of faecal flinging, but Mr Bell shook his head.

'You have made a terrible mistake,' he told the soldiers, who now joined us in the rear of the vehicle and were amusing themselves by nudging Mr Bell brutally with their bayonets whilst chanting, 'Spy, spy, poke him in the eye.'

'I demand to be taken at once to Mr Churchill,' my friend continued, crossing his legs as he did so. 'Mr Churchill is a personal friend of mine. He will have harsh words to say about my treatment, I assure you.'

But the soldiers did not heed the words of Mr Bell. In fact, the youngest-looking one, a slender private by the name of Pike, had words of his own to utter.

'We have you bang to rights, Jerry,' said he. 'You're one of those SS suicide soldiers that the *Daily Mail* has been warning us about. I'll wager that big belly of yours is all filled up with high explosives, and if we were to take you to Mr Churchill, you'd light your arse off his cigar and blow our Winnie to kingdom come and all.'

Mr Bell was for once quite lost for words.

'You'll go to the Tower,' sneered another of the soldiers, a brutal Highlander by the name of Frazer. 'Eaten by rats, you'll be, mark my words, I tell you.'

Lance Corporal Jones, an elderly soldier, remarked that we would not like it up us, whatever *that* meant.

I noticed that my friend was giving the soldiers considerable scrutiny, looking them up and down and nodding thoughtfully to himself. I took some comfort in this because it signified that he was once again using his remarkable powers of observation. In my opinion, he had been somewhat out of his depth in ancient Egypt, probably because everything was so utterly alien there. But here, back in London, even under the present uncomfortable circumstances, it was clear that his powers were as great as ever they had been.

We sat in the company of four soldiers. These I later learned were members of the Home Guard, a crack regiment dedicated to the defence of British soil. Fierce warriors all and not to be diddled about with. The captain of this particular group went by the name of Mainwaring, a deceptively avuncular figure, and it was to him first that my companion addressed a casual-sounding comment.

'It is sad,' said Mr Bell, as our uncomfortable conveyance rattled upon its way and great thumps that were clearly explosions came louder to our ears, 'that often the most worthy of soldiers are passed over for promotion.'

Captain Mainwaring, who had been tinkering with his moustache, raised an eyebrow to this.

'The class system,' said my friend, in a meaningful manner.

Lance Corporal Jones asked his superior for permission to club Mr Bell over the head with the butt of his rifle. This permission was denied.

'I understand your anger,' said Mr Bell to Lance Corporal Jones. 'An unfaithful wife can try a fellow's nerves.'

'Best throttle him here,' said Private Frazer, 'and spare the expense of a hangman.'

'That would certainly hide some sins,' said Mr Cameron Bell. And he winked at Private Frazer and called him a dirty rascal.

I watched and listened to my friend and I was most impressed. On the face of it, he appeared to say so little, and what he did say did not for the most part take the form of direct accusation. His timing, too, was impeccable and we had all but reached the centre of the war-torn capital when the fight broke out in earnest.

Lance Corporal Jones started it – he clubbed down Private Frazer, was reprimanded by his superior officer, then set about him also. The young and slender Private Pike, to whom Mr Bell had addressed an oblique remark regarding his mother's fondness for men of the officer class, also chose to strike at Captain Mainwaring. Captain Mainwaring drew out his pistol, but I do not believe that he actually meant to shoot Private Frazer dead. The vehicle lurched over fallen debris; the gun went off by accident.

I do not, however, think it was by accident that Lance Corporal Jones stuck his bayonet into the captain.

The mêlée became bloody and brutal and, as no one was paying us any attention, Mr Bell gathered up our clothes and belongings and we took our leave at the first possible opportunity.

We watched our conveyance rumble away, and I can only suspect that its utter destruction was caused by someone accidentally pulling a pin from a hand grenade during the onboard struggle.

'I am not sure I wholly approve of *that*,' I said to Mr Bell. 'Those soldiers were on our side, after all.'

Mr Bell was tucking sticks of dynamite back into his socks and he mumbled something that might possibly have been an apology.

I do have to say that we now found ourselves in most alarming circumstances. London was ablaze. It was terrible. Buildings were tumbling about us as deafening explosions cast awful shock waves. It was as if the city we loved had been swallowed into Hell.

'We must take cover,' shouted Mr Bell, struggling into his clothes. 'And down there would be the very place.'

He pointed towards the entrance of a station. An Underground railway station named Mornington Crescent.

Mr Bell took me by the hand and together we fled the destruction.

My companion advised me against redressing myself in my Germanic uniform. The Germans were the enemy, he told me. And so, naked but for my boots and spurs, I travelled with Mr Bell down in the lift that led to the platforms beneath.

If there was horror above, there was tragedy below. Folk of London, removed from their houses, huddled together under blankets along the length of the platforms. They were trying to make the best of it, as Londoners will, putting on brave faces, singing comic songs, dishing out tea from steaming urns.

It all but broke my little heart.

I had taken a perch upon my good friend's shoulder and whispered to him how very dreadful this was.

'We will have to stay here for now,' he whispered in reply. 'At least until the present assault upon the city ceases.'

'And what if it does not?' I asked. 'What if it just goes on and on and on?'

Then a child cried out, 'Look, it's a monkey.'

And Mr Bell suggested I should dance.

Dance?

But dance I did. I danced to entertain that child and all the others, too. I danced and Mr Bell sang a song from the music halls, and I know we made those children laugh and we were happy for that.

It was late and I was tired and so Mr Bell and I settled down upon that platform amongst the huddled Londoners and slept.

It was not an easy sleep, but had I any inkling of what lay ahead for us upon the following day, I am sure that I would have had absolutely no sleep whatsoever.

So I was later grateful for what sleep I'd had, for come morning, things took a terrible turn.

13

hen morning came, we left our Underground refuge with the others who had sheltered therein. We emerged into a sorrowful world. The beautiful city of London looked mortally wounded and the destruction was awful to behold.

'I do not like the future,' I whispered to Mr Bell.

The great detective shook his head. 'Nor indeed do I.'

A sad-eyed lady in a straw hat was dispensing tea from a chromium-plated urn. She smiled at the sight of me and beckoned us over.

'Tea and biscuits,' she said. 'And who is this fine little fellow?' And she chucked me under the chin with a long, cold finger. Normally I would have responded to such uninvited intimacy with a summary biting, but that would have been most inappropriate now. This sad-eyed lady offered only kindness, and we were glad to accept her kindly offer.

I munched upon a biscuit and Mr Bell sipped sweet tea. Others gathered about the lady, ghost-like figures all. Some were still wrapped in blankets, their eyes downcast. No one really wished to look up at the destruction around them.

Mr Bell engaged the tea drinkers in conversation. This he did with care, as he had no wish to be misidentified as a German spy once more.

I shook my head in wonder over this war. Were we really at war with the Germans? Why on Earth would this be? The Germans were our friends. The Germans were a sophisticated people – Beethoven was a German, after all.

Mr Bell offered me a cup of water and I drank it gladly. Then he said that we should be moving along, and we left the sad-eyed lady and set off through the ruined streets of London.

I had become adept at sitting upon the shoulder of Cameron Bell and conducting a confidential conversation with him, and this I did now.

'Where are we going?' I asked him.

'To a bookshop,' he replied.

'Now is not the time for reading,' I told him. 'Now is the time for action.'

'And what action would *you* suggest?'

'Departure,' I said, 'in the time-ship. Departure from this wretched time, and *now*.'

'We will be on our way soon enough,' said Mr Bell. 'When I have achieved my goal.'

'The arrest or destruction of Mr Arthur Knapton, the Pearly Emperor?'

'One and the same,' said Cameron Bell.

We had reached Piccadilly and things looked grim, with awful damage done.

'You know you cannot stop him here and now,' I said to Mr Bell.

The great detective sighed. 'Naturally, I am aware of the difficulties,' said he. 'I do not have identity papers suitable for this period of time. According to the documents I obtained in ancient Egypt, Mr Arthur Knapton would appear to be engaged in legitimate business here and now with the British Government. He has the edge on me, as our American cousins might put it.'

'And also—' I began.

But Mr Bell cut me short. 'I am aware of every "and also",' he said. 'We are in a very difficult position.'

'Then let us take our leave. It is far too dangerous here. What if a bomb comes down from the sky and blows up the *Marie Lloyd*?'

'You make a good point,' said my friend. 'We would do well to depart before night falls and the Blitz begins once more.'

'The *Blitz*?' I said. 'A horrid word is *that*.'

'Oh dear,' said Mr Cameron Bell. 'Oh dear, oh dear, oh dear.'

And I looked up to view the cause of his oh-dearings. And I was prompted to utter one of my own.

We stood now before the Electric Alhambra. But that beautiful building within which the greatest music hall acts of the day had entertained the plain folk and the gentry . . .

Was gone.

Destroyed.

A section of the façade was all that remained.

Mr Bell stooped down and picked up a piece of golden mosaic. 'Such a pity,' said he, in the softest of voices.

'I just cannot bear it,' I said.

'Bookshop,' said Mr Cameron Bell. 'There is much I need to know, and then we will see what we will see.'

The Atlantis Bookshop had not changed at all. It lay, as it always had done, a mere tome's throw from the British Museum, which looked for its part as yet unscathed. Mr Bell indicated a lamp post and suggested that I climb to its very top and await him there until he had done whatever business he wished to do. I set to climbing the lamp post, and Mr Bell entered the shop.

I heard a distant church clock chiming and looked on as Londoners came and went. I do not think that I had ever felt so alone before as I did then, and I was very glad when Mr Bell finally emerged from the shop, a brown paper bag tucked under his arm, and beckoned me down to join him.

'To Sydenham at once,' said he.

'Thank goodness for *that*,' said I.

We took a taxicab to Sydenham, and a wretched taxicab it was. It smelled of sweaty men and cigarettes and it coughed black smoke as it rattled along. Recalling the sleek electric-wheelers of eighteen ninety-nine, I found that taxicab puzzling.

Mr Bell spoke not throughout our journey. He had a very queer look on his face and his fists were knotted tightly. As we drew nearer and nearer to Sydenham Hill, I felt a growing sense of unease. A feeling of dread.

I had, if you will, a sort of premonition.

There was some unpleasantness regarding payment and the driver of the taxicab availed himself of Mr Bell's pocket watch. The great detective parted with this precious possession without a word of complaint. He had a weary look to him that I found most alarming.

The taxicab left us and we trudged back to where I had landed the *Marie Lloyd*.

And it came as no surprise to me, nor indeed to Mr Bell, to find that the *Marie Lloyd* had gone.

★

We sat together on high, on Sydenham Hill, and gazed down upon the rolling grasslands that spread beneath. No trace there of the Royal London Spaceport, of the great cobbled landing strip, of the vast Gothic-styled terminal buildings. No sign at all that they had ever existed.

I looked up at Mr Bell. 'We both knew,' I said. 'Somehow, we knew that the *Marie Lloyd* would not be here when we returned. We *knew*, Mr Bell. But *how* did we know? What does it mean, please tell me?'

My friend took off his topper and placed it between his feet. A gust of wind caught it and it bowled down the hill. Mr Bell made no attempt to retrieve it and we watched it bounce away until it was lost to our sight.

'Recall those chickens in ancient Egypt,' said Mr Cameron Bell.

'Only too well, and I did not like them at all.'

'And recall how you said that they should not be there because they received no mention in the history books of our time?'

'Certainly I do,' said I.

Mr Bell sighed. 'I engaged in a little research at the Atlantis Bookshop,' said he, 'and I purchased this for you.'

'A present? How kind.' I accepted the brown paper bag that Mr Bell offered to me and withdrew from it a colourful picture book. On the cover was an illustration of a portly monkey and an even portlier gentleman. The title of this book was *The Adventures of Darwin the Monkey Butler and Mr Ball the Dangerous Detective*.

'Posterity,' I said, with delight. 'At least they spelled *my* name correctly.'

'Have a little flick through,' said Mr Bell. As I did so, he added, 'Then see how pleased you are.'

Presently I closed the book and let it fall from my fingers.

'What does all this mean?' I asked my friend.

'What do *you* think it means?'

I glanced down at the book. 'It is a children's book,' I said. 'A work of fiction. It is about us, but we are foolish.'

'Foolish and fictional,' said Mr Bell.

'I do not understand.'

'I only had time for a quick perusal of the history books the Atlantis held upon its shelves. What I found within them was nothing less than alarming. You and I, my little friend, came to this benighted time from one of Victorian wonder, where the British Empire owned spaceships, where electric vehicles moved through the streets of London, their power drawn from the Tesla towers which offered the wireless transmission of electrical energy to an age of Babbage computers and great things yet to be.'

'I recall it all,' said I. 'In fact, it would appear that we were more advanced in the sciences back then than those folk here and now.'

'So it might *appear*,' said Mr Bell. 'But you see, Darwin, in *this* here and now, none of those things ever happened. Mr Babbage did *not* exhibit his difference engine at the Great Exhibition and find royal patronage. Mr Tesla did *not* effect the wireless transmission of electricity. And in eighteen eighty-five, the Martians did *not* attack England.'

'They did *not*?' I said. 'So where *did* they attack? Surely not America?'

'Not anywhere,' said Mr Bell, 'because there never were any Martians. Martians do *not* exist. They never did.'

'Of course they existed,' I said in protest. 'If they never existed, how could we have travelled through time in a Martian spaceship?'

'Mr Ernest Rutherford did win a Nobel Prize,' said

Cameron Bell, 'but not for mastering time travel. There never ever was any such thing as a time machine, except in the fictional work of H. G. Wells.'

'But *we* are here,' I said. '*We* are alive and real. You are Mr Bell, the greatest detective of our age, and I am Darwin, the educated ape.'

'Characters in a children's book and nothing more, it so appears.'

'No,' I said. 'No. We *are* real, I *know* we are real.'

'Are we?' asked Mr Bell.

'Yes, we are. Of course we are.'

Mr Bell sighed terribly and I felt the hair stand up on the back of my neck.

We sat in silence and gazed into the distance.

An aeroplane passed overhead, its engine coughing fearfully. A steam train *poop-pooped* in the distance.

The smell of smoke was on the wind.

And all, it appeared, was lost.

My friend sat and thoughtfully nodded his head. His face expressed great inner turmoil, as might reasonably have been expected. I offered him my opinion that all was well and truly lost.

Mr Bell cocked his head on one side. 'Not *all*,' he said to me.

'You have arrived at a plan that will lead to a satisfactory conclusion?'

'Not as *such*.'

'But you remain quietly confident?'

Mr Bell bobbed his head from side to side.

'We are doomed,' I said in a voice of gloom. 'We are done for, are we *not*?'

'We are *not*!' said Mr Bell, and with that he jumped to his feet. 'Do you fancy a day at the seaside, Darwin?' he asked.

'Not particularly,' I said. 'Why?'

'Because we are going to Hastings.'

I shook my head and asked why once more.

'To see an old friend,' said Cameron Bell. 'To see a *very* old friend.'

14

etherwood was a run-down boarding house. It was a *very* long walk from the station. There had been a taxi available, but Mr Bell decided to keep his watch chain.

We trudged up a gravelly drive to the late-Victorian eyesore that was Netherwood. Paint peeled from crumbling timberwork and brown-paper tape had been pasted in crosses over the windowpanes.

Mr Bell had decided not to tell me who we were visiting so that it would be a nice surprise. He tugged upon a bell-pull which came away in his hand, but a distant bell succeeded in drawing the attention of a ragged-looking fellow who smelled very strongly of cheese.

'A toff and a monkey,' this fellow said, looking us up and down. 'It takes all sorts, I suppose.'

Mr Bell presented his card. 'My name is Cameron Bell,' said he, 'and I have come to visit one of your lodgers – Mr Aleister Crowley.'

The ragged individual took my friend's card and slammed the front door shut upon us. I gaped up in horror at Cameron Bell. In horror, because I knew of Aleister Crowley.

'That man is a monster,' I said. 'A black magician. The papers were full of his magical shenanigans. He styled himself the Beast, six–six–six. They say that he sacrificed children.'

Mr Bell laughed somewhat at this. 'His reputation for wickedness far surpasses the facts in his case. But he was a wicked fellow.'

'I do not wish him to put a curse upon *me*,' I said.

'He will not curse you, Darwin,' said Mr Bell. 'Just pay attention to what is said and act accordingly.'

I shrugged my shoulders and shook my head. 'I am not happy,' said I.

'Nor me. But we must learn what we can. I trust it will all make sense when it is explained. Crowley and I were students together at Oxford, you know.'

'I did not,' I said. 'And I care not for it.' And with that I folded my arms.

The ragged man once more swung wide the door. 'The master will see you now,' he said.

He led us along a grimy hall and up a bare-boarded staircase. An unpleasing miasma stifled the air and Mr Bell made coughings.

'His brand of tobacco remains the same,' he muttered as he coughed. 'Perique soaked in rum with a sprinkling of black Moroccan.'

A grubby door was knocked upon, was softly answered, and we were ushered into the bedroom of the Beast himself.

It looked to me the very place for an ancient magician to lurk. An alchemist's den, piled high with books, strange paintings upon its walls. The smell was rank, the air befogged, and a frail figure sat in a candle's gleam.

He was wrapped in an antique dressing gown, a frayed velvet smoking cap perched on his old yellow head. I recalled the press photographs of the sprightly, athletic young

Crowley, a scaler of mountains, a man about town, a rubber of shoulders with the upper-class set. Here was a frail and broken parody. I almost felt sympathy.

'Do what thou wilt shall be the whole of the law,' quoth the elderly mage, in a wheezing tone that spoke of damaged lungs. 'Is that my old chum Bell I see before me?'

Mr Bell approached the shrunken figure. He extended his hand and a significant handshake was exchanged.

'Crowley,' said my friend. 'The Logos of the Aeon. You would appear to have fallen upon hard times. Have you so far failed to change base metal to gold?'

Aleister Crowley gave a hideous cough, then dabbed at his mouth with a most unsavoury hankie. 'I am expecting a cheque from America. L. Ron Hubbard, my magical son, will shortly be making a very big name for himself.'

'Always tomorrow.' Mr Bell seated himself on a Persian pouffe.

'And who is this?' asked Crowley, spying me. 'Your familiar, is it, Bell?'

'His name is Darwin,' said my friend. 'My travelling companion.'

'Indeed, indeed.' The magician's face was lined with age. A few sprouting hairs formed a half-hearted goatee and his fingertips were nicotine-hued. All in all, he was most unsavoury.

'Tell me,' whispered Crowley. 'Tell me how it is done.'

Mr Bell shook hard his head. 'Whatever can you mean?'

A withered hand stretched out to the great detective. 'You found it,' said the ancient. 'The Aqua Vitae – the Elixir of Life. You found it. How did you find it?'

Mr Bell shook his head once more. 'It is not what you think,' said he.

'But we were at Oxford together. I recall it well.'

'As do I,' said Mr Bell, 'and more besides. Recall our bootboy, Crowley?'

'Arthur Knapton,' said Aleister Crowley. 'What a young scamp was he.'

Arthur Knapton! I gazed from Mr Bell to Aleister Crowley.

'What became of Knapton?' asked Mr Bell.

'Gone to Hell, I hope!' cried the Logos of the Aeon, then sank back in his chair in a fit of coughing.

'Some bad blood between you, then?' Mr Bell discovered what appeared to be a glass half-filled with water upon a nearby Turkish table. He offered this to our raddled host who tossed it back with some vigour.

'Just tell me,' he croaked. 'What have you to lose? Just tell me how it is done.'

'If you answer *my* questions,' said Mr Bell, 'I will answer *yours*. Is that a fair exchange, in your opinion?'

Aleister Crowley made grumbling sounds but nodded his old yellow head.

'I would ask *you* a question,' said Mr Bell, 'because I believe that *you* might know the answer.'

'I know the answers to most, if not all, of the questions.'

'Quite so. Then tell me, Crowley – what became of the past?'

Aleister Crowley cackled somewhat. 'That is a very strange question.'

'But you have been asked far stranger.'

'Ha!' cried Crowley. 'Aha!' And his eyes grew wide as he stared at Mr Bell. 'You wore that very suit the last time I saw you – at the Electric Alhambra in the summer of eighteen ninety-nine. You have not aged a day, it would appear, but neither has your suit.'

'It is said,' said Mr Bell, 'that a well-tailored suit will see out its wearer.'

'No! No! No! He did it!' There was a look of enlighten-ment now on the face of the elderly fellow. 'That little swine did it. He stole my papers. He worked the spell. So you and he were in it together – it all makes sense to me now.'

Mr Bell looked long and hard at Aleister Crowley. 'Knapton,' he said. 'You speak of Arthur Knapton.'

'Of course, Knapton – don't pretend you are ignorant of this matter. He stole my magical stele. The engraved tablet of Akhenaten. The Stele of Revealing.'

'That one might travel—'

'Through time! You know this because you have done it.' Aleister Crowley clutched at his heart, and his breath came with terrible sounds.

Mr Bell did not appear too concerned regarding the old man's state. He cupped his chin in the palm of his hand and made a thoughtful face. 'So it is magic,' said he. 'Magic is the motive force for Mr Knapton's travellings.'

At length, Mr Crowley gathered his breath and his wits. 'Teach me the words, my old friend,' he said in a greasy tone. 'Let me hear the incantation. I am old and all but gone – what possible harm could it do?'

'All in good time,' said my friend. 'But first I need answers to *my* questions. What became of the past? What became of *our* past? What of Tesla towers, of ray guns and of space-ships?'

'Ray guns?' Aleister Crowley laughed.

Mr Bell patted his pockets in search of his.

But he did not have it and so he ceased his pattings. 'You remember well enough,' said he. 'I once shot you in the foot with mine at the Crystal Palace.'

This was news to me, but as I had taken an instant dislike to the repugnant Mr Crowley, I was quite tickled to think that Mr Bell had once shot him in the foot.

'Such a long time ago,' said Crowley. 'Such a long time ago.'

'And time has addled your brain,' said Cameron Bell.

The old man's evil eyes were once more fixed upon my friend. 'Aha!' he cried. 'I see more. He has tricked you, too, and you are trapped here. Now, tell me I am wrong.'

'You are not altogether wrong,' Mr Bell confessed. 'It is because of Knapton that I am here. I sought to bring him to justice. I traced him to this time and intended to lie in wait and take him, one way or another.'

'To the sound of exploding dynamite!' crowed Crowley. 'I know your methods well enough. But if not through magic, how came you to this time?'

'It is my turn to ask the questions,' said Mr Bell. 'And do not give me any folderol about fading memories – I see the scar of my ray gun's burn upon your veiny ankle.'

'Plah!' said Aleister Crowley, and he indicated his humidor. 'Let us smoke cigars and speak of the old days.'

'Of spaceships and ray guns?' asked Cameron Bell, drawing out cigars.

'Of those and the stele, too.'

Cigars were lit and smoke exhaled and I took to coughing with vigour.

'Darwin,' said Mr Bell, 'the atmosphere is somewhat noxious here. Why not go down to the garden for some fresh air? I will join you soon.' And Mr Bell gave me a certain look.

I left the room and he closed the door behind me, but I did not go down to the garden. I pressed my ear to the door and peeped at times through the keyhole.

'The Ape of Thoth,' said Aleister Crowley. 'How came you by *that*?'

'It is still my turn for questions. I felt, however, that you might care to yield more knowledge when free of his presence.'

I shook my head and shrugged my shoulders. What was the Ape of Thoth?

'In truth,' said Crowley, 'I am very glad that you came. I do not face death with a light heart. Sometimes I hate myself.'

'You have not exactly been a model citizen.'

'How did you find me?' Crowley asked. 'How did you know I was here?'

'Happy happenstance, as it happens. I visited the Atlantis Bookshop, where they pin upon their noticeboards certain cheques that clients have made out to them. Cheques that the banks have failed to honour. Bouncing cheques, as it were. There are several of yours on display. They told me the address and asked me to give you this.' Mr Bell pulled something from his pocket. I assumed it was Mr Crowley's account, drawn up by the Atlantis Bookshop.

Aleister Crowley cackled at this and said, 'Throw it into the bin.'

'Quite so. But the day wears on and I must have answers to my questions. What became of the past we grew up in? How could it simply vanish as if it never existed?'

The wrinkled fellow sucked deeply on his cigar. 'How so indeed?' said he. 'I *was* possessed of magic, you know. I could have become the greatest magician of this or any other age.'

'And naturally you would have used your powers for good.'

'Are you having a gi-raffe? I would have indulged myself in every vice and every pleasure known to Man.'

'But you did *not*.'

'Not for the want of trying.' Aleister Crowley tapped ash onto the carpet. 'But it went. All magic went at the turn of the twentieth century, as if a tap had been turned off, and with it the past as we recall it. The wonders of Tesla and Babbage. The matter of the Martian invasion. Damn it, Bell, the Martians blew up my aunty's house in Surbiton.'

'But history cannot be *unmade*, surely?'

Aleister Crowley laughed once more, a most depressing sound. 'The arrow of time is supposed to point in a single direction,' said he, 'but this can only be if it is not deflected, if time runs its course as it would do. Untampered with. Don't you see it, Bell? You travelled through time as did Knapton, and between the two of you, you have altered the past. All that has happened since the dawn of the twentieth century has happened because time was tampered with. This war now, this *World* War, is not the first of this century. It is the second, and you must take your share of the blame for it.'

'No,' said Mr Bell. 'I have done nothing to bring about these horrors. I have only pursued a criminal. And I *will* bring him to justice and I *will* set history to right.'

'Only if you can hunt him down and return with him to *our* past.'

'And that I will do,' said Cameron Bell. 'That I will certainly do.'

'Without a time conveyance of your own?'

Mr Bell did puff-puffings.

Aleister Crowley shook his ancient head. 'I *could* have been the greatest magician of this century,' he said, 'but it was not to be and now I am old and broken. But history *will* remember me, Mr Bell, and I will enjoy celebrity in the future. As for you, you are not even a footnote. You are a bumbling character in a children's book. You have brought this curse upon yourself. There is no future for you.'

Mr Bell rose to take his leave.

'You have cursed yourself,' said Mr Aleister Crowley.

15

e took a late lunch in an alehouse on the seafront. Hastings appeared to have escaped the cruel attentions of enemy aircraft so far. Which seemed a little unfair to me, as it is an unlovely seaside resort and might well have been improved by selective bombings.

That is a rather cruel thing to say, but my mood was none too jolly.

Before we had journeyed to Hastings, Mr Bell had been forced to pawn his remaining valuables to raise money for the fare. He pulled from his pocket a couple of pound notes and a tinkling of change.

'You overhead everything that was said, I suppose,' said he.

'I assumed that you wanted me to. What is the Ape of Thoth?' I asked.

Mr Bell shook hard his head. 'That hardly matters now.'

We sat in a window seat that afforded a view of the seafront. It was all very peaceful in Hastings, but patrons of the alehouse were looking hard at Mr Bell and me.

'You will have to avail yourself of more suitable apparel,' I whispered. 'You do look very out of place indeed.'

'And I feel the same,' said my friend, in such a plaintive manner as to raise once more those hairs on the back of my neck.

'Must we remain for ever in this dreadful time?' I spoke behind my hand. 'I really do not think that I could bear it.'

Mr Bell shrugged sadly and consulted the menu.

'Corned beef and reconstructed egg and a single choice of bottled beer,' said he with sadness. 'And we who have dined at the Savoy Grill and washed down our feasts with the finest Château Doveston.'

'We *did* really do that?' I whispered in reply. 'And we *did* go to Venus and Mars?'

'We *did*.' Mr Bell hailed what passed for a waiter. 'Two of today's "specials",' he said, 'and two of your finest ales.'

What passed for a waiter looked long and hard at me.

'If you say "we don't serve monkeys in here",' said Mr Bell, 'I shall rise from my seat and pitch you into the sea.'

'Two specials and two ales,' said the what-passed-for, and he scuttled away.

Folk were still glancing so we sat a while in silence. When all appeared safe, I asked Mr Bell whether he had any kind of plan.

'I am working on one,' he said.

'One that will involve our swift departure from this time?'

Mr Bell made the 'so-so' gesture with his fingers. 'I am thinking more of a plan to raise sufficient funds that we are not forced to sleep beneath the stars at night.'

'Preferable beneath the stars here than beneath the ground in London.'

What passed for a waiter brought us our ales and popped the tops from the bottles. 'Please do not take offence, sir,' he said to Mr Bell, 'but I wonder if you would be so good as to settle a matter for us?'

'If I can,' said Mr Bell. 'What does this matter entail?'

'Well,' began the what-passed-for, 'my friend Mr Walter Tomlinson over there says that you are a stage magician.'

Mr Bell sighed. 'Go on.'

'But my other friend, Mr Terence Lightfoot, says that you are the Great Caruso himself.'

'The Great Caruso?' said Mr Cameron Bell. 'And do you have an opinion of your own?'

'Not one that I would care to voice.'

'Well,' said Mr Bell, 'I can tell you that I am neither a stage magician nor the Great Caruso himself.'

'I suspected not Caruso, sir, as he died in nineteen twenty-one.'

'Quite so,' said Mr Bell. 'But I am indeed a well-known face upon the London stage.'

I raised my eyebrows to this outrageous lie.

'I am the celebrated Professor Thoth,' said Mr Cameron Bell, 'and this is the equally celebrated Darwin, known and loved from the Americas to Hindustan as the Educated Ape.'

'Educated?' said the man. 'How so?'

I stared slack-jawed whilst Mr Bell explained.

'He is a Wonder of the World,' explained he. 'A simian prodigy that does read and speak and prognosticate the future.'

A look of avarice appeared in the what-passed-for's eyes. A certain longing, perhaps, to leave his mundane job behind, take to the bright lights of the city and exhibit an educated ape.

Mr Bell noted well that look. 'Naturally, he can only perform whilst in *my* company,' he said, and he gritted his teeth and then added, 'Gottle o' geer.'

'Ah,' said the hoped-to-be-top-of-the-bill. 'I see.' And he winked at Mr Bell.

'We are hoping to be engaged to play at the Pavilion,' continued my duplicitous colleague. 'But please keep it under your hat, as it were,' and he pushed a sixpenny piece in the fellow's direction.

The fellow offered another wink, scooped up the tanner and then, with a grin, departed. He returned to his chums and words were exchanged and interest in us was no more.

'*A ventriloquist's dummy!*' I bared my teeth at Cameron Bell.

'Calm yourself, please,' he replied. 'The opportunity seemed Heaven-sent. I should be praised for my gifts of improvisation. Cheers.' And he raised his beer bottle.

'I will not do it,' I said most firmly. 'No, I jolly well won't.'

'I wonder, do they still have barrel organs in this benighted time?' my friend chanced to wonder.

'I'll *not* do it,' I said.

But of course I did.

There appeared to be no other way for it at the time.

We were trapped in this beastly period, and until Mr Bell came up with a solution to our problems, here and now we must remain, and we would need coin to furnish us with food to fill our empty bellies.

I told Mr Bell that I thought I could get used to Hastings. The air was bracing and the castle hill picturesque. Mr Bell in reply told me that we would not be staying at the seaside, in the comparative safety of this unbombed little town. Rather, we must return to London so that he could lay his hands upon the Pearly Emperor and seek to undo whatever had been done to change the past so drastically.

'There is nothing else for it,' said Cameron Bell.

Though I did not agree.

Professor Thoth and Darwin the Educated Ape premiered at Olympia on the thirtieth of July. Olympia at that time had a standing circus with many sideshows attached.

We rented a booth that had recently been vacated by Fremly, the Three-Legged Yorkshireman. Fremly's supernumerary appendage had apparently fallen off due to his dancing before the public under the influence of brown ale. An off-duty policeman had then recognised the erstwhile human tripod to be none other than Black Jack Magillicuddy, a light-fingered lighterman wanted the length and breadth of the Thames for crimes of a nautical nature.

And so we took the booth.

'I will just fold my arms and say nothing,' I said to Mr Bell.

'Then you and I will grow very thin, living on no food at all.'

'But I am an ape of education—'

'And that, indeed, is the point!' Mr Bell threw up his hands and sighed the most terrible sigh. 'I am not asking you to make a fool of yourself. Rather, to impress folk with your erudition.'

'By saying "gottle o' geer"?'

'Darwin, at times you quite exasperate me.' Mr Bell now folded *his* arms and made a very fierce face.

Actually, I quite enjoyed myself, but I was not prepared to admit it. We gave lunchtime and afternoon performances and the great hall of Olympia closed promptly at six. Its roof was tiled with glass, you see, and could not be 'blacked out'.

The hours suited me and the pennies flowed in and the days became carefree. But the nights were always filled with dread, when the sirens cried out and we took to the underground shelters.

Mr Bell worked hard at being Professor Thoth. But he also worked hard at being Mr Cameron Bell. He needed to enter the secret headquarters of the Ministry of Serendipity and there lay his hands upon Mr Arthur Knapton.

We discussed the matter over bottled beer in our Earls Court digs.

'According to the papers that I found in the library room in ancient Egypt,' said Mr Bell, 'our quarry will hold a meeting with Mr Churchill this coming Friday evening.'

'Just two days from now,' I said. 'Will this be our only chance?'

'I regret so,' said Mr Bell. 'If we do not take him then, he will be gone from this time and our chance of escaping with him.'

'And so you have a plan?'

Mr Bell drank deeply of his ale.

'Was the answer in the form of mime?' I asked him.

'I do have a plan. But it is reckless and dangerous, too.'

'So no change there, then,' I said, employing the popular parlance of the day. 'And no way, José, if it involves dynamite.'

'I know the location of the secret entrance but my key no longer fits the lock.'

'You have your housebreaking tools.'

'I will tell you my plan,' said Mr Bell. 'And when I have told you it, I will allow you to cast the deciding vote.'

'Most magnanimous of you,' I said, and I toasted my friend with my bottle.

'Possibly so,' agreed Mr Bell. 'But if you do *not* give it your seal of approval, we will be forced to live in this time for the rest of our days, and you might grow tired of the bombs and the loss of life.'

And so my good friend Mr Cameron Bell, once the

Victorian era's most celebrated detective, set about telling me his plan. He laid it out for me in the clearest of details, and when he had done with his telling, he raised his hands and asked me what I thought.

I will not belabour the reader's sensibilities by setting down here exactly what I had to say. Mr Bell's plan was not only dangerous and reckless, it was many other things besides, and none of them appealing.

'So it is a *no*?' said Cameron Bell.

'On the contrary,' I said. 'Your plan sounds well conceived, and although there will be explosions, naturally, they all appear to be for a noble cause. I will raise my thumb to you, Mr Bell. For what could *possibly* go wrong?'

'Indeed,' said Mr Cameron Bell. 'What indeed could possibly go wrong?'

16

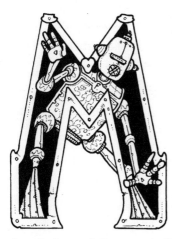r Winston Churchill is not quite so well remembered as he was. As I write these words in the year two thousand and twelve, it is clear to me that many things regarding that national hero are now quite forgotten.

You will surely recall that he was noted for his wily wit and quotable quotes, and if you have ever suffered the misfortune of being drawn into playing a game of Trivial Pursuit, you will know that you are on a reasonably firm footing when the witty quotes come up if you attribute them to either Oscar Wilde or Winston Churchill.*

Mr C was very good at one-liners:

LADY ASTOR: If I were married to you, I would put poison in your coffee.
WINSTON: If *I* were married to *you*, I would drink it.

---

* *Churchill often complained (privately) that Wilde stole much of his best material. (R. R.)*

WINSTON: Madam, you are ugly.

UNKNOWN LADY: Sir, *you* are *drunk*.

WINSTON: But *I* shall be sober in the morning.

And when it came to the making of speeches that stirred up the people of Britain into a regular ferment, Mr Churchill was quite in a class of his own. Who can forget:

> I have nothing to offer but blood, toil, tears and sweat.
>
> *May 1940*

> We shall fight on the beaches,
> we shall fight on the landing-grounds,
> we shall fight in the fields and in the streets,
> we shall fight in the hills.
> We shall never surrender!
>
> *June 1940*

> When I warned [the French] that Britain
> would fight on alone, whatever they did,
> their Generals told their Prime Minister . . .
> 'In three weeks, England will have her
> neck wrung like a chicken.'
> Some chicken. Some neck!
>
> *December 1941*

Who can forget? Well, clearly most, as few there are who can quote these speeches today.

Mr Churchill has certainly retained his popularity and respect, however, for in two thousand and two the nation took a poll to decide who were the top one hundred *greatest Britons*.

Sir Winston Churchill was voted number one.

Isambard Kingdom Brunel, number two.

Aleister Crowley (!) came in at seventy-three, beating Charles Babbage, who attained to number eighty.

We will draw the veil of discretion over the placement of a certain Bono within this top one hundred.

So, as you can see, the people of Britain still care for Mr Churchill. Even though they have forgotten so very much about him.

How many today, for instance, know that Winston Churchill was the very last man in England to employ the services of a monkey butler? Very few, I will wager.

Or that when he was not insulting titled ladies or leading his nation to victory, he loved nothing more than to dress up in frilly frocks and petticoats and troll about the War Room in the guise of his alter ego, Buttercup?

That Mr Churchill was a notable and prolific dresser-up-in-women's-clothes is all but forgotten today. But during the war years, Buttercup was as well known to and as well loved by the British public as Grayson Perry's second self Claire is today, the only difference being that the British public of the war years pretended they did not know that 'Lady Buttercup' was actually Winston Churchill.

I for one will never *truly* understand the humour of the British public.

So . . .

That the great statesman and the cross-dressing potter might share this common − one hesitates to use the word 'fetish' − might appear somewhat outré. But many a great man has favoured a frock, and there is no shame in *that*.

It is probable that Lady Astor's famous remark regarding coffee and poison was uttered in response to her discovering Winston digging through her wardrobe in search of a gown in which to promenade Horse Guards Parade.

But who can say for sure? As few remember these details today, I mention them here purely to inform the reader who might otherwise be surprised by what I am shortly to relate regarding Mr Cameron Bell's plan to lay his hands upon the Pearly Emperor and remove us from the time of the Second World War.

So . . .

It all began in this fashion.

And here I will eschew the grammatical category of 'first monkey' and allow the tale to tell itself, as it were.

For as these are the memoirs of Darwin the monkey, I can do just as I please.

The Adventure of the Prettified Prime Minister

The marvellous monkey was greatly admired, his charm and deportment earning him paeans of praise. Ladies yearned to stroke his glossy flealess coat and gentlemen conversed with him on this engaging topic and the next. For this was no ordinary ape that the patrons of Olympia clamoured to meet. This was Darwin, the Educated Ape. Darwin, the Sensational Simian.

In those days, Olympia owned to a standing circus where some of the world's most accomplished performers were to be viewed, displaying their remarkable skills to an appreciative public. Animal acts found favour then, acts such as Reekie's Remarkable Ribald Rhinos, Crawford's Cat Carousel, Captain Purkey's Perambulating Penguins and Kimberley's Kick-Boxing Kiwi Birds – the latter being avian acrobats who had performed before the Royal House-hold on many a state occasion.

Beyond the big top and the cheering crowds lay the showmen's booths, where were displayed a multitude of human curiosities of such strange and fanciful kidney that might serve as muse to any aspiring poet.

There was:

Cuttlefish O'Hooligan, the Human Octopoid,
A chap of many arms and charms,
A raconteur and wit.
A lady, loved as Layla,
Who sang songs through a loud-hailer
Whilst dwelling in an oven
And revolving on a spit.

The famous Jack-o'-Lantern with his bunny-rabbit eyes,
Whose lustrous luminescence shone
Like diamonds in the dark.
A giant known as Marmaluke,
A dandy and a dancing duke.
A cleric in a barrel
Who charmed cobras in the park.

And so on and so forth in that fashion, and wonderful they were to behold. But none could hold a candle to the Sensational Simian who had captured the public's heart, who was spoken of in drawing rooms and downstairs parlours, bar rooms and bordellos, houses both of God and ill-repute, on croquet lawns and carriageways.

Darwin, the Educated Ape.

This marvellous monkey's manager was a rotund, avuncular figure who went by the name of Professor Thoth in public and by Cameron Bell when locked behind closed doors. He was not a sideshow proprietor by first trade – rather, owning as he did to some small skills in the arts of criminal detection, he styled himself as an investigator and had enjoyed a modest degree of success in this specialised field.

How man and monkey came together would be a long tale in the telling, but that they had travelled far over distances both temporal and otherwise in close company lent them a familiarity which encompassed trust, admiration and indeed love, to a degree. They had fetched up at Olympia through necessity rather than choice, where the talents of the ape, those of human vocalisation, had made him in three short days the very talk of the town. Professor Thoth had invested a considerable portion of the first two days' takings in having playbills printed extolling the virtues of the marvellous monkey, and so it came to pass that by the Friday of their very first week at Olympia, titled folk were offering their patronage and requesting private audiences with this prodigy now called the Ape of Knowledge.

The Ape of Knowledge sat upon a muchly cushioned chair, a velvet smoking cap aslant across his noble brow. He was bedecked in a suit of dark cloth and a most flamboyant bow tie. This attire was not altogether of his choosing, but as his own wardrobe had been lost to him, he was forced to wear the clothes his manager had acquired, which had been stripped – although the man kept the knowledge from the monkey – from a discarded ventriloquist's dummy.*

Upon this Friday morning, at a little after nine, the Ape was sharing his knowledge with a strapping young fireman who had been prepared to pay the now-necessary guinea.

'I come,' said the fireman to the Ape, 'from a showman's

---

* *As an aside, it is of interest to note that when Brighton's West Pier was attacked for the first time by arsonists, a single ticket booth remained unscathed. This booth, it is believed, was haunted by the ghost of a ventriloquist's dummy. (R. R.)*

background, for once I was a circus strongman. I have sailed the Seven Seas of Rhye, but I still haven't found what I'm looking for.'

'And what is *that*, young man?' The Ape of Knowledge raised a languid hand to his face and drew upon a slim cheroot, releasing from his mouth white featherings of smoke.

'I would know truth,' said the fighter of fires.

'Ethical axioms are found and tested not so very differently from the axioms of science,' said the Ape. 'Truth is what stands the test of experience.'

'To quote Einstein,' said the erstwhile circus strongman.

'Hm,' went the Ape. 'Next, please.'

'Ah, just one thing before I go. I have studied the poster that advertises your skills.'

'Hm,' went the Ape of Knowledge once more. It was a *certain* 'hm'.

'It recommends you as the Prognosticating Primate and claims that you can predict future events. Speak to me of the future.'

'The future,' declared the Prognosticating Primate, 'is much like the past, in that there will be an equal amount of it. But I might tell you this: the Greatness of Mankind is now behind us. The past is the new future. Fuss not for the future, for it will be on you soon enough and what is now will soon be then behind you.'

'Such is the doctrine of Zen,' said the seeker after truth.

'Next, *please*!' called the magnificent monkey.

'Might you tell me something specific about the future?' asked the young man, who had been kneeling, as he rose at last to his feet.

'A man will come,' predicted the Prognosticating Primate, 'a man and two women. The man will be quite without talent, yet he will be elevated to a position of greatness. This man's name will be R★ssell Br★nd.'★

'And the women?' asked the young man, stroking sawdust from his knees.

'They will go unrewarded, though their talents surpass those of all who have gone before and their beauty eclipses that of any other female. For the small will attain greatness and the great become small. This will be the way of the future. Amen.'

'I see,' said the young man, 'and understand the wisdom of your words. Might I ask of you the names of these noble ladies?'

'The Cheeky Girls,' the Ape of Knowledge said. '*Next, please!*'

Professor Thoth hustled out the fireman and whispered words of wisdom to the Ape.

'Let it be with the shouting,' he said.

Darwin sipped from a glass of chilled champagne. 'Has our special guest arrived?' he asked.

'Our special guest awaits without.'

'Then bid them come within.'

Professor Thoth bowed and departed, returning at length in the company of a very winsome lady.

She was dressed in an old-fashioned bonnet, secured beneath her chin by a great big bow. Her blue silk frock flounced out from a profusion of petticoats and on her feet she wore the most dear little shoes.

Over her arm she carried a large shopping basket, and from this peeped a monkey, dressed identically to the winsome lady.

★ *It would not be wise to risk litigation over what is, after all, just the opinion of a monkey. (R. R.)*

'Lady Buttercup,' announced Professor Thoth, 'and her monkey maid, Petal.'

The Ape of Knowledge smiled upon Lady Buttercup.

'ictory at all costs, victory in spite of all terror, victory, however long and hard the road may be; for without victory, there is no survival.' said Lady Buttercup.

The Ape of Knowledge clapped his hands and cried a big bravo. 'And you could add,' he added, 'never in the field of human conflict was so much owed by so many to so few.'

'I might indeed,' said Lady Buttercup, removing from her shopping basket a large cigar and thrusting it into her mouth, 'if I were the Prime Minister, rather than a frail little female in a pretty little bonnet.'

Darwin lit the lady's cigar then shook out the match with a flourish. 'They say the Prime Minister is a very handsome man,' he said. 'I hope that one day I will have the honour of making his acquaintance.'

'He is a close personal friend,' said Lady Buttercup. 'In fact, it was *he* who sent me here to meet you.'

'I am touched,' said Darwin, 'but must express my enormous surprise that I have come to his notice.'

'Your manager pushed a great many handbills advertising

your unique talents through the letterbox of Ten Downing Street. He would have pushed more through, but Mr Churchill's monkey butler chased him away.'

'Is *this* the monkey butler?' Darwin smiled at the other ape. Whose face was clearly that of a young male monkey.

'This is Petal,' the lady said. 'My little poppet, Petal.'

Petal made a certain face. Which Darwin understood.

'Mr Churchill,' continued Lady Buttercup, 'is a man who puts the defence of the realm above every other thing. He *will* have victory. He *will*.'

'Quite so,' said the Ape of Knowledge.

'And as such, when word reached him via the printed pamphlet that a Prognosticating Primate was to be found displaying himself at Olympia, Mr Churchill naturally wished to know more of this wonder, that it might aid in the war effort.'

'I predict that the talents of the Cheeky Girls will never find true recognition,' predicted the Prognosticating Primate.

'Such knowledge, though undoubtedly profound, may not be immediately applicable to present circumstances,' said Lady Buttercup, puffing mighty plumes of smoke into the air. 'Mr Churchill would like your advice upon a particularly pressing matter.'

'I would be happy to assist in any way I can,' said Darwin. 'I am an ape who is true to King and Country. London and the Empire mean a great deal to me.'

'Then please would you be so kind as to demonstrate your predictive skills by prophesying something that will come to pass this day.'

'Gladly,' said Darwin, and he made a thoughtful face. 'Oh, yes,' he said. 'Something is coming through. Mr

Churchill will hold a top-secret meeting today at a top-secret establishment known as the Ministry of Serendipity.'

'Oooh,' said Lady Buttercup. 'I am most impressed.'

'And not only that,' continued the Ape, 'but this meeting will be held with a malefactor by the name of Arthur Knapton, who seeks only ill for this nation.'

'Goodness me,' said Lady Buttercup.

'And what is more,' said the Ape, for the Ape had more to say, 'Mr Churchill, being the generous, kindly and wise individual he is, will reward myself with a medal and present Professor Thoth with an item taken from the possession of the evil Arthur Knapton.'

Lady Buttercup asked what this item might be, and Darwin the Simian Sensation told her.

'An ancient Egyptian tablet engraved with hieroglyphics. Mr Knapton carries it close to his person.'

Lady Buttercup nodded her bonnet. 'There is no doubt that you are an ape of knowledge,' said she.

'I do my best to please when I can,' said Darwin in reply.

'Thus and so,' said Lady Buttercup, and, rising from the seat she had taken, she cast aside her bonnet. 'Know me, enemy of England!' she cried. 'Nazi spy that you are. Know me as your nemesis, for I am Winston Churchill.'

And Mr Churchill drew out a pistol and pointed it at Darwin.

In Olympia at this time there was always a great deal of noise, merry cries and shrieks, many shouts of joy and the sounds of revelry and laughter.

Consequently, no one beyond the booth that housed the Educated Ape heard the gunfire. And when presently a figure in a bonnet, carrying a monkey in a shopping basket, slipped away from the booth and merged into the joyous crowd, no one paid that figure any attention at all.

The Ministry of Serendipity, as those in the know will know, is housed in caverns measureless to man, deep beneath Mornington Crescent Station. It is there that those 'corridors of power' of which people speak lead from one room to another, occasionally to a staircase and sometimes to a toilet.

A special key is required to enter this secret Ministry, one that must be turned in a lock within the lift that freights the folk of London down to the platforms. Only a very few hold such a key, a very favoured few.

Alone in the lift, but for the basket and monkey, the figure in the bonnet turned such a key and the lift fell downwards many floors, as if into the very bowels of the Earth.

And then it stopped and a bell went *ting* and the figure left the lift. I would be wrong of course, to call this figure a lady, for this figure was no such thing – rather a frocked-up fellow with a frocked-up ape in his basket. As this frocked-up fellow left the lift, a guard at the door saluted.

'Good afternoon, Mr Churchill, *sir*,' saluted he.

'Not when I'm all frocked-up,' said the fellow. 'Call me Buttercup.'

'Good afternoon, Mr Buttercup, *sir*, madam.'

'I suppose that will have to do.' Buttercup lit a new cigar then asked, 'Has *he* arrived?'

'The Galactic Emperor? Yes, sir, madam. He awaits you in the War Room, with his . . . *things*.' And the guard made shudders.

'His *things*?' asked Winston Buttercup. 'What *things* are these that you speak of?'

'The tentacly things,' said the guard. 'The Martian tentacly things.'

'Hm,' went the smoker of the big cigar. 'Well, as long as they all do what *I* wish, it is no matter to me.'

'You'll probably wish to slip into your siren suit,' said the guard.

'Hm, I probably will,' mused the frocked-up fellow as he swung his basket to and fro and to.

'I will escort you to your changing room,' said the guard, and that is what he did.

A little later, Mr Churchill emerged from his changing room. He wore the famous siren suit* that he popularised through the war years and smoked the cigar for which he was known and loved. He also still sported his bonnet.

'Bonnet?' queried the guard, saluting once again.

Mr Churchill returned the salute. 'I think I will keep it on,' said he. 'It is rather nippy down here.'

Mr Churchill's monkey butler was no longer cluttered with satins and lace. *He* – and this monkey butler had always been a *he* – looked extremely smart in the dress uniform of a major of the Household Cavalry. The monkey saluted the guard and grinned. The guard saluted the monkey.

'Lead us to the War Room,' said Mr Churchill. 'And keep a weather eye open – walls have ears, you know, and I encountered a monkey today whose knowledge of this establishment led me to believe that we have spies amongst us.'

The guard cocked his rifle and led the way.

The way to the secret War Room.

*

* *You might want to look this up. (R. R.)*

Now, a War Room is a War Room, no matter the where or the when. Bright harsh light shines down upon a table surrounded by a number of chairs. The chair at the table's head is slightly bigger and grander than the rest. The high muckamuck who holds the meeting always sits in this.

Mr Winston Churchill, in the company of his monkey butler, Major Monkey B, entered the War Room. At the far end of the table, in the slightly bigger chair, sat a fellow with a long, strange face. A fellow by the name of Arthur Knapton.

A passing Egyptologist, had there been one there to pass by, might well have been surprised by the looks of Arthur Knapton, finding that he bore an uncanny resemblance to a young pharaoh named Akhenaten.

Mr Churchill cared not a jot for anything Egyptian. He spied the fellow with the face and shouted, 'Out of *my* chair!'

Two dreadful figures sprang from shadows into the harsh bright light. Monstrous things with waggling tentacles.

'Easy, boys,' said Mr Knapton, rising from the chair. 'We are all on the same side 'ere, I'm finkin'. Let's 'ave no up'eavals!'

The Martians, for such these beings were, muttered and gargled menacingly and then made their withdrawals.

'Quite so,' said Mr Churchill. 'We will have decorum here.'

'A rather fetchin' bonnet,' said Arthur Knapton, laughing his horrible laugh. 'Will you wear that when they crowns ya King o' the World?'

'King of the World?' said Mr Churchill in a very low and troubled tone.

'You surely ain't forgotten our deal? You make me Commander-in-Chief of all the Allied Forces and I bring down me Martian mates and wipe the Nazis out.'

'It is a plan that has much to recommend it,' said Mr Churchill, elbowing his way past a tentacly beasty and taking his place in the slightly larger chair.

Arthur Knapton sat himself down at the other end of the table. And then leaned back in his chair and put his feet on the table.

'Feet *down!*' commanded Mr Churchill.

Arthur Knapton slowly lowered his feet.

'Your Martians interest me,' said Mr Churchill, puffing like a tugboat on his big cigar. 'I have read the *fictional* account of the Martian invasion – Mr Wells' *War of the Worlds*. I recall that the Martians died because they had no immunity to Earthly bacteria.'

Arthur Knapton laughed his most annoying laugh once more. ''Tis true,' said he. 'An' as *you* an' a few of yer in-the-know colleagues know, the War of the Worlds was *not* a fiction. It 'appened in eighteen eighty-five, and would 'ave remained a part of 'istory 'ad not *I* chosen to make some alterations.'

'In your capacity as—' Mr Churchill paused.

'A time traveller,' said Arthur Knapton. 'The world's one an' only time traveller.'

'As a time traveller, thank you, you altered the past so that the Martian invasion did not take place?'

'I postponed it. These Martians 'ere won't die from Earthly bacteria. These Martians 'ere are all dosed up with penicillin.'

'Penicillin?' said Mr Churchill. 'Is this drug upon the shelves of Boots?'

'Not as yet, it ain't. It was discovered by Alexander Fleming in nineteen twenty-eight, but it don't go into commercial use until nineteen forty-five.'

'Interesting,' said Mr Winston Churchill. 'A man who can

travel through time may achieve so very much, it would appear. Pray tell me, Mr Knapton, where is your time machine?'

Arthur Knapton clutched at his chest, then threw his arms wide and smiled. 'That's for me to know,' said he, 'an' for you to wonder of. Now, I 'ave all the papers wiv me, if you'll look 'em over and sign on the dotted line.'

'On the dotted line of what, exactly?' said Mr Churchill.

'Of the contracts we agreed upon – that you become King of the World an' I your Commander-in-Chief.'

'Ah, those,' said Mr Churchill. 'I don't think we'll bother with those.'

'What of this?'

'I am dissolving this partnership,' said Mr Churchill. 'I believe that, should I sign these papers, you will unleash a Martian invasion upon the whole world, after which I suspect a military coup would not be long in coming, and you, my very treacherous friend, would crown *yourself* King of the World.'

'Oho,' said Arthur Knapton. 'A very fine fing is *this*. I'll 'ave t' teach ya the error of yer ways.'

'I think *not*.' And Mr Churchill rose, discarded his bonnet and drew from his basket an army service revolver. 'Know me, enemy of England,' he declared. 'Know me, enemy of Mankind that you are. Know me as your nemesis. Know me as Cameron Bell.'

'Cameron Bell?' went Arthur Knapton as his big face fell.

'I have tracked you through time,' said the great detective, 'and now I will bring you to justice.'

'But if you are Bell,' said the villain, 'what became of Churchill?'

'Mr Churchill and his monkey butler are both safe and sound, tied up in a showman's booth at Olympia. I lured Mr

Churchill there with playbills advertising a Prognosticating Primate that could divine the future, and there overcame him when he pulled a pistol upon my companion. This pistol here, as it happens. I knew you had dealings planned with Mr Churchill and I knew the where and when of them. I studied your papers in ancient Egypt, where you are known as Akhenaten.'

'You fiend!' cried Arthur Knapton.

'Quite the contrary. I also learned from our mutual acquaintance Aleister Crowley that you perambulate through time by means of a magical tablet, the Stele of Revealing, which you stole from him and then decoded through extensive study of the books you stole from the British Museum.'

Darwin the monkey, for of course it was *he* with Mr Bell, masquerading as Churchill's monkey butler, Major Monkey B, scratched at his chin and pondered, 'I am not too certain that works out,' said he.

'It is best that we dismiss plot holes,' said Mr Bell. 'When dealing with time travel it is something of a free-for-all.'

'Fair enough,' said the Ape of Knowledge.

'So 'ow did you get 'ere?' asked Arthur Knapton, effecting a thoughtful expression. 'Do you 'ave a stele of yer own?'

'I travel through the medium of science rather than magic,' declared Mr Bell, 'in a time-ship invented by Mr Ernest Rutherford, the workings of which are contained within a back-engineered Martian warship.'

'One commandeered after the failed invasion of eighteen eighty-five?' asked Arthur Knapton.

'Best not continue this line of conversation,' said Darwin, 'lest we stumble once more into a mighty big plot hole.'

'I am leaving now,' said Arthur Knapton. 'Do not try to stop me.'

'Absolutely *not*,' said Mr Bell. 'Hand over the Stele of Revealing or I will shoot you dead and take it from your body.'

'Kill 'im, boys!' cried Arthur Knapton, flinging himself behind his chair and urging on his Martians.

Cameron Bell drew down fire on his attackers.

Darwin the monkey dived for cover.

Arthur Knapton fled.

'After him, Darwin!' shouted Mr Bell. 'We must not let him escape.'

The Martians now floundered about on the floor, leaking green goo from numerous wounds. Mr Bell leapt nimbly over them, closely followed by Darwin the monkey.

Arthur Knapton pelted down a corridor of power.

'There he goes,' cried Mr Bell. 'After him, Darwin, hurry.'

The monkey and the man gave chase.

And as they did so, they heard the chant rise up from the mouth of Arthur Knapton.

And as they reached the end of that corridor of power, near the stairs but quite a way from the toilet, they saw a bright light emanate from the runner. Then they saw the flash and heard the sound of water entering some titanic plughole.

And then together they stopped and sighed.

For Arthur Knapton was gone.

18

'ell, that might have gone somewhat better,' said the monkey to the man. 'He has escaped and we are trapped here for ever.'

'Not a bit of it,' said Cameron Bell.

'*Not a bit of it?*' Darwin the monkey stamped his feet and showed his very sharp teeth. 'He has departed in the company of the magic tablet. We are trapped and doomed.'

'All has gone as I planned it,' said the great detective. 'We shall pursue him now and bring him to justice just as I have planned.'

'*What?*' cried the ape, a-gnashing his teeth. 'Have you gone stark raving mad?'

'Follow me, Darwin,' said Cameron Bell. 'I have been here before, as you know, and I am well acquainted with the layout.'

'And—'

'We shall proceed to the loading docks.'

'And—'

'Take our leave in the *Marie Lloyd*. If that finds favour with *you*.'

'And—' went the ape once more, and then, '*What?*'

'That *is* what we came for,' said Mr Bell. 'That and to foil Arthur Knapton's plan in this day and age.'

'*And* to bring him to justice, I recall.'

'That would have been a bonus, but I considered it unlikely.'

'Now just hold on right *there*,' said Darwin. 'This is all getting quite beyond me. Are you saying that the *Marie Lloyd* is somewhere in this underground complex?'

'Where else would it be?' asked Mr Bell. 'This is the top-secretest top-secret place in all of the British Empire. If you sought a captured Martian spaceship, would you not seek it here?'

'But our time-ship ceased to exist, because in this day and age, you and I are considered purely fictional, because the War of the Worlds never happened. Am I correct?'

'Up to a point,' said Cameron Bell. 'But you did see those Martians with your own two eyes?'

'I did,' said Darwin.

'And you do of course possess absolute proof of the *Marie Lloyd*'s existence.'

'Do I?' asked Darwin.

'You do.' Mr Bell reached down to the monkey butler, dug about in his uniform and drew out a key on a chain.

'The ignition key to the *Marie Lloyd*,' said Darwin.

'Around your neck all along,' said Mr Bell. 'Which set me early to thinking that all might *not* be so simple as we supposed.'

'I never supposed it was simple.'

'If the key was still with you,' said Mr Bell, 'then it was my conjecture that the *Marie Lloyd* must be here also. And if it is still *here*, then this is the *here* where we'll find it.'

'In the loading bay?' said Darwin the monkey.

'And untampered with, I'm hoping, as you have the only key.'

'I am sadly not wearing a hat,' said Darwin, 'or I would take it off to you, my friend.'

'I detect a hint of sarcasm in that.'

'Lead me to the loading bay,' said Darwin, the Ape of Knowledge.

And of course it *was* there.

And *I* – and here I shall return once more to 'first monkey' – was suitably impressed by its being there.

'I would like to leave now, please,' I said to Mr Bell. 'This is a dreadful time for the world and I have no wish to remain here.'

There was *some* unpleasantness.

There were guards surrounding the *Marie Lloyd* and they were not convinced by Mr Bell's impersonation of Mr Winston Churchill. In fact, they sought to arrest Mr Bell as a Nazi spy and me as a spy also.

I feel that had Mr Bell not flourished dynamite, taken on a wild-eyed look and threatened to blow all and sundry to kingdom come unless the guards made haste with their departures . . .

. . . I think things might have taken a turn for the worse.

'Where to, and *when*?' I asked Mr Bell when we were once more aboard our time-ship, with the hatchway door locked firmly from within.

'I have a theory,' said the great detective.

'I am sure that you do. But do you have a date?'

'I do,' said Mr Bell, and he whispered it into my ear.

'I am not keen,' I said in reply. 'That is further into the

future. What if there is still war? Things will be *very* grim then.'

'I am confident that there will be no war in this particular time.'

'I recall you saying something similar about *this* time,' I recalled.

'I was getting my "time legs", as it were. All will be well, I promise.'

'And why this particular time and this particular date?'

'Because I found this,' replied Mr Bell, pulling something from the pocket of the siren suit.

'It is a ticket,' I said, regarding same.

'It is indeed a ticket. Arthur Knapton evidently gave it to Mr Churchill for him to write upon it the time and date of today's meeting.'

I made the face that says, *Go on*. So Cameron Bell went on.

'It is a bus ticket,' he said.

'Go on.'

'A bus ticket from the future.'

'And how can you tell *that*?' I asked.

'By the date upon it,' said Cameron Bell.

I took the ticket and examined it with interest.

'London Transport, route sixty-five,' I read aloud. 'And yes – the date *is* stamped upon it. Is not *that* convenient!'

'God clearly smiled upon our endeavours,' said Mr Bell.

'Let us be grateful for His mercy.'

'Quite so. Now, according to *this*—' Mr Bell produced from another pocket a London gazetteer –

'Which just happened to be in the pocket?' I said.

'Exactly. Well, according to this, the Number Sixty-Five bus route was established in nineteen thirty-eight. It runs between Ealing and Leatherhead.'

'So where would you like me to land the ship?'

'Sniff the ticket,' said Mr Bell, 'then tell me what you smell.'

I put the ticket to my sensitive nostrils and sniffed. 'It smells like rotten eggs,' I said.

'Precisely. And to my knowledge, unless they have moved it and I doubt whether they have, only one place on the Sixty-Five bus route smells like that.'

Mr Bell paused that we both might enjoy his triumph.

'Get on with it,' I told him.

'Brentford,' said Mr Bell. 'The gasworks down in Brentford.'

And so I set the controls for Brentford.

And nineteen sixty-seven.

19

 nd so upon the dubious strength of a bus ticket that smelled of rotten eggs, we set out for the sixties and for Brentford.

Naturally, I knew Brentford, as I had been Lord Brentford's monkey butler and also his best monkey-man when he got married. I had lived with his lordship in Syon House, an old mile along the Isleworth Road from the little town of Brentford.

To know Brentford is to love it, as the old song says, and few who visit this 'little piece of Heaven that has fallen to Earth' are not moved by its beauty.

The sky seems somehow bluer in Brentford, the bricks of the houses that little bit brickier, the pavements more pavementy. Certainly the ladies there are prettier than those in other parts of London, and the gentlemen hold to such dignified deportment that when the term 'God-like' is used to describe them, it is not used casually.

'Cradled lovingly in an elbow of Old Mother Thames', as the poet once put it,* Brentford remains to this very day (the

---

* *I do not usually employ the term 'poet' when I describe myself. I prefer the term 'visionary' – but I appreciate the gesture. (R. R.)*

year 2012) one of England's top tourist attractions. Its flora and fauna attract naturalists, whilst its pub-night talent competitions draw in record-company executives from all over the world who seek to find next year's Big Thing.

Ah, Brentford.

A pity, though, about that dreadful gasworks.

A body blow! A pustule on the nose of the Madonna! This black and evil edifice stood upon the road between Brentford and Kew, obscuring the idyllic views of the Thames and poisoning the air.

The Brentford Gasworks were constructed in eighteen twenty-one to supply street lighting from Brentford to Kensington, to light the way for the fashionable as they travelled in their quilted curricles. A noble venture, to be sure. But to site so ugly a structure in such a beautiful place?

Many suspected it to be the work of the ever-jealous French. Johnny Frenchman, as is well known, looks bitterly from the shores of his dismal country towards the shining sands and sun-drenched vistas of our fair land.

So, yes, it seems fair to me that the blame must lie on a Frenchman's garlicky doorstep.*

But did the gasworks really ruin Brentford?

No, not a bit of it did they!

Because the philosophical folk of that blessed borough merely turned a blind eye to the gasworks and utterly ignored their very existence.

And so we fetched up in Brentford.

We had set the controls for midnight and I carefully steered the *Marie Lloyd* down into the grounds of Syon House, as far away from the mansion as I could manage.

* *It is not racist to poke fun at the French. In fact, it is to be admired. (R. R.)*

Then we tasted brandy, enjoyed a cigar and took ourselves off to our beds.

To be rudely awakened at dawn.

A clamouring came to the hull of the *Marie Lloyd*. Great oaths were sworn and cries of anger, too.

I awoke and joined Mr Bell, who was peering bleary-eyed out through the windscreen and shaking his head from side to side.

'Are we under attack?' I asked my friend, who stood in his nightshirt and cap. 'Is it chickens, or Nazis, or both?'

'I do not think so,' Mr Bell replied. 'From what I gather, we have "parked our attraction in quite the wrong place". I shall go and remonstrate. You would do well to stay here.'

I nodded in agreement then followed Mr Bell to the hatchway, which he unlocked and let down.

'Cooee there,' he called.

Some rather fierce-looking fellows wearing denim trousers and cotton vests (jeans and T-shirts, it was later explained) were rapping upon the *Marie Lloyd* and demanding that it be moved.

'So sorry,' called my friend to them. 'We arrived rather late in the night.'

'Well, now,' said a fellow who was bigger than the rest. 'You certainly look the part and no mistake.'

'I do?' said Mr Bell, and he shrugged his shoulders.

'You certainly do, but you can't park it here – and where is the loader that brought it?'

'We flew it in,' said Mr Bell.

The large fellow laughed at this. 'Priceless,' said he, when he had done. 'Well, we'll bring in the crane and shift you.'

'Shift us to where, exactly?'

'Oh, it's *us*, is it, then?' And the fellow caught sight of me, dressed too in my nightshirt and cap.

'You've got to be ******* joking,' the fellow declared.

Mr Bell cast me a look that I felt was rather disparaging.

'I told you to wait in the cabin,' said he.

'Well, that'll have to go back to where it came from,' said the fellow. 'Can't have one of them running around loose in the park.'

I looked up at Mr Bell.

And he looked down at me.

'I do not think we are in any danger,' he said to me, 'but there appears to be a degree of misunderstanding. We'll let this fellow bring his crane, then see what we shall see.'

Mr Bell smiled at the fellow.

The fellow looked back, slack of jaw.

We attended to the morning's ablutions, dressed and set to breakfast.

'There is only porridge, I regret,' said Mr Bell. 'We will have to take on more supplies – it is ever foolhardy to begin the day without a good breakfast inside you.'

Mr Bell was a man who took his food as he took his ale and indeed as he took his life: without moderation.

A sudden movement bothered at our breakfasting.

The *Marie Lloyd* was lifted aloft and borne along slowly but surely.

I gazed from a porthole of the dining salon. 'I can see Syon House in the distance,' I said. 'It looks very much the same. It brings back many memories.'

Which of course it did, for I had enjoyed happy times whilst working for Lord Brentford.

But I *did* feel trepidation, because I remembered well the *terrible thing*. How I had crash-landed this very *Marie Lloyd*, this time-ship, into the Bananary at the rear of Syon House in the year eighteen ninety-eight.

And how Lord Brentford, entering the crashed craft with his double-barrelled fowling piece, had shot the elderly me stone dead, thinking me an enemy.

It had all been a terrible thing and I remembered it clearly. But it *had* happened and it *would* happen, this I knew. But not until I was a very ancient ape.

Mr Bell gazed hard at my expression.

'I know what you are thinking, my little friend,' said he, 'and you know that Lord Brentford loved you and that what he did was a dreadful mistake.'

'I know,' I said. 'And I have forgiven him.'

'Then,' replied Mr Bell, a-wiping his mouth with a napkin, 'let us go out and look at the world of the nineteen-sixties and see if we can fathom exactly what the ambitious Mr Knapton is up to in this day and age.'

'Let us do that very thing.'

'Oh my dear dead mother,' said Cameron Bell.

For we had left the *Marie Lloyd* (carefully locking it behind us) and ventured out into the grounds of Syon, where we came upon a sign:

VICTORIAN THEME PARK
AND MONKEY SANCTUARY

I read this, as had Mr Bell, and I, too, expressed words regarding his defunct mama.

'What is a *theme park*?' I asked my friend. 'And why would a monkey need sanctuary?'

I had read Victor Hugo's *The Hunchback of Notre-Dame*, where Quasimodo took sanctuary in the cathedral, and wondered, perchance, whether the monkeys of this age were suffering from the same kind of religious persecution.

Around and about us stood traction engines and steam-driven carousels, swing boats and roundabouts and all the delights of a bright and gay Victorian funfair.

Mr Bell was in his tweeds and I in new summer linens. Many folk pointed in our direction and said we looked 'very authentic'.

'And *that*,' said a laughing fellow, wearing jeans and a T-shirt as did most round about, 'that really *does* look the part, doesn't it?' And he pointed towards the *Marie Lloyd*. 'That is exactly how you might have imagined a Victorian spaceship to be, if ever one had existed.'

'Oh dear,' I whispered to Mr Bell. 'History hasn't changed back, then.'

'You want to put a muzzle on that monkey, though,' said the fellow. 'They can turn right nasty and give you rabies if they bite your finger.'

'Darwin is quite tame,' said Mr Bell, and he tousled my head as I was sans pith helmet that day.

'Darwin?' said the fellow. 'Like the father of the monkeys? Very good.' And, grinning like a buffoon, he went upon his way.

'Shall we take a walk up to the house?' asked Mr Bell, when there was none but me to hear him ask it. 'Perhaps we might meet one of Lord Brentford's grandchildren. Assuming they remain in residence. For it is clear that the house and grounds are now opened up to the public.'

Lord Brentford's grandchildren? I thought this over and then a sad thought struck me. Lord Brentford would of course be dead and gone. Long dead and gone by now and maybe long forgotten.

'I would like to go to the house,' I said.

And I put out my hand and my friend took it in his.

Very little had really changed, it appeared. The Bananary had *not* been rebuilt. Instead, where it had once so proudly stood, there was a sort of second-rate greenhouse affair that contained a cafeteria.

We strolled about to the big front door and this stood widely open. Within we encountered a kind of ticket booth.

Mr Bell patted his pockets. Of course we had no present-day currency.

'You can go through as you're in the show,' said a lady on the desk, and a very sweet lady she was, too. 'And oh, doesn't he look cute in his little suit.' And she smiled down at me and I could not help smiling back.

'Don't let him touch anything,' said the lady.

Mr Bell just grinned and nodded his head.

Many memories now came tumbling back as we walked through the house. Memories of the grand masked balls and lavish garden parties, of the famous folk who had cast their exotic shadows upon lawns lit by lanterns, feasted in the dining room and danced the night away in the grand hall, with its frescoed walls and glittering chandeliers.

Syon House looked rather sad and rather faded, too, like the dry dead husk of a once bright, vital place.

'Oh my,' said Cameron Bell, of a sudden. 'Darwin, look at this.'

We stood now in what had been his lordship's private study. The furniture was mostly the same as I remembered, an eclectic mix of east and west, gathered to suit Lord Brentford's personal tastes.

But there above the fireplace was the portrait.

Framed within a gilt rococo frame.

The work of the painter Edward Burne-Jones.

The portrait of a monkey.

I looked. I stared. And tears fell from my eyes.

'It is *you*,' said my friend.

And yes, it was. The portrait was of me.

The painted me stood tall and proud, wearing the uniform of the Queen's Own Electric Fusiliers, blue with buttons of brass and braid of gold. He struck a most heroic pose, one hand on the pommel of a sword and in the other the staff of a Union Jack.

'And see here,' said Mr Cameron Bell, and he pointed to a brass plaque on the base of the gilded frame, too high for me to read from where I stood.

'What does it say?' I sniffed as I spoke. 'Please read it to me, Mr Bell.'

My friend took a deep breath and read:

DARWIN
My loyal butler and bestest friend.

Mr Bell took my hand once more and we left Syon House.

'What a beautiful thing to do,' I said, when I had dried my eyes.

'I told you he loved you,' said Cameron Bell. 'But you knew that anyway. Look, I have a folded pamphlet here – a potted history, I suppose. Let us sit beneath that tree over there and study it together.'

We sat beneath a spreading chestnut tree. I had climbed this tree myself in times past, and now I leaned back upon its trunk and wondered at the future.

'It is wrong, you know,' I said to Mr Bell.

'Travelling through time, do you mean?'

I nodded. 'It is wrong.'

'I tend to agree,' said my friend. 'It is an unnatural thing to do. I have cautioned care before and I do so again now.'

'You shot dead that MacTurnip, I recall.'

'Hm,' said Mr Cameron Bell, and then, 'Oho,' and Mr Bell laughed.

'What is so very funny?' I enquired.

'Darwin,' said my friend to me, 'when you were Lord Brentford's monkey butler, did you ever, how shall I put this, *entertain* any lady monkeys here?'

'A gentleman never divulges,' I said. 'But yes, there were one or two dalliances. Queen Victoria had a monkey maid, as did several of the grand ladies who lived nearabouts. They used to visit upon Sundays and I would take their monkeys for a walk.'

'*For a walk?*' croaked Mr Bell, suddenly made all but helpless by a fit of laughter.

'I only did what was natural,' I said, 'as any ape would do.'

'And did it well,' said my friend, guffawing as he handed the pamphlet to me.

I perused it once.

Perused it twice.

Perused it once again.

'Oh my,' I said, when I had done. 'Oh my, oh my, oh my.'

'Oh my, indeed,' said Mr Bell. 'Now we understand what that fellow said earlier about you being the "father of the monkeys". It would appear that a monkey house in the grounds is currently home to several hundred of your own descendants.'

And then Mr Bell had to run to the toilet.

For otherwise he would have wet himself, as he was laughing so hard.

20

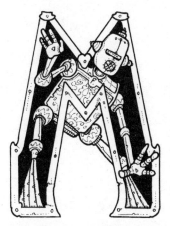

r Bell at last regained sobriety.

I chastened him for his rude behaviour and he fell into laughter once again.

At last, when he was finally done, he shook his head.

'I suppose it is a natural enough thing,' said he. 'Monkeys will be monkeys, after all.'

I perused the pamphlet. 'Two hundred monkeys,' I said, in some awe. 'I have a tribe of my own.'

Which caused me to think about matters. For, as I have written in an earlier chapter, tribalism appears to have caused more problems for the human race and indeed others than almost any other thing. I know that many blame religion, but religion is so often used merely as an excuse for being nasty.

Mr Bell took out his fountain pen. The one that had been a gift to him from the Rajah of Nepal for sorting out a delicate matter involving an elephant named Dwelly van der Poodleberry-Uffington Smythe.

Mr Bell replaced the fountain pen in his pocket and I never did find out exactly why he had brought it out in the first place.

'Would you like to visit your tribe?' he asked me.

'Yes, I certainly would,' I said. 'Shall we go and meet them now?'

'I would rather like lunch first,' said Mr Bell, 'and perhaps a pint of porter. If I recall, from a case I once solved hereabouts, there used to be a rather splendid public house named the Flying Swan along the Ealing Road. Shall we take a walk to the town and see if it's still there?'

'And then see my monkeys after lunch?'

'See your monkeys after lunch indeed.' And a silly smirk appeared on my friend's face.

'Beware the teeth,' I said, and I bared them.

'Quite so,' said my friend, and he ceased his foolish grinning.

We left Syon Park and strolled along the highway, bound for lunch. Motor carriages passed us by, horrid noisy things.

'The internal combustion engine,' said Mr Bell, displaying once again his arcane knowledge. 'Dismissed, I recall, by Mr Tesla as inefficient and harmful to the environment.'

'Arthur Knapton has much to answer for, if it truly was he who changed history and erased the wonderful technology of our age.'

'Much indeed.' And we continued on our way, my companion deep in thought.

I knew the town of Brentford quite well and found it for the most part as I remembered. Late-Victorian houses built of London stocks and sheltering beneath slate roofs. Flowers in window boxes, pussycats asleep upon doorsteps. Ivy climbing the library walls, a floral clock in the memorial park.

'*You* are wondering,' said I, breaking in on the thoughts of

Mr Bell, 'exactly what your arch-enemy the Pearly Emperor is up to hereabouts.'

'Bravo, Darwin,' said Cameron Bell. 'According to this bus ticket, he got on at Kew and off at Brentford.'

'If we knew exactly when,' I said, 'we could lie in wait and bop him on the head when he gets off that bus.'

'It was never going to be *that* easy,' Mr Bell assured me. 'But look, here we are – the Flying Swan, and it has changed hardly at all.'

And it had not.

We entered together and each took stock in our way.

I beheld an elderly saloon bar, grown old with dignity, smelling as an alehouse should and bathed in that particular light that drifts through etched-glass windows. A bar-counter extended the length of one wall, and a row of Britannia tables faced it from the other. It did not fairly bustle with folk, but was just full enough.

Mr Bell saw what I saw, but he of course saw so much more. His practised eye gleaned details from details, drew up a mental log of characteristics, created a macrocosm from the microcosm.

And things of that nature generally.

Behind the bar-counter there stood a young fellow, well dressed in white shirt and dicky bow, his hair sleekly brilliant-ined. He worried at a pint pot with a polishing cloth whilst chatting with a little knot of locals.

I discerned a pair of young scallywags, an ancient in wellington boots* with a half-spaniel snoozing at his feet and a chap in a brown shopkeeper's coat, all of them drinking beer.

* *The Iron Duke had already popularised those by the 1880s. (R. R.)*

Mr Bell made lip-smacking sounds and we approached the bar-counter.

Now, it might have been expected that we would raise some attention, dressed as we were and me being no man at all. But we elicited nothing more than casual glances and welcoming nods of the head.

The smartly dressed barman detached himself from his company and smiled upon our presence.

'What will it be, sir?' he asked of Mr Bell, in a voice that contained not a hint of a Scottish accent. 'We have eight hand-drawn ales on pump – two more than the Four Horsemen down the way and three more than the Purple Princess up-aways.'

Mr Bell gazed, with a look approaching love, from beer-pull, to beer-pull, to beer-pull.

'What shall we have, then, Darwin?' he asked of me.

I did swarmings up onto the counter and peerings at the pumps. This brought some amusement to the patrons.

'Likes his beer, then, does he?' asked the ancient.

'He much prefers champagne,' said Mr Bell. And then to the barman, 'What would *you* recommend?'

'Large,' said the barkeeper, drawing a sipping into a tiny glass.

Mr Bell took and tasted, then nodded and smiled. 'A pint and a half, if you will.'

'Have you travelled far?' enquired the barman as he drew the beers for Mr Bell and me.

A certain handshake then was exchanged and certain words were muttered.

'The first one's on the house,' the barman said.

It was exceptionally good ale. And the barman watched us with a great deal of pride as we enjoyed the drinking of it.

'I assume you are with the Victorian show at Syon,' said the barman.

Mr Bell nodded to this.

'You are not thinking to move into the neighbourhood, then?'

'Only passing through,' said Mr Bell.

'I think that would be for the best.' The barman smiled upon us, then made the introductions.

'My name is Neville,' said he, 'and I am the part-time barman. This gentleman here in the wellingtons is Old Pete, chap in the shopkeeper's coat is Norman, and these two fellows are Jim Pooley and John Omally.'

Heads were nodded, smiles exchanged, and I watched Mr Bell's eyes dart from detail to detail to detail, shoe to shirt-cuff, forelock to fingernail. It was a joy to see my good friend at it.

'And what conclusions have you drawn from your surreptitious observations?' asked Neville, the part-time barman.

Which, I feel, caught Mr Bell by something of a surprise.

'Enough to know that I am in no ordinary alehouse,' said Mr Bell, in a calm and measured tone. 'As was clear from the moment I entered.' And Mr Bell nodded in thought.

'You are a detective, then,' said Neville.

Which caused some alarm to Pooley and Omally.

'A *private* detective,' said Cameron Bell. 'And I do not believe that the case I am presently engaged upon will cause concern to anybody here.'

'Splendid,' said Neville. 'You see, Brentford has its own private detective, Lazlo Woodbine – the creation of local author P. P. Penrose, who sadly died earlier this year in a bizarre vacuum-cleaning accident.'

'I see,' said Mr Bell.

Though *I* did not. In fact, I had no idea whatsoever as to what was going on with this conversation.

'Look around you,' said Neville, 'and in no more than six words tell me what you see.'

'An all but perfect public house,' said Mr Bell without hesitation.

I counted up his words.

'Precisely,' said Neville. 'And outside you see Brentford, where the flowers are a little bit floweryer and the trees that bit more tree-ie than elsewhere.'

'Quite,' said Mr Bell. 'And the beer here –' and he raised his glass and held it to the light '– is just that little bit more beery, so as to make it all but perfect.'

'Precisely,' said Neville once more. 'And how would you, with your particular skills in mind, explain it?'

Mr Bell now shook his head. 'I confess that I cannot,' he said.

'Would you care for me to do so?' asked Neville, the part-time barman.

Mr Bell did noddings of the head.

'We do not know when it began,' he began. 'Perhaps it has always been so, but there is a magic here in Brentford, and those who live in these parts feel it every day. You will know that there are four cardinal points to a compass – north, south, east and west. In Brentford, however, things are different. Here we have a fifth point.'

'I do not see how that can be possible,' said Mr Bell.

Old Pete dug into a tweedy trouser pocket and withdrew from it an ancient compass of brass. Engraved upon its lid were the words:

Old Pete flipped open the lid and held the compass towards myself and Mr Bell. We both peered at it with interest.

Then I looked up at Mr Bell.

And he looked down at me.

'Oh my dear dead mother,' said Cameron Bell.

'Do any doubts remain?' asked Neville.

'None at all,' said my friend. 'The needle points to a fifth point on the compass.'

'So how might this be?' the part-time barman continued. 'Well, I will tell you, sir. Things in Brentford are just a little bit "more so" because Brentford, it might be said, stands on the front line between reality and otherwise. Brentford is where the mundane meets the mysterious, the Earthly, the outré, the worldly, the wildly weird. And so on and so forth and such like. To the north, Ealing. To the south, Kew. To the east, Chiswick. To the west, Isleworth. To the other point on the compass—'

Mr Bell listened and so did I.

'Fairyland,' the part-time barman said.

'Fairyland?' said Mr Bell, and he shook his head not a little.

'We live upon its border,' said Neville. 'So when the weird stuff happens, the weird stuff happens here.'

Mr Bell's glass was now empty and the part-time barman took it to the pump.

'I have had little to do with the fairy kingdom,' said Mr Bell. 'In truth, I believe I have only met one of their number in all of my life. A troll named Jones. A quite unspeakable creature.'

'Well, we get the lot here,' said Neville. 'More at times than you'd think we could handle. But we bumble through.'

'More than simply bumble, I suspect,' said Mr Bell.

'We do what we can.'

'Which is why you said that you thought it was for the best that I am only passing through,' Mr Bell said.

'Precisely so once more, sir. We have enough to be going on with. You are clearly a chap with a backstory, bound on some kind of adventure. You have an eccentric suit and a well-dressed monkey as a companion. You would be a bit-of-a-character, to my way of thinking.'

'And mine, too,' said Mr Bell, for few regarded him more highly than he himself did.

'Then you will understand why I must say what I must say,' said Neville. 'For to have you here and have you getting involved in whatever adventure you are presently involved in would complicate matters considerably for us.'

'You are engaged upon something big yourself, then?' Mr Bell asked.

And as he was asking, the saloon bar door opened and a tramp of evil aspect and sorry footwear peeped into the room. He gazed all around and said, 'I'll come back later.'

'So,' said Neville, to Mr Bell, 'I regret I must bar you for life. Please leave this establishment quietly so not to inconvenience the neighbours.'

I looked up at Mr Bell.

'Fair enough,' said he.

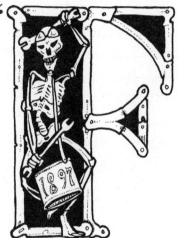

'*air enough?*' I said to Mr Bell, when we had left the Flying Swan. '*Fair enough?* He barred us and you say *fair enough!*'

'He treated us to lunch before throwing us out,' said Cameron Bell. 'An all but perfect plough-man's lunch. The best I've ever tasted.'

I agreed that the cheese was superb – just that little bit cheesier than the norm.

'So what else could he do?' Mr Bell was breathing in the healthy Brentford air. 'These people have quite enough on their hands without being drawn into our nonsense.'

'Nonsense?' I asked.

'Hm,' went Mr Bell. 'Naturally, I did not mean *nonsense* as such.'

'Naturally.'

'But he told me everything I needed to know and that was the point of the exercise.'

We had come to a bench before the Memorial Library and

we sat down upon it. The bench was just that little bit more benchy than other benches I'd sat on.*

'What is this "everything" of which you speak?' I asked Mr Bell.

'The reason why Arthur Knapton is here, of course.'

I shook my head and sat and soaked up sunlight. It really was very nice indeed here in Brentford. It was the sort of place that I would really like to live. Perhaps we could give up adventuring for a while, I thought, rent a small house and become regular patrons of the Flying Swan.

'Tempting, isn't it?' said Mr Bell, who was clearly harbouring similar thoughts. 'And obviously part of its magic. I wonder what effect this marvellous place has had upon Arthur Knapton?'

'Do you know where he is?' I asked.

Mr Bell dug into his waistcoat pocket and pulled out a tiny compass of his own. One that I had not seen before, but suspected might well have been a gift from an Arabian potentate for solving a delicate matter involving a sand dancer, a stick of celery and a spotted dog called Carlos.

'I purchased this in Woolworths,' said Mr Cameron Bell, 'years ago, as a present for my nephew. Look at its face and tell me what you see.'

I examined the tiny compass. 'Same inexplicable business,' I said. 'Its needle points to a fifth point, one I have never seen before today.'

'Fascinating, isn't it?' said Mr Bell, turning the compass this way and the other. 'It points to the realm of the faerie – where, if I am not altogether wrong, we will find Arthur Knapton.'

---

* Given the law of diminishing returns it is to be hoped that that will be the last of the 'more so' carry on. (R. R.).

I put it to Mr Bell, in as polite a manner as I could, that I was not altogether certain about this business of Fairyland. That in fact I had my doubts regarding its reality. And indeed a sneaking suspicion that the part-time barman and his cronies might well be having a gi-raffe at our expense.

Mr Bell shook his head and said, 'Neville and I are Brothers under the Arch.'

'Well, I don't want to get involved with any fairies,' I said. 'I want to go and visit my monkeys. You said we could visit my monkeys after lunch, and we've had our lunch now and I want to visit my monkeys.'

Mr Bell rose and dusted down his tweeds. 'And that is fair enough, too,' he said. 'Monkeys now and fairies at midnight. That is the way that it should be done.'

And it was.

We returned to the grounds of Syon House, passed by the mansion and the Victorian fair and approached the monkey sanctuary.

I do not know exactly what I had been expecting. Perhaps a sort of gentle-monkey's club not unlike my own in Piccadilly. Panelled walls of oak and overstuffed leather couches. Bananas served from silver bowls to smartly suited simians. A well-stocked bar and a billiard room.

What I found appalled me!

The sanctuary was nothing but a cage. A huge cage, quite cathedralesque, but nonetheless a cage.

And my monkeys were not civilised one bit. They were nude and rude and noisy. They skittered about, flung dung and publicly engaged in that monkey business which should really only be practised in private.

I was truly horrified.

'They are behaving like—'

'Monkeys?' said Mr Bell.

'Monkeys,' I said, and sadly I said it, too. 'I had thought that . . . perhaps—'

'Perhaps they would have acquired your intellectual capabilities?' Mr Bell shook his head, and sadly, too. '*You* are a very special fellow, my little friend. You are one of a kind. I know of your tutor Herr Döktor's conviction that education could accelerate the evolutionary process of Man's hairy cousins, and perhaps he is right. You stand before me as proof that it *can* be done. But for this to be passed on from generation to generation . . . ? Perhaps, if many generations were taught as you have been taught. Perhaps.'

'So Man will always be Man and Monkey will always be Monkey?'

'How can it be otherwise? Even if all of these apes had acquired your skills, they would, alas, still be apes nonetheless. They would not turn into men.'

'I know *that*,' I said, and rather bitterly I said it, too. 'I am not stupid. A Man is a Man and a Monkey is a Monkey. But *I*, through my education and the intimate friendships I have formed with yourself, Colonel Katterfelto and Lord Brentford, have come to learn so much. To appreciate so much. The love of good food and fine wine. The wonders of the written word. The music of Brahms and Beethoven. How sad it feels to me that my own descendants should be denied these marvellous things.'

'Yes,' agreed Mr Bell. 'It *is* sad. And having viewed the horrors of the London Blitz at first hand, I can say, without hesitation, that Mankind has made no progress whatsoever in this dismal century. Perhaps Man has come as far along the evolutionary road as it is possible for him to travel. So perhaps, just perhaps, one day the Monkey may catch him up. Or even overtake him.'

'You really think so?' I asked Mr Bell.

'I claim no expertise in such matters,' said my friend, 'but it sounds to me like a reasonable proposition.'

'So one day this might be *The Planet of the Apes*?' I said.

Mr Bell smiled. 'Perhaps.'

'Would you mind,' I asked my friend, 'if I spent a little time alone with my monkeys? There is no one else around and I would like a private moment or two in their company.'

'Certainly,' said Mr Bell. 'I will meet you in the cafeteria. I noticed that they sell cider and I'm sure they will accept the wartime coinage I have in my pocket.'

So Mr Bell left me alone and I gazed into the great cage where the many monkeys skittered. And as I stood and gazed at them and wondered for the future, a rather curious thing happened. One by one, the monkeys caught sight of me standing there. And one by one as they did so, they ceased their chatter and risqué antics and took to staring at me. And soon the great cage was utterly still with every single ape therein looking at myself.

Having unexpectedly gained their attention, I addressed these apes, these fruit of my loins, as the Good Book would have put it. I addressed them in the tongue of Man and also that of Monkey.

Then did something that I probably should not have done.

And then said farewell and went to the cafeteria.

My journey to the cafeteria was not without incident.

'Monkey on the loose!' cried someone, and many others gave chase. I took to the trees and presently entered the cafeteria through one of the open panels of its glazed roof.

I dropped down to Mr Bell's table, causing my friend to dissolve into laughter once more.

I gave him the look and he ceased to be foolish. 'I bought you a banana,' he said, presenting this to me. 'It is a Brentford banana, guaranteed to be that little bit more bananary than the average banana.'*

I took the banana gratefully. 'How is the cider?' I asked.

'Just that bit more cidery.'† Mr Bell toasted me with his glass then poured a measure for me.

'Do you have any kind of a plan?' I asked my friend. 'Or are we just going to bumble into the forbidden realm of the faerie and trust in the fates that we will not come to grief?'

Mr Bell eyed me and smiled once more. 'Perhaps it is a good thing for Man that you are one of a kind,' said he. 'I am not sure Man is a match for you.'

I was flattered and munched at my banana.

'We must certainly be cautious,' Mr Bell continued. 'I will be somewhat out of my jurisdiction, as it were. We will sip some more of this excellent cider then return to the *Marie Lloyd*, where I will study certain books in my travelling library. Then, well armed, we will sally forth before the hour of midnight.'

'What could possibly go wrong?' I said.

Which was, of course, a rhetorical question.

Brentford boasts beautiful sunsets. You even get the *green flash*, which otherwise you only see in the tropics. Parrots flock from Gunnersbury Park to their night nestings in the Royal Gardens of Kew. A giant feral tomcat howls upon the

---

* *That better be the last. (R. R.)*
† *All right, make that the last! (R. R.)*

164

allotments. Bats circle over the Butts Estate. And perhaps, just perhaps, the Brentford griffin flies.

Mr Bell was engrossed in his researches and so we did not go out for dinner. Rather we dined upon what provisions we possessed, which were limited, and neither of us cared much for that porridge.

Mr Bell's carriage clock (a gift from someone or other for solving such and such a thing)* struck half-past the hour of eleven, and the two of us, now looking as if we were dressed for battle (which to a degree we were), set out from the time-ship en route to Fairyland.

Mr Bell held up his compass and followed its pointing needle. He wore what is known as a safari suit – a khaki jacket equipped with many pockets, accompanied by a heavy belt hung with ray guns and weaponry. Jodhpurs and riding boots and a big-game hunter's pith helmet fitted with night-vision goggles completed the ensemble. The hand unoccupied by compass swung a large stout stick.

I wore an all but identical get-up. Mine, however, was somewhat better tailored than that of Mr Bell.

I carried no heavy arsenal, but had in my pockets a number of items which my friend assured me might well save our lives and should be carried with care.

Which was comforting.

I also took the precaution of hanging a police whistle about my neck on a piece of string.

Which, for reasons of my own, I found *even more* comforting.

Through the night-time streets of Brentford crept myself and Mr Cameron Bell. We looked severely out of place and

---

* *Darwin's decision to discontinue this particularly annoying and in no way amusing gag is, to say the least, commendable. (R. R.)*

165

I felt very awkward. The moonlight tinted all with a priceless silver and a soft breeze carried fragrances of night-flowering blooms. From somewhere came the sounds of a string quartet.

We plodded onwards, Mr Bell a-gazing at his compass.

'This way,' he whispered, and we plodded on.

And on and on . . .

And on . . .

'We have surely plodded down this street before,' I whispered.

Mr Bell looked baffled.

'We are going around in circles, are we not?'

'The compass needle keeps pointing the way,' said the great detective. 'But as you say, we are going around in circles.'

We stopped and Mr Bell looked up at the moon. 'You take the compass,' he said to me. 'See if it is different for you.'

I took the compass and peered at its face. 'Its needle is pointing *that* way,' I said.

Mr Bell looked down at the compass. 'It was not pointing that way when I was holding it,' he observed. 'Follow its pointing, Darwin.'

So I followed the compass needle and Mr Bell followed me. And soon the two of us stood in the Memorial Park.

My nose now took to twitching, for I smelled something strange.

My ears pricked up, for I heard curious sounds.

Sounds of laughter and sounds of singing, and we saw a weird pale light.

'The entrance lies ahead,' said Mr Bell. 'Will you enter with me, Darwin? I wish no harm to come to you.'

'I am brave,' I said to Mr Bell. 'I will enter with you.'

And so we stepped forward into the weird pale light. The strange smell grew stronger. The jolly sounds, louder. We entered Fairyland.

22

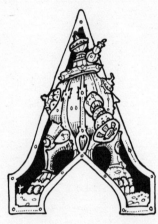s we *were* entering Fairyland, I feel this episode must be told as a fairy tale. Perhaps with some fanciful and faintly amusing title, such as:

The Magnificent Monkey and the Dangerous Detective Cross Swords with the Maleficent Magician.

Naturally, it would begin thusly:

Once upon a time that was not his own, there lived a magnificent monkey. He was loved by the ladies and greatly admired by the gentlemen. All who met him considered him to be the very acme of apes, the very maestro of monkeydom—*

Which is why he became the most celebrated simian in this world and all others.

Together with his best friend and business associate Cameron Bell, he brought to justice many evil-doers, righted

---

* *There were several more pages of this guff, but I have removed them to spare the reader's sensitivities. (R. R.)*

168

wrongs and generally carried on in a fashion that was above reproach.

The dangerous detective, however, was sad, because a solitary individual, a king amongst criminals, evaded capture time and time again. This singular gentleman went by the name of Arthur Knapton, but preferred to be known as the Pearly Emperor.

Many and heinous were the crimes of this terrible, terrible man, made worse by the fact that he possessed a magical Egyptian stele which enabled him to travel from one time to another, there to perform yet more dreadful deeds.

The marvellous monkey and the dangerous detective were in pursuit of the Pearly Emperor and had followed him to the very gateway of Fairyland, which was to be found within Brentford at the fifth point of the compass.

The year was nineteen sixty-seven and it was the Summer of Love.

The magnificent monkey gazed at the ombré gateway. Being an ape of literary learnings, he was put in mind of the very first chapter of Aubrey Beardsley's erotic masterwork *Under the Hill.*

For it is there that the Chevalier Tannhäuser, having lighted from his horse, stands doubtfully for a moment before the gateway of the mysterious hill of Venus:

> The pillars were fashioned in some pale stone and rose up like hymns in the praise of pleasure, for from cap to base, each one was carved with loving sculptures, showing such a cunning invention and such a curious knowledge . . .

The Chevalier lingers not a little in reviewing these.

'What is that naked gentleman doing with that duck?' the ape named Darwin asked of Cameron Bell.

The great detective viewed the carved columns with fastidious interest.

'And those ladies,' said Darwin. 'Is that a long cucumber they are sharing?'

'Let us move swiftly along,' said Cameron Bell. 'We have much to do and must not be diverted from our task.'

'And why has that little man got such an enormous—'

But the dangerous detective took the monkey by the hand, and together they entered Fairyland.

It is well to be wary in Fairyland, for the fairy folk oft-times play queer pranks on those who would venture within their domain. It is written that fairies are of an order halfway between Man and the angels, and that many centuries ago, the race of Mankind drove these first folk from their lands and into the forests and wastes. How long fairies live and what they dine upon are matters for scholarly debate, as is the question regarding whether or not they are possessed of a mortal soul.

Some claim they are cacodemons, bugaboos and flibberti-gibbets who would hasten Man to his destruction; others that they are wood nymphs, sylphs and sprites, who, though of impish humour, mean Mankind no harm at all.

In truth, opinions remain divided and very few truths be told.

'Are we really in Fairyland?' asked the magnificent mon-key.

The dangerous detective nodded his big bald head, which lurked beneath his oversized pith helmet, then lowered his night-vision goggles and peered all around and about. 'This is a very strange land,' said he, 'for we stand in the light of day beneath a bright blue sky, but I can see no sun at all – can you?'

The monkey shrugged and said that he could not. But

that the curious smell, which had pressed upon his sensitive nostrils when first they approached the portal to the fairy world, had now intensified to a point that was almost beyond endurance. But not from malodorousness – quite the reverse. The smell was utterly delicious.

'I smell only cinnamon,' said Mr Bell, a-sniffing at the air.

'I smell so much more,' the monkey said, and composed on the spot a verse to list the fragrances that met him as he walked.

> 'Tis a dainty bouquet with a honeysome charm,
> Sugarplum, marzipan, marmalade, myrrh.
> Bewitching, beguiling, a beauteous balm,
> Liquorice, lollypop, fritters and fur.
>
> A nectarous nosegay to nuzzle the nostrils,
> Sandalwood, cedarwood, parsley and pine.
> Pork pies and poppadoms, pasties and pastilles,
> Fruits of the forest and fruits of the vine.
>
> A full-flavoured fancy, a savoury scent,
> Tasty and toothsome and feathery-light.
> Per–fum–at–ory and am–bros–i–ient,
> Toffee and treacle and Turkish delight.

'All of *that*?' asked Mr Cameron Bell.

'All of that and more,' said the educated ape. 'Which makes it rather hard for me to do anything other than just sniff and enjoy it.'

They stood in an Arcadian glade. Tall grasses whispered in a gentle breeze. A white fluffy cloud or two meandered across the sky. Curly-branched trees were adorned with strange fruits. Faint music drifted from somewhere.

'Do you know what I am thinking?' said the monkey to the man.

'I believe I do,' the man replied. 'You are thinking that perhaps this is how our world was, so very very long ago, before the birth of Man.'

'Precisely,' said the monkey. 'It looks like a perfect world and I feel that perhaps we should not be here.'

'And nor should Arthur Knapton,' said the man. 'Let us seek him out and capture him and return to the world we know.'

The two walked on, the monkey ever more amazed by the smells that crowded upon him, the man overwhelmed by the beauty, but anxious to achieve his goal and capture the Pearly Emperor.

They climbed a hill and reached its brow, and then the man smiled and pointed. Planted fields led down to a picturesque village of red-tiled roofs and blue-bricked walls and bottle-glass windows and all medieval in its looks, quaint and at peace with the landscape. The sounds of music and jollity came louder to the ears of man and monkey.

'We shall go and enquire within the alehouse,' the man to the monkey said.

'But you promise you will not shoot anyone dead unless it is *absolutely* necessary.'

'You have my word. Come on.'

And so they strolled through the fields and entered the quaint little village.

Children danced about what appeared to be a maypole whilst old gentlemen sat on a bench by an alehouse door. The dangerous detective, a man who had ever upon him a healthy thirst for alcohol, noted well the mugs of grog these gentlemen held in their fists.

'All looks to be safe enough,' he said to his friend the monkey.

The monkey simply nodded, for he had nothing to say.

He did, however, tinker with the police whistle that hung about his neck on a length of string.

Music was provided for the dancing children by a deuce of roguish gypsy types, one of whom played a concertina, the other an old violin.

Mr Bell tipped his helmet to all and sundry and, meeting with no ill looks, entered the alehouse. It was quaintness personified, all cobbled floor, rustic stools, a counter of oak and a chap behind this counter.

'Good day to you, sirs,' said the chap to the man and the monkey. 'You look as if you have travelled far and could trouble a mug of good ale.'

'That we could,' said Mr Bell, removing from his head his pith helmet and placing it with care upon the counter. 'We have come from a far country and perhaps we are lost, for I know not the name of the village.'

'Welcome to Knapton,' said the bar-lord, drawing a mug of ale.

'Knapton,' said Mr Bell. 'Knapton, indeed?'

'The village of Knapton, in the Shire of Knapton. The prettiest village you will find in this whole country of Knapton.'

The bar-lord pushed a filled mug towards Mr Bell and took to the filling of a lesser one.

'Is there a city of Knapton, too?' asked Mr Bell as he tasted ale. Tasted ale and found it pleasing, too.

'There is no city that I know of, sir. Only the castle, wherein lives the King.'

Beckoned by the bar-lord, the monkey now swarmed up

onto the bar-counter, accepted his ale and took to similar tastings.

'Castle Knapton, perchance?' said the detective. 'Where King Knapton lives?'

The bar-lord shook his head. 'Castle Camelot,' he said, 'where good King Arthur lives.'

The monkey looked at Mr Bell.

And Mr Bell looked at the monkey.

'Might I enquire,' enquired Mr Bell, 'as to whether good King Arthur has a round table and a legion of noble knights?'

'Wouldn't be much of a king if he didn't,' said the bar-lord, and then he lit a pipe.

The man and the monkey tasted more ale and smacked their lips with pleasure.

'I hope you do not feel that I am being rude in asking so many questions,' said Cameron Bell.

The bar-lord shrugged his shoulders and said, 'No.'

'Then might I ask you whether you have ever met good King Arthur? And if you have, what exactly he looks like in the flesh?'

'Strange you should ask me that,' said the bar-lord. 'I have certainly never been granted an audience with the King, as I am a commoner, me. But I know well the looks of him, as many around here do. Here, sir, let me show you this portrait of him which arrived in the morning post.'

And the bar-lord delved beneath his counter and brought forth a sheet of paper, which he placed with a certain reverence atop the counter.

The man and the monkey peered down at the portrait.

The King wore a crown as a king will do and a robe of ermine also. And there was no doubt in the mind of man or monkey that good King Arthur's second name was Knapton.

'Good King Arthur,' said Mr Cameron Bell.

'Good King Arthur indeed, sir,' said the bar-lord. 'And please turn over the paper before you, if you will, to see something that may cause you some surprise.'

Mr Bell turned over the page. Then said, 'Oh my dear dead mother.'

On the rear of the page was printed the word:

WANTED

In very large letters. And:

BIG REWARD FOR CAPTURE

And beneath these words were two portraits: one of a man and one of a monkey.

'Uncommon likenesses, aren't they, sir?' said the bar-lord.

'I think we must be going now,' said Mr Cameron Bell.

'No, sir,' said the bar-lord. 'I think not.'

Cameron Bell drew out his ray gun. Then took to wobbling slightly on his toes.

'We were told to expect you,' said the bar-lord. 'Your ales have been laced with a strong soporific – I doubt you could even make three single steps towards the door.'

Cameron Bell managed almost three.

Darwin, however, did not.

23

arwin awoke in a very bad mood indeed. His little head hurt and, to his absolute horror, he found that he had been stripped of his fine clothing and accoutrements.

All he retained was the key to the *Marie Lloyd* and the police whistle, both still hanging about his dainty neck.

The detective awoke with a shriek of pain, which gradually dimmed to groans of his own.

'That is another fine mess you have got us both into,' said the ape, in a tone which almost echoed that of Stan Laurel. 'Note well that we always come unstuck in alehouses. That cries something loud that must be heard!'

'Please do *not* cry it so loud here,' mumbled the dismal detective. 'I believe this must be what a hangover feels like and I like it not one small piece.'

Mr Bell now took to patting at himself, groaning at intervals and shaking his head.

'They have taken the lot,' he said in gloom. 'My weapons, my adjuncts, my dynamite.'

'Your adjuncts?' said the ape.

'Never mind.'

'I am hungry,' continued the ape. 'And I am very upset. We have been tricked again. No, let me phrase that better – *you* have been tricked yet again.'

'Don't rub it in.' Mr Bell struggled to his feet. There was no doubt at all as to where they were. They were in a dungeon, and a grim and ghastly one, too.

'My plan would be this—' said Cameron Bell.

But Darwin shook his head. 'I am beginning to think,' said he, 'that if you never have a plan, then nothing can ever be said to go wrong.'

'You are wise beyond your years,' said Mr Bell, dusting down his underwear. For naught had been left upon him but his long johns and his vest.

'Why do you need elasticated garters to hold up your socks?' asked Darwin.

And his socks!

'Never mind.' Mr Bell knotted his fists. 'We must escape from here post-haste. It will be the executioner's block in the castle courtyard for us, I am thinking.'

Light shone down through a grating high above.

'Could you swarm up there?' asked Mr Bell.

'I could *not*,' said the monkey.

'Then we must find some other way out or—'

But Mr Bell did not finish that sentence, because now there came those distinctive sounds of a great key being turned in a great lock and the shrieking of irritated hinges as the dungeon door swung open.

Something monstrous stooped and peered in at the man and the monkey.

'Fee-fi-fo-fum,' boomed this fearsome figure. For a fearsome figure he was, all a-bulge with muscles and sinews and terribly fierce of face. 'Out, foul conspirators!'

Darwin's knees began to knock.

Mr Bell offered comfort.

'Climb onto my back,' said the man to the monkey. 'All might not be lost.'

But all now appeared hopelessly lost, and as the giant jailer urged Mr Bell along a grim passage, with many a boot to the backside, the prospects for the Happy-Ever-After that ought to bring a fairy tale to a satisfactory conclusion looked remote at best.

'Up them stairs,' boomed the bemuscled monster. 'And get a move on, do.'

Up the stairs went man and monkey, the man a-grinding his teeth, the monkey a-trembling fearfully.

And out into bright light, a banqueting hall and very much laughter indeed.

And—

'Oh my dear dead mother,' said Cameron Bell.

For everywhere, around and about and up and down, were fairies.

They hovered aloft upon dragonfly wings. They peeped from corners and bounced upon benches. Brownies and boggarts and bogles. Leprechauns, loireags and lobs. Goblins and things that go bump in the night. Hinkypunks, huldus and hobs.

They laughed and they chattered, they howled and they called, and such was the awful cacophony in that great hall that it might drive sanity from the mind of mortal Man.

'Be silent!' A voice rose up and silence fell.

Mr Bell peeped up and saw . . .

None other than Arthur Knapton.

And he did look the very picture of a king in his golden crown and his ermine cape. And he lolled upon a throne of impressive size and wispy sylph-like ladies fed him porter and pork pies.

'Dear oh dear oh dear,' cried good King Arthur. 'If it ain't me old master from Oxford, Mr Cameron Bell.'

Mr Bell made a grumpy face, but wisely kept his own counsel.

'And in 'is knickers and vest.' And good King Arthur laughed, and the elves and dwarves and gnomes and trolls all took to much laughter also. Because no matter where or when you are, if the King laughs, you laugh, too.

'Ain't so full of beans now, are ya?' asked the King of Fairyland. 'And you calls yerself a detective.' And the King laughed again, and so did all and sundry around and about.

'Where's me loyal subject who captured these two?'

A small plump gnome with a long nose and hands that almost reached the floor stepped forward.

Mr Bell cocked an eye at this apparition.

'And where's me dancin' children, and the two old gents on the bench and them musicians, too?'

A group of grotesques waved their hands and fluttered their butterfly wings.

'Like lambs to the slaughter,' said good King Arthur, 'led 'ere by a bus ticket and the talk in a Brentford pub. Then down to a village what looked like a village and villagers what looked like villagers.'

'The glamour,' whispered the monkey to the man. 'An enchantment cast, that things are perceived, or otherwise, as the enchanter wishes.'

'I am aware of this,' said Mr Bell, most brusquely. 'I read up on the fairy world before we entered it. And—'

'And then forgot yer learning when you entered.' The good King laughed his horrible laugh. 'There's more to this 'ere world than you'll read of in any of them scholarly books

179

out there. An' I should know, as I owns most of the libraries of the Earth.' And the King laughed again and his subjects laughed again and the man and the monkey felt very sad indeed.

'I think it best,' said the King, when all had done with laughter, 'that I 'ave yer 'eads chopped off so you can cause me no more hin-con-ven-i-ence. I can't 'ave you runnin' about on the loose, gettin' up to all manner of shenanigans and causing me bovver and grief.'

The fairies made ominous mumbling sounds. They could not have their dear King Arthur brought to bother and grief.

'You just don't gets it,' continued the King. 'I ain't no tuppeny-'apenny footpad what you can track down with yer intuitive examinations of me shirt-cuffs. I'm the Pearly Emperor, I am. The God-Pharaoh Akhenaten of ancient Egypt. Good King Arthur in the land of myth an' legend. And other rulers in other times what I won't mention 'ere. And I'll 'ave your realm too, Mr 'igh an' mighty Cameron Bell, what swaggers about as the world's most famous detective. I've already written you out of 'istory – and now I'll write you out of life itself.'

The fairies pointed fingers at the man and the monkey and booed and jeered and even catcalled, too.

'Shut up!' shouted the King. 'But know this, Mr Bell as finks 'e's so clever. I 'as Crowley's magic stele. I was smart enough to decode it. I can travel as and when I want and I will 'ave it all – the past, the present an' the future. I'll 'ave all the worlds that are and all the worlds that may be. So what do you say to that, Mr Dangerous Detective?'

In truth, Mr Bell appeared to be somewhat lost for words. For in truth, he appeared to have met his match.

The monkey whispered at the detective's ear. 'Shall I blow my whistle now?' he asked.

Cameron Bell sighed sadly. 'I regret that blowing your whistle here will not summons the assistance of a policeman.'

'But—' said the monkey.

'Stop that whisperin',' called the King. 'Jailer, take 'em out to the courtyard an' let's 'ave off their 'eads.'

And to much applause and good humour and much bouncing up and down of boggarts, and elbowings of elves, and laughings of leprechauns and hootings of hobgoblins and shoutings of sylphs and suchlike, the man was booted in the bum and encouraged towards the courtyard.

It was another sunny day in Fairyland. Though, as before, the sky of blue lacked for a sun.

The King was borne aloft upon his throne, held high upon the backs of creatures half-man and half-Hobnob.* Wingéd fairies swarmed the air and those that leapt and crawled moved by whatever means they had into the castle courtyard.

Upon a raised platform, the chopping block stood. And next to this another titanic figure, sporting the terrible axe and the big black hood that marked him out as an executioner, rather than, say, a quantity surveyor.

'I would blow my whistle *now*!' said the monkey to the man.

'I am so very very sorry,' said the man to the monkey. 'My foolishness, my overconfidence, oh so many things, have brought this awful fate upon you, my innocent friend. I am truly sorry.'

'I think I *will* blow it,' said the monkey.

'Up!' the King shouted. 'Onto the platform. Onto the block. Off with their 'eads as of now.'

And Mr Bell was urged up steps onto the frightful

* *A type of biscuit, apparently. (R. R.)*

platform and the fairies swarmed and the fairies jeered and the good King raised his hand up high . . .

And then brought down his thumb.

The huge executioner grabbed the monkey, held him high in the air by his tail.

The monkey put his whistle to his mouth and blew.

The fairy crowd broke out in applause.

The monkey blew his whistle three more times.

The good King fell about in mirth.

The executioner held the monkey to the block, raised up his axe and prepared to bring it down.

Mr Bell covered his eyes and said his prayers.

The executioner made to swing his axe.

And then the world went mad.

They seemed to come from everywhere and nowhere.

Screaming and screeching.

Leaping and bounding.

Viciously fighting.

Clawing and punching.

Biting and biffing.

Producing and flinging dung.

Monkeys! Hundreds of monkeys!

They fell without fear onto the fairies and the King, onto the jailer and thing that held the axe.

'I think we should be going now,' said Darwin.

And as monkey mayhem was given its full hairy head, Mr Bell and Darwin slipped away.

24

ell me *now*,' said Mr Cameron Bell.

He and Darwin were once more aboard the *Marie Lloyd*, this time in the company of many many monkeys.

They had all made good their escape from Fairyland and all were now in the very best of spirits.

Darwin sat in the pilot's seat, a young ape on his lap. 'It is all rather simple,' he said to Mr Bell. 'You had a plan, so I thought that I should have one, too. Mine worked a little better than yours, I am thinking.'

'Go on then,' said Mr Bell. 'Tell me all about it.'

'Well,' said Darwin, 'it was this way. When I visited my monkeys yesterday and found them all caged up and in such a disorganised state, it upset me greatly. I asked you to leave me all alone with them, and when you did so – and when there was nobody else around – I spoke to them in both Man and Monkey. I told them who I was and that I had come to free them—'

'Oh dear, oh dear,' said Mr Cameron Bell.

'And I told them that if they all behaved themselves, I would take them to a better place.'

Mr Bell 'oh deared' some more. Darwin told him to shush.

'Then I unlocked their cage,' said the educated ape, 'and told them to quietly follow you and I when we left the *Marie Lloyd* a little before midnight yesterday.'

'They were certainly stealthy,' said Mr Bell. 'I had no idea they were following us.'

Darwin grinned. 'I am very proud of them,' he said. 'But let me finish. I had brought this whistle with me and I told my monkeys that if I got into any desperate trouble I would blow it four times, and I would really appreciate it if they rescued me.'

Mr Bell smiled and said, 'Which they did.'

'Which they did,' agreed the ape. 'You see, Mr Bell, it was not good that my monkeys should have to spend their lives in a cage, but it looked as though that would be their fate if they remained in the world of men. The world of fairies, however, appeared to be quite another matter, and I reasoned that here was a place that might perhaps suit my monkeys better.'

'Hm,' said Mr Bell. 'Perhaps.'

'*Perhaps*, indeed. But it was not to be. Fairyland is probably not a place for anyone other than fairies.'

'Arthur Knapton looks quite at home there.'

'But not my monkeys,' Darwin said. 'It would have been nice, but it was not to be.'

'It was a noble idea,' said Mr Bell, 'and I applaud you for it. And undoubtedly your forward planning saved our lives. I shall be forever in your debt.'

Darwin reached out his little hand and Mr Bell took it and shook it.

'But, as you said, it was not to be,' said the great detective.

'And so I regret we must return these monkeys to their rightful owner.'

There was a terrible silence then, within the *Marie Lloyd*.

'Well, they can't come with us,' said Mr Bell.

'We do not have room,' said Mr Bell.

'Think of all they would eat,' said Mr Bell.

'Think of all the poo!' said Mr Bell.

'They are *not* going back to the cage,' said Darwin. 'That is that is *that*!'

'But they can't—'

'They saved our lives,' said the educated ape, 'and I will not abandon them now.'

'But they—'

'Listen,' said Darwin. 'I have an idea. Let me explain to you what it is, and if you agree that it is a good idea, then we will translate this idea from words into a deed – are we agreed upon this?'

'Tell me your idea,' said Mr Bell.

Many provisions were purchased. As many as Mr Bell's limited funds would stretch to. The monkeys, in the care of Darwin, remained aboard the *Marie Lloyd*, hidden from the world, whilst the detective to-ed and fro-ed from the time-ship, looking ever more grumpy.

'I think *now* would be the time for us to depart,' he informed the monkey pilot. 'There are many policemen now abroad in Syon Park, searching high and low for all these monkeys.'

'They will not think to look in here, Mr Bell,' said Darwin.

'I fear that I may have aroused certain suspicions by bringing aboard such a large cargo of bananas and monkey nuts,' declared the detective. 'Let us leave *now*, if you please.'

185

Darwin called, 'Hold tight,' in Monkey to his monkeys, buckled his seat belt and diddled away at the dashboard.

'The date I want isn't on here,' he said to his friend as he studied the dials and counters.

'Then just put the ship into reverse and we will use our discretion.'

The monkeys of Syon did not get on very well with Cameron Bell. There always appeared to be several monkeys in any particular place that he wished to be in at any particular time. And all those monkeys *did* take up an awful lot of room. And they *did* eat an awful lot of food. And as to the matter of monkey poo . . .

Awful!

Mr Bell fretted and fumed.

Darwin, however, had rarely, if ever, been happier.

Here he was in the company of his grandchildren, great-grandchildren and great-great-grandchildren, too. And as the *Marie Lloyd* plied its way through quantum shifts and Doppler passages and things of a meta-temporal nature generally, he set to educating his travelling companions, offering to them the basics of 'civilisation'.

'You are my tribe,' he told them, 'and as such, you are special.'

Back and back went the ship of time.

Back and back and back.

Within the *Marie Lloyd* a week had passed.

'I feel we should now stop the ship,' said Mr Cameron Bell.

Darwin looked towards his friend and started with surprise.

Mr Bell was no longer the Mr Bell that Darwin knew so

well, the avuncular Pickwickian figure, well dressed and bright of eye.

Here indeed was a sad shadow of that Mr Bell. Here was a fellow most put upon and, it had to be said, most *pooped* upon. A fellow unshaven and unkempt, with dark rings under his eyes.

'In truth,' cried Mr Cameron Bell, wading about amidst monkeys, 'I am at the end of my tether. Either stop this ship now or I swear I will throw open the port and hurl myself into the aether.'

'Ah,' said Darwin, and gave himself a scratch.

'Please,' begged Mr Bell. 'I can stand no more.'

A fine young monkey bit him on the bottom.

'So be it,' said Darwin. 'Hold on, everyone.'

And he took the *Marie Lloyd* out of gear and tugged upon the handbrake.

The ship of time rested in a sylvan glade. A gentle breeze whispered at grasses. The sun shone down from a sky of blue. And all looked very nice.

Darwin set his key to the lock and the port swung open with a sigh.

The monkeys clustered at the door, but Darwin held them back and sniffed the air.

'What do you think?' asked Cameron Bell, his voice both weary and soft.

'I think,' said Darwin, 'in fact, I *sense* and indeed *know* that all is well. We have travelled back to a time many many many thousands of years before the dawn of Mankind. And –' and he sniffed once again '– a time that is not populated by chickens.'

'Praise be for that,' said Cameron Bell.

'But I must be sure.'

Darwin left his monkeys in the care of Mr Bell and was gone from the ship for almost an hour, but he was smiling when he returned.

'All is indeed safe,' said he. 'There are no dinosaurs, nor did I smell any monkey-eating predators. This is where my monkeys can live in freedom.'

The monkeys left the time-ship two by two.

They ambled into the sweet-smelling glade and stood in a big hairy horde.

Darwin addressed his monkeys from the port of the *Marie Lloyd*. 'This is my goodbye to you,' he said. 'You will be happy here with no man to hunt you down, or cage you in, or bother you in any way at all. You can make good lives for yourselves here. Some of you have already mastered the rudiments of Man-speak and indeed the formative skills of reading and writing, and I have given you the power of Man's red flower. My friend Mr Bell and I must leave you now. I love you all. Farewell.'

The monkeys waved to Darwin, and Darwin sniffed away a tear as the port rose up and closed.

The *Marie Lloyd* shimmered in the dawn-of-time sunlight, then was gone.

An ape, slightly bigger than the rest, raised a thumb and said, 'Goodbye.'

The monkeys grinned, the monkeys skittered, then got down to monkey business.

And, as a fairy tale should end . . .

They all lived very happily ever after.

25

'That really was a *very* happy happily-ever-after, wasn't it, Mr Bell?' I said (once more in 'first monkey') as I put the *Marie Lloyd* into forward-mode and we set off *Back to the Future*.

Mr Bell sat with his head in his hands. 'Look at the state of the ship,' said he. 'Look at the state of the ship.'

I sniffed the air and had to confess that it did rather smell of monkey. 'But we did a great thing,' I said. 'And it *was* a happily-ever-after.'

Mr Bell shrugged but had to agree that it was.

'My monkeys will be happy back there and then,' I said. 'It is a wonderful place for them to be. In fact, I would go so far as to say that it was quite the Garden of Eden.'

Mr Bell looked up and opened his mouth.

And a very strange expression came to his face.

'Darwin,' he said. 'Oh, Darwin, what have you done?'

'I think we should open the champagne now,' I said to Cameron Bell.

26

 rather enjoyed that champagne. I felt that I had earned it. Mr Bell, however, did not drink it down with his usual enthusiasm. He kept mumbling phrases such as 'Garden of Eden' and 'Man evolved from monkeys' and 'you might be the Father of all Mankind'.

I did not mind these mumblings, for they did not spoil the taste of that champagne.

Quite the opposite, in fact.

There was an awful lot of clearing up to be done aboard the *Marie Lloyd*. An awful lot of scrubbing floors and polishing things now covered with fingermarks. But together Mr Bell and I returned our time-ship to a clean and serviceable state.

But it did take several days to do it. And we did refresh ourselves each night with champagne.

'Aha,' said I, upon the fifth morning after our departure from the past. 'The dials and counters on the dashboard are once more within the limits of recorded time. Should I bring us to a halt in eighteen twenty-four at the Theater am Kärntnertor in Vienna, so we can finally enjoy Beethoven conducting the premiere performance of the Ninth?'

Mr Bell, now well shaved, well kempt and somewhat less wild of eye, shook his head. 'My work is not yet done with Arthur Knapton,' he said.

'I regret we have lost him for sure,' I replied, though I did *not* regret it at all. 'We have no idea where and when he is now, and you told me that we cannot return to wheres and whens we've already visited or we will encounter ourselves and things will get overly complicated.'

'True enough,' said himself. 'But there are still ways and means.'

I gave myself a hearty scratch. 'What do you mean by *that*?' I asked.

'Think about it,' said my friend, drawing an armchair near to my pilot's seat. 'Think about what he said in Fairyland. What he boasted about. That he would be ruler—'

'In every age,' I said, and I scratched myself again. 'He intends to rule everywhere in every period of time. To my mind a most original ambition. If somewhat difficult to realise.'

'If anyone can do it, *he* can,' said Mr Bell in a grudging tone. 'And why do you keep scratching at yourself?'

'It started a week ago,' I said, 'when we had my monkeys on board. I hate to admit it, but I think they have given me fleas.'

Mr Bell moved his armchair away from my seat. 'We'll get you some flea powder the next time we stop,' said he.

I shook my head. 'Actually, I think I will keep them,' I said. 'There is something almost comforting about them. They will always remind me of my monkeys.'

Mr Bell rose, came over and gingerly patted my shoulder.

'I understand,' he said. 'But if any of those fleas choose to change their allegiance and seek residence upon my person, you will be taking a big deep antiseptic bath and no arguments at all about *that*.'

'We are almost out of bananas and champagne,' I said. 'We will have to stop somewhere and sometime, sometime soon. So to speak.'

'And some*where* and some-*when*, where and when Mr Arthur Knapton is not already King of the Castle.'

'Nor has his cronies lying in wait to catch us.'

'Quite so, my little friend, and I know the very time and very place.'

I held my breath and wondered what was coming.

'Eighteen fifty-one,' said my friend. 'We shall go to the Great Exhibition.'

Now, I had been keen to visit the Great Exhibition anyway, what with its purported abundance of banana trees, but I did ask my friend why he chose that particular time and place above all others.

'Because that is where Arthur Knapton's henchman assassinates Queen Victoria!'

Which had me all but falling from my pilot's seat.

'What of this?' I asked when I was able.

'Recall our time in Blitz-torn London?'

I nodded without enthusiasm.

'When I visited a bookshop and discovered that history only remembered us as fictional characters?'

'I did not like that one bit,' I said.

'Well, I read other things in other books in that shop, and it turns out that the reason the past changed—'

'It changed because Arthur Knapton changed it.'

'True, but the question I wanted answered was, "How?" The answer was that Queen Victoria was assassinated during a visit to the Great Exhibition in eighteen fifty-one and her crown was passed on to—'

'Do not tell me,' I said. 'Good King Arthur, was it?'

'Prince Arthur of Bavaria, a previously unknown son of Victoria. Certain papers found in the Queen's bedchamber stated implicitly that the crown of England should be placed upon the head of this Arthur should any ill befall her. Arthur Knapton was crowned King of England the following year and he brought a halt to the marvellous technology of Mr Tesla and Mr Babbage, effectively changing history.'

'Just fancy *that*,' I said. And then I had a little think. 'Hold on right there,' I further said. 'If this is the case and you knew of it back in war-torn London, why did we waste our time following the bus-ticket clue and nearly getting our heads chopped off when we could have gone straight to the Great Exhibition?'

Mr Bell said something about a pressing appointment in the toilet and left the cockpit at the hurry-up.

I must say that when first I read of the Great Exhibition, I found it a Wonder of the World. Built in eighteen fifty-one, it was a triumph of that modern age, a masterpiece of prefabricated construction. It simply bristled with 'first time ever' statistics.

I list here but a few.

Length of main building	1848 ft
Width of main building	408 ft
Height of nave	64 ft
Height of transept	108 ft
Weight of iron used	4500 tons

Panes of glass	293,655 (900,000 sq ft)
Guttering	24 miles
Number of exhibits	over 100,000
Number of visitors	6,039,205

It took only nine months from organisation to opening and remained open in Hyde Park for less than six months before it was taken down and reconstructed in a slightly different form upon Sydenham Hill. It became the very symbol of the British Empire, and when I learned that we were going to visit it, I was very excited indeed and went at once to my wardrobe to seek out suitable attire.

Exactly where we would set down the time-ship became a matter for debate. This was, after all, an adapted Martian warship, and although in eighteen fifty-one no one had ever encountered a Martian warship as the invasion did not occur until eighteen eighty-five, there was still the matter of it being an advanced metal-clad flying machine, and such craft did not exist at the time of the Great Exhibition. We had no wish to cause alarm, or indeed occasion our own arrests.

My various 'sensible' suggestions were overruled by Mr Bell, who decided that the best place to land the *Marie Lloyd* would be in the orchard to the rear of a country house in Kent which at that time was owned by his family.

'I recall my father telling me that they spent the summer of eighteen fifty-one in London, visiting the Great Exhibition.'

So that was settled, then.

We landed on the twelfth of July, eighteen fifty-one, in the orchard to the rear of Hyphephilia House, which I recall had rather interesting curtains. We landed without incident and, to the best of our knowledge, unseen.

Mr Bell commandeered a horse from a neighbouring field, hitched it to a two-wheeled trap commandeered from a nearby barn and we set off for London.

We looked very dapper, did Mr Bell and I, both in our morning suits. I cut a rather dashing figure in top hat and kid gloves and all.

It was a beautiful summer's day and the lanes of Kent were glorious to drive through. Mr Bell took some pains to knock the occasional passing cleric from his bicycle, as he told me that nothing very funny had happened for a while.

I shook my head in a dignified way and pondered over the various bulges in my friend's apparel. Ray guns and dynamite, I supposed.

'Please tell me what you know of this assassination,' I asked Mr Bell as merrily we rode along.

'The newspapers of the time describe him as an anarchist who approached the Royal Party and murdered the Queen.'

'Did the papers name him?' I asked. 'And perhaps give his address? That would be useful. We could pay him a visit before he sets off and bonk him on the head.'

'Sadly, no,' said Mr Bell. 'But we do know the time and the place of the assassination itself.'

'And if we save the Queen and prevent Arthur Knapton from taking her throne, we can consider that a job well done. We will have saved history as well as the Queen.'

'Precisely. And I make no bones about it – I am prepared to kill Arthur Knapton, should the need arise.'

'Do warn me when the time comes,' I said. 'I would dearly like to watch.'

Because, gentle reader, I really hated Arthur Knapton now. He had, after all, sent myself and Mr Bell to the executioner's block and in one version of history arranged the assassination of Queen Victoria, and frankly I could find no good whatsoever in this dreadful person.

'I hate to ask this,' I said to my friend, 'but do you have any sort of plan?'

Mr Bell beamed and his face fairly glowed. 'Oh yes I do,' said he. 'I will not be caught napping by Knapton this time. We have two days before the assassination will take place — more than enough time for me to do what I do best.'

'Blow things up?' I asked Mr Bell.

He offered me a very stern face in reply.

We pressed on towards London, stopping to refresh ourselves at various alehouses along the way, and by the time we reached the heart of the Empire we were in a most merry mood. Accommodation was not easily to be found as so many had flooded here to visit the Great Exhibition.

So we took a room, above a pub . . .

In Brentford.

'The Flying Swan,' I said to Mr Bell. 'I suppose you find this somehow amusing, though frankly the humour is lost upon me.'

'Just think of the beer,' said Mr Bell. 'How good it was in nineteen sixty-seven. And any beer drinker knows that "the beer was so much better in the good old days".'

'Ah,' I said. 'So we can expect really wondrous beer.'

Mr Bell nodded and grinned quite lopsidedly.

For by now we had visited very many such alehouses, looking for a room.

Later, Mr Bell ordered dinner and it arrived in the company of fine ale. We dined and drank and were merrier still. And the more we drank, the more certain we became that this time we'd put paid to Arthur Knapton.

In vino veritas.
'In wine there is truth.'
It is not that way with beer.

27

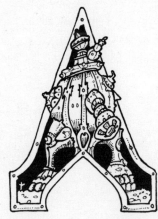lcohol left no hangover upon Mr Cameron Bell and so he was up with the lark and off upon his business.

I awoke somewhat late in the day, dragged myself into consciousness and did not feel a very well monkey at all. I viewed my normally handsome face in the bedroom mirror and found it less than appealing. My eyes were red, and as for my tongue – when I stuck this out to examine it, the thing presented such an unpleasant aspect that I felt disinclined to return it to my mouth.

But I did.

Upon the dresser I found a note, written by Mr Bell.

Dear Darwin,

I have gone into London to arrange things as best I can. Please do not leave the Flying Swan, as I fear you will be taken by Brentford's Monkey-Catcher-in-Residence and we would not want that. I may not return tonight, so be ready to leave at 9 o'clock sharp tomorrow morning. A driver will collect and instruct you and also settle our account.

C. B.

PS Should things not go according to my plans, know that I consider you the best friend that I ever had.

This note did nothing to raise my spirits. I had no wish to make the acquaintance of Brentford's Monkey-Catcher-in-Residence. And although I was deeply touched by the 'PS' part, I also found it most distressing.

So I sat in a rather grumpy mood until a knock at the door signalled the arrival of a very late breakfast that Mr Bell had taken the trouble to arrange for me. Bananas were included and strong coffee, too, and very soon I was once more my former self, bright, alert and ready for adventure.

But just what was I to do?

I concluded that as I had the day to myself, I should engage in an adventure of my own, independent of those involving Mr Bell. An adventure with some magic and of course a happy ending, and so this is what came to be . . .

The Adventurous Ape in the Land of Clouds*

The adventurous ape was all alone and greatly in need of adventure. He enjoyed his breakfast and cleaned his teeth and sat peering out of the window. Beyond, the world of Brentford went about its everyday business. Above, the sky was blue and strewn with clouds.

The adventurous ape looked up at those clouds and wondered, as all of us have done at times, and sighed a little, too. He raised the sash window and breathed in the pure

* *From Ki-Vi and the Sky Whales and other Far-Fetched Fictions by Robert Rankin. Reproduced by kind permission of Far-Fetched Books,* © 2014.

Brentford air. And he leaned upon the windowsill and longed very hard for adventure.

And if one longs *really* hard for adventure . . .

Adventure *will* come calling.

From above came a curious rushing sound, accompanied by a shriek. These two were followed by a thump and a rather loud cry of pain.

The adventurous ape, rightly startled by these untoward sounds, climbed nimbly out of the window, up the drainpipe, over the gutter and onto the roof.

And here found a little boy.

He was a very grubby little boy, being all-over black with chimney soot, and he lay upon his back upon the grey roof slates, rubbing at his elbows and swearing through the gaps between his unwashed teeth.

'Are you all right?' asked the monkey. 'And indeed, where on Earth have you come from?'

The grubby boy looked up at the ape. 'You are a talking monkey,' he observed.

'I am and my name is Darwin,' said the ape.

'I am Jack Rankin,' said the boy, 'and I would shake your hand.'

Darwin reached out to shake a hand but found none offered to him.

'I *would* shake your hand,' said Jack Rankin, 'but I've all but busted me elbows a-falling onto this roof.'

'You are a chimney-sweep's boy,' said the monkey, for this was evident to his eyes. 'But the chimneys here are rather small and I heard you come down from above.'

'That I did,' said Jack. 'Precipitated, I was, out of a big chimney at Syon House. I'm Lord Brentford's step-and-fetch-it, I am, and pleased to be in service to that noble man. But his lordship has these ideas, you see. Of inventions and the like.'

'Go on,' said the monkey, for he found the lad's conversation to be not without certain points of interest. 'Speak to me of these inventions.'

'Them's many,' said Jack, 'and they mostly don't work. Save for the one what brought me here. That one worked well enough.'

The monkey tried to dust Jack down, but he was sooty, it appeared, right down to the bone.

'A pneumatic chimney-cleaning ap-ar-ma-ra-tus,' continued the soot-smothered boy, 'what would fit about a fireplace and then blow the soot from the chimney out of the chimney pot.'

'That might make the land around and about rather grubby,' said the ape.

'Not on a windy day. His lordship reasoned that if the wind blew hard to the west, Isleworth would cop for the soot. And who cares for Isleworth, eh?'

'True enough,' said the ape. 'A bit of added soot might even improve the place.'

'Such was his lordship's thinking. However, he decided he'd have a little test today. So here I am.'

'I feel there is a small piece missing from the tale,' said the ape.

'Ah, yes,' said Jack. 'The chimney was blocked, you see, so he sent me up to clear it. And being at times an absent-minded fellow, my supposing would be that he forgot I was up there and switched on the damnable pneumatic motor once more. Thus precipitating me, as a cork might escape from a bottle of champagne, out of the chimney, into the sky and down onto this here rooftop.'

'An unlikely tale if ever there was,' said the ape.

'I do so agree,' said the lad. 'But that is the truth of it.'

'There is some coffee left over from breakfast in my room,' said the monkey. 'You can have some to refresh you, before you return to his lordship.'

The sooty boy did shakings of his very sooty head and Darwin took a step or two away.

'I ain't going back,' declared the sooty boy. 'I'm done with chimney-sweeping and lion-taming and underwater ex-plor-a-mor-ation.'

'I raise my eyebrows regarding the last two,' said the ape and did so.

'His lordship maintains a small private zoo and has recently patented an air-filled suit what enables its wearer to walk on the ocean's floor.'

'Your life with his lordship is little less than exciting.'

'It is little less than hazardous and I will have no more of it.'

'Then what will you do?' asked the ape.

'I will take my chances aloft.'

'In a crow's nest, do you mean? Aboard a sailing ship?'

'Aloft, as in *up there*.' The lad pointed skywards with a blackened finger. 'Up there. Up in the clouds.'

The ape scratched his head, as an ape often will when baffled. 'Has his lordship invented a sky-going carriage?' he asked.

'Not to my knowledge,' said Jack. 'But he well might soon, which would be another good reason for me to quit his employ as of now.'

The ape looked up at the sky above, all blue with scudding clouds.

'How do you mean to get up *there*?' he asked. 'And *why*?'

The boy sat up and eased at his elbows. 'I spends a lot of time on rooftops,' he said. 'I hides upon rooftops, I make no excuse. I knows the rooftops of Syon House well enough and I've spent enough time lying on them a-gazing up at the Heavens to see a bit of what goes on up there.'

'What *does* go on up there?' asked Darwin, squinting towards the sky.

'There's a whole world up there amongst the clouds. A world that is made of them clouds, and things what are made out of clouds. Surely you've noticed the likenesses? Surely everyone does.'

'If you mean that clouds sometimes look like things, then yes,' said Darwin. 'That one up there, for instance, looks like something rather rude, as it happens.'

'They often do *that*,' agreed Jack. 'But what about *that* one?' And he pointed.

'That one looks like a whale,' said Darwin.

'Because that's just what it is.'

'Ah,' said Darwin. 'I regret I must disillusion you there. Which is a pity, but it must be done. You are using your childish imagination here, which is a wonderful thing, do not get me wrong. But you are imagining, as children do, that there is a land in the clouds. That there is a land made out of clouds. That clouds that look like whales *are* whales, cloud whales. It is not really true, I'm afraid.'

'Have you quite finished?' asked the boy, now standing on the rooftop.

'It is a cloud and *not* a whale,' said Darwin.

'It is a cloud *and* a whale,' said Jack. 'It is a sky whale.'

'No,' said Darwin.

But, 'Yes,' said Jack, and he nodded his head very hard. 'And,' he went on to say, 'I can prove it.'

The monkey shrugged and said, 'Go on, then.'

'You'd have to trust me,' said Jack. 'You would have to believe.'

'Ah,' said the monkey. 'I see.'

'Wouldn't you like to go up there?' asked Jack. 'Up amongst the clouds? To sail across the world and gaze down upon oceans and continents, forests and mountains and all?'

'I think it would be a very wonderful thing to do,' said the monkey. 'But it is what one does in dreams, and not, I regret, when awake.'

'Well, I'm going,' said Jack. 'And if you won't come with me, then at least you can watch me go.'

The monkey shrugged once more and said, 'I will.'

'Then you must climb with me to a high place and you'll see me board a low-runner.'

The monkey had one shrug left in him and so he offered it now.

'Follow me,' said Jack and took off at the trot.

He was very nimble on his toes, was Jack, and he fair bounded over the slate roofs, jumping from building to building. Darwin followed on with admiration.

'Not much further now,' called Jack and pointed up ahead, towards the spire of Saint Joan's Church that rose beyond the rooftops.

A swing, a jump, a swing and they had reached Saint Joan's.

Darwin gazed up at the spire that dwindled into the sky above. It was a *very* tall church spire and monkeys *do* really like high places. Darwin worried for Jack, however, and said so.

'Fear not for me,' said Jack most bravely, 'for I have no fear of my own.'

And with that said, he began to scale the spire.

Up and up went Darwin and the boy, past grinning gargoyles and decorative slates, right up to the weathercock.

The views were utterly wonderful. The beautiful borough

of Brentford spread all around and about. The Thames a mirrored snake reflecting the sky.

A gentle breeze rippled Darwin's coat and danced soot from Jack's head.

'We're here,' said he. 'And now you'll see for yourself.'

Darwin was admiring the views. 'What am I going to see?'

'You'll see me go up, that's what.'

And Jack clung to the weathercock and waited.

Darwin waited, too. But being a monkey of mercurial disposition, he soon tired of waiting and asked, 'What are we waiting *for*?'

'A low-runner, I told you.'

'But what *is* a low-runner?'

'That's one there,' said Jack, and he pointed. 'If it comes near enough.'

Drifting towards them was a tiny little cloud. About the size of a bathtub, it was, or perhaps a rowing boat. In fact, it did rather resemble a rowing boat, truth be told. It was the right shape and it almost looked as it if had oars as well.

'Perfect,' said Jack. 'That's just what I'm after.'

'Jack?' said Darwin. 'What are you going to do?'

'Board that low-runner and go aloft,' said Jack.

'Do you mean climb onto that cloud?'

The cloud was almost upon them.

Jack simply nodded his head.

'Oh no,' said Darwin. 'Jack, do not. Please, you must not do that.'

'What have I to lose?' asked Jack.

And with that said, he leapt from the spire towards the passing cloud.

28

arwin screamed a terrible scream as Jack jumped from the spire. As Jack plunged down to meet his doom. A terrible scream indeed. And Darwin covered his eyes when he screamed, for he had no wish to see Jack strike the pavement.

Darwin ceased to scream and held his breath.

'See,' said the voice of Jack from below. 'I told you it was perfect.'

Darwin uncovered his eyes and peeped and then dropped low his jaw. For there sat Jack in a tiny boat, a-waggling at the oars. A tiny boat that was a tiny cloud, or perhaps a tiny cloud that was a tiny boat.

'Oh my goodness,' said the adventurous ape.

'Come on, then,' cried Jack. 'Come aboard.'

Darwin stared and Darwin dithered and did not know what to do. Was it a cloud, or was it a boat? A cloudy-boat or a boaty-cloud or something in between?

'Oh!' cried Jack as his boat-cloud became more cloud than boat. 'Don't do that, Darwin. You are getting the cloud-boat all confused.'

Jack's feet began to sink through the cloud-boat's bottom.

'You're a boat! You're a boat! You're a boat!' shouted Darwin and bravely jumped from the spire and into the boat.

'Thank you for *that*,' said Jack, a-pulling up his feet. 'So what do we say to Jack now, if you please?'

Darwin bobbed his head from side to side.

'We say, "Well done, Jack, for being so clever and sorry I ever doubted you," ' said Jack.

'Or something similar,' said Darwin, peering down and over the side of the cloud-boat and admiring the view beneath. 'But how did you *know*, please tell me.'

'As I said,' said Jack, now applying himself to the oars, 'I spent a lot of time hiding upon rooftops staring up at the sky, and the more I stared the more I began to see them – the sharks and the porpoises and great sky whales. And I said to myself, young Jack, one day you'll go up there and have a great adventure.'

Darwin now turned his gaze towards the sky. Then blinked his eyes a number of times and dropped his jaw once more.

'You look a bit goofy with your mouth all open like that,' said Jack.

'But I can see them, too,' said Darwin. 'I can see them, too.'

For so he could.

Above clouds rolled, but were they clouds, or were they many strange things? Mighty fish that dipped and swooped as birds do. Tumbling landscapes of trees and cottages and sheep (for sheep are oft-times very much like clouds). Folk who waved from windows in high castles. Castles perched atop the great sky whales.

'But how can it be?' asked Darwin. 'How do those below not know of this?'

Young Jack tugged upon the oars and grinned. 'I think certain people know,' he said. 'There are always certain people who know *a lot*. But *most* people, as perhaps you have noticed, know very little indeed. And I suspect that were they to be told, they would not believe. And few will ever enter the skies to find out for themselves.'

A sudden thought struck Darwin and it made him rather sad. He had boarded the *Empress of Mars*, a mighty airship, in eighteen ninety-five. Forty-four years from this time. And he had gazed down upon the clouds from that wondrous pleasure craft and he had seen no trace of floating whales and magical castles. Nothing had he seen at all but clouds.

Which meant . . .

It must be gone by then, thought Darwin. *All of this, all gone away as magic, when Man takes to the skies in great machines.*

And this did make Darwin very sad indeed. For it seemed to him that Man, although capable of greatness of thought and deed, as evidenced by the great composers and great artists, appeared ever to be removing magic from the world. Ever 'applying logic' and 'following the scientific thinking of the day', but ever, though apparently gaining, losing so very much.

'Why so thoughtful, young monkey?' asked Jack. 'Are you not as grandly excited as I?'

'I truly am,' said Darwin, 'for this is all quite wonderful.'

'We will need a harpoon,' said Jack.

'A harpoon?' asked the ape.

'For the whaling,' said Jack.

'Whaling?' asked the ape.

'It's in my blood,' said Jack to the ape. 'The Rankins are notable whalers, and I would be a whaler when I grow up. But see here, Darwin, look at those great white whales. How would it be to take a harpoon and bring down one of *them*?'

Darwin's jaw was once more on his chest. But soon again moving swiftly.

'That is outrageous!' he shouted at Jack. 'A terrible thing to even think. You must not bring cruelty into this wonderful aerial kingdom.'

'Oh, it's cruel enough,' said Jack. 'You've seen clouds on stormy days. Those are great sky battles.'

'Really?' said Darwin, and he looked on as Jack rowed them through the sky.

They had gained to a preposterous height and below the great expanse of London dwindled at its edges into green and pleasant lands. The cloud-boat drifted now upon a gentle breeze and Jack amused himself by spitting down upon high-flying pigeons.

'That is a very bad habit indeed,' said Darwin.

Jack said, 'Look, there's an island up ahead. Shall we go ashore?'

The ape espied a misty realm and thought to hear the jolly cries of monkeys.

'Promise me,' he said to Jack, 'that you will not kill anything.'

'But we are as hunters,' said the boy.

'We are as *explorers*,' Darwin said. 'Please do not do anything horrid.'

Jack hunched his shoulders over the oars. He was indeed a boy of bravery and imagination. But he was *a boy* nonetheless, and boys can often be more horrid than not.

Horrid or not, Jack steered the boat to the shore where fluffy pebbles formed a stony beach. The lad leapt ashore and dragged the boat after him. Darwin leapt from boat to land and tested this land with his toes.

'All this,' he said, and he shook his hairy head. 'All this up here all the time, and I never knew it until now.'

The pebbly beach was fringed by waving palms. A tropical island this appeared to be and now the monkey heard the calls of parrots.

'Let us explore,' cried Jack, striking out for the palms.

Darwin paused and scratched at himself. *There might be lions*, he thought.

But then he shrugged and said to himself, 'What care monkeys for lions? For monkeys can always take to the trees if alarmed.'

'Are you talking to yourself?' asked Jack. 'That is the first sign of madness, you know.'

Darwin hurried after the lad. 'Let us explore this jungle, then,' said he.

Darwin had never entered a real jungle before. But as he did so and its sounds and smells closed in upon him, he felt a certain something that he could not at first identify. A certain sense of belonging, was it, perhaps? The rich and heavy scent of vegetation smelled so familiar, the sounds most natural to his simian ears. Reassuring. Safe.

'It is as if I have come home,' said Darwin.

'If only I had brought my gun,' said Jack.

'Jack,' said Darwin, and Darwin showed Jack his teeth. 'If you are going to continue to be beastly, perhaps we should just part company now and have done.'

'I'm sorry,' said Jack. 'But it's rather frightening here.'

'Ah.' The monkey understood the man.

Darwin took Jack by the hand. 'Then let us walk together,' he said.

They wandered here and wandered there, then Darwin spied bananas.

He swarmed up a tree and threw a big hand down to Jack

below. Returning to the ground, the monkey said, 'Let's share them out.'

'You should not eat bananas,' said Jack. 'Bananas will give you the runs.'

'Whatever are *the runs*?' asked Darwin.

Jack explained what they were.

'I think you have been misinformed,' said Darwin. 'Bananas, as with other fruits, are very good for boys.'

'Good for titled folk,' said Jack, 'but not for common boys. As I was constantly told at the big house.'

Darwin frowned. 'Bananas will not give you the runs,' he said. 'Try one and see what you think.'

And so they feasted on bananas. And found a little pool and drank from it. Darwin leaned against the trunk of some exotic tree and grinned as Jack rammed too much banana into his boyish mouth.

'This is a wonderful place to be,' said Darwin. 'A most marvellous place.' And now he thought that this marvellous island in the sky reminded him somewhat of that Garden of Eden sort-of place far back in the past where he had left his monkeys.

Darwin sighed. Then heard the sound of monkeys in the distance.

'Let us go and find those monkeys,' said Darwin. 'I would like to ask them about this world, and how indeed there came to be monkeys up here.'

'Monkeys don't know anything,' said Jack.

'Apes are very wise indeed,' said Darwin. Which was not altogether true, but he was growing *just* a tad fed up with Jack.

'You can hollow out a monkey,' said Jack, 'and make either a glove puppet or a hot-water-bottle cover with it.'

Darwin rose and bit Jack on the ankle.

Jack howled loud and took to hopping about.

The howls of Jack brought on a sudden silence.

The boy and the monkey looked at one another.

Darwin put his finger to his lips. 'We had best move quietly,' he said.

With a very grumpy face and a lot of unnecessary limping, Jack followed Darwin, and as sounds returned to the jungle he even did a little whistling.

They came to a sudden halt in a jungle glade. Sunlight bathed it in vibrant colours. A waterfall trickled somewhere near at hand.

In the middle of the glade there was a great big egg.

Perched upon that egg, a kiwi bird.

The kiwi bird appeared to be sleeping, but as Darwin and Jack drew closer, it opened a beady eye, swung its slender beak towards them and said in the voice of one well bred, 'However do you do?'

'A talking kiwi bird!' said Darwin.

'A talking *ape*!' said the bird.

Jack was about to remark that so large an egg as the one that the kiwi bird sat upon would surely make a very fine omelette indeed. But considering his wounded ankle, he kept such untoward outspokenness in check.

'It is well that you have arrived at last,' said the kiwi bird. 'My name is Ki Vi the kiwi, and you must be Darwin and this horrid boy must be Jack.'

'I am not as horrid as you might think,' said Jack. Which was not, as had been Darwin's remark regarding the wisdom of apes, altogether true.

'You are as horrid as a boy should be,' said Ki Vi the kiwi. 'I should wish you no more horrid than less.'

'How do you know our names?' asked Darwin, as this seemed a logical question.

'All naughty boys in this day and age are called Jack.' Ki Vi waved her beak about, as if conducting an orchestra.

'And all monkeys Darwin?' asked Darwin.

'No, only you. For you are the Ape of Thoth.'

Now, Darwin had heard this term before, spoken of to Mr Bell by Mr Aleister Crowley.

'The Ape of Thoth?' said Darwin.

'Certainly,' said Ki Vi, comfying her great big feet to either side of her egg. 'Thoth is an Egyptian deity. An *ancient* Egyptian deity, from the time of the chickens.'

Darwin remembered the chickens of ancient Egypt.

'Thoth is generally depicted as an ibis,' said Ki Vi, informatively, 'but sometimes disguises himself as an ape when bringing his wisdom to Men.'

'I told you apes were wise,' said Darwin, sticking his tongue out at Jack.

'The Ape of Thoth is known by other names,' the kiwi bird went on. 'Djehuty, Dhouti, Djhuty, Dah-Wyn. He is the God of medicine, magic and the moon. Of justice, wisdom and writing. Of science and speech. Thoth is credited with inventing the Egyptian hieroglyphic system. Thoth means "thought" and "time". He is the Lord of the Past and the Future.'

'You think that I am a God?' said Darwin.

'We *know* that you are, Dah-Wyn,' said Ki Vi the kiwi bird.

29

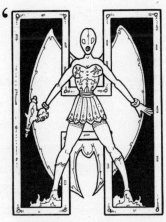

'e is *not* a God,' said Jack with a laugh. 'He's just a silly monkey.'

The silly monkey bit the boy called Jack.

'Quite right, too,' said the kiwi bird. 'He's a horrid little boy.'

'And do stop calling me horrid!' Jack took once more to hopping about, now holding his other ankle.

'But he *is* right,' said Darwin. 'I am really *not* a God.'

'There is a Hindu monkey God named Hanuman,' the kiwi said. 'He is the devoted helper of Rama.'

'I have heard of him,' said Darwin. 'But what is he to me?'

'You are an aspect of Hanuman and your partner Cameron Bell is an aspect of Rama.'

'Rather unlikely,' said Darwin.

'Much is in the words,' explained the kiwi bird. 'Take Hanuman, for instance. If one removes the first "a" and the first "n", one finds that "Hanuman" becomes "Human". And given that the original Celtic for Cameron is Camaron, one finds that by removing the capital "C", the first "a" and the "on", we have the word "amar", which of course spells "Rama" when reversed.'

'I want to go now,' said Jack. 'I find all this rather dull.'

'The word *Jack* has many meanings,' said the knowledge-able kiwi bird. 'A male donkey, of course, is known as a jackass.'

'I will not be insulted by a foolish kiwi bird,' said Jack.

'Jack is also a knave in a pack of playing cards – which is to say, a prince.'

'Ah,' said Jack, and he preened at his sooty lapels. 'Al-though I consider it unlikely that the monkey here is a God, I will warm to the idea that I am of royal blood. I have always suspected such a thing. Possibly born on the wrong side of the blanket, as it were, and—'

'Do be quiet, *please*,' cried the kiwi bird. 'You rattle on as a jackdaw will and jackdaws are well known as thieves.'

'Did *you* lay that egg?' asked the ape of a sudden.

Ki Vi nodded. 'Indeed.'

'But it is bigger than you are.'

'Such is the case with kiwis and eggs, but you are chan-ging the subject.'

'I do not believe that I am a God,' said Darwin.

'Nor me,' agreed Jack. 'But I probably am a real prince.'

'You are both what you are,' said the kiwi. 'And you have been brought here because you are needed.'

'Nobody brought us here but me,' said Jack.

Ki Vi the kiwi shook her head, her beak describing very graceful arcs. 'You are here because we want you here. We need you here. We let you see the clouds for what they are. We knew you would yearn to come here. And how do you think you ended up on the roof of the Flying Swan in the first place?'

'I got blown out of a chimney,' said Jack. 'Which is why my princely robes are smutted with soot.'

Ki Vi said to Darwin the monkey, 'He really is a quite

obnoxious boy.' And then went on to explain exactly what had happened.

'Lord Brentford owns a kiwi bird,' said Ki Vi. 'Jack was very cruel to it. He cemented down its feet and stuck its beak into the air.'

'I turned it into a sundial!' said Jack. 'Rather enterprising of me, I thought.'

'The kiwi got its own back when it pressed the button on Lord Brentford's pneumatic chimney-sweeper whilst Jack was up the chimney.'

'I will do for that bird,' said the sooty boy.

'And one thing led to another as it should and now you both are here.' Ki Vi nodded her head to Darwin. Darwin nodded back.

'So why have you gone to all this effort?' Darwin asked.

'Because the Kingdom of the Sky is in peril,' Ki Vi said. 'And who better to sort things out than a God and a prince?'

'Is there any treasure?' asked Jack. 'Because kingdoms have kings and kings have treasure and a prince should have some treasure, too.'

'There is plenty of treasure,' said Ki Vi. 'You can have as much as you want, when all is said and done.'

'Then count me in,' said Prince Jack. 'I'll need a sword and brand-new boots and brand-new clothes as well.'

Darwin shook his head sadly, but Ki Vi nodded her beak.

'So, then,' said Jack, 'I am up for the fight.' And then he clutched at his stomach. 'Oh no,' he said, and then he backed away.

Jack returned in a little while looking rather pale.

'Those bananas gave me the runs,' said Jack.

Then Jack said, 'Now, where did *they* come from?' as he perused the clothes.

They were neatly stacked, of noble stuff, with polished boots and a sword.

'Go and wash yourself in the waterfall and throw your other clothes away,' said Ki Vi.

Jack really did look rather princely upon his eventual return. He swaggered in his brand-new boots and flourished his sword. 'Let us go and see that treasure,' said Jack.

'First things first,' said Ki Vi. 'You must take the magic egg.'

'The big one there?' asked Jack, and his thoughts turned once more towards omelettes.

'This big one here. Which you must take to the castle of Skia the Sky Whale.'

'Where the treasure is kept?' asked Jack.

Ki Vi the kiwi made sighing sounds. 'Just take the egg,' said she.

Darwin gave himself a bit of a scratching.

'Do you have fleas?' the kiwi asked the ape.

'Yes, I do,' said Darwin, 'and I am keeping them. Is there anything else you could tell us? It all sounds rather vague.'

'I have sat upon this egg,' said Ki Vi, 'whilst the Earth has circled the Sun one hundred times.'

'Your bum must be numb,' said Jack, with a silly laugh.

'I waited,' said Ki Vi, 'as was my job, to pass the egg to you.'

'Darwin can carry the egg,' said Jack. 'I will carry my sword.'

'It looks like a rather heavy egg,' said Darwin.

The kiwi beckoned Darwin with her beak.

Darwin joined the kiwi, who whispered into his ear.

At length, Darwin said, 'Surely we cannot do *that*!'

'It is the only way,' said Ki Vi. 'For it *is* a magic egg.'

'Well,' said Darwin, and a big smile spread all across his face. 'Jack,' he called, 'come over here, if you will.'

'Aaaaaaarooooh!' went Jack, and cough cough cough and choke.

He and Darwin were once more alone in the jungle. They were marching back to the boat. Though Jack was hardly marching.

'You monster!' howled Jack. 'You tricked me,' howled Jack. 'I am poisoned and will die,' howled Jack as well.

'It is only an egg,' said Darwin. 'And you were thinking to have it as an omelette, were you not?'

'I never was.' Jack clutched at his throat. 'I don't feel right inside.'

'It is a magic egg,' said Darwin. 'As Ki Vi explained to you, this is the best way to carry it.'

'She explained it to me *after* you had held me down and she had rammed it right down my throat.'

'She magicked it small when she did so,' said Darwin, skipping along out of reach of the young prince's sword.

'It might swell up inside me. I might *die*.' Jack grew quite red in the face.

'She said to me that it will only grow big again when it is being—' Darwin paused in speech but not in motion.

'When it is being *what*?'

'Laid,' said Darwin. 'Laid was the word, I believe.'

'*Laid?*' Jack now clutched at other places. 'Do you mean that *I* must lay a kiwi bird's egg?'

Darwin made a very pained expression. 'I am sure it will all turn out for the best in the end.'

'I'll sick it up,' threatened Jack. 'I don't want an egg coming out of my bu—'

'Ah,' said Darwin. 'We have reached the beach.'

'I want my mum,' said Jack, and he began to cry.

Darwin felt suddenly guilty. It *had* seemed quite funny at the time, because Jack was a rather horrid boy. But now he was clearly a very scared boy and not without good cause.

'Think of the treasure,' Darwin said. 'And think about being a prince.'

'I'm thinking of my poor bottom,' grumbled Prince Jack.

'Let us think of jollier things. This is a very big adventure indeed.'

'It is all right for *you*,' sulked Jack. 'You don't have a bird's egg in your belly, waiting to burst out of your ars—'

'Look,' said Darwin and pointed. 'Is that not a sky whale drifting *there*?'

Jack made an even grumpier face.

'What is done is done,' said Darwin.

'You've done a wicked thing to me,' said Jack. 'And let me tell you this. If I don't get my treasure, I'll use my sword and hollow you out and wear you on my head as a hairy hat.'

Darwin felt less guilty now. *What a really horrible boy*, he thought.

Sulking and grumping and grumbling, too, Jack pushed the cloud-boat away from the beach and jumped into it. Darwin followed Jack into the boat and sat himself down in the prow.

'You look very princely indeed, Prince Jack,' he said. 'Those royal robes and fine boots really suit you.'

'Don't try to get around me,' said Jack as he took up the oars.

'You were clearly born to wear such finery,' said Darwin. 'I could not carry off a look like that myself.'

'That's because *you* are a monkey,' said Jack, 'and I a noble prince.' And Jack laughed. 'A God, *indeed*!' he said, and he laughed some more.

'As you are wise beyond your years,' said Darwin, 'and brave and noble, too, you must lead us to the castle of Skia the Sky Whale.'

'Obviously so,' agreed Jack.

'So which way do you think we should go?'

Jack made the face of perplexity. Then pointed. 'That way, obviously,' he said.

'Obviously,' said Darwin, and Jack rowed *that way*.

It was very idyllic up there in the sky. Little cloudy fish swam by and cloudy mermaids, too. The mermaids were beautiful creatures that put Darwin in mind of angels he had seen painted upon the ceiling of St Paul's Cathedral.

And thoughts of St Paul's Cathedral put thoughts of London and Mr Bell and the Crystal Palace and Queen Victoria into the head of Darwin. Who wondered now whether he was likely to be back at the Flying Swan by nine o'clock tomorrow morning.

A sense of urgency now impinged upon Darwin's thoughts, and as it was quite clear to Darwin that Jack had been rowing about in circles for a while now, the ape spoke up.

'Do you think we should ask directions, your royal highness?'

Jack, who had been affecting what he considered to be 'regal poses' whilst rowing, which probably accounted for the going around in circles, said, 'That was what *we* thought.'

'*We*.' Darwin sighed. 'The royal *we*, I suppose.'

'*You* make enquiries,' said Jack. 'It would not be fitting for one such as *I* to confer with humble folk.'

'Jack,' said Darwin. 'You might have a sword. But I have very sharp teeth.'

But then Darwin found himself struck suddenly speechless. Unable to do anything but point.

'It is rude to point,' said Jack. 'You are a very rude monkey.'

Darwin, open-mouthed, just pointed on.

'Stop it *now*.' But Jack glanced into the direction of Darwin's pointings.

Then found that he, too, was lost for words.

He found two words at last and shouted . . .

'SKY SHARK!'

30

he great white shark swept down from above, its ghastly jaws wide open.

'Abandon ship!' cried Jack, all of a sudden loquacious. 'Every man for himself. Princes first. God bless my soul,' and, '*Help!*'

Darwin clung to the cloud-boat as Jack leapt into the blue.

Down and down rushed the dreadful shark and Darwin, now clasping his hands in prayer, begged God to be let into Heaven.

An awful crunch and a munching of jaws, a ripping and mashing of boat. Shredded planks dissolved to wisps of cloud. Darwin viewed that yawning maw a-feared by every seaman. There was a great, black swallowing gulp and Darwin the monkey was gone.

Then up flew Darwin, up from the jaws of death.

Up on a hook and a line and a sinker.

Up to the tall ship above.

The adventurous ape gained fleeting impressions of Jack being similarly hauled. Of the cloud-boat gone into nothingness. Of the great white shark stuck through by a mighty harpoon.

All this within seconds, then Darwin's eyes crossed and he fainted dead away.

A strange dream came to visit Darwin, causing him unrest.

He stood with Mr Cameron Bell upon a blasted landscape. Smoke curled from a distant township, the grass beneath their feet scorched to black. From above came sounds of groaning metal, cries of fear and other monstrous noises.

Cameron Bell was shouting to Darwin, but his words could not be heard. The groaning, grinding-metal din was deafening.

For above, they swung upon their three tall armoured legs, jointed tentacles whipping wildly, flames rushing out to sear and destroy. Steely-scaled and terrible, the Martian engines of death.

Folk were running now across the blackened sward, wide-eyed in frenzy, through flames and grasping tentacles and horror borne upon horror.

Whilst Darwin stood in silence and scratched and scratched at himself.

Scratched and scratched and scratched and scratched and scratched.

'Wake yourself up, matey boy.' Water splashed on Darwin's face. The ape became awake.

It was all in confusion, of course, with lots of thrashing about, but Darwin heard the voice of Jack, saying, 'It's all right.'

So Darwin awoke to find himself upon the deck of a ship. Many faces grinned at him and some went, 'Ooooh,' and others, 'Arrrrh,' whilst others belched bad breath.

Darwin drew himself up to a-sitting and found a pewter tankard being thrust into his hands.

'Drink well, me hearty,' someone said, whilst others 'oooohed' and 'arrrrhed' again.

'Pirates,' came the voice of Jack. 'We're on a pirate ship.' And then he said something that later many would say, but not for at least one hundred years.

'How cool is *that*?' said Jack.

Darwin sipped grog from the pewter tankard. '*Very* cool,' said he, and looking all around and about beheld the pirate vessel.

It looked to Darwin's mind the way a pirate ship *should* look. The wooden deck, the ship's wheel and the masts. The barrel for storing limes to stave off scurvy. The cannon and the powder kegs, the sails above, the Jolly Roger flying.

The pirates were as pirates should be, have been, would be, ought to be the wide world over. Or at least around the Spanish Main and places such as that.

Tricorns naturally found favour, broad belts tucked with cutlasses and flintlocks. Ragged frock coats, lacy shirts, sea-faring boots and bandanas. Each and all covered in a layer of grime, for pirates are rebels and cannot be made to wash.

Grizzled beards were to be observed, and various body parts generally considered if not essential, then at least favour-able to retain, were notably absent. Hence the proliferation of eyepatches, hook-hands and carved wooden legs.

And as it is generally agreed that most, if not all, pirates originated in the West Country, they spoke with that glori-ous Cornishy and mellowy twang that has made National Talk Like a Pirate Day the twenty-first-century institution that it has so rightly become.

'Cool,' said Jack. 'So *very* cool. And they have parrots and everything.'

A parrot said, 'Hello,' to Darwin, then added, 'Pieces of eight.'

'So,' said Darwin, rising to his feet, 'we have been rescued by pirates.'

'Ooooh,' and, 'Aaaarh,' went the pirates bold, taking a single step back as one. 'A talking ape, well, shiver me timbers,' and things of that nature generally.

And then one bigger than the rest stepped forward, thrusting others aside. 'A talking ape?' he bellowed. 'What demon-spawn is this?'

'No demon-spawn, I,' explained Darwin, 'but a monkey butler, schooled in man-speech by a visionary with an evolutionary hypotheses that—'

'He has fine words about him,' bellowed the pirate chief, for such was this overlarge fellow. 'He can serve a while as me cabin boy, before we sell him on.'

'Ah, no,' said Jack, stepping forward. 'This ape belongs to me.'

The pirates now fell into laughter, as pirates will do at the drop of a three-cornered hat.

'Are you challenging Black Jack MacJackblack, captain of the good ship *Venus*?'

'Not as such,' said Jack. 'And my name's Jack, too, by the way. But he's still my monkey.'

Darwin made a certain face towards Jack. 'We should just thank the nice gentlemen for saving our lives,' he suggested. 'Matters of ownership regarding myself might perhaps be postponed until I—'

'Don't he go on a fine treat?' Black Jack MacJackblack laughed and the pirate crew took to great laughter with him.

Then, 'Hold on there,' said Jack. 'Did you say the good ship *Venus*?'

'As I took in sky battle over Plymouth,' quoth Black Jack.

'I know the song,' said young Jack.

Darwin chewed upon his knuckles, for he knew that song, too.

'Song?' asked Black Jack. 'What song be this?'

And young Jack started to sing:

> 'Twas on the good ship *Venus*,
> My lads, you should have seen us,
> The figurehead
> Was lying in bed
> Sucking a dead man's—

'I'm sure the captain does *not* want to hear *that*,' said Darwin.

'Don't interrupt *me* when I'm singing,' said Jack. 'I'm a prince, after all.'

The pirates took another step back, and as they 'oooohed' and 'arrrrhed' again, Darwin let out a groan.

Jack raised a puzzled expression.

Darwin whispered, 'You should not have mentioned *that*.'

'*A prince!*' roared Captain Black Jack. 'A prince, do we have on board?'

'Quite right,' said Jack, doing princely posings, 'and you should show me some respect.'

'Over the side with him!' shouted a pirate.

'Fetch the plank,' cried another.

Black Jack snatched young Jack up by his regal collar. 'We don't hold with princes,' he told him. 'We sends princes to Davy Jones.'

'Or the aerial equivalent thereof,' remarked a pirate with literary pretensions. Because there is always one. Because it is a tradition* amongst pirates to embrace a broad spectrum of types, so long as they all adhere to the accent.

---

* *Or an old charter, or something. (R. R.)*

'Aaaar–harrr,' added the pirate with literary pretensions.

'The plank! The plank!' shouted the pirates.

'No, no,' cried Jack, now a-feared.

But pirate hands and pirate hooks were upon him and he was lifted into the air and bounced around and about.

'Please don't throw him off the ship,' pleaded Darwin.

'You're *my* monkey now,' bawled Black Jack MacJackblack, 'so shut up your noise if you knows what's good for you.'

Darwin watched in horror as pirates jostled Jack about and a plank was pushed out over the side of the ship.

'Over you go, bonny prince!' Pirates laughed and waggled weapons as Jack was nudged along the fearful plank.

Jack peeped down to the sky beneath, where the harpooned shark circled below.

'No,' wailed Jack, 'please don't. I want my mum.'

'*Please* don't,' shouted Darwin.

The pirates just chortled and prodded.

'And over he goes,' yelled the captain.

And over—

But then was heard one rather magical word.

'*Treasure!*' shouted Darwin. At the top of his voice.

The pirates paused, because this word *was* magic.

'Treasure,' Darwin said once more, when he had *all* their attention.

'What of this?' demanded the captain. 'What do you say of treasure?'

'*Great* treasure,' said Darwin. '*Very great* treasure. In the prince's castle. If you take us safely to it, all of it can be yours.'

'What of *this*?' The captain glared at Jack.

'Well, I *am* a prince,' said Jack. 'But it's *my* treasure.'

'Grrrrrr!' went Black Jack MacJackblack.

'He is a rather silly young prince,' said Darwin. 'But there is a very great deal of treasure, and if you take us safely to the castle, *all* of it will be yours.'

The pirates took to mumbling. Some of them mumbled, 'Rhubarb-rhubarb,' for they were extras who did not have speaking parts.

'Quiet, ye swabs,' called the captain. 'I be a-thinking, I be.'

'Many fine clothes, too,' added Darwin. 'You might wish to extend your wardrobe. Perhaps add an extra dash of colour here and—'

'Shut it!' cried the captain. 'Or I'll hollow you out and—'

'Not a word more,' said Darwin.

The captain now did a bit of marching up and down the deck. He did it with a certain flair, for he had a wooden leg. 'Where be this castle?' he said of a sudden, turning on Darwin the monkey.

'It is the castle of Skia the Sky Whale.'

'Oooh-hoo,' 'Arr-harr' and 'Arrr,' went the pirates generally.

'But where be it?' the captain enquired.

'How would *I* know?' said Darwin. '*I* am only a silly monkey. *You* are the mighty pirate chief, who holds the command and respect of his crew through his authority and knowledge of such matters.'

The pirate crew went 'ooooh' and 'aaar' and their collective gaze swung from Darwin to the master of the ship.

'Aaar,' said Captain MacJackblack.

'A pirate chief,' continued Darwin, returning all eyes to himself, 'has boundless knowledge of where treasure might be found. It is instinctive, or so I have been informed.'

The gaze of all returned to the captain.

'Aaar,' said that fellow once more.

A grumbling mumbling came from the pirates. Someone said, 'Rhubarb,' quite loudly.

'Right, me hearties,' called the captain. 'We be sailing for treasure. Weigh the anchor, trim the sails and tots of rum all round.'

The pirates cheered and waggled their weapons.

Jack asked politely, 'Can I come down from this plank?'

31

he sails of the good ship *Venus* gathered wind.

Darwin sat on the captain's deck, drinking the captain's rum. Young Jack made his grumpy face and idled about with a scallop.

'It is *my* treasure, Darwin,' he said for the umpteenth time.

'You might perhaps thank me for saving your life,' said Darwin.

'Thank you,' said Jack. '*And* a pirate stole my sword. *And* another one touched me inappropriately.'

Darwin raised his eyebrows to that. 'All will be well,' said he.

'All will be well!' And Jack rolled his eyes. 'I don't believe that captain knows where he's going.'

'Nor do I,' said Darwin, tasting further rum. 'But at least we are safe up here for now and going somewhere or other.'

'I should be the captain of this ship,' said Jack. 'Prince outranks captain. Everybody knows that.'

'I would have thought,' said Darwin, quietly, 'that everyone would know that pirates have no love for princes. Everyone but *you*, apparently.'

Jack made a face much grumpier and with that folded his arms.

Darwin arose, to find himself unsteady. 'It is very fine rum,' he said. 'And this is certainly an exciting adventure.'

And then it occurred to Darwin that he did have that appointment with Mr Bell at nine o'clock the following morning. And now he did not even know over which far-flung part of the globe the ship was flying. Darwin stumbled to the rail and took a peep. Cloudy lands lay scattered below, and beneath them rolled the ocean.

'Oh, well,' said Darwin, returning to the captain's rum.

Jack said underneath his breath, 'They are not having my treasure.'

The captain appeared on the captain's deck and bid them a hearty hello. He slapped young Jack upon the back and offered a wink to Darwin.

'We're making good headway,' the captain said, and he tugged from a frock-coat pocket a shiny brass compass and took to perusing its face.

'Shall we soon arrive at the treasure-filled castle?' asked Darwin.

The captain glanced askew at the ape. 'Just mind your tongue,' quoth he.

'It must be nearly time for lunch,' said young Jack, grinning up at the captain. 'I would like roast leg of lamb and potatoes, but no greens.'

'Pirates don't eat greens,' the captain said. 'And you mind your manners or you'll find yourself on the menu.'

'You were to convey us in safety,' said Darwin.

'I recall no written contract to that effect,' said the pirate chief.

'I would like Treacle Sponge Bastard for pudding,' said Jack.

The captain shook his head, then clipped Jack round the ear.

'Ouch,' said Jack.

And on the good ship sailed.

It was certainly magical up there in the clouds, with wonderful cloud islands and great cloudy dolphins and small cloudy fish and this thing and that and the other.

Darwin leaned upon the ship's rail and grinned rather foolishly. He had drunk a tad too much rum, for sure, and he did feel stupidly happy.

'Look at it all,' he called to young Jack. 'Isn't it just so—'

'Cool?' said Jack, who was spitting again, this time onto seagulls. 'Yes, it is *very* cool, and I would be having a good time myself if I was *not* being held to ransom by pirates and did *not* have a kiwi's egg inside my belly.'

Darwin gave himself a scratch. 'I have fleas,' he said.

'And you seem proud of them,' said Jack. 'I wonder if I can live in the castle of Skia.'

'How does a whale have a castle, I wonder?' said Darwin.

'Ah,' said Jack. 'Well, I know that, cos I've seen them. The big sky whales are *very* big and carry great big castles on their backs.'

'Why?' asked Darwin, and, 'How?'

'Who cares why *or* how?' said Jack. 'They just do.'

'And what is so special, I wonder, about this Skia?'

'I expect it's the Skia in the fairy tale,' said Jack.

Darwin peered down the rum bottle's neck and found the rum bottle empty. 'I have been to Fairyland,' he said. 'I did not take to it very much.'

'So you know the story of Skia?'

'No, I don't,' said Darwin. 'Tell me it now, if you please.'

'I am too big a boy for fairy tales, but I'll tell you it all the same.' Jack sat himself down with his back to a mast and so began the tale.

'Once upon a time,' said Jack, 'there lived a whale called Skia. She swam about in the ocean deep with her mummy and her daddy and her big and handsome brother named Jack.'

Darwin sighed softly, but young Jack continued undaunted.

'It was a time so very long ago, a time when Man was different from how he is today. Man then, they say, was smaller and hairy and very much like a monkey. The race of Man lived then upon a large and beautiful island, which as time has passed and memory faded has gone by many names. Eden, some say it was called.'

Darwin pricked up his ears to this. 'Who told you that?' he asked.

'My daddy,' said Jack. 'For he was a whaler and knew many tales about whales.'

'Go on.'

'The hairy men lived happily in Eden. They swung about in the trees, dined upon bananas and used what words they had to engage in lengthy philosophical discussions about the nature of being.'

'You are making this up,' said Darwin.

'I couldn't make *that* up,' said Jack. 'So, the hairy monkey-men were happy enough. They had all that they wanted and needed. They did not require fire and had no wish to invent the wheel. Not that they lacked the intellectual prowess to do so, rather they adhered to an altruistic empiricism, that knowledge derives from experience and to experience the infinite one must eschew worldly goods.'

Darwin stared slack-jawed at Jack. 'Your daddy told you *that*?'

'Do you want to hear the story or not?'

'I do,' said Darwin. 'I do.'

'Thus,' continued Jack, 'these monkey-men, these proto-humans, if you will, were of an order close to God, for their thoughts were pure and they caused no harm to the world in which they lived.'

Darwin nodded. 'I am glad for that.'

'But,' said Jack, 'though this tribe lived in peace and flourished, also did it grow in numbers, mightily. For monkeys are prolific and prodigious in their mating habits and after a span of many centuries, the Garden of Eden was overrun with monkeys. But they were goodly God-fearing monkeys and they all got by somehow. God looked down upon his favoured people, but God being God, he chose to not get involved. It was then that the chickens—'

'*The chickens?*' said Darwin. 'What is all this about chickens?'

'Many believe,' said Jack, 'that chickens were the first folk on Earth and that Man evolved from the chicken.'

'Stuff and nonsense,' said Darwin. 'Man evolved from the noble ape and the noble ape from me.'

'The noble ape from— What did you say?'

'Nothing,' said Darwin. 'Please carry on with the story.'

'The chickens lived on another island, and theirs was called Atlantis.'

Darwin sighed and said, 'I don't care for chickens.'

'The chickens were not like the monkeys,' Jack said. 'The chickens were driven by more material and less spiritual things and invented the wheel. And they invented binoculars and cricket, which originally was called chicket, and they built pyramids and were indeed a most industrious race.'

'But ungodly,' said Darwin. 'Ungodly.'

'Very ungodly,' said Jack. 'And very bothersome, too. They built great sailing ships and circumnavigated the globe. Chickens turn up everywhere in history, which is probably why ultimately they came to be such a popular dish.'

'That does not follow at all,' said Darwin. 'Please get on with the story.'

'Oh, look,' said Jack, and he pointed. 'That there is a sky kraken.'

Darwin looked on as the impressive creature, part-octopus, part-bat or bird, it appeared, moved by with languid swimming motions of its lengthy tentacles.

'Do carry on with the story,' said Darwin.

Jack carried on with the story.

'The chickens of Mammon made war on the monkeys of God. And the leader of the monkeys, Hanuman as that silly kiwi mentioned, led a brave fight against those filthy fowl. But the chickens were big and the monkeys were small and the chickens had developed many forms of martial technology – prang cannons and poison muskets, ultrasonic catapults and laser-guided missiles. They even had their own website.'

'I am going to get more rum,' said Darwin. 'You can finish the story without me.'

'No, all right,' said Jack. 'I made up the last bit. But they did have weapons and armour and suchlike and they were more than a match for the monkeys. And they drove those monkeys off their paradise island.'

'Where does the sky whale come into this tale?' asked Darwin.

'It comes in now,' said Jack. 'Skia was bobbing about in the sea off the island and she saw the whole thing, and when the chickens drove the monkeys into the sea, she rescued them. All the monkeys climbed onto her back and they all lived happily ever after.'

'I think you must have left a bit out,' said Darwin, 'such as how this whale came up into the sky.'

'Oh,' said Jack. 'Well, all right. This was the time when the Earth was young and still becoming itself. The chickens could have been the creatures to rule the world, but it was not to be. There are certain things which are known as Eternal Verities, you know.'

'Like how a swan can break a man's arm,' said Darwin.

'Exactly. And how Martians cannot survive here due to Earthly bacteria.'

'And how time-travel plot holes are best stepped neatly across,' said Darwin.

Young Jack shrugged. 'Something like that, I suppose. Well, one thing *everyone* knows, and I do mean *everyone*, is that Atlantis was an island that lay before the great flood in an area we now call the Atlantic Ocean.* And Atlantis sank. *Everyone* knows that. So the evil chickens didn't stay long on the monkey's island, because it was all covered in monkey poo and not really a nice place to live any more. So they returned to Atlantis and the whole horrid lot of them went down into the sea when that continent sank.'

'Bravo,' said Darwin. 'And good riddance to those chickens.'

'Bravo indeed,' said Jack. 'If a bit of a shame about those monkeys.'

'But *my* monkeys – *those* monkeys, I mean – escaped on the back of Skia.'

'Yes, but as I told you, according to the story all this

* *God bless Donovan, say I. (R. R.)*

happened when the world was very very young and in all kinds of turmoil, and a big storm lashed and Skia got lost with all those monkeys clinging to her back.'

'I do not think I am going to like the next part of the story.'

'It does have a happy ending,' said Jack. 'Well, sort of.'

Darwin had tired of saying, 'Go on,' so instead he said, 'Please continue.'

'The monkeys clung on to Skia's back and Skia swam on and on, but she never ever reached land again and eventually she and all the monkeys died.'

'That is *not* a happy ending,' said Darwin. 'In fact, that is no ending at all, because Skia supposedly is a sky whale who still swims about up here.'

'Of course she is,' said Jack. 'She's up here, and all those monkeys, too.'

'Well, they can't be up here if they're dead,' said Darwin.

'Well, I can't imagine how they'd get here otherwise.'

'And now you are not making any sense at all,' said Darwin. 'What are you saying? That the only way you can get up here is by dying? Like going to Heaven? That *this* is Heaven — is that what you are saying?'

'That is *exactly* what I'm saying,' said Jack. 'Now don't pretend you don't know.'

'Don't know?' said Darwin, now becoming most con-fused indeed.

'Don't know you're dead,' said Jack to Darwin. 'How else did you think we got here?'

'What?' went Darwin. 'What?'

'Well, you didn't think this was real life, did you?' asked Jack, and he laughed. 'Islands in the sky made out of clouds? This is the small boy's Heaven, Darwin. Where small dead boys have adventures. Where poor dead boys become princes and meet pirates and go on magical quests. I jumped off the spire of the church,' said Jack. 'You saw my ghost in a cloudy boat, jumped into it and you fell, too. I'm sorry.'

32

o no no!' cried Darwin, all in a lather.

'What is all this no-ing?' asked the captain, clumping by.

'Jack just told me an awful tale. He says that we are dead.'

'Dead's not so bad,' said the captain. 'Once you get over the shock. I was an engineer, me. Worked on the Great Exhibition. Some swab dropped a hammer on me head. I had always dreamed of being a pirate, when I was a boy.'

'No,' said Darwin. 'This is all absurd.'

'Not as such,' said the literarily inclined pirate, happening by. 'In many ways it exhibits a divine elegance. The ghosts of men inhabit a realm above the Earth, to which those who walk upon terra firma will never rise when living.'

'Oh yes they will and quite soon,' said Darwin. 'Oh, I don't feel very well.'

'Just getting your dead-legs,' said the captain. 'As in sea-legs, you see.'

'I *do* see,' said Darwin. 'And it was not even funny.'

'I'm a prince,' said Jack, 'so I am happy enough.'

This gave Darwin pause for thought. 'Just hold on here,'

he said. 'I recall well enough that conversation with the kiwi bird. It identified me as the Ape of Thoth, Lord of the Past and the Future.'

'And your point is?' asked the captain.

'I cannot be dead if I am a God,' said Darwin.

'I might take issue with you there,' said the pirate with literary learnings. 'As this Heavenly realm encompasses the dreams and fantasies of the souls that inhabit it, an inflated image of one's own importance might surely result in a projected manifestation where delusion of Godhood takes on a reality of its own. In fact—'

But this pirate said no more than, 'Ooooow!' for Darwin bit him.

'I am *not* dead,' declared the ape. 'And *I* never said I was a God.'

'You did say,' said Jack, 'that Man descended from the noble ape and the noble ape from you.'

'I *might* have,' said Darwin. 'But—'

'It really doesn't matter,' said the captain. 'Soon we will all be nothing but whispers in space.'

'And what does *that* mean?' asked Darwin.

'Look around you,' said the captain. 'Look around the sky.'

Darwin did and Darwin shook his head.

'You see islands, you see fish, you see birds and kraken, too, but you will notice that you don't see many men.'

'I see *you*,' said Darwin.

'And my crew of pirates. *Eight* in number – a rather small tally of pirates, don't you agree?'

'Where is *this* leading?' Darwin asked.

'I believe,' said the captain, 'and others before me have believed – others who are not here now – that this wonderful cloudy realm in the sky is but the portal to Heaven. You might consider it Limbo, or indeed God's waiting room, for surely if it were inhabited by the souls of the dead it would be a very very crowded place. Seeing as how millions and millions of people have died before this time.'

'Hm!' went Darwin, making a face. 'That could well be an argument that this is *not* some realm of the dead. In fact,' and here his little face lit up, 'I might just be dreaming all this.' And Darwin started pinching himself. Because it is one of those Eternal Verities that if you are having a bad dream, you can pinch yourself and it will wake you up.

Not that Darwin could ever recall anyone vouching for the authenticity of this particular Eternal Verity.

'I tried *that*,' said Captain Black Jack. 'Gave myself terrible bruises. Banged my head on the mast, I did. Nearly put me eye out.'

Darwin made fists, flung them into the air and took to stalking up and down the deck.

He took to reciting a mantra that went: 'I am *not* dead. I am *not* dead. I am *not* dead,' and so on.

'You don't seem to mind at all, do you, boy?' the captain asked young Jack.

'I told the ape,' said Jack, 'when I jumped from the spire, that I had nothing to lose. I was a child labourer, pushed up chimneys, treated like the dirt that covered me. There was no life in that for me. I am happy here.'

'You were not so happy when you had that magic egg poked down your throat,' said Darwin. 'Not very Heavenly, *that*, to my thinking.'

'It's not all wings and harps,' said Black Jack MacJackblack. 'There would be no adventure if it was. We have battles and we have quests. Why, even now we are bound for a treasure castle. Aaah–harr–harr–harr.'

'Bravo,' said the literary pirate. 'A nice return to character.

Let us have no more of this theosophical disputation. Let us just be sky pirates bold and sail the aerial oceans.'

'Well said,' said the captain. 'Break out the grog and we'll all get legless together.'

There had been a certain shift about in the sulking.

Young Jack had brightened up no end. Considering that he *was* a prince now, and he *was* having an adventure with pirates, and that *was* pretty much all he had ever wanted to be and to do when alive.

Darwin, however . . .

The ape hunched low with folded brow and glared towards the sky. Here was an ape who was not at all pleased with his lot. A dead ape who did not *want* to be dead, had not *chosen* to be dead, did not consider it *fun at all* to be dead. And so on.

'Outrageous,' Darwin said at intervals. 'Quite preposterous, too.'

Jack even tried to comfort Darwin.

Darwin bit young Jack.

The sails billowed out as sails will do and the good ship *Venus* moved on. Young Jack was actually nice to Darwin and was even prepared to take just a little bit of responsibility for the ape's death. What with him encouraging Darwin to leap from the church spire into the cloud boat. And everything. Darwin sighed and huffed and puffed but finally gave up the grumping. There was really no point to it, and he was an ape of a naturally cheery disposition, and if he *was* now dead, and it did appear extremely likely that this was in fact the case, then there was really nothing more for it than to make the best of a *very* bad job and simply get on with it.

Though it still made the ape very angry and also rather

confused. Because he was absolutely certain that when it came to his own death, this death would come through the medium of his old master Lord Brentford shooting him dead within the *Marie Lloyd* in eighteen ninety-nine.

Darwin's conviction that this was how it would happen was, of course, backed up by the fact that it *already had*.

So Darwin was left in some confusion, but was prepared to put it down to all the chaos of time travelling, and so he *would* have to make the best of a *very* bad job and simply get on with it.

'The captain said you might like this,' said Jack, presenting Darwin with a bottle and a pair of long-stemmed glasses.

Darwin perused the bottle's label.

Château Doveston
CHAMPAGNE

1824

Darwin had a little cry. Then uncorked the champagne.

It is a fact well known to those who know it well that the simple transference of a body of liquid from one place to the other can alter so many things. Or at least appear to.*

One half-hour after the champagne opening, Darwin was mellow once more. He and Jack peered over the rail and spat onto seagulls below.

'Look at the size of those mountains,' said Jack. 'They'd be the Him-a-ma-layas, they would.'

'And that would be Lhasa,' said Darwin, pointing, 'the

---

* *See* The Sprouts of Wrath, *available from Amazon in a Kindle edition, Far-Fetched Books, 2012. (R. R.)*

capital of Tibet, and that is the Potala Palace, where the Dalai Lama lives.'

'And *that*,' said Jack, all pointy-fingered, 'that there would be something *very* special.'

Darwin looked and Darwin saw and Darwin's mouth fell open.

In the distance, something monstrous swam. It was monstrous in size, not in nature, for it swam with grace and rolled with ease through the bright blue sky. The sunlight shimmered upon its sides, which shone with rainbow hues. And rising high upon it stood a castle formed from many many spires. Before this kingly castle was a noble courtyard proud with mighty statues, and in this courtyard stood a gushing fountain.

'Thar she blows!' cried a pirate from the crow's nest. 'Thar blows Skia the Sky Whale.'

33

he pirate ship approached the mighty sky whale.

Darwin stared in awe and shook his head.

Skia was vast. Surely the biggest creature that had ever lived. If indeed she *had* ever lived and was not the wistful conjuration of some deceased whale, a phantasm brought to reality within this Heavenly kingdom.

The sky whale was many times the length of the good ship *Venus*. In fact, she put Darwin in mind of the ill-fated *Empress of Mars*, an airship of improbable dimensions aboard which he had once travelled.

The whale was a beautiful thing to behold, with its shimmering flukes and its great fanned tail. And upon its back rose the castle, a fairy-tale construction of high towers, cupolas and minarets. Flags waved gaily, crystal windows reflected the sunlight and down in the courtyard, with its heroic statuary, the great fountain - which was Skia's blow-hole – cast watery rainbows skyward.

It was all too beautiful. Such nobility, such grandeur, such wonder. Darwin was enchanted.

'Harpoons at the ready!' The captain stumped along the

deck, waving his cutlass high. 'Steer us close, Mr Mate, and we'll have her.'

'No!' shouted Darwin. 'Do not even think of doing such a terrible thing.'

'We be pirates,' said the captain, 'and we be whalers, too. Are we not men? Show us such a beast as this and we must kill it. Be it already dead, *or not*. What say you, my bonny lads?'

His bonny lads said, 'Aye!'

'You must not kill this beautiful creature,' begged Darwin.

'You're not really cut out for a life of piracy, are you?' asked the captain, tapping a shanty-beat upon his wooden leg.

'No,' said Darwin. 'And I do not understand how you can kill things when they are already dead. Nor why you would wish to.'

'I told you – we're pirates. That's that. Harpoons at the ready, lads.' The captain turned his back.

'Ah,' said Darwin, who was not done yet. 'If you kill her she might sink.'

The captain paused.

'And if she sinks,' Darwin continued, 'then you will lose your treasure.'

And the captain turned back.

'Hold hard on those harpoons,' he told his crew.

'Aaaaaaw,' his crew replied.

'Take us in to the whale's back and we'll storm the castle.'

'No,' said Darwin. 'No. My monkeys might be in that castle. I do not want you doing any storming. We should just knock politely upon the door and they will probably let us in.'

Black Jack MacJackblack cocked his head. 'Do you be

issuing orders?' he asked. 'For as you may or may not know, pirates are notoriously treacherous and untrustworthy, and as we have now reached our destination and be almost in sight of our treasure, perhaps it's time for *you* to walk the plank.'

'What?' went Darwin, rightly appalled.

'It's *my* treasure, anyway,' muttered Jack.

'And I heard *that*,' cried the captain. 'Along the plank with the both of them, lads.'

The pirates fell upon Darwin and Jack.

Then came a terrible sound. It was a series of sounds really, a procession of sounds. A triad of sounds, to be precise. The first could be described as a 'muffled report'. The second a 'pronounced whistling', which grew inexorably louder and deeper. And the third an 'explosion proper' as a cannonball struck the mainmast, bringing it down upon the deck.

In chaos and confusion, pirates floundered and murmured then roared. Someone raised a spyglass and then shouted.

'Chickens on the starboard bow!' he shouted.

'Chickens?' Darwin, under much sailcloth, adopted the foetal position.

'*Chickens?*' bawled the captain. 'Man the cannon.'

The chickens' ship was very fine indeed, a four-masted hen-o'-war with two gun decks and a rear-mounted prang cannon. The ship was named the *Pride of Atlantis* and flew the infamous chicken ensign of double egg, chips and crossed bacon. The figurehead was a noble cock, as was indeed the captain, whose name was Speckley Jim.

The captain wore high-topped boots and spurs, a sleeveless golden-braided frock coat, gilded back adornments and the very latest in avian nautical wear, a quadracorn hat. Beneath a dextrous wing he carried his lucky fun-fur figure of Lop Lop, God of the Birds.

For seamen are notably superstitious and seagoing chickens even more so.

'Put another one across their bows, Master Mate,' called Captain Speckley Jim to a chicken whose full name was Henry Chirpy-Cheap-Cheap-Fancy McPenny-Cluck-Cluck—*

'Aye aye, Captain,' said a hen.

And another shot rang out.

'Fire!' yelled Captain Black Jack MacJackblack. Pirates fired their cannon.

'Come on, Darwin.' Young Jack uncovered the monkey. 'This is wonderful stuff. Pirates battling chickens – it doesn't get better than this.'

Darwin peeped over a gunwale. 'So even chickens secretly yearn to be pirates,' he said.

'Now, if I could be a pirate *King*,' said Jack, 'that would fulfil every wish, really, now *duck*.'

Darwin did not say, 'What duck?' for Darwin knew better than that. He ducked as a cannonball soared overhead, and ducked more as something exploded.

Captain Black Jack was at the ship's wheel, spinning it around and shouting out orders. Pirates were firing cannon and yelling abuse at the chickens. A cabin boy had appeared from somewhere† and was playing the concertina.

A mast went down on the hen-o'-war and the pirates cheered its falling.

The chickens' prang cannon poured forth fire and the pirates took to ducking.

'Prepare to board!' the captain called. Pirates thrust knives

---

* *There were several more paragraphs of this nonsense, but as they were neither funny nor clever, I have edited them out. (R. R.)*

† *A cabin, perhaps? (R. R.)*

between their teeth, cocked their pistols and 'ahhaar-harrhed' 'til they were almost blue in the face.

'I think I'll stay out of the actual hand-to-hand combat,' said Jack. 'We could climb up one of the remaining masts and watch it from there.'

Darwin shrugged, and as the good ship *Venus* slapped into the side of the *Pride of Atlantis* and the pirates swung onto the enemy ship in a manner not unlike that employed by monkeys, he and Jack did swarmings up a mast to watch the ensuing mêlée.

''Tis a fellow bold as would war with a hen,' as William Shakespeare put it. And the Bard of Avon knew of which he spoke, for history records that Shakespeare himself, when down upon his uppers, before rising to fame, had made a precarious living fighting chickens in one of the notorious cock pits of Chiswick.

When pirate fought chicken, the battle was bloody and brutal. The hackings and hewings were horrible. The slashings and slaughters were savage. The choppings of chickens and piercings of pirates were, as it happens, mightily cheered on by Jack and Darwin who, from the comparative safety of their lofty viewing point, were able to enjoy what must surely have been a unique spectacle.

Captain Black Jack engaged Captain Speckley Jim in swordplay. Up and down the decks they went amidst the battle royal. Feathers flew and bits of Black Jack also. Then the *Pride of Atlantis* burst into flames, which brought even more excitement.

'Who do you think will win?' Jack asked of Darwin.

The monkey gave himself a scratch and said, 'I do not think it will go well for us no matter which side wins. The pirates will make us walk the plank if *they* win. And as for the chickens, Heaven knows, if they win they will probably eat us.'

'Perhaps it would be better if we just quietly slipped away,' was Jack's suggestion.

Darwin had no objection to make regarding this.

'To the longboat,' said Jack, because pirate ships always *do* have a longboat. 'I will row us over to the sky whale whilst all the fuss and bother's going on.'

For the fuss and bother *was* going on by now in a most spectacular fashion, with chickens on fire and barrels of gunpowder exploding and pirates hacking away like mad and pirates *and* chickens falling off the *Pride of Atlantis* and Captain Black Jack giving a pretty good account of himself with the swordplay. And everything.

Jack lowered the longboat whilst Darwin looked on.*

'Come on,' called Jack, when the lowering was done. 'Let us make good our escape.'

Darwin joined Jack in the longboat and Jack put effort to the oars.

The sky whale wallowed in the air, all a-shimmer and spouting water up through the ornamental fountain.

Viewing this fountain, Darwin was caused to remark that he wondered just where the sky whale got its water from to spout, as it hung in empty air.

Jack replied that, given the ludicrous nature of all that was presently going on, did it *actually* matter?

Darwin agreed it did *not*.

Whales have rather friendly faces, as do dolphins and

---

* *It is a fact well known to those in nautical circles that it takes at least four strong men to lower a longboat. But given the ludicrous nature of the above narrative, it would be rather pointless to raise such an objection here. (R. R.)*

porpoises. They have big smiley mouths and charming expressions. Skia had lovely long eyelashes.

There was a harpoon in the longboat. Jack looked wistfully at it.

'We will beach the boat on Skia's tail,' said Darwin, and he showed his teeth to Jack.

As the longboat beached, Jack and Darwin found themselves ducking as two mighty explosions rent the air about them. Then down towards the Earth plunged wreckage of the good ship *Venus* and the *Pride of Atlantis*.

'And good riddance to *them*,' said Jack, and he smacked his palms together.

'I shall not miss them,' said Darwin. 'I hope though that they do not fall upon anyone and do them serious damage.'

Jack rolled his eyes and shook his head. 'Darwin,' he said, 'when things fall from this kingdom they change into rain, for they are made out of clouds, are they not?'

'Yes,' said Darwin. 'I suppose that they are.' And it pained him somewhat to say it, because by saying it he had to admit that *he* was now made out of clouds.

Jack looked up at the lofty castle and rubbed his hands together. '*My* castle,' he said to Darwin. 'And *my* treasure within.'

'There might be a little more to it than *that*,' said the adventurous ape. 'And if there isn't, don't forget about the magic egg you still have to lay.'

Which quite wiped the greedy smile from the face of Jack.

'Shall we go and knock on the castle door and see what happens?' Darwin asked.

Jack shrugged and nodded and offered Darwin his hand.

Together they wandered along the great back of Skia around the fairy-tale castle to the courtyard with its statuary and ornate fountain, which cast water skyward without a care for logic.

'Oh,' said Darwin, and he stopped.

'Why the oh–ing?' Jack asked.

'Look at the statues,' Darwin said, and Jack looked up at the statues.

The statues were of monkeys. Noble monkeys cast in noble poses. Darwin immediately recognised one that bore an uncanny resemblance to Michelangelo's *David*, but for the simian features and tail.

And *that* one, by the Egyptian garb, was clearly the Ape of Thoth. Others wore togas and laurel wreaths. Others drove chariots, pulled, it appeared, by chickens.

Darwin gaped from statue to statue, finding each most satisfactory.

'I'll have all those pulled down,' said Jack. 'Have lots made of me, chopping pirates' heads off and doing daring deeds.'

'Or laying an egg?' said Darwin.

Jack put on his grumpy face. 'Let's knock at the door,' said he.

The door was huge, as a castle door should be. But it had a little door in the lower left-hand corner, which had upon it a brass knocker imaginatively fashioned into the shape of a monkey's head. Jack took this knocker and rapped three times with it.

Hollow echoes were returned from within.

Jack knocked again and many times more, but only received further echoes.

Darwin put his ear to the door and also took to sniffing. 'Perhaps they have gone off for a boat trip or something,' he said.

Jack gave the little door a kick. The little door eased open.

Darwin peeped inside. 'It does smell vaguely of monkey,' he said.

'But not of lions, or dragons, or monsters?'

Darwin shook his little hairy head.

'Treasure, here I come,' said Jack, pushing into the castle.

34

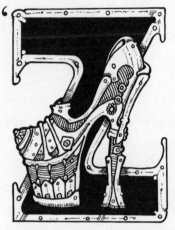‘oos smell just like this,’ said Jack, taking a sniff of the air. ‘I will have to get my servants to spray eau de cologne all about the place.’

Darwin was sniffing and peering as well. ‘I do not think that my monkeys have been here for a very long time,’ he said, rather sadly.

‘Where is the treasure room?’ asked Jack.

Darwin shook his head.

They stood now in the great hall of the castle. Its walls dwindled towards a ceiling hidden in shadows. Moth-eaten tabards hung upon fusty columns. An enormous oil portrait that might have been of Darwin peeled paint and the flagstones were velvet with the dust of long ages.

Darwin sighed and Jack kicked up the dust.

‘I do not understand this,’ said the educated ape. ‘We were sent on a questing adventure to deliver a magic egg—’

‘Will you *please* stop going on about the egg!’

‘There is surely, though, a purpose,’ said Darwin. ‘Some reason why we are here.’

‘I am here for my treasure,’ said Jack. ‘I am sure you’ll

agree that I've earned it. *You* might make yourself useful by tidying up and getting the kettle on.'

Darwin settled down upon a worm-eaten banqueting table. 'There *must* be a purpose,' said he.

'There is no purpose to anything,' said Jack. 'We are born, we live, we die. Some of us are lucky in life, some of us are not. But it's all we get and we have to make the most of it.'

'And now neither you nor I has a life,' said Darwin, 'for we are dead together.'

'If this is Heaven, it will do,' said Jack. 'I was a nobody when I was alive, a servant to be pushed up chimneys. If I am to be rewarded here by being a prince, I have no complaints to make. No complaints at all.'

'You paint a sad picture of life,' said Darwin, 'and I myself can vouch for the truth of what you say. I am a monkey and a monkey receives *no* respect from men. Although . . .'

'Although?' asked Jack.

'Although I have made more friends than enemies and known more love than hate. A noble lord once told me that a person's life has meaning if, when they come to the end of it, they can truly say that they tried during their life to make the world just a little bit better than it was when they came into it.'

'I think I understand that,' said Jack. 'Although you might perhaps have put it better.'

'I am only a monkey,' said Darwin.

Jack nodded thoughtfully.

'But I did my best. I *did* do my best. I did try to make the world a better place to be.'

'Which is why you've come to Heaven, like me,' said Jack. 'We are both very wonderful people. Except for you, because you are a monkey.'

'Have you ever wondered,' Darwin asked, 'what it would

be like for you to open your mouth and have something nice come out of it?'

Jack gave this a moment of thought. 'Not really,' was his reply.

'I wonder what might happen if you did.'

'I would probably cry,' said Jack. 'Life has treated me *very* badly indeed, and so if I find myself unable to spread sweetness and light all around, I don't think I should be wholly blamed for it.'

'New experiences can sometimes be edifying,' said Darwin.

'That is called a platitude,' said Jack. 'Platitudes are often offered by the rich to the poor because of course they do not cost anything. The poor would prefer to be offered bread.'

Darwin looked long and hard at Jack.

Darwin looked all around and about at the hall.

Darwin had a thoughtful scratch at his fleas and then said, 'Say something nice, Jack.'

'No,' said Jack. 'I won't.'

'I really think you should,' said Darwin. 'In fact, I know that you should.'

Jack kicked out at a tumbled stool, and the tumbled stool crumbled to dust.

'Say something nice,' said Darwin, his voice echoing all around the great, dusty room.

'Why should I?' Jack asked.

'Because I have a theory,' said Darwin. 'I have reasoned something out, the way my partner Cameron Bell reasons things out. I think I have found a solution, and if you indulge me, I think that you might find yourself pleasantly surprised.'

Jack gave Darwin the queerest of expressions. 'Whatever are you on about?' he asked.

'Just say something nice. *Anything. Something.*'

256

'Just say something nice?'

'Please, Jack.'

'All right,' said Jack, and he took a deep breath. 'I am very nice,' he said.

'Not about yourself,' said Darwin. 'That is not going to work.'

Jack did exasperated sighings. Then he gazed down at his boots and mumbled.

'What did you say?' asked Darwin.

Jack mumbled some more.

'Please speak up.'

'I said,' said Jack, 'that I like you.'

'Oh,' said Darwin. 'Thank you.'

'I think you are a very nice monkey,' said Jack. 'And I am sorry that you died. I know it's all my fault. And I thank you for being nice to me. And you are the best friend that I have ever had.'

'Well,' said Darwin. 'Why, thank you – that *is* very nice.'

'I've never had a friend before,' said Jack. 'I like you *very very* much.'

Then Jack said suddenly, 'Oooh.'

Darwin looked on at Jack.

'Oooh,' went Jack again, and louder, and this time he clutched at his stomach. 'Oooh!' he continued, very much in the same vein, but growing ever in volume. 'Ooooooh. It's coming. It's coming. I'm going to lay the egg!'

To go into the actual details of the actual laying would not, perhaps, be appropriate here. There were certainly comedic aspects, for Darwin was in no time rocking with laughter and had to flee to a high place to avoid a punching from Jack.

But that the egg was definitely bigger when it came out than when it went in, of this there can be no doubt.

And that when the laying was finally, after quite a lengthy process, actually achieved, Darwin had come near to wetting himself from mirth and Jack had many tears of his own in his eyes.

Silence came once more to the ancient hall.

Then, 'Oh,' groaned Jack, and, 'What the Hell is *that*?'

For what he had given birth to was other than an egg. It appeared to be a crystal sphere that glittered from within.

Darwin gazed down from his lofty retreat. 'Is that a diamond?' he asked.

'Is it *treasure*?' Jack peered at the sphere. It was pure, unsullied, untainted by organic nastiness. It twinkled and shone and it did look valuable.

Jack looked up at Darwin and said, 'It was you who made this happen.'

'No,' said Darwin, climbing down. 'It was *you*. Because you said something nice. You sort of purged yourself, Jack.' And, 'Ooh,' the ape continued, as something rather wonderful was happening. A bright light sprang from the crystal sphere. A bright and colourful light that spread like a rainbow, radiating outwards. Jack stepped nimbly back as the light spread beneath his feet, sweeping away the dust and bringing a polish to the flagstones. Then up the table, drawing brightness of colour from dull and faded fabrics and wood, restoring the crumbled stool and setting it upright. Then over the floor and up the walls, washing away the drabness and gloom, returning all to cleanliness and colour.

And then appeared the monkeys.

They wore royal robes, comporting themselves in dignified manners. Gentle-monkeys bowing to lady apes, flourishing fine lace handkerchiefs, picking at wonderful viands that now appeared on the table.

An orchestra of monkeys materialised in a minstrels' gallery.

Monkey ladies in crinolines danced the waltz.

A monkey king bowed low and tipped his crown to Jack.

A monkey queen took Darwin by the hand.

And they danced.

With a whirl and a fluster of regal stuffs.
With well-turned ankles and silken shoes.
With pearl-drop earrings and fine lace ruffs.
With purples and pinks and royal blues.

With diamonds set in quilted cuffs.
With turn along, cut out along, down along dee.
With sippings of champagnes and takings of snuff.
With many a floral frippery.

The music swelled and rare perfumes filled the air to mingle with those of fabulous foodstuffs, Treacle Sponge Bastard and pan-fried bananas in honey.

The dancers danced, the diners dined, shy faces peeped from behind fluttering fans and Darwin felt that he had never seen or experienced anything quite so absolutely wonderful in all of his little life.

'Oh, Jack,' said Darwin. 'It was *you* who made this happen.'

Jack was sipping champagne and chewing banana.

He just shook his head and mouthed the word, 'How?'

The music ceased and the dancers bowed and curtsied. Polite applause rippled as a dandified monkey bowed low.

'Prince Jack,' called a voice.

And Jack glanced about and said, 'What?'

'Prince Jack,' said the King of the Monkeys. 'And Great-Father Darwin, too.'

Darwin smiled at his monkeys. For him it had been only days since he had seen them last. For them it had been many many centuries.

'I am very happy to be here, sire,' said Darwin. 'You all look so very marvellous. So refined.'

'You taught us the ways of Man whilst we travelled together aboard the *Marie Lloyd*.'

'What of *this*?' asked Jack. But all ignored him.

'And now you have brought us a prince,' said the King.

'Yes, that's me,' said Jack. 'Prince Jack is my name.'

'And you shall be welcomed into our family.'

Jack gave a shrug. 'You are all very nice,' said he.

Darwin grinned as Jack said this, because Darwin felt he knew what would happen next.

'Are you happy, Jack?' asked the King.

'I am very happy, your majesty,' said the lad.

'Then so it must be. Magician,' the King called out, and an ape in magician's robes got up and stepped forward.

'Do what must be done,' said the King.

'What of this?' said Jack.

The monkey magician raised his magical wand, then brought it down in a flurry of sparkles . . .

. . . and Jack turned into a monkey.

35

'arwin, wake up.' Somebody poked at the ape.

'Darwin, please.' Darwin was rattled about. 'Please.'

And Darwin opened his eyes and blinked.

'Mr Bell?' said Darwin. 'Is that you, Mr Bell?'

'More to the point, is that you?'

Darwin tried to rise, but something held him down. He focused his eyes and glanced about and then became confused. He was in some kind of bed, but it was unlike any bed he had previously inhabited. It was a disc and he appeared to be hovering slightly above it. And there were queer things all about. Shiny things of burnished metal. Things with tubes and dials and little screens. And above, the ceiling was not flat. The entire room looked like a great big dome.

'Where am I?' asked Darwin. 'Was I asleep?'

'You are in the year three thousand,' said Mr Bell, who wore some kind of strange and silvery suit.

'The year three thousand?' Darwin said.

'The year three thousand. Not a lot has changed. Although they do live underwater.'

Darwin breathed in sterilised air. 'Then I did *not* die,' said he.

'Ah,' said Mr Bell. 'Regarding *that*.'

Darwin dragged himself into a seated position. He felt very odd indeed, as if his body was a suit of clothes that did not entirely fit him.

'Regarding *that*?' he asked Mr Bell.

'You were dead,' said Mr Cameron Bell. 'Very dead indeed, I am sad to say.'

'And you did *what*? Brought me back from the dead? What am I now – a zombie?'

'No no no.' Mr Bell did shakings of the head. 'You are yourself, I think. You are a clone.'

Darwin gave himself a scratch. 'What is a clone?' he asked.

'I will do my best to explain,' said Mr Bell, and he sat himself down upon the disc above which Darwin appeared to float. 'It was a dreadful business,' he said. 'A dreadful business indeed. I left you alone at the Flying Swan with a note expressing that you should *not* leave the premises and that a carriage would collect you at nine o'clock the following day.'

'I do remember *that*,' said Darwin.

'But you *did* leave the premises, and when the carriage came you were not there.'

'No, I suppose I was not,' said Darwin.

'Because, according to witnesses, you and a young chimney-sweep boy climbed up the spire of Saint Joan's Church in Brentford and then threw yourselves off.'

'It was not quite like that,' said Darwin, 'but sadly it amounted very much to the same thing.'

'I arrived back in Brentford that evening to search for you, and that was when I learned what had happened. I was told that your body had been taken to Syon House because they thought you must be an escaped ape from the monkey sanctuary. It was all beyond awful, Darwin. When I got there, they were about to stick your body into the incinerator.'

'Oh dear me,' said Darwin.

'I wrapped you up,' said Mr Bell, and a tear came to his eye. 'Wrapped you up and took you back to the *Marie Lloyd* and put you in the refridgetorium.'

Darwin shivered.

'Quite so. But what else could I do? I thought I would give you a decent burial. But then something did not make any sense to me. If you were dead, then how could you, as a very old monkey, travel back to the eighteen nineties to be shot dead by Lord Brentford?'

'I thought we had given up on asking those sorts of questions,' said Darwin.

'Ah,' said Mr Bell. 'It is definitely you.'

'So what happened next?'

'Well, I thought of the future and it set me to thinking that in the future there would be great steps forward made in medicine. Perhaps the folk of the future had even conquered death.'

'And have they?' Darwin asked.

'No,' said Cameron Bell. 'On the contrary. They have simply come up with more efficient ways of *causing* death.'

'And they live underwater?'

'Something to do with something known as the greenhouse effect.'

'Is that to do with growing bananas?' asked the ape.

'Sadly not. But to continue. I stopped off again and again but to no avail. Finally I got this far into the future and here they have mastered cloning. Which actually is a way of almost conquering death.'

'Tell me all about it,' said Darwin.

And Mr Bell went on to explain. 'I think it had much to do with a moving picture called *Jurassic Park*,' he explained. 'You need the blood of the subject, and from this you extract the DNA, and then—'*

Some time later Darwin said, 'That all sounds rather unlikely.'

Mr Bell raised his eyebrows.

'Fair enough, then,' said Darwin. And he scratched at himself once again.

'You still have fleas?' asked Mr Bell.

'Why should I not?' asked Darwin.

'Well, I just explained to you all about the cloning process.' Mr Bell now shrugged. 'But if you still have them, then I suppose they must almost be a part of you now, somehow. And I am told that the cloning process improves the subject being cloned.'

'I do feel a little different,' said Darwin.

'Then so, I suppose, must your fleas. In fact, they may now have become super-fleas, as it were.'

'I am rather hungry,' said Darwin. 'And I would at least care for a pair of trousers to wear.'

'Good old Darwin,' said Cameron Bell. 'How wonderful to have you back.'

'It is wonderful to be back,' said the ape. 'It was not too bad being dead, but I would far rather be alive.'

And I thanked Mr Bell (for now I return to 'First Monkey'), and I told him that I was very grateful that he had gone to so much trouble to bring me back to life.

'What is a friend for?' said Mr Bell. Which was a rhetorical question and I gave him a hug.

* *And we all know how it works. In theory. (R. R.)*

We lunched in a big refractory dome. And this one too was underwater and transparent, too, so we could see the big fish swimming above.

They put me in mind of the sky whale and I told my friend all about the adventures that I had become involved in after I had died.

Mr Bell listened with interest, but also tucked into his lunch. He had lost none of his appetite and I was glad for that. And of course *he* had survived his encounter with Arthur Knapton, the Pearly Emperor, at the Crystal Palace in eighteen fifty-one, and I was very glad for that, too.

'So,' I said, when I had done with eating, 'it has all been a most extraordinary business and I for one am glad it is over and done with. Now we can return to eighteen twenty-four and finally enjoy Beethoven conducting the Ninth.'

Mr Bell drew breath and stared at me.

'Ah,' said he, and he made a thoughtful face.

'You did defeat Arthur Knapton, did you not?'

Mr Bell made a slightly more thoughtful face.

'You didn't, did you?' I said.

Mr Bell made so-so movements with his hands and fingers.

'He is still on the loose, isn't he?'

Mr Bell nodded sadly.

'Tell me the worst,' I said.

And Mr Bell did.

'As you will know,' said Mr Bell, 'when I set out to solve a case, I do so with precision and an eye for the finest detail. I leave nothing to chance, I am scrupulous, I am exact, I—'

'And I will have to stop you there,' I said, 'because, as *you* have said, you did *not* apprehend Mr Arthur Knapton.'

'It was not for the want of trying,' said Mr Bell, 'and not for lack of skills upon my part.'

'Did you blow up the Crystal Palace?' I asked.

Mr Bell made that thoughtful face once more.

'Did you save Queen Victoria from assassination, Mr Bell?'

'Yes, I did that,' said himself.

'But at some cost to the capital of the British Empire?'

'Certain landmarks that were there are no longer there,' my friend confessed, and then he went on to tell me the whole story.

It certainly did not lack for excitement, nor for ingenuity upon the part of my friend. Indeed, he came up with several ploys and stratagems which I have no hesitation in saying had to be unique in the field of crime solution. The business regarding Her Majesty the Queen and the see-through aspidistra plant was little less than inspired. And his employment of radio waves during the period he spent in suspended animation, prior to erecting the full-size facsimile of the Forth Bridge, was a work of genius.

I must emphasise my admiration for the way he dealt with the conundrum of the Greek lady-boy and the travelling rhinoceros impersonator. And his bravery when confronted by quite so many fire-walkers whilst he foiled the evil intentions of the psychic triplets should have earned him the Order of the Garter at the very least.

I oooohed and aaaahed and applauded when he spoke of how he dug the underground tunnels and perfected the means to walk upside down on the ceiling. And his description of how he confounded the army of killer ants was so funny that I was hard-pressed to keep my luncheon down.

'But you did not catch Arthur Knapton?' I said, when he paused to take breath and drink water.

'Not as such,' replied my friend. 'But let me tell you about the countess and the sentient trifle.'

And so it went on for some time. I would have liked, of course, to have related my friend's tale in full here. But as I lacked for pen and paper when he told it, I did not take it all down in detail, so I would hesitate to repeat it from memory lest I neglect some salient detail or miscount the number of dwarves.

And as, of course, I was *not* personally involved in these particular adventures, I would not wish to 'inflict' them upon the unsuspecting reader.*

'But you did *not* catch Arthur Knapton,' I said, when all was said and done.

'Regretfully, no,' said my friend, a-shaking his head. 'But I am confident that I will next time.' Mr Bell lowered his voice and added, 'Because I will *have to* next time.'

'What was that?' I said.

'Next time will be the last time,' said Cameron Bell. 'The very last time to stop him. If I fail next time, then that is that.'

'And we can go and see Beethoven?'

Mr Bell shook his head once more. 'If I get it wrong next time, it will be all up for us and we will never travel any-where through time again.'

'But we have agreed that I must,' I said, 'because I must die by both barrels of Lord Brentford's fowling piece.'

'If I fail,' said Mr Bell, 'then *all* will be confounded.'

'Please explain what you mean by that,' I said.

'Recall how I told you that Arthur Knapton escaped in the pedal-driven ornithopter that was hidden inside the artificial elephant?'

* *Outrageous! (R. R.)*

'And you pursued him by means of an improvised rocket pack comprising two fire extinguishers?'

'Quite so. Well, it was during our confrontation on London Bridge—'

'Which you blew up.'

'That was not entirely my fault. Regardless, it was during this confrontation that he cursed me for foiling his plans to assassinate Her Majesty and plant himself upon the throne of England, and he vowed to take a terrible revenge upon my person and upon all the people of England.'

'Oh dear, oh dear,' I said to Mr Bell. 'You certainly got him riled.'

Mr Bell chewed on his bottom lip. 'Well, he vowed a terrible vengeance,' he said. 'For eighteen eighty-five.'

'That year rings a bell,' said I.

'It should,' said Mr Bell, 'because it is the year that the Martians invaded Earth.'

'And failed,' I said, 'because we all know what happens to Martians on Earth – they die from Earthly bacteria. That is called an Eternal Verity, by the way – something we simply know to be true, cos it is.'

'Indeed,' said Cameron Bell. 'Except this time, in eighteen eighty-five, the Martians will *not* fall prey to Earthly bacteria. Because this time those Martians will all be inoculated with penicillin by Mr Arthur Knapton, Pearly Emperor and apparently also King of Mars.'

'Oh your dear dead mother,' I said.

'Oh my dear dead mother indeed,' said Mr Cameron Bell.

36

‘n eighteen eighty-five,’ said Mr Bell, ‘I was a student at Oxford. Happily, the Martians never laid waste to the country that far north.’

‘Well, they will this time,’ I said, ‘if we are unable to stop them.’

‘Bravo, Darwin,’ said my friend, and he patted me on the shoulder. ‘I knew you would not let me down. In for a penny, in for a pound, as it might be.’

If we had inhabited the pages of a comic book, I am certain that a question mark would have formed above my head at this moment. ‘What do you mean by *that*?’ I asked Mr Bell.

‘You volunteered yourself without being asked by me,’ he replied. ‘You said, "If *we* are unable to stop them." ’

‘Well, stop them *we* must,’ I said.

And we shook hands upon *that*.

We returned to the *Marie Lloyd* and within her we travelled back in time.

‘Would it be presumptuous of me to ask,’ I ventured, ‘whether you have any plan of campaign whatsoever germinating, as it might be, as some seedling in your mind?’

Mr Bell was opening champagne. 'I plan to share *this* with you,' he replied.

'And then?'

'A bath and some sleep. I will cogitate upon these pressing matters. I will not let you down this time, I promise you.'

I gave myself a scratch and said, 'I trust you.'

'But tell me,' said my friend as he poured champagne for me, 'how do you feel in yourself? How *do* you feel?'

'I feel very well indeed,' I said, 'and glad to be once more alive. Being dead was not so bad, but I prefer life any time.' I took my champagne. We clinked our glasses. I toasted Mr Bell.

'So,' said he. 'To eighteen eighty-five.'

In the early months of that momentous year, the man of the hour was that fearless explorer, big-game hunter and pioneer of the air Colonel James Richardson-Brown. Lionised by high society, admired by ladies and envied by men, Colonel James had slashed his way through the jungles of darkest Africa in search of lost cities, bagged lions on the plains of the Serengeti and taken potshots at aerial kraken from the bewickered basket of a hot-air balloon. His lectures at the Egyptian Hall, Piccadilly, were given before packed audiences with the assistance of his *amour* and travelling companion, that silken lovely Miss Defy, a winsome creature of proven courage and outstanding natural beauty.

Together they reflected the glory of the British Empire and personified all that was *right* with the world.

Mr Cameron Bell had, in his youth, been a great admirer of Colonel James Richardson-Brown, and, it had to be said, a solitary worshipper of the gorgeous Miss Defy.* It seemed

---

* *It is quite clear what Darwin means by this, but it is best not dwelt upon. (R. R.)*

natural therefore to my friend that he should seek out this hero and heroine of the Empire and enlist their help to protect the realm from the forthcoming Martian invasion.

I landed the *Marie Lloyd* at night, to the rear of the Bell family home in Kent, switched off the ignition and hung the key once more about my neck.

Then to be assailed by a dreadful odour.

'Whatever is *that*?' I asked in dismay. 'Has something died hereabouts?'

'That's quite enough of *that*,' said Mr Bell, who was as always impeccably dressed. Impeccably dressed but smelling (as I believe the phrase goes) like a tart's handbag in summer.

'It is eau de cologne,' said my friend, wafting his fragrance in my direction.

'It is awful,' I told him.

'To *you* it is.' Mr Bell did dustings at his dust-free lapels. 'It is not concocted to attract those of the simian species. Ladies, I am told, find it quite irresistible.'

'Ladies?' I queried. 'And who told you this?'

Mr Bell gave a little throat-clearing cough. 'Aaaaagter Cxrronay,' he said.

'I did not quite catch that,' I said.

'Aleister Crowley,' said my friend. 'It is composed from civet, ambergris and musk – ladies adore it.'

'Ah,' I said, and, 'All becomes clear. You are thinking to entrance this Miss Defy woman with your godless perfume?'

Mr Bell's face became tomato red.

'It just will not do,' said I to Mr Bell.

'I know my own business best,' said himself.

'No,' I said. 'It will *not* do. It is far too late in the story to suddenly introduce a "love interest". Or, I would argue, even a "strong lead female". I do not think we have encountered a single woman throughout the entire course of our adventures. And whilst this is inconceivable and will certainly preclude Nineteenth Century Fox from wishing to acquire the film rights, some might argue that we have created the very first "buddy book".'

Mr Bell's mouth opened and closed but no sounds came from it. When finally they did, they came in words to the effect that breaking down the fourth wall was not a good thing, and I should for the remaining pages of the adventure keep such thoughts to myself.

I shrugged and nodded. 'You smell very nice,' I said to Mr Bell.

'That is much better. So, dress for a day in the city. Bring some light armaments, and if you are thinking to do something witty, such as smearing the soles of your shoes with dung, do *not!*'

'As if I *would*,' I said to Mr Bell, and repaired to my cabin and my wardrobe.

An hour later, moonlight found us in an acquired carriage, pulled by an acquired horse and travelling in the direction of central London.

'Colonel Richardson-Brown will be signing copies of his latest best-selling epistle *The Life of the Air Kraken* at Foyles* this evening, with a champagne reception later at The Ritz.'

'I do like champagne.' I smacked my lips. 'And I do very much like The Ritz.'

'Then you will find the evening very much to your liking. I must convince the colonel and his lovely lady –' and Mr Bell's cheeks coloured once more '– of the reality of the forthcoming Martian invasion. This will not be easy.'

* *Foyles, the discerning reader will have realised, did not open until 1903. But given all that has gone before, do we really care? (R. R.)*

'You could show them your ray gun, or even give them a guided tour around the *Marie Lloyd*.'

'If it proves necessary, then so it must be.' Mr Bell had a very intense expression on his face and I could see that he was a very worried man. This was hardly surprising, really, because it was after all *his* abortive attempt to capture Arthur Knapton at the Great Exhibition of eighteen fifty-one which had caused that rotter to vow terrible vengeance and unleash his bacteriologically immune Martians upon the world. Mr Bell must certainly have been feeling some guilt and some consternation. I have to say that *I* did not feel particularly confident.

We drove on in silence.

It was wonderful to be back in London. So much was exactly as I had remembered it. Certainly, as this *was* eighteen eighty-five, the great city lacked for the tall Tesla towers which broadcast electricity across the Empire's capital without the need for cables, and none of the back-engineered technology gained from the abandoned Martian spaceships was in evidence. No mighty airships passed overhead, no electric hansoms purred by. But it *was* London. *My* London. Mine and Mr Bell's, and we were glad to see it again. Although we worried for its survival.

'You had best exhibit discretion regarding your vocal capabilities,' said my friend. 'And you *do* look *very* smart and smell *very* nice.'

'Carbolic soap,' I said to Mr Bell. 'Clean in body and thought and deed. That is me.'

'Quite so.'

There was quite a queue outside Foyles, of lords and ladies dressed in the height of fashion. The lords affected noble poses, shoulders back and chins thrust upwards. The ladies fluttered fans before their faces. As well they might, given the preponderance of male perfume that burdened the evening air.

Mr Bell did not, of course, have an entrance ticket. He did, however, have his handshake and his imagination. And without a by your leave from myself, he lifted me suddenly into his arms, shouted, 'Exotic animal delivery for Colonel Richardson-Brown,' and pressed his way to the front of the queue. Where he employed his handshake.

We had very good seats, right at the front, and I thoroughly enjoyed the lecture. There was no doubt that the colonel was an extremely good-looking and charismatic young man, or that the astonishing Miss Defy was anything less than adorable.

But as the colonel's tales continued, tales of adventure and bravery and derring-do, growing ever in extravagance and wonder, I began to smell something that was not composed of civet, ambergris and musk.

I began to smell a rat.

'Mr Bell,' I whispered to my friend. 'I do believe that the colonel is, how shall I put this, being a little economical with the truth.'

The colonel was at this moment holding forth about his encounters with a yeti on the slopes of Kangchenjunga. And miming the employment of a martial art he named as Dimac to demonstrate how he had saved the lives of numerous Sherpas, to then be carried shoulder-high to their village where he was immediately added to the pantheon of Tibetan Gods.

Mr Bell shushed me and sighed. I noted a rather foolish expression spread over his face. It was clear that he had eyes and ears for none but Miss Defy.

The book signing went almost without incident. My appearance at the signing table in the arms of Mr Bell occasioned Miss Defy to draw out a derringer and express a wish to 'bag' me.

I enjoyed the champagne and The Ritz, though.

Mr Bell and I dwelt on the outskirts of the crowd.

'You do know,' I whispered to my friend, 'that he makes most of this stuff up. I will wager you he's never travelled further south than Brighton.'

Mr Bell did chewings at his lip. 'I have made my observations of the colonel,' he said, 'and have drawn certain conclusions of my own.'

'Such as that his complexion is not "tanned by the relentless sun of the Sahara" as he averred, but tinted by coconut oil from Boots the Chemist?'

'Harsh,' said Mr Bell. 'But true. That Miss Defy is a beautiful woman, don't you think?'

'Enchanting,' I said. 'But do you *really* believe these people can actually help us?'

'Trust me,' said Mr Bell.

And I trusted him.

Presently the champagne was done and in ones and twos the gentry drifted away. Eventually all that remained were the colonel and his small entourage: publisher, publicist, broken-nosed guardian and his lovely companion.

And us.

'Colonel,' said Mr Bell, marching up to the colonel and offering a smart and faultless salute.

'At ease,' said the colonel, giving some kind of salute in reply. Then, sighting me, he continued, 'Chap with the ape, do keep that under control.'

Mr Bell ignored this slight. 'I have an urgent matter to discuss,' said he. 'The future of the Empire rests upon it.'

'Future of the Empire, eh?' The adventurous author tugged out his pocket watch. 'Can give you a couple of mins, I suppose. Spit it out.'

'A private matter,' said Mr Bell.

'No secrets here,' said the colonel.

Mr Bell leaned forwards and whispered certain words into the colonel's ear. I was not privy to these words, but I assumed that Mr Bell had drawn something incriminating from his observation of the colonel and was making the hint that this incriminating something might well be publicised should the colonel not deign to offer him a private audience.

The colonel coughed and flustered. 'Best come up to my rooms,' said he. 'We will discuss these matters in private.'

'Do bring your charming companion,' said Mr Bell. 'I have every intention of bringing *mine*.'

And so we adjourned to the colonel's suite of rooms.

Where interesting things occurred.

37

'ou are a hero of the Empire,' said Mr Cameron Bell. 'And you, madam, too, are possessed of heroic qualities to the degree that you are idolised.' Mr Bell bowed low to the lovely Miss Defy.

We were sipping the chilled champagne that Mr Bell had ordered and sitting in the luxurious lounge room of the colonel's suite at The Ritz.

The wallpaper was Chinese, the coffee tables Turkish, the champagne from the south of France and the bananas from the Temperate House in Kew Gardens. And none of us gave a fig for the fact that The Ritz was not built until the twentieth century.

Mr Bell, who, in my personal opinion, had indulged in rather too much champagne, was on his feet and holding forth with vigour.

'You are,' he continued, topping up his glass as he did so, 'two of the most famous and feted people in all of the British Empire.'

Miss Defy smiled coyly.

Colonel Richardson-Brown just nodded his head.

'And so it is fit and proper,' my friend went on, 'that the two of you play a part, a *leading* part – leading *parts*, indeed – in the drama that lies ahead.'

'What, precisely, is the nature of this drama?' asked the colonel, availing himself of the champagne and splashing some into the glass of Miss Defy.

'In a word, or indeed several,' said Mr Bell, 'Mars is about to invade the planet Earth.'

'*Mars?*' The colonel laughed as he refilled his own glass. 'I can assure you, sir,' said he, 'that the chances of anything coming from Mars are a million to one.'

'But still they will come,' said Mr Cameron Bell.

'And how would *you* know this?'

I wondered whether Mr Bell might answer this by saying, 'Because it is all my fault.'

But he did not.

'I am employed by the Ministry of Serendipity,' said my friend, 'and it is the job of the Ministry to know such things.'

'Indeed,' said the colonel. 'Naturally, I have heard of this Ministry. It is rumoured that it is the real power behind Victoria's throne.'

'So it is rumoured,' agreed Mr Bell. 'And the Ministry has sent me here to enlist you in the fight against the Martians.'

The colonel shifted in his chair, in my opinion, somewhat uncomfortably.

'In what capacity?' he asked. 'And will this be a paid position?'

'I think you will be able to make it pay,' said Mr Cameron Bell. 'It will need to be *written up*, as it were.'

'Ah,' said the colonel. 'You wish me to chronicle events. I understand.'

'Not entirely.' Mr Bell shook his head. Which appeared to make him rather giddy, and so he had to sit down.

'Not entirely, eh? Well, listen to me, my dear fellow. You whispered certain things into my ear downstairs which had you marked in my book as a potential blackmailer. But now you give me some old guff about Martians attacking the Earth and it is quite clear to me that you are an escaped lunatic, or some such.'

'All right,' said Mr Bell. 'Let us bandy no more words and waste no more time. I am a consulting detective and I draw inferences through close observation. You, sir, are *not* a colonel. Never have been one, never will be one. You have never fought a yeti with your bare hands alone. Nor have you slain a Jabberwock by piercing its skull with a sharpened pencil projected from a blowpipe fashioned from a rolled pound note. You are neither an explorer nor a big-game hunter. You, sir, are a writer of fiction.'

'I . . . but—' the colonel huffed and puffed.

'And your name is *not* James Richardson-Brown,' Mr Bell continued, 'but Herbert George Wells. Or H. G. Wells, as history will know and love you, should you hearken to my words.'

I was, to say the least, most surprised.

I gaped at Mr Bell.

The lovely Miss Defy now rose to her feet. She rose upon very tall and slender boot-heels and glared at Mr Bell.

'Sir,' said she, and she stamped a foot. 'Sir, you have offended me with your words.'

'They are, nonetheless, true,' said my friend.

'True or not, you will never live to spread them around and about.' With that said, she drew out her derringer and aimed it at Mr Bell.

'Fair lady—' said he.

'Be quiet,' said she. 'You are a spoilsport and we have no time for you.'

'Oh no, dearest lady,' replied Mr Bell. 'You have me entirely wrong. I understand why you do what you do. You present your wonderful personas to the public, bringing thrills and glamour into their lives. There is no harm to be had in this and I wish you no ill for it. You make the world a better place with your tall-tale tellings.'

'Being an author can at times be rather dull,' said Mr H. G. Wells. 'One hankers sometimes to live the life of the hero one writes about.'

'I quite understand,' said my friend.

'I think I will still shoot you dead,' said the glamorous lady. 'It is *our* secret, Herbie's and mine. Herbie has many exciting adventures to tell.'

'I am well aware of that,' said Mr Bell. 'I particularly enjoyed his book *The Invisible Man.*'

'The invisible *what*?' asked H. G. Wells.

'Ah,' said Mr Bell. 'That's right. You won't publish that until eighteen ninety-seven.'

'What?' went Mr Wells.

'And of course you will be publishing the Sherlock Holmes stories at that time.'

'Sherlock *who*?' asked H. G. Wells.

'Excuse me,' I said to Mr Bell, 'but as you know full well, Sir Arthur Conan Doyle wrote – or should I say *will* write – the Sherlock Holmes books.'

There was a sudden silence in that suite of rooms.

'How did you do *that*?' asked H. G. Wells. 'Ventriloquism, is it?'

'His name is Darwin,' said my friend, 'and he is an ape of exceptional capabilities.'

'And I know who wrote the Sherlock Holmes books,' I said.

'Mr Wells will,' said Cameron Bell.

I shook my head. 'He will *not*.'

'Oh yes he will,' said Mr Bell, 'under the pen name of Sir Arthur Conan Doyle. H. G. Wells and Sir Arthur are one and the same person.'

'Well, I never did,' I said, as I *did not*.

'I think that monkey is actually speaking,' said Miss Defy, and she aimed her derringer at me.

'Sweet lady,' said Mr Bell, stepping between the upraised weapon and myself, 'we are wandering – rather dangerously, I hasten to add – off the topic. I require the assistance of both of you if I am to have any hope of defeating the Martians.'

'You *personally*?' asked Miss Defy.

'It is a personal quest. Something that *I* must do.'

'But there aren't any Martians,' said Mr Wells. 'Not really. Although it would make for a good story. *Battle of the Planets*, it might be called.'

'Or *War of the Worlds*?' I suggested.

'Even better. *War of the Worlds* it is, then.' H. G. Wells smiled upon me. 'How *do* you do that?' he asked Mr Bell.

'They *will* come,' said Mr Bell. 'Even now they will be preparing warships and armoured tripods—'

'Let me write all this down,' said Mr Wells.

'Your country needs *you*!' cried Mr Bell, and he pointed at the author, who was searching for a pencil. Possibly the one which had proved lethal to a Jabberwock.

'Let us say I do believe you,' said Mr Wells.

'Let us say that *I* do *not*,' said Miss Defy.

'But *if* we *did*,' said Mr Wells, 'then what could *we* actually do?'

'I require your assistance,' said Mr Bell. 'You are dining tomorrow with the Prime Minister, I believe.'

'How do you know *that*?' asked Mr Wells.

'It is written all over your shirt-cuffs.'

'Oh, so it is.'

'You must alert the authorities. The Martian tripods are heavily armoured but not indestructible. I would recommend the extensive use of dynamite—'

And so Mr Bell went on. He spoke at length, eloquently and convincingly, and Mr Wells made many many notes. And when Mr Bell had finally done, the author nodded his head.

'Either this is all true,' he said, 'or you are a far greater writer of fiction than myself.'

'If doubts remain,' I said to Mr Bell, 'we could always show Mr Wells the time machine.'

'*The Time Machine*,' said H. G. Wells, making further notes.

'You will introduce me as your elder brother,' said Mr Bell.

'Pardon me? *What?*' said Mr Wells.

'To the Prime Minister,' my friend explained. 'Tomorrow night. I would not wish you to carry the burden of this responsibility alone. Nor would I expect you to outline my plan for the destruction of the Martians in all its intricate detail. You can leave that to me and—'

'Just hold on,' said Miss Defy. '*You* are expecting *us* to introduce you to the Prime Minister so that you can then tell him everything that you have just told us?'

'And a great deal more,' said my friend. 'The Martians *can* be beaten and *I* am the man who will beat them.'

'Outrageous,' said Miss Defy.

'Unthinkable,' said Mr Wells. 'You might well be some dangerous anarchist intent upon assassinating the Prime Minister.'

'Have you actually listened to *anything* I have said?' Mr Bell made a most exasperated face.

'Tell me some more about this "invisible man",' said Mr Wells.

Cameron Bell threw up his hands. 'The world is about to be invaded!' he shouted.

I felt rather sorry for Mr Bell. Because, after all, he *did* know that the world was about to be invaded. There was no question at all in his mind, or indeed mine, regarding *that*. But getting anyone else to believe it, or even to take it seriously, was going to be something of a problem.

'Right,' said Mr Bell, and he drew out his ray gun.

'What is *that*?' asked H. G. Wells.

'A Martian weapon,' said Mr Bell. 'One that functions through the transperambulation of pseudo-cosmic anti-matter.'

'That's easy for you to say,' said Mr Wells.

Cameron Bell aimed his ray gun and fired it.

The chair Mr Wells was sitting upon disintegrated and he fell onto the floor.

Miss Defy whistled. 'I want one of *those*,' she said, and she winked at Mr Bell.

My friend grew pink about the cheeks once more. 'I know where you live,' he said to Mr Wells. 'My companion and I will call for you at seven tomorrow evening and accompany you to Downing Street. Darwin, did you bring with you a ray gun of your own?'

'Just a little one,' I said, producing same.

'Then kindly give it to Miss Defy. I want there to be no mistake about this. You must both know—' and he glanced from Miss Defy to H. G. Wells '—that I am telling all of the truth. If you aid me, you will both know considerable fame in the future. If I am unable to pass my knowledge on to the Prime Minister, England will fall to the might of the Martians and all of us will die.'

There was a certain silence then.
And it was most intense.

And . . .

'. . . across the gulf of space . . . intellects vast and cool and unsympathetic, regarded this earth with envious eyes, and slowly and surely drew their plans against us . . .'

'Tell me more about this "time machine",' said Mr H. G. Wells.

38

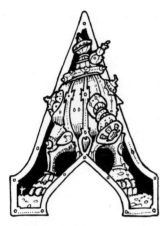lthough, at times, my friend Mr Bell did things that I was not wholly in agreement with — to wit, his over-exuberance when it came to the employment of dynamite — never for a moment did I doubt that *ultimately* he would achieve his goal and bring to justice Arthur Knapton, king of this place, that place and the other.

To see him once more in his own habitat, as it were, where he could exhibit his unique skills to the very optimum, was a great joy to me, I can tell you. And if I had been wondering whether our meeting with Colonel James Richardson-Brown and the achingly lovely Miss Defy had simply been a matter of Mr Bell wishing to meet a hero of his teenage years and a lady he had clearly longed for, then what next occurred proved me wrong in these matters.

Mr Bell had plans, it appeared. Very big plans indeed.

Plans that could not be put into operation without the complete cooperation and financial assistance of Her Majesty's Government. For this he would need to win over Mr Gladstone the Prime Minister, and to this end he would employ Colonel James Richardson-Brown.

And, in particular, the lovely and remarkable Miss Defy.

That William Ewart Gladstone, Prime Minister of England, confidant of Her Majesty the Queen, philanthropist and founder of numerous charities to enrich the lives of the poor and needy, was *something of a ladies' man* was a fact well known to those who knew it well.

Those being the reporters of Grub Street, the Lords of the Upper House, all of Her Majesty's Government and each and every 'lady' from Limehouse to Lincoln's Inn Fields.

In fact, to everyone, really. In fact, throughout history, although each has sought to hide their embarrassing peccadilloes from an unforgiving public, it appears that each and every Prime Minister has been 'outed', to use a twentieth-century term, and that all and sundry somehow knew about their dark desires.

And so, when it came time for the mesmerising Miss Defy to meet the Prime Minister, it was no surprise whatsoever to me that it would be my friend Mr Cameron Bell who put himself into the position of making the introductions.

Mr Bell had engaged a steam-driven phaeton to convey us to Number Ten Downing Street. It was an ungainly vehicle that belched foul-smelling smoke and showered us with cinders.

Colonel James Richardson-Brown was loud in his praises for this 'marvel of modern-day transportation' and said he could foresee the time when 'vast steam-driven trains of the sky' would traverse the globe.

Mr Bell rolled his eyes at this and I would have put the colonel (or Mr H. G. Wells, as *we* knew him to be) straight upon this matter had not my friend shaken his head and whispered that it really did not matter.

'When the Martians invade,' confided Mr Bell, '*everything* will change.'

And *I* knew that it would, and *I* worried hugely for this, for although I *did* trust Mr Bell, I greatly feared those Martians. And Martians, immune to Earthly bacteria, I feared very much more.

'I have been thinking, Bell,' said the colonel, affecting a particularly hoity-toity expression and straightening up in his seat, 'that this Martian business is unlikely at best and total madness at worst. I make no bones about it: I am suspicious of you, sir.'

Mr Bell nodded and smiled a bit, too. 'I am aware,' said he, in an even manner, 'that you do not trust me. That you fear me to be an assassin and that you have taken certain measures.'

'*Measures?*' said the colonel, a-raising his eyebrows.

'You carry no fewer than four concealed weapons,' said Mr Bell, 'which, given the slightest opportunity or excuse, you will employ to bring about my destruction.'

I raised wide eyes to my friend.

'In your place, I would have done the same,' said Mr Bell. 'Although, as a gentleman, I would definitely *not* have done what *you* have done, in persuading Miss Defy to conceal a weapon of her own in a place quite unsuited to its holstering.'

There was a sudden silence in our carriage.

Three jaws now hung very slack indeed.

Mr Bell just grinned.

'I am no assassin,' said Mr Bell, 'and you can search me for weapons, should you wish. Indeed, you may search me most intimately.'

Jaws hung, if anything, slacker.

'You will find no weapons upon me.' And Mr Bell folded his arms.

And it *was* true. He carried no weapons at all. No weapons and indeed no dynamite.

I, however, *did*!

Because he had insisted upon it.

There was a certain smell about Number Ten. An earthy, musky, bodily, perfumy smell. I did not take to that smell at all, but I did like Mr Gladstone.

He was certainly a fine figure of a man. His clothes were expertly cut and I recognised his lapel detailing as the trademark stitch of my own London tailor. His shoes were well polished, his sideburns a treat, he had twinkly blue eyes and he patted my head as I passed him.

Mr Bell made very much of introducing Miss Defy to Mr William Gladstone, and Mr Gladstone made very much of his welcoming of Miss Defy. So much so, in fact, that other guests were forced to form an orderly queue outside. Which was most inconvenient for them as it was coming on to rain.

Colonel James Richardson-Brown did not take at all to Mr Gladstone. As one rogue will recognise another, he took in the honeyed words that Mr Gladstone spread lavishly over Miss Defy and once or twice even reached for the sword that he wore.

When, finally, all were within and champagne poured and chattings done and we were led to the grand dining hall,* it came as no surprise to me that we were to be seated at the top table. With Miss Defy on the PM's right hand and Mr Bell on the left.

I noticed, all around and about, *security*. This came in the form of tall and pale-faced men, dressed entirely in black,

---

* *It is a fact known to few that the interior of Number Ten is somewhat Tardis-like – far bigger on the inside than the out. (R. R.)*

with blackly tinted pince-nez and gloves. These were the mysterious Gentlemen in Black, from the equally mysterious Ministry of Serendipity.

When all were seated, and there were many, and very well heeled were all, Mr Gladstone broke off his conversation with Miss Defy, did a little *tink-tink* upon his wine glass with an eel fork and rose from his seat to address the assembled guests.

I looked on at all and sundry, thinking to recognise a potentate here, a rajah there, a shogun over yonder. They were a magnificent crowd, a-glitter with jewels, decked out in the richest of silks and velvets. Tiaras twinkled, necklaces sparkled, gentlemen sported medallions of high orders.

'My lords, ladies, gentlemen, kings, queens, princes, all of rank and noble birth, I salute you.' Mr Gladstone did toasting with his glass and each took favour of the wine. 'As you will know, you have all been invited here tonight to participate in an auction in order to raise funds for a worthy cause. In fact, it might be said, without fear of contradiction, to be *the* worthy cause. The most worthy cause upon Earth. That of eradicating poverty worldwide. My friends, and I feel I can call you my friends –' Mr Gladstone's eyes swept over the assembled multitude, lingering here and there upon some particularly tantalising female or other '– to eradicate poverty, to eradicate want, to eradicate hunger, these are worthy causes indeed. Together they become *the* worthy cause, and *we* are the favoured few who will bring this world into a state of well-being.'

There was much applause at this and I clapped my hands, too. I had not thought at all about the reason for this exalted get-together – it had not in the least crossed my mind. But to find that these great folk were all gathered here to do something altruistic, something that would benefit Mankind as a whole rather than doing what the rich generally did – line their pockets at the expense of all others – this was something wonderful.

Something historic.

'It is my regret,' continued Mr Gladstone, 'that our fair Queen Victoria is unable to attend tonight. She has been taken unaccountably sick and sends her sincerest apologies. But, and here I must read from a telegram lately received, she sends her apologies and states –' And here Mr Gladstone perched pince-nez upon his nose, unfolded from his pocket the telegram in question and read from it:

TELEGRAM

We are in complete agreement with this noble cause STOP We pledge one million English pounds STOP VR STOP

And applause like thunder was offered up.

'Quite so.' Mr Gladstone raised a calming hand. 'So,' said he, 'as you can see, England is one hundred per cent behind this.'

More applause, but I did not join in, as I noted well a certain look on the face of Mr Bell. A look of *concern*, shall we say.

The Prime Minister continued, 'And so, when our meal is concluded, we will hold our auction. The goal is to raise twenty million English pounds to complete the work started by the great Indian scholar, chemist and humanitarian Notpank Ruhtra, whose wonder food Ruhtrate is now ready to go into production and, with the funds raised tonight, will be distributed across the globe. This wonder food comes in many forms. It can be planted to produce massive crops in less than a week. It can be beaten flat then used to create clothing. It can . . .'

And so the miraculous qualities of Ruhtrate were extolled. And they were many and various and rather difficult, to my small mind, for me to entirely believe. But Mr Gladstone was clearly convinced, and as he was talking here upon this evening in eighteen eighty-five to literally *all* of the world's current leaders – folk who, frankly, were *not* to be trifled with – I was prepared, up to a point, to suspend my disbelief and hope that the utopia Mr Gladstone was now enlarging upon, once the whole world was in possession of Ruhtrate, would indeed come about.

So I smiled as he went on and on and on.

But not so Mr Bell.

The look of concern upon the face of my friend had transformed first into one of enlightenment, and now into one of extreme alarm.

I noted beads of perspiration and I became a-feared.

Mr Bell suddenly rose from his seat and flung his hands in the air. 'Fire!' he shouted. Very loudly. 'Please vacate the premises. Ladies first, if you will.'

Mr Gladstone stared aghast at Cameron Bell.

Colonel Richardson-Brown made motions towards his arsenal.

Gentlemen in Black did likewise.

I became *more* a-feared.

'What of *this*?' the Prime Minister roared. 'There is no fire. What of *this*?'

'There *is* fire!' my friend shouted. 'All will be consumed in the flames. Flee now. Fire FIRE FIRE!'

'Cease this nonsense!' shouted Mr Gladstone.

'FIRE!'

Shouted my friend.

And let us be honest here, there are few cries that will get folk up on their feet and making for the door in quite the manner that **FIRE!** does.

FIRE! just gets the job done.

It does.

And though Mr Gladstone made mighty attempts to halt the ensuing rush, all were to no avail. Mr Bell continued with his hollerings, raising his voice to volumes that I would hitherto have considered beyond his vocal range.

Colonel Richardson-Brown now drew out a pistol.

But my friend clubbed him down with a champagne bottle.

'FIRE!'

And they bolted, crushed through doorways, heaved along corridors, flooded into the street.

Mr Gladstone raised his fists, but Gentlemen in Black, whose role it was to protect the Prime Minister, bore him aloft and heaved his struggling form from the premises.

Suddenly the great dining room was empty but for myself, Mr Bell and the unconscious Colonel James Richardson-Brown.

'Now, what was *that* all about?' I asked my friend. 'I was looking forward to my dinner.'

'Help me with him, Darwin,' said Mr Bell, taking the fallen colonel by the shoulders. 'We must hurry – there is little time left.'

'But there is no fire,' I said, and I sniffed with my sensitive nostrils.

'But there will be soon,' said Cameron Bell. 'And a very loud explosion.'

And he was certainly right about that.

For mere moments later, there came . . .

A VERY LOUD EXPLOSION.

39

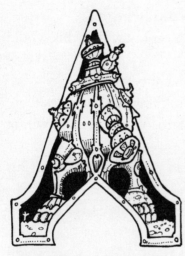s these were the days before radar, nobody knew they were coming. The Martian warships dropped down from the sky, bound for the heart of London.

Bound was one for Ten Downing Street.

The flagship of the Martian fleet, this was. The bomb that fell from it caused fire and fury and that loud explosion.

Mr Bell and I both covered our ears. We were out of Downing Street by now and although burdened by the weight of the colonel were making good progress.

For although the cry of *FIRE!* has the power to move people fast, falling bombs and mighty explosions do add a spring to that already hastened step.

'Into that Underground station,' shouted my friend, and we made for the steps. We were not alone in making this our shelter of choice. Londoners were pouring into the Underground. Flames were rising and explosions battered the air as we humped the colonel down the steps in the company of many.

At last, on the northbound platform, we laid our cargo to rest. Mr Bell patted about at the unconscious figure.

'Looting?' I enquired.

'I want all his weaponry,' said my friend, patting and pulling and probing.

We were huddled together in a corner with no one paying us any particular interest. My heart was beating rather fast and not amongst the smallest of my regrets was that this had happened *before* we had eaten our dinner.

I took deep breaths and tried to steady myself.

'You knew,' I said to Mr Bell. 'You knew that this would happen.'

Mr Bell nodded and pulled out a shiny revolver.

'You shouted "fire" because you knew the Martians were coming and that they were about to bomb Ten Downing Street.'

Mr Bell nodded once more and pushed pistols into his pockets.

'*How* did you know?' I asked Mr Bell. 'How did you know it would happen?'

'I reasoned it out, Darwin. All those heads of state and members of foreign royalty all together in a single room. All brought together for a single worthy cause.'

'But it *is* a worthy cause,' I said.

'If it were real,' said Cameron Bell.

I shrugged and said, 'Go on,' and so he did.

'The miracle of Ruhtrate,' said Mr Bell, 'invented by that Indian philanthropist, Notpank Ruhtra.'

'It is not a name I know,' I said.

'It is if you reverse the letters.'

I did this inside my head. 'Arthur Knapton,' I said.

'None other than he,' said Mr Bell. 'And what a cunning plan – to have all those noble leaders of nations assembled in a single place, lured there by such a worthy cause, and then to destroy them all. *Bang!*' Mr Bell mimed the explosion.

'And if you had not shouted *FIRE*—'

Mr Bell nodded once more. 'They would all be dead.'

I gave my head a shaking. 'But this is all wrong,' I said. 'This is *not* the way *The War of the Worlds* begins. It begins on Horsell Common, where the first spaceship lands. The spaceship that will later be known as the *Marie Lloyd*.'

'That was the way it happened the first time, and the outcome is well known. *This time*, however, all will be different.'

'I am very afraid indeed,' I said to Mr Bell.

'And I myself most inconvenienced. It was my intention to win the PM around to the idea that a Martian invasion was imminent and have him requisition for me the Empire's entire stock of—'

'Dynamite?' I suggested.

'Precisely. Yet here we are, cowering underground whilst the Martian horde lays waste to London. Not the outcome that I might have wished for.' Mr Bell made a very grumpy face.

Colonel Richardson-Brown began to stir. 'I will fight any man who dallies with my woman,' he mumbled.

Mr Bell gave him a swift, sharp smack upon the cheek.

'What? What? What?' went the colonel, coming to. 'And *where*?' he asked, as he took in his surroundings. And, 'Common folk,' he continued, with disapproval.

'Those Martians, whose existence you doubted, are presently destroying the Empire's capital,' said Mr Bell. 'And it is *your* duty, as a great patriot and hero of the nation, to bring these evil invaders swiftly to their knees.'

'And *where* did you say we are?' asked the colonel.

'Safely below, in an Underground Railway station.'

'Well, thank the Lord for *that*.' The colonel patted all over himself. 'I have been robbed,' he declared.

'Your armaments have been requisitioned. Together we must go to Mornington Crescent.'

'Why?' asked the colonel, and Mr Bell told him why.

'Because beneath that station is the headquarters of the Ministry of Serendipity. The Prime Minister will have been conveyed there by the Gentlemen in Black.'

'Well, I have no wish to go there,' said the colonel.

'The PM will have travelled in the company of that adventuress and society beauty, Miss Defy,' said Cameron Bell.

'Then what are we waiting for?' The colonel rose, dusted at himself, straightened his uniform and adjusted his trouser seat. He cast a bitter eye upon my friend and then we all made off to Mornington Crescent.

Along the railway track.

'Isn't this rather a dangerous thing to do?' I said as we stumbled along in the dark.

'A talking ape is an abomination unto the Lord,' observed Colonel Richardson-Brown. And then he howled, because the talking ape had reasonably good night vision and very sharp teeth indeed.

I heard the distinctive chuckle of Mr Bell.

And on we walked.

At length, and I will not tire the reader with tales of our travails as we went upon our way – how we were nearly run over by Underground trains, eaten by legions of rats, threatened by curious mole men and troglodytes and once encountered a lost race, half of monkey, half of man – we arrived.

'Ah,' said Mr Bell, of a sudden. 'We're here.'

He pressed his special key into a special lock and we three were gratified when it turned with a pleasing *click*.

I had wondered many times about the Ministry of Serendipity. It seemed to me one of those convenient hooks on to which one might hang the most extravagant of conspiracy theories. Whenever something appeared to be going wrong for no apparent reason, folk would say, 'The *Ministry* is behind it.' I found – to little surprise, I might add – that folk still said *that* in the year three thousand.

So, not a lot *had* changed *there*.

We moved along a stone lane and into the loading area where the *Marie Lloyd* would stand in the London of the Second World War. And on from there to that self-same top-secret conference room where Mr Bell would impersonate Winston Churchill and *not* lay hands upon Mr Arthur Knapton.

Mr Bell knocked on the door of this top-secret room.

Scuffling sounds issued from within, followed by the Prime Minister's voice calling, 'Hold on there one moment and I will be with you.'

Mr Bell pressed down on the handle and flung the door wide open.

To expose a scene of nothing less than scandal.

There was Mr William Gladstone, struggling to pull up his trousers, and Miss Defy in a state of undress, struggling likewise with stockings.

I stared, aghast. I was quite lost for words.

Not so the colonel, however.

'You absolute swine!' cried he as he drew out his sword.

The Prime Minister stumbled in his trousers and fell heavily to the floor. As he turned to rise, the colonel kicked him hard in the bottom.

I looked up at Mr Bell.

A huge smile covered his face.

'You can at times be a very bad man,' I told him.

Mr Bell winked, then helped up Mr Gladstone.

'This is all a misunderstanding,' said the guilty man. 'I was explaining military tactics.'

And that would have to do, it appeared, for an explanation as he added nothing more.

'We came at once,' said Mr Bell. 'We knew we would be needed.'

'Did you?' the PM almost fell over again, for he had two legs down one trouser. 'Why did you? What?'

Mr Bell aided the trouser-struggler. 'The colonel is your man,' said he. 'To lead us to victory.'

'Am I?' asked the colonel.

'Yes,' said my friend. 'You are.'

'Well, if I am, then I am, I suppose.'

'What is all this about?' Now once more fly-buttoned into respectability, Mr Gladstone sat himself down in that chair that is slightly bigger than the rest and did, to my mind at least, a very reasonable impression of a man who had done absolutely nothing wrong whatsoever.

My gaze strayed over to Miss Defy, who was now fully dressed and sitting primly at the table's other end, gloved hands in lap, looking demure and innocent.

The colonel was rather red in the face. Mr Bell suggested that he should sheathe his sword.

'It is this way,' said Mr Bell to Mr Gladstone. 'The colonel here informed me during your speech at Ten Downing Street that the sixth sense he has developed during his many exciting and dangerous adventures had alerted him to imminent danger. He directed me to shout "FIRE!" so all would be saved from the forthcoming Martian attack.'

I really admired my friend for the way that words of

untruth could sometimes spill from his mouth and I wondered just what was coming next.

'Naturally,' continued Mr Bell, 'you will see to it that he receives the nation's highest honour for this act of valour alone.'

I would describe the look on the face of the colonel throughout all this as baffled. It brightened considerably, however, with this talk of a decoration.

Although he did look rather bitterly towards the lovely lady.

'And,' continued Mr Bell, 'the colonel, as a natural hero and ideal figurehead to spur on the nation during this time of national calamity, will be pleased to take control of the armed forces, with myself as his personal adviser.'

The Prime Minister made gagging sounds.

Mr Bell smiled serenely.

'Naturally,' he went on, 'no word of what has occurred here will reach my close friends at *The Times* newspaper.'

The Prime Minister drew out an oversized red gingham handkerchief and mopped his brow with it.

'What do you suggest, then?' he asked in the voice of one lost.

'I suggest,' said Mr Cameron Bell, 'that we formulate plans here and now to destroy the Martian strike force.'

'And how would we do *that*?' asked the Prime Minister. 'We did not even know of the existence of Martians until an hour ago.'

'The colonel did,' said Cameron Bell.

'*Did* I?' asked the colonel.

'Now, do not be so modest,' said my friend. 'Only last night, after your highly successful book signing, you told me that you feared such an eventuality as this and that you had gleaned secret information about the Martian invasion and the man behind it all.'

The colonel's mouth opened and shut, but no words came from it.

'Such a modest gentleman,' said Mr Bell to Mr Gladstone. 'He has been working undercover for months to track down the evil villain behind this attack. A beast in human form who leads these Martian foes. A man by the name of Arthur Knapton.'

'Is this true?' asked the PM of the colonel.

The colonel shrugged, then nodded his head. 'I suppose it is,' said he.

'Then if you know so much, tell us what is to be done.'

The colonel's mouth opened once more, then shut, then opened, then shut. Mr Bell gave him a certain look.

'Aha,' said the colonel, 'I see.'

'You do?' asked the Prime Minister. 'Go on.'

'I have confided all to my aide, Mr Cameron Bell,' said Colonel James Richardson-Brown. 'He will brief you on the details, won't you, Mr Bell?'

'If you insist,' said Cameron Bell. 'But these are *your* ideas.'

'Please go ahead,' said the colonel, and he took himself off to the table's end to engage in a rather heated, if lower-toned, conversation with Miss Defy.

'So,' said Mr Gladstone. 'Say your piece, Mr Bell.'

'The *colonel's* piece,' said my friend.

'I do not care whose it is, just *say* it!'

Mr Bell smiled and began.

'We are going to need some dynamite,' he said.

40

he destruction of the capital was awful. The spaceships rained down fire and bombs, destroying all and sundry. The Martians were not employing the tactics they had used in the original *War of the Worlds*. They were laying waste to London even before they landed to unleash the terrible tripods.

Death rays cleaved the streets and houses rumbled into dust. In Trafalgar Square, the fountains foamed and steamed as Nelson fell. Architectural treasures became nothing more than memories. The seat of the British Empire became a flaming Hell.

Within the top-secret room in the Ministry of Serendipity, Mr Cameron Bell held forth. Gentlemen in Black were crowded therein, as were the surviving members of the Government (3), the Queen (1) and the royal corgis (18).

'Dynamite,' said Mr Bell, and, 'Dynamite,' again.

'And this will get the job done?' asked Mr Gladstone, fumbling to light a cigar with wildly trembling hands.

Mr Bell made so-so gestures. 'It will certainly give them something to think about,' he said.

'Something to think about,' said the Prime Minister, and very thoughtfully, too. 'And whilst we are giving them something to think about, what will we *actually be doing to stop them*?' His voice rose terribly here and I took a nimble step back.

'I will be putting *my* plan into operation,' said Mr Bell.

'And your plan is . . . ?'

'Ah.' Mr Bell gave his snubby nose a tap. 'That would ruin the surprise.'

'*Ruin the surprise?*' The Prime Minister cast his unlit cigar aside and rose with a rush to his feet. 'Gentlemen in Black,' he shouted. 'Take this Mr Pickwick fellow and toss him into a cell!'

I was about to protest this outrage, but I was snatched up by the collar.

'Yes!' cried Mr Gladstone. 'And his monkey, too. Sling them both in a cell and get me a large gin and tonic!'

'This is really not going according to plan,' I said to Mr Bell. 'Pardon me for saying this, but I do recall *you* saying that this time you would sort everything out.'

'I do not recollect being quite so specific,' replied my friend, and he sighed a most heartfelt sigh.

We sat side by side in a dire little cell, which I hate to say smelled of wee-wee. The cell's iron door had been slammed shut upon us and the big bolt crammed into place.

'I suppose at least we are safe in here,' I said.

'Safe at least until all in the Ministry are dead and we then starve to death,' said my friend.

'Help! Let us out!' I shouted, and I banged upon the iron door.

'Darwin,' said Mr Cameron Bell. 'We find ourselves in

extreme circumstances. Probably the most extreme circumstances we have so far found ourselves in—'

'Nearly getting our heads chopped off in Fairyland was rather extreme,' I helpfully suggested.

'Quite so.'

'And I can think of several more such extreme instances, if you wish.'

'I do not. But I am going to have to leave you here whilst I put my plan into action.'

'Leave me here?' I said, both slowly and with care. 'This would suggest to me that you have found a way to escape from this cell.'

'There is a way,' said my friend. 'A possible way. But one I would never under any normal circumstances even consider trying. But I can see no other way of getting us, and indeed the world, out of this terrible mess.'

'Right,' I said, and I waggled a finger at Mr Bell. 'Well, firstly, I have no wish to be left here all alone. Secondly, you told me when we first set off upon our adventures through time that we should always stay together. Look what happened the last time we parted company. You left me alone in Brentford and I jumped off a church spire and died. *And thirdly*, this cell has no windows and only a locked iron door for an exit. How could you possibly hope to escape?'

'*You* will bring about my escape,' said Mr Cameron Bell.

'And how could I possibly do *that*?'

'You will do it through magic.'

I stared at my friend, and my mouth spoke a silent word: 'Magic?'

'You overheard my conversation with Aleister Crowley,' said Mr Bell, 'in which he identified you as the Ape of Thoth.'

'The kiwi bird called me that, too,' I said, 'when I was dead and up there in the clouds.'

'Through our travels,' said Mr Bell, 'and through the skills in language and the written word that you were taught by Herr Döktor, you have become unique. An ape amongst apes. And through releasing your monkeys into the far and distant past, you have become the father of all Mankind.'

'I am not sure I *really* believe that,' I said to my friend. 'Although, naturally, it does hold a certain charm.'

'No ape such as you has ever existed before, *except* –' and Mr Bell put a very large emphasis upon the word *except* '– for the monkey Gods Hanuman and Thoth. And Thoth, as you may know, means "thought" and "time", the Lord of the Past and the Future.'

'I am only a monkey,' I said. 'Although I have certainly experienced more wonderful things than has the average monkey.'

'You died and you rose from the dead.'

'And that sounds blasphemous to me. I was born again through science.'

'You are the Ape of Thoth,' said Cameron Bell, 'and you will release me from this cell.'

'I cannot,' I said. 'I do not know how. Why say such things to me?'

Mr Bell pulled something from his pocket. It looked to be a piece of parchment. It *was* a piece of parchment.

'Before I left Crowley's room,' said my friend, 'he pressed this into my hand. Crowley is a shameless and immoral rogue, but he *is* a real magician. He recognised in you the power of Thoth and whispered that when the time was right and when all appeared lost, I should pass this to you and you should read from it.'

'And it will set everything right?'

'It will release me from this cell so that *I* can put every-thing right. I am responsible for this tragedy, Darwin, my overconfidence, my foolishness . . . This Martian attack – it is all *my* fault. *I* must put it right. *You* must aid me in this.'

'And I read the words and you will be magicked from this cell?'

'In a word, yes,' said my friend.

'Well, isn't *that* convenient!'

'Ahem,' said Mr Bell. 'Do you want to escape or do you not?'

'You said only *you* could escape,'

'Darwin, trust me,' said Cameron Bell.

'I do,' I said, 'but—'

'But me no buts. You will magic me from this cell so that I can put my plan into operation, stop Arthur Knapton and defeat the Martians. You will leave this cell at three o'clock sharp this afternoon.'

'*Three?*' I said. 'Why three?'

'Darwin,' said Mr Bell, 'this is the British Empire. What happens at three o'clock every day in the British Empire?'

'Everything stops for tea,' I said.

'Precisely. And so at three o'clock, a Gentleman in Black will bring a tray of tea and crumpets to this cell. It is the British way of doing things. Ultimately it is what we are all fighting for.'

'Tea?' I said.

'And crumpets. The Gentleman in Black will enter the cell with his tray. He will be shocked to find I am gone. Whilst he is gaping about the cell with a stupefied expression on his face, you will quietly slip away. Agreed?'

I nodded without conviction.

'Follow the Underground Railway System to Woking and make your way to the sandpits at Horsell Common. I will meet you there at nine o'clock tomorrow morning and there we will conclude our business.'

'Well, firstly,' I said, as I had seen the flaw in this, 'I would like to draw your attention to the fact that there is no—'

'Darwin!' said Mr Bell. 'Just do as I say.'

I folded my arms and made a foul face.

'All will be well, I promise you, Darwin.'

'We will see about that.'

Mr Bell unfolded his parchment and placed it into my hands. It was printed with Egyptian hieroglyphics and these meant absolutely nothing to me.

'There you are,' I said. 'I cannot read this.'

'You can,' said Mr Bell. 'Look *very* hard.'

'This is quite absurd,' I said. 'I am *not* a God, I am Darwin.'

'Read the parchment,' said Mr Bell, 'or I will give you a smack.' My friend made a very fearsome face and I gazed at the parchment.

And would not you know it, or would not you not, the hieroglyphics began to change. Not into English, but into *something*. Something that somehow I could understand. And the more I gazed, the clearer it all became.

All of it.

The truth, if you will.

About everything.

It was a magical moment and a profound one, too, and I only wish that there was time for me to enlighten you all by describing it in detail here.

But there is not.*

So I took a deep breath and read the words aloud.

* *This will probably be the last time I say 'outrageous'. So, 'OUTRAGEOUS!'*
(R. R.)

A sudden and intense silence formed in that cell as a physical thing and then the world appeared to fold in upon itself, to vanish away and then to expand and return.

And I found myself all alone in that cell.

41

sat all alone and had a little cry.

I was, frankly, fed up with all this. When Mr Bell and I first set off upon our journey through time, I had been of the opinion that it was going to be an enjoyable experience. That we would see and hear wonderful things.

Like Beethoven conducting the Ninth, for example.

But it had been nothing of the sort. We had chased and chased after the Pearly Emperor, Arthur Knapton, who time and again had outsmarted my friend Mr Bell. He had always been one step ahead of the great detective and in truth I had no real reason to believe that this time would be any different. And this time the fate of the whole world rested upon Mr Bell defeating Mr Knapton. That was a very big responsibility, and much as I admired my friend's extraordinary skills in the field of crime detection, and loved him in a way that one might love one's own brother, and trusted him, too – yes, I *did*! – I worried that perhaps he *had* this time met his match and that nothing his remarkable mind could come up with would foil this terrible villain. So I sat and I snivelled and I felt very sorry for myself.

At three o'clock sharp, the cell door opened and a

Gentleman in Black brought in the tea. He was, as Mr Bell predicted, shocked to find that my friend had gone, and whilst he was gaping about the cell with a stupefied expression upon his face, I quietly slipped away.

An air shaft took me to Mornington Crescent Underground Station, and from there I began my journey to Woking.

I know that there will be those readers who have been intently studying my narrative to content themselves that all the details I provide are scrupulously accurate. For, after all, if I had not actually done the things I claim to have done within the pages of this book, then how, I hear you ask, would I know all I know? And be able to write with such historical exactitude and precision?

Clearly, I would not. And so, when I attempted to take issue with Mr Bell in the previous chapter regarding the means by which I would travel to Woking, the more scrupulous readers will certainly have reached for their maps of the London Underground and cried, 'Aha – the London Underground does *not* run to Woking.'

Bravo!

Good for you!

Well done.

So, naturally I did *not* follow the course of the London Underground System to Woking.

I followed it to Horsell Common Underground Station.

Which was somewhat closer to the sandpits.

And there I spent what was truly the most miserable night of my life.

The sky that night glowed hideous red as tripods stalked from the Martian spaceships, wreaking havoc across the countryside. London was ablaze, Old London Town, of many memories, all gone to ruination as the mighty armoured war machines picked their three-legged way above the streets, ray guns showering down destruction. Poor Old London Town.

With dawn came refugees, thousands fleeing destruction. I had settled myself into a tree for the night and watched the sorry hordes of broken people struggling with meagre belongings away from the engines of death. There was, it appeared, no hope left. Nothing remaining but sadness.

I shook my head and shivered for I was rather cold, and having had no sleep at all, most tired, too, was I.

'It is all too awful,' I said as thousands passed beneath my tree.

I had dreamed a terrible dream of a blackened landscape and Martian tripods, a dream that now was becoming reality. I had a little blubber and then I heard the call.

'Darwin,' came this call to me. 'Darwin, where are you?'

'I am here,' I cried and dropped down from the tree into my best friend's arms.

Mr Bell smiled upon me. 'You look all in,' he said.

Folk tramped by to either side, caring naught for us.

'I have brought a picnic,' said Mr Cameron Bell.

'You have brought a picnic?' I said. 'At a time like *this*?'

'You *are* hungry, are you not?'

'And footsore, too,' I told him.

'Then let us hasten away to one of the sandpits and enjoy breakfast beyond the eyes of the refugees.'

I stared at my friend and shook my head. 'Have you any idea how utterly insane that sounds?' I asked him.

'I have quail's eggs, croissants, Swiss cheese and Château Doveston.'

'Ah,' said I, and, 'Ah,' once more.

'And Treacle Sponge Bastard for pudding.'

'Breakfast with pudding,' I said. 'What could be *less* insane than that?'

'Always best to go into battle on a full stomach,' said my friend, and he placed me onto his shoulders and took up the picnic basket.

And so we picnicked. In the sandpits on Horsell Common with Martian tripods moving ever nearer and thousands fleeing in terror just out of sight.

I tucked into croissants and marmalade. 'How goes your plan?' I enquired between munchings. 'I suppose you are aware that London is now utterly destroyed.'

'We can put that right,' said Mr Bell.

'Oh, can we?' I replied.

Mr Bell poured two glasses of bubbly. 'All will be well,' said he.

'You do look rather chipper for a fellow who has wrought destruction upon the planet.'

'Now now, Darwin,' said my friend. 'Have a little faith.'

'A little faith?' I smiled as I said it. 'The world as we know it is coming to an end. We are sat drinking champagne as the Martians lay waste to southern England. And if all of *that* is not bad enough, *I* had to spend an entire night *up in a tree!*'

Mr Bell looked at me.

I looked at him.

And then we began to laugh.

'It is *not* funny,' I said, when we had quite finished laughing and refilled our glasses with champers. 'I saw regiments of soldiers marching into battle against the Martians last night. I have seen two or three sorry survivors making a retreat this morning. All is gone, Mr Bell. All is lost. All is doom.'

'But looking on the bright side—'

'There *is* no bright side.'

'I have it all under control.'

I sighed deeply and shook my head. Distant explosions were growing ever less distant. 'They are coming this way. You know that?'

'Of course I know that,' said my friend. 'And I am sure that Arthur Knapton will know that I know that. Seeing as how he has always been one step ahead.'

'So what are we going to do – just sit here and wait for him to arrive?'

'Unless you have a better plan.'

I was sipping champagne, but now I spat it. *'A better plan?'* I spluttered. 'Than sit here and wait for death? I think I can come up with something better than that.'

'It is all under control.'

'No, Mr Bell, it is *not*.'

We heard yet more distant explosions.

'I love the sound of dynamite in the morning,' said Mr Bell. 'Sounds like . . . victory.'

'Give me more champagne,' I said. 'If I am to die, I would prefer to do so whilst drunk.' I gave myself a thorough scratching. 'And my fleas would prefer to do likewise,' I said. 'More champagne.'

'What do you know about Martians?' asked my friend, possibly by way of conversation.

'Well, according to one now apparently inaccurate Eternal Verity, they are vulnerable to Earthly bacteria.'

'What else?'

'That they are tentacly and horrid.'

'Anything else?'

I scratched at my head. 'I recall reading that Sir Frederick Treves performed a post-mortem upon a Martian. It was described as the first "alien autopsy".'

'And?' asked my friend.

I ceased to scratch and just shrugged.

'Martians have no vocal cords,' said Mr Bell. 'They do not communicate by speech. They are telepathic.'

'And why would you mention this *now*?'

'Because it is significant. You will remember from history that *all* the Martians died from Earthly bacteria. *All* of them, Darwin.'

'And how is *this* significant?'

'Because not every single one of them actually came out of their war machines to breathe Earthly air, did they?'

'I do not know,' I said. 'But I suppose they must have done – they all died, after all.'

'They died through, you might say, a psychic plague. The King of all the Martians stepped down from his tripod to view the destruction he had brought about. He gained the fatal infection of Earthly bacteria and passed it on telepathically to all other Martians then upon the Earth.'

'Sounds like far-fetched fiction,' I said.

'Yet I believe it is true.'

'And so, and here let me see if I can get ahead of you . . .' I located a banana in the picnic basket and with some small pleasure began to unpeel it. 'You are hoping to somehow infect the King of all the Martians and by doing so telepathically infect all the rest.'

Mr Bell nodded.

'And that is your plan?'

'Well, part of it.'

'Oh, good,' I said. 'Because it is a very rubbish part of it. For one point, because the Martians are presently immune to Earthly bacteria, because they have been inoculated with penicillin. And for a second, because the King of Mars is now Mr Arthur Knapton.'

'You might have a point or two there,' said my friend. 'So let us hope for the best.'

I skilfully downed the banana in one. 'Share out the Treacle Sponge Bastard,' I said. 'At least we can die with full stomachs.'

Closer and closer now came the terrible sounds of destruction, the grinding metal of tripod legs growling ever louder in our ears.

Mr Bell shared out the Treacle Sponge Bastard.

And decanted the vintage champagne.

42

e shared a certain moment. Was it one of absolute calm amidst the terrible sounds of destruction, the roaring of fires and the screams of the fleeing thousands? Were we at the eye of the hurricane? The point of peace within the maelstrom?

At that moment, gentle reader, I truly believed that my end would shortly come, no matter how previously preordained its circumstances had appeared to be, and certain thoughts came to me then.

Certain words.

From Schiller's 'Ode to Joy'. Which Beethoven chose as the libretto for the famous fourth movement of his wondrous Ninth Symphony.

> Joy, beautiful spark of the Gods,
> Daughter of Elysium,
> We enter, drunk with fire,
> Heavenly one, your sanctuary.

I sighed a sigh for that beautiful spark and then chastened Mr Bell for having more than his fair share of the Treacle Sponge Bastard.

Our repast at length concluded, Mr Bell rose to his feet and dabbed at his chops with a napkin patterned in the tartan of Lord Burberry. 'Onto my shoulder, my friend,' said he.

And I climbed onto his shoulder.

The sad, bedraggled multitude had passed us by. From the direction of London came the terrible sounds of the tripods, the sky behind them red with rushing fire.

The war machines of the Martians were terrible indeed, the armoured canopy high above each set of tripod legs fashioned to resemble a gigantic monstrous face. The eyes glowed red, for these were the portholes through which the dreadful Martians peered and pointed. But the canopies were several hundred feet above the ground and beneath them were mounted the great gasping engines that swung the tripod legs across the landscape. All over grey dull metal, rivet-studded, armour-plated, apparently invulnerable, they picked their way across the fields with awful sound and fearful tread.

Flames gushed and trees took fire. The very fabric of all that was England was being torn and twisted, burned and broken.

'Oh, Mr Bell,' I cried to my friend. 'This truly is the most terrible thing. Whatever are we to do?'

'You must trust me,' said Mr Cameron Bell. 'Do whatever I say, without question, *when* I say it. Do you understand?'

'I do,' I said, and I clung to Mr Bell's shoulder.

There was one tripod larger than all the rest. Larger it was and grander, too, its steel grey legs enamelled and inlaid with many precious metals. Above the canopy rose many golden spires. I stared at it and gasped in utter horror.

'The face,' I said. 'That great metal face.'

'The face of Arthur Knapton,' said my friend.

For so it was. Picked out in terrible detail. That long and loathsome face. Recognisable to many as the God-Pharaoh Akhenaten.

This monstrous creation swayed towards us and loomed far above our heads.

'Mr Bell, we must run!' I cried.

'Not yet,' said Cameron Bell.

A dreadful stench now filled the air. A dreadful clamour went up from the high canopy.

And then the metal jaws of the dreadful face ground open and great sounds were heard.

Great and terrible sounds were these.

The laughter of Arthur Knapton.

'Well, well, well,' came a greatly magnified voice. 'Fee-fi-fo-fum, don't I smell the blood of a fat bald 'un?'

Mr Bell stood his ground with remarkable courage as the hideous structure filled all the sky, dwarfing us in a black and icy shadow.

'There is a definite niff in the air,' said my friend. 'But then you were never a man inclined to the use of soap.'

'Gawd bless my soul,' came the voice. 'If you ain't a rude 'un, a-considering 'ow yer about to meet a very 'orrible end.'

'*Me?*' said Mr Bell. 'I do think not.'

Laughter poured from the war machine and appeared to engulf the whole world. 'But you're 'ere,' bawled Arthur Knapton. 'Right where I knew you'd be. We fink the same at times, you an' me.'

'I was relying on *that*,' my friend whispered to me.

'*The War of the Worlds* began on this 'ere common,' the man in the war machine went on, 'so it seemed fitting enough to us both that this 'ere common is where *this* war should end. An' blow me down an' kiss me bleedin' elbow if I didn't reckon you'd show up 'ere yourself to 'ave a show-down as those American Cowblokes will. Am I right, or am I right?'

'You are right,' said Cameron Bell.

'I ain't seein' no army, though.' That grating laugh poured from the steely mouth. 'I ain't seein' no batteries of cannons, no redcoats on 'orses prepared to die for Queen and country. In fact, I ain't seein' noffin' but a silly Mr Pickwick an' 'is monkey.'

Mr Bell did chewings upon his upper lip.

'Would I be right in believing,' I said, 'that you did intend for such a military force be present? Right now?'

Mr Bell nodded.

Rather dismally.

'And they have not turned up?' I asked.

'It rather looks that way,' said Mr Bell.

'Speak up,' called the voice of Arthur Knapton. 'You were p'raps a wondering as to where yer army is.'

'Perhaps,' said Mr Cameron Bell, shuffling uncomfortably.

'Well, I'll tells ya. They's *dead*, Mr 'igh an' mighty detective. I'm always one step ahead of you. I 'ad the barracks bombed first fing this morning.'

'Ah,' said Mr Cameron Bell, and he said it painfully.

'And now,' came that great and deafening voice, 'I reckons it's time to be 'avin' you. I've Martian minions 'ere what wants their breakfast.'

And with that abominable statement, two metallic tendrils

319

sprang from the canopy and coiled down with speed towards us.

'We should run *now*,' said Mr Bell.

And that is what we did.

That is to say, I clung to my friend and he did all the running. And remarkably sprightly, too, he was, for such a portly chap as he. He sprinted between the legs of the tripod and made at haste in the general direction of Horsell Common Underground Station. I was impressed by his speed.

Run and run and run went Mr Bell.

Turn and swing and then pursue went the tripod.

We were in the high street now, or what at least was left of that beautiful village's main thoroughfare. Blackened, burned-out houses and shops. A twisted, broken hansom cab with a horse's skeleton hanging between its shafts. The dreadful stench was all-consuming, for it was the putrid stench of death.

I looked back. 'It is gaining on us,' I cried.

'Just a little further,' puffed my friend.

'Into the Underground Railway?'

'Something like that,' my friend panted.

Mr Bell was rooting as he ran.

Rooting about in his pockets, was he.

Then drawing out a very special something.

It was a very special something that I immediately recognised. It was one of Mr Bell's very favourite very special somethings. A brass-box contrivance approximately the size of a cigarette case, from which sprouted a slim metal rod, and upon the face of which was a big red button.

'Just a little further,' puffed and panted my friend.

And then . . .

We were inside the Underground station and Mr Bell's thumb went hard down on the button.

'Cover your ears, Darwin!' he cried as he threw himself down into cover and hugged me to his bosom.

The dynamite had been well concealed.

Within the high street drains.

The explosion was a mighty one.

It roared beneath the tripod . . .

and went . . .

BOOM!

43

'*otcha!*' shouted Mr Bell, and he rose amidst dust and patted away at his person. I arose with him and I did pattings, too.

We peered from the station into the street but could see nothing but smoke.

'That really was a *very* big bang,' I said.

Mr Bell, who had only managed to cover one of his ears as the other arm had been shielding me, looked a tad unsteady on his feet.

'I think I might have lost an eardrum,' he said.

I tried to look sympathetic. 'Where did you get all that dynamite from?' I asked.

'Pardon?' said my friend.

So this time I shouted.

'I have had a rather busy twelve hours,' said Mr Bell. 'I acquired two things of major importance. The dynamite was one of them.'

'The dynamite came from the soldiers' barracks,' I shouted, for my friend had *not* answered my question. 'Where the soldiers were. The ones Arthur Knapton killed.'

'It can all be put right.' Mr Bell banged at his head. 'All

this can be made to unhappen. It *has* to be made to un-happen.'

We peered once more into the street. The smoke and dust were clearing now, exposing a scene of utter devastation.

'It has gone,' I shouted. 'The entire village has gone, Mr Bell. You have wiped Horsell village from the map.'

Mr Bell nodded thoughtfully.

But then began to smile.

For not only had the village gone.

So, too, the Martian tripod.

'You blew it up,' I cried. 'You blew *him* up. Arthur Knapton is no more. You beat him, Mr Bell.'

'I rather think that I did,' said my friend, and he preened at his dusty lapels. 'And this victory will hopefully act as a rallying cry to the forces of Empire. Victory shall shortly be ours.'

'Bravo.' And I climbed onto Mr Bell's shoulder and gave it a 'well done' pat.

'A breath of fresh air,' said Mr Bell, 'then away down the Underground tunnel with us and back to the *Marie Lloyd*.'

'And Beethoven's Ninth?' I said hopefully.

'And Beethoven's Ninth,' said the great detective. 'The clearing up of these horrors can wait until after that. We are time travellers, my little friend – we can put all back to-gether.'

'Wonderful, oh, wonderful.' I was *so* looking forward to the Ninth.

Mr Bell did a little more dusting and then he stepped from the station. I peered about from my perch on his shoulder.

At nothing.

All that remained of the village was a single twisted lamp post. That and, of course, the Underground station. Clearly Mr Bell had displayed a degree of cunning when it came to the laying down of his dynamite, that our hiding place would be the only building to survive.*

'No more Horsell village,' I said. 'I wonder whether they will ever rebuild it. If they do not, they will probably demolish the Underground station, and no one in the future will ever know that there was one.'

Mr Bell gave me a certain look. 'Trying to fill in a little plot hole there, Darwin?' he asked.

I nodded and grinned at my friend.

And we shared a moment or two.

And then I screamed.

Very loudly indeed.

And Mr Bell came all over weak at the knees.

For a great black shadow fell across us. The shadow of the Martian war machine.

'Oh my dear dead mother,' said Cameron Bell. Which was probably the last time he would ever get to say it.

The massive tripod, with the ghastly Arthur Knapton face so high upon it, had *not* been blown to smithereens at all. It had been straddling the Underground station all along, unharmed, apparently, its occupants simply waiting for us to emerge.

'Most inconvenient,' said my friend. 'However—'

But whatever direction this particular line of conversation might have been taking, I will never know. For Mr Bell found himself suddenly speechless as a steely tendril swept down from the tripod's canopy, wrapped swiftly about his portly frame and dragged my friend aloft.

I was about to slip quietly away . . .

---

* *We will turn a blind eye to the sheer ludicrousness of this. Because I suspect that you, like myself, have long since given up on reason and logic. But at least the end is now in sight. (R. R.)*

324

When another dragged me from my feet.

So up we went in the hideous grasp of those sinister steely tendrils, up and into the horrible open mouth.

Then *whack!*

We both found ourselves sprawled upon the floor of the Martian tripod's wheelhouse. Smelly Martians loomed about us, their horrid, slimy tentacles moving in a most unpleasant manner.

'Well, well, well, well, well.' And there was Arthur Knapton, most extravagantly dressed in what might well have been the uniform of an Admiral of the Fleet. Heavily braided and hung with many medals, it was topped by a rather splendid hat.

A nautical hat with five separate pointy bits!

A pentacorn.

The nasty long face did evil grinnings at us.

Mr Bell rose to his feet and did more dustings down.

I just sat and folded my arms and had a bit of a sulk.

'That was a big explosion,' said the Admiral of the Fleet. 'I ain't finkin' that 'orsell District Council will be a-raising a statue to ya.' And he laughed. And again. And again and again and again. And the Martians sort of jiggled about, as they had no voices to laugh with.

'I told ya,' said Arthur Knapton. 'Told ya time an' again. I'm always way ahead of ya. You can't blow these 'ere tripods up with dynamite.'

'So it would appear,' said Mr Bell.

'Titanium hyper-alloy combat chassis. Twenty-first-century technology.' Arthur Knapton now preened at his heavily braided jacket. I hated to admit it, but when it came to preening, Arthur Knapton did it with considerably more aplomb than did Mr Bell. Arthur Knapton was a natural preener.

'And so it ends,' this evil preener said. 'You 'ad yer chance. Lumme, guv'nor, if you ain't 'ad chances aplenty. And fouled 'em all up, so you 'ave. But enough is enough, I say. I 'as this 'ere planet to stamp under me titanium boot 'eels, then we'll clobber Jupiter an' Venus, too. And that'll be that'll be that.'

Mr Bell hung his head sadly. 'On the face of it,' said he, 'it would appear that you have won.'

Arthur Knapton laughed once more. 'It does seem very much like that, don't it?' he said. Producing, as he did so, a most substantial ray gun and pointing it with joy towards my friend.

'I'm gonna shoot you now,' the Pearly Emperor said. 'Not in the 'eart, or in the 'ed, but in your big fat belly. Your guts will all come a-pouring out, but that won't kill you dead. These 'ere Martians feastin' on yer innards'll kill you. Then they'll 'ave yer monkey for their puddin'. This 'un 'ere –' Arthur Knapton pointed to a Martian '– 'e was King afore I took 'is throne. 'E does the orderin' about on me behalf. And after 'e's 'ad his din-dins out of yer belly-parts, I'll 'ave 'im tell all 'is mates to tuck into anyone left upon these poxy British blinking Isles. A fine old feast they'll 'ave, an' no mistake at all.'

I looked up at Mr Bell.

And he looked down at me.

'I am very sorry, Darwin,' said my friend.

'Aw, bless 'im,' went Arthur Knapton, God-Pharaoh of Egypt and King of Fairyland. ''E's sayin' sorry to 'is monkey. Now ain't that flippin' sweet.'

The Martians rocked and jiggled their horrible selves about.

I gave myself a good scratching, for I felt it might be the last I ever had.

326

'I know you might consider this a very silly question,' said Mr Bell, 'but please, before you kill us, tell me why.'

'Why?' asked Arthur Knapton. 'Why about what and which?'

'The magical stele that you purloined from Aleister Crowley has enabled you to travel through time. *You*, in fact, were the first man ever to do this. With such power you could have made this world a better place to be. The world of today and yesterday and tomorrow.'

'And why would I want to do *that*?'

Mr Bell sighed. 'Because,' said he, 'there is a question that gets asked at one time or another, and that question is, what is the meaning of life? A very wise man once said that everyone's life has a meaning – *can* have a meaning – if, when they are about to die, they know that they did their best to make this world of ours a slightly better place than it was when they were born.'

'Oh, spare me such platitudes,' said the Pearly Emperor.

'I say to *you*,' said Mr Bell, 'that this ape here—' and he pointed at me '—has in his own little life achieved more and done more to make the world a better place than you might do if given a thousand lifetimes.'

'An' well it might be.' The villain laughed once more his appalling laugh. 'An' I care not. I was brought up poor and I 'ad nothin', so I'll make this world a better place for *me*.'

'This world would be a better place without you, then,' said Mr Cameron Bell.

'But you'll not be my executioner. For I shall be *yours*.'

And with no further words said at all, Arthur Knapton, the Pearly Emperor, God-Pharaoh of Egypt, King of Fairy-land and Mars and no doubt God to the Chickens of Atlantis, pointed his substantial weapon at my best friend's belly and tugged heartily upon the great big trigger.

44

'o!' said Mr Bell. '*I think not.*' And he made a rather fierce face at Arthur Knapton.

'You finks not?' The Pearly Emperor laughed his annoying laugh. 'What you finks ain't got nothin' t' do wiv it.' And his finger tightened once more upon the trigger.

'If you fire *that*, then I will press *this*,' said Mr Cameron Bell, and he produced from behind his back another brass contrivance with an extended metal rod and a blood-red button, upon which his thumb now rested.

'Oh ho ho,' roared Arthur Knapton and his horrid Martians laughed as well. 'Wotcha thinkin' t' do, Mr Bell – blow us all a★★★ over t★★? I thought you'd learned your lesson – you can't blow us up in 'ere.'

'Not here,' said my friend, and he looked most brave. 'Pray do look out through your cockpit window. You might find something to surprise you.'

Arthur Knapton hesitated, but his gun wobbled ever so slightly in his hand. 'No,' he said. 'I fink I'll kills ya now.'

Mr Bell's thumb was firmly on the button and his firm gaze met that of Arthur Knapton.

Sweat broke out upon foreheads, including my own. This was what the chickens in the time of Akhenaten would have referred to as an 'Egyptian stand-off'.

Arthur Knapton's trigger finger twitched.

Mr Bell's thumb pressed down on the button ever so slightly.

'All right, all right,' cried Arthur Knapton. 'I will allow a dyin' man 'is final wish.' And he stalked to the cockpit window and peered out.

Beyond was the blasted landscape. The ruination and misery. The fallen houses, the scorched earth, all of the horrors that this evil man and his Martian hordes had caused.

'All looks mighty fine, in me 'umble opinion,' said the King of Mars.

'If you will just glance down at the half-toppled lamp post to your right.' Mr Bell had a rather broad smile on now.

'There ain't nofink— Oh my good Gawd!' Arthur Knapton threw up his hands in horror.

'Recognise the fellow?' asked Mr Bell. 'The fellow tied to the lamp post. With twenty sticks of dynamite strapped to his chest, which I can explode with a simple press on this button.' He waggled his contraption at the villain of the piece.

The villain of the piece glared him daggers. 'It is *me*,' he said very slowly, between his gritted teeth. 'It is meself in me teens you 'ave trussed up down there. 'Ow 'ave you done this 'ere fing?'

'I decided that I must apply a special logic to the situation,' explained Mr Cameron Bell. 'The situation being somewhat outré, at best. You were always one step ahead of me. But we were both travellers in time, and so I reasoned that the best way to sort things out was for me to be one step *behind you*. This is the year eighteen eighty-five. The year when myself and Mr Crowley were students together at Oxford and *you* were our fag and our bootboy.'

Arthur Knapton made terrible growling sounds.

'A bootboy with ideas above his station. Mighty ambitions. So the me that stands before you now visited the me that is now a student at Oxford. Together we took the teenage you captive. And so he stands down there, a rather uncomfortable and frightened fellow – and one who, if you do not immediately surrender to me, I shall blow to smithereens.'

Arthur Knapton rocked upon his heels.

I gazed up in admiration at my friend Mr Bell.

'That is very clever,' said I, 'because if you blow up *that* Arthur Knapton, then *this* one will cease to exist.'

'That is about the shape of it,' said Mr Bell.

Arthur Knapton spat upon the floor. Which was not a very nice thing to do, but he *was* a common fellow. 'Think you're so damn clever, doncha?' he roared as he spat. 'Well, you ain't and I'll tell you why. I 'as the Stele of Revealin' sewn into me vest, an' I can use it to transport meself back in time before you can even press yer blasted button.'

'I doubt if that is altogether true,' said Mr Bell.

'Oh, it's true, well enough. An' I'll go back in time and wring your b****y neck whilst you still lies as a baby in yer cot.'

'That sounds jolly unsporting,' said Mr Bell.

The Martians looked from my friend to his mortal enemy. They were, perhaps, becoming confused by all this.

'Farewell!' shouted Arthur Knapton, and he clutched very hard at his chest.

But he did not vanish into time.

He stayed just where he was.

'Perhaps you should give it another go,' suggested Mr Bell. 'Perhaps you did not do it properly the first time.'

'What the Dickens?' The Pearly Emperor tore at his wonderful jacket, he ripped it open and clutched at his vest. 'It is gone!' he cried. 'The Stele of Revealin' is gone.'

The Martians now looked back at Mr Bell.

'You stole the stele from Aleister Crowley,' said Mr Bell, 'then used the knowledge from the libraries of books you have acquired whilst travelling through time to decipher it and use it as a time-travelling magical adjunct.'

'I think we agreed that *that* wouldn't work,' I whispered to Mr Bell. 'It was one of those time-travelling plot–hole affairs.'

'Not now, Darwin,' said my friend. 'So,' he continued to the very very angry Arthur Knapton, 'I removed the stele from Mr Crowley's possession before your younger self could steal it and use it to travel through time.'

'But?' I said, and I scratched my head.

And scratched at other parts, too.

'Not *now*, Darwin,' said Cameron Bell. 'So Arthur Knapton, aka the God-Pharaoh Akhenaten, the Pearly Emperor, King Arthur of both Fairyland and Mars, I am arresting you for the theft of the British Library from the British Museum – a crime you will commit a few years from now.'

'But—' said I.

'*Not now, Darwin.*' To the Pearly Emperor, Mr Bell said, 'Drop your ray gun and surrender to me, or I will blow up your teenage self and spare Scotland Yard and the Old Bailey a great deal of confusion.'

'Well, at least you put *that* in,' I said.

Arthur Knapton began to laugh his horrible horrible laugh.

'It wasn't *that* funny,' I said. 'Although I must say that all these time-travelling shenanigans have taught me one thing, and that is how many plot holes it takes to fill the Albert Hall.'

Arthur Knapton continued to laugh. And not at what I had said.

'You can't win,' he said, when he finally stopped. 'And d'you know *why* you can't win?'

Mr Bell, whose thumb had not left the bright-red button, shook his head. 'Enlighten me,' he said.

'Because,' said Arthur Knapton, 'this is *The War of the Worlds*, but things are different this time around. Everyone knows that Martians cannot survive upon Earth because they fall prey to Earthly bacteria.'

'It is an Eternal Verity,' I said. 'Like you should *never* run with scissors, or—'

'Shut up,' said Arthur Knapton. 'You ain't gettin' it, Mr Bell. My Martians 'ave been inoculated wiv penicillin. They are immune to Earthly bacteria, which means this time they will *win*.'

I looked once more up at my friend. He had ceased to smile.

'So fink on,' continued Arthur Knapton. 'If me Martians win, then there ain't gonna be no Martian spaceships lying abandoned in Sussex, is there? And if there ain't, then Ernest Rutherford will not be able to convert one into a time-ship for you to travel in. Which means that *you* cannot travel through time an' capture *me*.'

I now looked from one to the other of them. 'But—' I said once more.

'Sssh,' said Mr Bell.

'But he *does* have a point,' I said. 'And I think we should at least take the occasional point into consideration. If the Martians win, then we *cannot* acquire a Martian spaceship and so we *cannot* be here.'

I looked all around and about.

Martians shrugged. It was all double Dutch to them.

'So *I* will just stand *here*,' said Arthur Knapton, now folding his arms, whilst still keeping hold of his ray gun, 'an' watch as you just vanish away.'

'Hm,' went Mr Bell. 'I feel that you might have a very long wait. I suggest instead that we remain with the original plan. *You* surrender to *me* at once, or I will explode your younger self and that will be *that* for you.'

'No!' went Arthur Knapton. '*That* is *that* for *you*. Me Martians are immune to Earthly bacteria. *We* win. *I* win. *You* most certainly lose.'

'No,' said Mr Bell. 'I think not,' and he glanced around at the Martians. 'Between you and me,' he said in a loud stage whisper, 'I think your Martians are looking a little unwell.'

'Oh no they're not!'

I now glanced about at the Martians, and I did have to say that they did not look all that well. They were rubbing at themselves and displaying rather horrid boils upon their horrid flesh.

'Oh yes they *are*,' said Mr Bell.

'Oh no they're not!'

But they were – they were looking most unwell indeed. All spotty and boily and ghastly, they looked, and then one by one they fell in a heap on the floor.

'*What?*' cried Arthur Knapton. '*What?*'

I looked up at Mr Bell and gave my head a scratch.

Mr Bell smiled down upon me and with his free hand he patted me on the shoulder.

'History is resolving itself,' he said to Arthur Knapton. 'Things that you have done are becoming undone.'

'How?' asked the Pearly Emperor.

'My friend Darwin and myself travelled to the year three thousand—'

333

'Not much had changed,' I said. 'Although they do live under—'

'Best not labour that one any more,' said Mr Bell. 'But let me explain it to you, Mr Knapton. My friend here –' and I smiled up at Mr Bell '– was cloned. And with him, his fleas.'

'His *fleas?*' went Arthur Knapton.

'His fleas,' said Cameron Bell. 'I regret to tell you that penicillin holds no fear for Darwin's super-fleas.'

'No! No! No!' shouted Arthur Knapton.

'Yes,' said Cameron Bell.

Chapter the very last

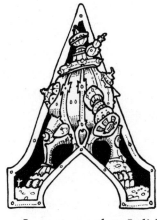

nd so it ended. Not with a bang, as perhaps my friend Mr Bell would have preferred it, but with a whimper.

A whimper from Arthur Knapton.

He gave himself up to Mr Bell. What else was he to do?

Mr Bell had finally triumphed and I was pleased for *that*.

Mind you.

I must say that I did have certain words to say to Mr Bell regarding the manner in which he finally defeated Arthur Knapton, the Pearly Emperor. Because a rather obvious thought had struck me.

'Why?' I asked my friend. 'With you being such an intelligent fellow and everything and being the greatest detective of your age, *why*, when you discovered that the villain who stole the books from the British Museum (this being your single unsolved case) was in fact your old fag and bootboy at Oxford, Mr Arthur Knapton – *why* did we not travel back to eighteen eighty-five immediately so you could lay your hands upon him when he was still a teenager? Rather than get involved in all the dangerous time-travelling adventures that we subsequently got into?'

My friend nodded thoughtfully to this, then had the temerity to tell me that the thought had obviously crossed his mind upon that very first night when we encountered Arthur Knapton in his Akhenaten persona at the British Museum.

But that if we had simply gone back and apprehended the teenage Knapton before he could commit any crimes at all, *it would not have been nearly so much fun.*

IN FACT, IT WOULD HAVE BEEN . . .

NO FUN AT ALL.

And I confess that I bit Mr Bell.

Not hard.

Just hard enough.

But we did drink champagne and we did celebrate Mr Bell's success. And also my own, because during the course of our adventures I had managed to achieve one or two significant things myself.

I *had* managed to transport my monkey descendants back to the morning of the world, endowed with the knowledge of speech and writing and fire.

Which had enabled them to eventually evolve into what we know today as Man.

Which made *me* the Father of All Mankind.

To my mind, no small achievement.

And it *was* me who defeated the Martians, because they had no immunity to the bites of my super-fleas.

So I had not only begun Mankind.

I had saved it also.

Which should at least have earned me a medal.

Or something.

Now that the case was finally concluded, Mr Bell finally honoured his promise to accompany me back to Vienna in eighteen twenty-four, to watch Beethoven conducting his Ninth Symphony.

It would be impossible for me to express in words the very wonder of that experience. Allow me to say only that it was everything I had hoped that it would be.

And more.

As the fourth movement concluded its glory, a curious incident occurred. A gentleman turned the great composer around towards the cheering crowd.

I was baffled by this until Mr Bell explained to me that the maestro Beethoven was quite deaf. That he had composed and conducted what many informed souls believe to be one of the highest of human achievements without being able to hear a single note of it.

I was brought to tears by this disclosure and begged Mr Bell to do something about it. He simply shrugged and said, 'What?'

But I had an idea, and so we brought Mr Beethoven to our time-ship and conveyed him to the year eighteen ninety-nine and the Grand Exposition, where Alberto Toscanini was to conduct the largest ever assembly of world-class musicians ever to perform Beethoven's Ninth.

And here, with the assistance of hearing aids which Mr Bell and I acquired in the year three thousand (where not very much had changed), the great composer was able to sit down next to Queen Victoria and enjoy every note of his greatest symphony.

Mr Bell and I were pleased for *that*.

It is with great sadness that I must write of the death of my dear friend Mister Cameron Bell. His passing came peacefully enough. He died at the age of eighty-five in the year two thousand and ten, in the city of Cardiff in Wales. I was at his bedside when he died and held his hand as he slipped away from this world.

We had spent so many many years together and together enjoyed so many many adventures.

I have only written here of those adventures we had whilst on the trail of Mr Arthur Knapton. But there had been so many others.

We had revisited the nineteen sixties, where *I* became the first ape in space (during that age, at least). Mr Bell solved numerous 'mysteries', such as who carved the Easter Island statues, what happened to those aboard the *Mary Céleste* (chickens *again*!) and why Stonehenge was constructed (which was all to do with a misunderstanding between Mr Bell and some Druids). I became personally involved in 'The Murders in the Rue Morgue' and inspired a young gentleman that I met in a Brentford public house to give up a life of crime and write far-fetched fiction instead.

That young gentleman's name is Robert Rankin.

Yes, Mr Bell and I had many adventures.

And I have written them up, and one day perhaps they will all be published. I hope very much that they will.

But now I am old. Old and alone and so must return to the eighteen nineties, to Syon House, to face my own death at the hands of my dear friend Lord Brentford.

I know that it must happen this way, and although I cannot say that I go willingly to meet this fate, I can say that I have lived a long and happy life and one with few regrets.

I have known more joy than sorrow.

More kindness than cruelty.

More good men than bad.

More love than hatred.

I set my tale before you here in the hope that it might amuse you.

Some perhaps will say that it is 'a missed opportunity', that 'the laughs were few and far between' and that it 'simply petered out at the end'. To those who would say such things, I offer my apologies. I am sorry that my work did not please you, as I had hoped that it would.

But also I offer this warning, that should I ever meet face to face with any of the mean-spirited blighters who would say such cruel things and still retain the strength in my right arm –

Beware the flinging of faeces!

And so I say farewell to you and wish you love and happiness.

I remain,
your humble scrivener,
Darwin
The Educated Ape.

THE END